The Hempen Widow

Harper Quinn

PublishAmerica
Baltimore

ISBN: 1-4137-3814-1
PUBLISHED BY PUBLISHAMERICA, LLLP
www.publishamerica.com
Baltimore

Printed in the United States of America

Prologue

1883

The Candyman stood in the doorway. He wore boots so big and wide at the toes that it looked as though he had clown's feet. He handed the bedraggled little girl a peppermint stick. She hungrily bit into the candy, wax wrapper and all. "Your mama's dead," the Candyman said. "Do you know what that means?"

She nodded while the sweet, minty drool ran down her chin. It meant that her mother's body stank like decaying meat and that flies were attracted to her arms and legs. It also meant that her mother had stopped talking to her many days ago, and though her eyes were still open, acted like she was asleep. Still. Silent. Heavy on the cot. Covered in flies—more flies every day. And smelling like garbage. It made Mary's stomach sick.

The Candyman dragged the corpse across the dirt floor. "Where's she going?" Mary asked.

"In the ground," he said. Not, "to heaven" or "home to God"—but in the ground, where the worms, not the flies, would feast upon her flesh. She watched him dig the hole and drop the body down, then fill it back up with dirt.

The Candyman drove Mary back into town. His house was bursting with children. The younger ones brought Mary up to the attic to play. One boy asked, "Are you sad that your mamma's dead?"

Mary shrugged. "Not really." Inside she was ripped and bruised.

The smells drifted up from the kitchen's enormous copper kettles, delicious aromas of caramel and chocolate, maple and peppermint. The molded chocolates were shipped in pretty pink boxes to neighboring counties and sold in the glass cases of fine restaurants and general stores, even in the Sears Catalog. Each of the Candyman's fifteen children received their very own box of hand-dipped nut clusters at Christmas time, Mary included.

She didn't see the Candyman very much; he was always working on the farm while his skinny, anxious wife made the candy in the kitchen, barking orders for the children to help. When Mary was bad, she got the switch just like the other children, and when she was good, she sometimes received an affectionate rub on the head. That family was her favorite; she stayed with them for almost five years, but the business went bankrupt one summer and Mary was sent away.

After that, she stayed with a mean old woman who could never have children of her own, and when she ran away from her, she was taken by the authorities to a home for orphans, where she stayed for several months, until another large farm family brought her to live with them. She worked like an indentured servant for several families. One time, she got lice in her hair from one of the children at school and had to have her head soaked in scorching hot water that burnt her scalp and caused pussy yellow blisters to form.

She wore hand-me-down clothing, the material worn through at the elbows and knees, revealing the individual strands of thread. The elastic on the waist of her petticoat was old and stretched to the point where it wasn't really elastic anymore, but more like dangling cord. The night Billy proposed, he gave her a pink gingham dress with a lacy white collar and a white satin sash wrapped around its waist.

When she looked in the mirror, the reflection that stared back at her was not that of dirty-faced Mary, her hair, dull with grease, hanging like cracked straw about her plain, freckled face. For Billy had also given her two seashell combs—pink and silver, to match the dress. Her hair was neatly assembled into a fine, dignified bun at the top of her head.

The dress was a paragon of perfection, clinging at the right parts and gracefully falling to her ankles in a curtain of impeccability. When she swung in a circle the skirt lifted, even danced, around her flowering form. The other girls envied her at the party that night. Billy's gift made her a princess, and for that, she was forever indebted to him. Of course she would be his wife…yes, yes! She kissed him, tender and grateful, and he pressed her against the wall, smelling of liquor and animal desire.

1

1895—Twelve Years Later

Mary stopped. The baby bore down hard against her pelvis, brute and relentless in force. It gripped her womb, held it in a vise that tightened with uncompromising strength, then gradually released. Seconds passed...the pain subsided.

She resumed walking along the winding dirt road, walled in by a towering sea of ripe sweet corn, its verdant husks rippling in the hot summer breeze. The road widened into a field with rolling waves of hay and clover that reached straight up to the sky as if physically yearning for the sun's nurturing light. The sky overhead appeared dusty, hazed in clouds of grey.

She wiped her brow with the back of her hand, removed a flask from her carpetbag, and thirstily drank from her diminishing water supply. The man at the train station had told her that Bately was less than a five-mile walk. When she set out earlier that morning her labor was light and tolerable, the mild cramps occurring every twenty minutes or so. By mid-morning the cramps were stronger, tighter; by noon they were no longer isolated to her lower regions, but rushed through her entire body in potent, punishing waves with only a minute's break spacing each one.

She staggered up a hill, dropped the flask and carpetbag, and fell to her knees. The baby's head was pressing to come out. She crawled to a cluster of alder bushes that grew along the edge of a sloping ditch and crouched, instinctively, into the birthing position. Tearing off her undergarments, she pushed with all of her might. Her moans, raw and primal, rose like heat from the ground, winding through the cascade of crooked alder branches, embracing each fragile, swaying leaf. They drifted higher, even higher, up to the blistering sun. A black ant crawled across her bootlace. The birth canal stretched to the point of tearing as the head came forth.

Mary's hands gripped hold of each knee and squeezed until her knuckles turned white. She released one final cry, not unlike the howl of a mortally-wounded animal, as the baby's head pressed forward, pulled back, pressed forward even farther, then suddenly slipped out, to be caught in Mary's trembling hands. She collapsed into the ditch, still holding the wet, warm head. Another push, this one easier, expelled the newborn's shoulders, torso and legs. Mary laughed for joy and lifted the infant to her chest.

She looked down at the tiny blue face. The cord was wrapped around its neck. Her fingers worked with the skill of a surgeon as she untangled the slippery noose. "Please God…" Her prayer was desperate and yet more focused than any prayer she had made in her life. She sensed a soft fluttering that encircled the baby's motionless form; a timorous dance of shadows blending into whitened light. Time froze. The leaves were still. In the distance, a deer watched on.

Mary lifted the cord from the infant's head. The purple mouth opened wide and released a piercing, victorious cry. She pressed the baby to her chest, softly weeping tears of relief and gratitude. She felt small and insignificant; her soul shrouded in heavy layers of mystery.

The baby cried louder. Mary unbuttoned her shirt and lifted her undershirt, which was thoroughly soaked through in perspiration. She placed her nipple into the newborn's mouth. The infant sucked with instinctive vigor. Closing her eyes, Mary felt another hard contraction as the afterbirth emerged and soaked her wool skirt with even more blood. She gently tilted the infant's bottom and peered down at its genitals. Her heart leaped—a girl!

She was frightened by the prospect of cutting the umbilical cord but knew that it had to be done soon. There were scissors in her carpetbag. If only she could get to it, but in her present situation it was impossible to move. She once heard that Indian women would bite the cord with their teeth if they gave birth in the forest where no sharp objects could be found. She considered just how she would go about doing this, when she saw a horse-drawn cart emerging in the distance.

Mary ceased nursing and pulled down her shirt. Her legs remained open in a v-shape on the ground with the coiled-cord stretched between them, a tight, little rope of flesh framed by her muddied skirt. She tried pulling her knees together and attempted to stand, but fell back, groaning in pain.

The horse grunted as it pulled the cart up the hill. A young farmer stood at the seat, energetically snapping the reins. He rode over to the ditch and jumped down.

"Get back!" Mary screamed.

He stopped. "Just trying to help, ma'am." His voice resonated with calmness and concern.

She stroked her baby's head, spreading the chalk-like mucus over her fingers and palm. The man took a step forward and Mary recoiled, overcome by vulnerability and fear. "I said get back!"

"I'm not going to hurt you. Where's your husband? Has anyone gone to find help?"

Her breathing was light, strangled. "Don't take her."

"I won't." He walked forward slowly.

The sense of threat engulfed her. She squeezed the infant in her arms, whispering, "No, no, no..." She pressed her eyes shut and wished the stranger away.

When she looked up, he stood directly before her, his entire body emanating a dazzling sapphire light with hues of silver-grey that rolled and shimmered from his limbs, fading, then re-creating and fading once again. She blinked several times, wondering if this were all a strange dream...

He knelt down. "I'm going to cut the cord, ma'am, is that alright?"

She focused on his colors. "Yes."

He took a small knife from his pocket and sliced through the thick tissue at the base of the cord. He tied the baby's end with a piece of twine, then went back to the cart and returned with a burlap sack and a wool blanket. He handed the sack to Mary. "You'd better wrap her up." Mary's hands shook as she swaddled the infant's shivering body in the rough burlap material. The farmer tossed the blanket at Mary's feet. "Put this over you," he said.

She placed the baby on the ground and attempted to remove her ankle-length walking skirt, the buttons of which were located at the back. Her legs felt anesthetized as she rolled about in the ditch. Seeing her discomfort, the farmer helped Mary to a standing position, undid the imitation pearl buttons, and draped the blanket around her bloated waist. He tied a large, loose knot over her left hip.

"There," he said, "you're ready for the ball."

Mary hadn't the strength to laugh. She picked up the baby and held the farmer's arm as he walked her to the cart.

"By the way, my name is Jacob Zane." He placed the baby on the floor and lifted Mary up onto the bench.

She forced a weary smile. "I'm Mary."

The horse released a satisfied snort.

Jacob fetched her belongings from the ditch, remembering to pick up the flask and carpetbag from the middle of the road, and joined Mary on the cart. Dizzy and mildly nauseated, she reached for her baby and placed her on her lap. The infant was in a deep, postpartum sleep, her half-moon eyes lightly twitching with dark, comforting memories of water and the womb.

"All set?" Jacob asked.

"Where are we going?"

He looked at her. "Isn't your home around here?"

She shook her head. "I took the train to Cincinnati this morning. I heard there was work for a seamstress in these parts. I thought I could find a job and a cheap place to live."

"A woman in your condition shouldn't be worried about a job. Where's your husband?"

"Dead."

If her reply surprised him, he didn't show it. "I'll take you into Bately. We'll get you some help there."

2

Mary didn't tell Jacob that Bately was the town where she was initially headed, nor that it was the town where her dead husband's mother supposedly lived. She decided to forget about Bonnie Turner. At least forget about her for today.

The road was merciless in its bumps and shallow ditches. Tears welled up in Mary's eyes but these too were stoically suppressed. Jacob frequently glanced over at mother and child, his boyish face alight with an almost paternal pride.

"That must have been quite a scare."

"How did you know where to cut the cord?" she asked.

"My wife had all three without a doctor."

"So you have children?"

He winced. "Not yet. They were all stillborn. Tara just found out she's pregnant again." His eyes, an unsettling blend of hazel and grey, revealed a raw, childlike need for empathy.

The road came to a crossing. Jacob steered east, thankfully taking the cart onto a macadam surface. The ride into town was easier after that, although with the tremendous loss of blood, Mary grew weak. Her body craved a soft bed covered in quilts with a goose pillow beneath her head.

Mary's first glimpse of Bately came as they rode to the peak of a steep hill that overlooked the village below. A string of houses traced its circumference, forming a white, wooden fortress. In one part of the circle there stood a grouping of two-story commercial buildings, mostly farm-related businesses and one restaurant attached to a general store. Behind these, a square strip of larger, luxurious homes sat back on a hill.

The sprawling green commons was located in the center of the village.

Today it was crowded with people and booths in celebration of the Strawberry Festival which Bately celebrated on this particular day in July, each year for the last forty years, a piece of town history that Jacob explained to Mary as they approached. Mary shuddered that such an event would be occurring on the very day that she entered the town with a bloodied blanket looped around her waist and a newborn baby in her arms. Her timing was hideous.

Jacob pulled the horse to a halt in front of a white steepled church a safe distance from the festival. "I'm going to look for someone who can take you into their home. Do you mind?"

Mary's heart raced. "What about your house? Would your wife mind?"

"Seeing that baby might upset Tara. You know, stillborns and all…"

She watched him walk over to the festival and talk to individuals one at a time. Her heart no longer raced, but felt to be burning in her chest. No one seemed keen on the idea of helping her. Many stared at Mary, even stepped forward to have a closer look, only to back off and speak again to Jacob, evidently making an excuse. A thin waif of a man limped about the festival with a scrawny dog trailing his side, its tail only a fast-wagging, hairless stub. He was evidently unaware of the three little girls that followed him. They huddled together, covering their mouths, giggling while cruelly imitating his limp.

Mary yawned and slumped her body down on the bench. Her lower back ached and her bottom was extremely sore; the torn birth canal still flowed with warm, sticky blood. She was in the early stages of sleep, random images darting about the black canvas of her mind, when a shrill yet earthy voice pulled her back to reality. Mary opened her eyes, initially blinded by the brilliance of the sun, and looked down at the heavily rouged face of a plump woman, about her age, perhaps a little older, staring up at her with absorbed fascination.

"Oh my, did you just give birth to that *child*?" The word "child" was emphasized in a way which suggested that the baby herself was a negative thing and if Mary had only produced a different item, a monkey perhaps, then the situation would not appear so…so what? So scandalous.

Mary sat up straight and turned in the direction of the festival. Where did Jacob go? What was she to say to this nosey creature staring up at her, a smile of derision brightening her purple mouth? She chose to say nothing and simply allowed the woman to shamelessly gape, as if watching a circus sideshow, her dark eyes shifting from Mary's macabre skirt to the baby's sleeping form, then back to the skirt.

Jacob returned with three people. He introduced them as the town doctor and his wife, and the church sexton, Hannah Graf. He turned to the young woman who, in such a short time, Mary had grown to despise.

"Go on, Azalea." It sounded like he was disciplining a child, or better yet, a dog.

Her hands dropped to her wide hips. "I have just as much right to be standing here as you do, Jacob Zane. Maybe more."

Dr. Smith helped Mary down from the wagon. Hannah smiled at the baby in Mary's arms. "So this is her!" she gushed, scant traces of a German accent dotting her southern Ohio speech. She tenderly stroked the baby's cap of furry, black hair. "Do you mind if I hold her?"

Mary suddenly needed to vomit. She quickly handed her daughter to Hannah. "Can I lie down somewhere?"

"Of course," Dr. Smith said. "We'll take you up to Hannah's apartment."

As if sensing that Mary's legs were buckling under, he lifted her entire body in his arms and carried her up the church's front steps and through the tall, whitewashed doors. They went down the wood-planked aisle, around the pulpit, through a second set of tall, stained-glass doors, then up a narrow stairway that led to a small, dark wood door. Mary leaned into Dr. Smith's shoulder and heard the high-pitched chattering of Azalea in the sanctuary, asking Jacob how on earth he got tangled up in this kind of mess. Who was the baby's father? She *needed* to know.

"It's unlocked!" Hanna called up from the foot of the stairway.

Unlike the spacious, sunlit interior of the church sanctuary, Hannah's apartment was a dark, enclosed space, Spartan in décor. Dr. Smith placed Mary down on the green wicker daybed in the front room. She sank into its goose-feathered mattress, moaning. Hannah handed the baby to Kate, then went into the small kitchen where she filled a copper kettle with water from the pump. Within fifteen minutes the baby's first bath was prepared.

Kate lay the infant on the kitchen table and delicately removed the layers of burlap that kept her warm. Thomas took some items from his black bag and examined the sleeping child. He lifted her in his large, gentle hands and lowered her into the shallow water. The baby stirred slightly as the doctor moved a soapy cloth over the perfectly formed limbs; the crusts of blood and mucus disappeared beneath liquid clouds of soap. Washed clean, the baby's bottom was neatly diapered with a cotton dishcloth by Hannah and her fragile pink limbs tenderly swaddled in an embroidered shawl.

Hannah presented the cooing package to her mother. Mary rolled onto her side and accepted the baby in her arms, breathing in the sweet, vinegar scent with animal delight. Dr. Smith kneaded Mary's belly with his fists.

Jacob arrived in the doorway, speaking angrily over his shoulder at Azalea. "That's enough! You're not coming in."

Azalea protested from the top step. Jacob closed the door in her face and entered the room, shaking his head at Azalea's brazen ways. He looked surprised to find the peaceful scene before him. Hannah and Kate spoke softly in the kitchen, while Dr. Smith sat beside Mary on the bed, jotting down notes in his small black record book. Jacob sat across from Mary in the rocking chair.

"I'm sorry about Azalea," he apologized. "She's the minister's daughter—thinks she can say and do anything she pleases and get away with it."

Dr. Smith raised his eyebrows. "And usually she does."

Mary smiled. To have this small network of support in her midst made Azalea's obnoxious behavior seem trivial. "Does Hannah mind that I'm here?"

Dr. Smith shook his head. "She's glad to help, and you're welcome to stay as long as you want."

Hannah came into the front room holding a makeshift bassinet, her finest handmade quilt serving as a mattress folded into an empty drawer. She put the drawer on top of a trunk and pushed it next to Mary's bed. "You can put the baby in here when you're through feeding her."

"How are you feeling now, Mary?" Kate asked from the kitchen. Her words were pointed and with purpose, English and refined.

"Tired."

Kate went to the door, dabbing the corners of her mouth with a pink handkerchief. "I didn't see Tara at the festival," she said to Jacob. "Is her stomach still weak?"

He rose from the chair. "She feels awful."

"That might be a good sign," Dr. Smith remarked. He turned to Mary. "If you need anything in the next while…"

"Yes, anything," Kate agreed coughing.

"Thank you," Mary said.

The group left with the exception of Hannah. Mary closed her eyes and nestled into her baby. She heard the muffled noises of the Strawberry Festival outside: echoed announcements of the winners of the pie-eating contest, bursts of laughter enveloped in blankets of applause, and muted songs played on a fiddle and another instrument that Mary did not recognize. Her breathing slowed to match that of her daughter's. Her head tipped back and every aching muscle of her body went limp as she tumbled into a deep, well-deserved sleep.

She was awakened in the night by a loud clap of thunder. She opened her eyes with a start, unsure of where she was. Then it all came back to her; the dirt road, the baby, Jacob lifting her into the cart. Her arms were empty. She sat up. The baby slept peacefully in the drawer beside her, evidently placed there by Hannah earlier in the night. A flash of lightning lit up the small room, followed by a deafening burst of thunder. The baby did not stir.

Mary crawled to the base of the bed and stood on her own for the first time since before the delivery. She fell forward and grabbed the rocking chair to retrieve her balance. Hannah appeared at the room's entrance, her stout form filling the doorway. "Are you all right, Mary?"

"Yes, I didn't mean to wake you."

"You didn't. It's only eight o'clock."

"That's all? I thought it was the middle of the night."

Hannah helped Mary back to bed. "The sky is dark from the storm. Did the thunder wake you?"

Mary nodded. "Could I have a glass of water?"

"Of course." Hannah went to the kitchen and returned with a pewter mug. She sat in the rocking chair and watched Mary drink. "I remember how difficult my first one was. His feet were in the wrong direction, it took forever to get him out."

Mary handed the empty mug to Hannah. "I hope my being here isn't a burden."

"Hardly. My husband passed away last winter. It's good to have a guest." She removed a large metal pail from the kitchen cupboard. "Would you like to get washed? I wish that I could offer you a big tub but all I have is this." She helped Mary into the kitchen and filled the metal pail with warm water from the stove.

Mary stepped into the pail. The water rose halfway to her calves. She washed herself with the sponge that Hannah provided, then bent over and managed to sit. It felt good to soak her wounds in the water. She stared down at her sagging breasts and dimpled thighs, the backs of which were covered in hideous purple and blue varicose veins. Her body had changed significantly in recent months, transforming from a slender, well-toned figure into a plump, ill-proportioned vessel whose sole purpose was to accommodate the rapidly forming life within its womb.

As Mary left the pail, her hand reached for the lower rim of her belly to rub her empty womb. The habit would take several weeks to disappear. Hannah handed her a loose-fitting cotton nightgown and undergarments with extra padding to absorb the blood.

"I'll make us some tea," she said.

Mary limped back to the bed and sat against its frame. The baby's eyes opened and squinted at the wall of the drawer. As if suddenly realizing her lonely predicament, she released a fierce, demanding cry. Mary scooped the bundle to her breast. The thunder and lightning stopped, replaced by pouring rain. Hannah returned with two cups of tea. Mary traced the shape of her daughter's blotched pink face with her fingertips, listening to the rain.

Hannah sat down. "Did you grow up in these parts?"

Mary reached for her tea. "No, but my husband Billy did. That's why I'm here." She paused, sipping. "He once told me to go back to his mother if I ever needed help."

"What's her name?"

"Bonnie Turner."

Hannah's face darkened. "I know her well."

"Could you take me to see her?"

"Bonnie doesn't live in Bately anymore, but trust me, you're better off without her. I don't mean to put down your husband's mother, it's just that Bonnie Turner was a hard drinker. She even tried running a brothel at the outskirts of town, but the God-fearing people ran her out."

Mary looked down at her child. The tiny pink mouth encircled the entire tip of her nipple, the small cheeks forming steady, sucking movements.

"Where's Billy?" Hannah asked.

Mary switched the baby onto her other breast. "He's dead."

"Dead? How?"

"He was hung last month in Louisville. I read about it in the newspaper. Seems he killed a sheriff—shot him three times in the head. That's another reason why I came to see Bonnie, she probably doesn't even know about it."

"You weren't there to see him hang?"

"No. I left Billy last November. I'm relieved that he's dead, now I don't have to worry about him hunting me down."

"Did he hurt you, Mary?"

"Yes."

"Maybe you should return to your own family."

"I don't have a family. I've lived with more people over the years than I care to recall. Then Billy came along."

"How old are you, dear?"

"Seventeen."

Hannah stood from her chair and walked to the window. "This storm should clear soon. We've been getting them almost every night. I'm just glad that we had good weather for the festival today." She went to Mary and showed her how to burp the infant, but the child had already slipped back into sleep. Mary placed her daughter in the drawer and lay back down herself.

"Can I get you something to eat?" Hannah asked.

"If you don't mind, I'd like to sleep."

"You go right ahead. I'll make you a farmer's breakfast in the morning, complete with strips of sausage and hot coffee. Do you like coffee?"

"Yes," Mary lied. She had never had a cup of coffee in her life. It was too expensive a treat. She inwardly wondered how Hannah could afford to drink coffee and eat meat on a sexton's modest salary.

"Good then. You sleep while you can, that child will have you up through the night if she's anything like mine were at that age."

The baby awoke at midnight. Mary was startled by the sudden cry that shot across the darkness, jolting her from a dream. She unbuttoned the nightdress and pulled her daughter to her side, then fell back to sleep as the baby fed. When the baby awoke two hours later, Mary simply latched her back onto her breast. She repeated the procedure at dawn and awoke at seven a.m. feeling somewhat rested herself.

Hannah was in the kitchen, preparing the promised farmer's breakfast. She proudly presented the new mother with a heaping stack of buckwheat pancakes, so big that they hung over the rim of the ironware plate, a cup of strong, piping hot coffee, and a side-plate covered in strips of ham and sausage links. Mary ate everything with ravenous appetite and even accepted a second helping of ham and another cup of coffee.

Hannah bent over and energetically straightened the covers of Mary's bed. She looked fresher than the night before, brighter. She wore a yellow calico dress of a light cotton material. The flowers were orange with spots of kelly green. A starched white apron trailed the front of her soft bosom and melted into her thick, round waist. Her cheeks were rosy, like shiny apples on her wrinkled face, and framed by curly brown wisps of thinning hair, tied into a pretzel-shaped knot at the back of her head.

"How did you sleep?" she asked.

"Good. I had some cramps, but I was too tired to care."

Hannah pulled the bulky green drapes back from the main window of the room. Streams of sunlight poured across the apartment, immediately lifting Mary's spirits. The baby awoke and she quickly took her to the breast. Her milk had come in earlier that morning, drenching her nightgown and leaving a large, embarrassing spot on the mattress. The baby drank with insatiable thirst, thriving on the new dimension of sweet nourishment.

"If you just give me a day or two," Mary said, sheepish with guilt, "then I'll be on my way."

Hannah's eyes widened. "Where would you go?"

"I'm not sure."

"Don't talk nonsense, dear. You're welcome to stay here for as long as you like."

"The baby will wake you up at night."

"I don't mind."

"Are you sure?"

Hannah smiled. "I'm sure." She cleared the dishes, then left to do some cleaning in the church basement.

Mary moved the rocking chair to the window and sat down. She looked at her baby. The peculiar little creature resembled Mary with her long, sandy brown lashes and a deep crevice of a dimple on the cleft of her heart-shaped chin. Her skin was pale and, like Mary's, would easily burn when directly exposed to the sun. Her eyes, though typically dark blue, already showed hints of gold and green. But where did the black hair come from? Perhaps from Billy's side of the family, or maybe it was temporary and would fall away in a matter of weeks and come in an entirely different color.

Mary's heart swelled with wonder. For nine months she had carried the growing child in her womb and yet, in all of that time, she could not imagine the face that would present itself, nor the soft, pliable limbs, the meticulously chiseled fingers and toes. Something born out of nothing, water changed into wine. For the fist time in her life Mary felt that she had done something right, more than right, something miraculous and wholly pure.

She rocked her daughter, basking in the steady stream of light. She thought of names for the child, assorted sounds and syllables that mixed together well. *Elizabeth.* The name came to her like a beam of light.

She whispered in the little ear, "Good morning, Elizabeth."

3

Mary slipped Elizabeth into the secure confines of the padded drawer. Her lower regions itched and burned as a result of the natural healing that was taking place. She limped over to the pump and filled a stoneware crock with water. Hannah kept the washcloths and towels neatly stacked on the shelf above the sink. Mary took several of the smaller towels and the bowl of water into Hannah's bedroom, placing them on the bureau.

Jacob had deposited Mary's carpetbag at the foot of Hannah's bed the day before. She reached inside and removed its contents: scissors and a spool of brown thread, a pair of well-worn grey stockings, undergarments, a comb, a toothbrush and a small container of baking soda to clean her teeth. She went to the dresser and splashed handfuls of water onto her face, her hands, and her slender, freckled arms. It was invigorating. Her reflection stared back at her in the mirror above the dresser. The youthful complexion was without blemish and the eyes, usually stricken and distressed, shone with frail tinges of joy. *It's Elizabeth*, Mary thought, amazed.

She washed her long hair with a bar of soap, then brushed her teeth with baking soda. Despite the years of poverty her teeth were in good condition. She rarely ate sweets and brushed them each night. She remembered the teeth of one of her many guardians, black and rotting in her head. Mary refused to suffer the same fate.

She sat on Hannah's bed and gazed out the window at the bustling village below. Farmers drove their carts over the macadam and cobblestone roads, stopping briefly to greet one another and engage in friendly conversation. Women walked about with baskets in hand while children floated through the streets like little guppies in a pond—moving in schools, then breaking off into smaller groupings of two or three. They played marbles and hopscotch. Four little girls jumped rope in the commons, beneath a drooping willow tree. Mary felt distanced, not just physically, but in every other way, from this respectable world of marriage and family.

Footsteps sounded from the stairwell and the front door opened. Mary jumped up, worried that Hannah would be upset if she discovered her guest lazily lounging on the bed. Hannah was brimming with excitement when she came into the room. "Come with me, Mary, I have a present for you."

Mary followed Hannah down the hallway. It hardly seemed possible that someone would want to buy her a present, especially an elderly sexton whose wages were small. She grew suspicious. The last gift she had received was the dress from Billy, and look where that landed her. In the kitchen, Hannah proudly presented Mary with not just one box, but *six* wrapped boxes. Mary stared at the pile of presents on the table, speechless.

"Open them," Hannah said. Mary looked up with confusion. Hannah lightly, delicately, touched a coiled strand of Mary's wet hair. "Open them."

She opened the first of the gifts. It was a simply tailored lavender skirt and a white blouse that ruffled to chin level. Mary's mouth dropped open. "I can't—"

Hannah smiled. "You can."

"How can you afford—"

"My sons send me money," Hannah replied.

Mary opened the second of the gifts. Each one was so beautifully wrapped that she hesitated before tearing off the paper. Inside she found a walking dress of pale, yellow chine with tiny, blurred flowers in rose-colored shades, and beneath this, a brown plaid walking dress.

"You see, I was thinking of your hair and eyes," Hannah said. "Women of your coloring look good in yellows and browns. It brings out the lightness of their features."

"I can't take these gifts."

"Alright." Hannah took the two dresses, a gleam of mischief in her eyes. "Then you'll just have to wear my nightdresses when you go into town, unless you prefer to wear the skirt that Jacob brought back yesterday. That is all of the clothing that you own, right?"

Mary held back a smile. "You win." The remaining boxes contained silk stockings and undergarments, plus cotton nightgowns and diapers for Elizabeth. Mary thanked Hanna several times.

For lunch they ate a meal of boiled cabbage and potatoes and pork chops with a thin coating of brown gravy. Mary's bladder ached. It occurred to her that she had not visited the outhouse since early that morning. She excused herself from the table and went to the latrine behind the church. Walking back, she passed one of the tall windows and saw a group of older men sitting around a meeting table. Their faces were sour and they frowned as they spoke. A lean, balding man sat at the table's head. He reminded Mary of a vulture with his long, pointed nose, his narrow eyes, and sinuous mouth. Mary shuddered as she entered the church. She went quickly upstairs, back to the refuge of Hannah's apartment.

Hannah was holding Elizabeth on the daybed, beside the stack of gifts. Mary sat down. "I named her this morning."

"What did you choose?"

"Elizabeth. I'm not sure of the middle name yet."

"Elizabeth—that's lovely." Hannah's arms wound around the baby's soft form. "They're so innocent at this age, aren't they? So untouched...." She rocked the newborn infant in her arms, singing a lullaby. Minutes passed and she handed the baby back to Mary. "I have to go downstairs and polish the sanctuary. Do you mind being alone in the apartment?"

"No," Mary said. Her body ached for her baby and she was glad to have some time alone, though after Hannah left, dark waves of melancholy swept over her as she nursed.

Only the morning before she was riding on the train, nine months pregnant and uncomfortable, but also free from obligation. Within the space of several hours, the baby had emerged and thrown Mary's world upside down. She could no longer go where she wanted to go and sleep when she wanted to sleep, but had to first consider this dependent little creature's needs before her own. She had assumed, wrongly, that even with a baby to care for, she could find work seamstressing in Bately, thus enabling her to earn an income and support her child. She did not anticipate the overwhelming drama of giving birth, nor the period of physical recovery, nor the tied-down aspect of motherhood. Mary felt like a helpless infant herself.

These revelations came upon her in waves. Her shoulders drooped as she bowed her head to cry. The hot tears splashed down on Elizabeth's face, bathing it in her mother's grief. Mary sniffed loudly, shifted in the chair, and straightened her new chine dress. It was too loose around the shoulders and would need to be taken in, though the small waist pinched around Mary's protruding belly with the strength of a corset two sizes too small. Even Mary's figure was beyond control, like some kind of foreign being that she no longer recognized.

Elizabeth pulled back from Mary's nipple and released a sweet, melodious moan of satisfaction. It was enough to pull Mary out of her depression. *She is a precious thing. Thank heavens she didn't die. The man Jacob was like an angel, the way he found me and brought me here. And his colors! He's a good man, a kind man.* Mary smiled down at her daughter. It was a tremendous relief not to have to seek Bonnie Turner's help. Mary had only met her mother-in-law once. At the time, the woman was full of drink and judgment because Mary "stole her little boy," as if Billy was a costly commodity to be seized!

But now Billy and his mother were the past. Elizabeth and Hannah were the future. Mary glanced around the tidy little flat, drying her tears with the back of her hand. She was never so thankful for a home in her life.

Dr. Smith had finished his work and brought back the day's income in the back of his wagon: a large sack of apples, a few prime cuts of beef, and two dozen fresh eggs. Rarely did he get cash for his services, only from Bately's wealthy resident living on "The Hill," but somehow he and Kate always managed to get by. The inheritance that they received twenty years earlier was a significant help, raising their standard of living overnight.

He turned north at an intersection and took his rickety old vehicle onto the dirt road that went by the Zane farm and eventually led to his land. The sun slipped behind a mass of dark, puffy clouds. A light drizzle began to fall, creating small, dew-like droplets on the matted brown hair of Mr. Smith's horse, Colonel Scott. A slender, dark figure walked ahead, cutting across the distant fields of wheat and corn. Dr. Smith snapped at the reins and caught up to the figure, which gradually took the shape of Mickey Jenson.

"Afternoon, Mickey. Need a lift?"

The younger man looked at the wagon's right wheel, then over his shoulder, his eyes returning to Dr. Smith. "Well, I don't know. Maybe, sir, if it's not a bother."

"No bother at all, Mickey."

Mickey joined Dr. Smith on the bench. "Where you headed?" Dr. Smith asked.

"The Zane farm. Jacob asked for help."

They rode in silence. The two men had known one another for many years, beginning with the morning when Dr. Smith delivered Mickey as a premature infant from his elderly mother's womb—elderly, in that Carol Jenson gave birth to her last son at the incredible age of fifty-one, a modern-day Sarah.

The next day Dr. Smith's little boy Tommy died of smallpox. The two events were always linked in Dr. Smith's memory, simply by virtue of the fact that they happened within the same dramatic space of time.

Dr. Smith glanced over at Mickey, who sat motionless on the bench, staring at the road ahead. To this day, he still did not look quite "right"—as if a crucial amount of blood had been drained from him while he rested all too briefly in his mother's tired womb, and his limbs had not been given adequate time to develop. Mickey had his share of sickness. For a time, it seemed Dr. Smith was at the Jenson farm every day, treating Mickey's various viruses and obscure diseases that kept him referring to the latest medical journals to find the cures. Not a winter passed when Mickey was not on death's doorstep at least once. Miraculously, he always recovered, despite his poor constitution, a cruel reminder to Dr. Smith of poor little Tommy's fate.

Tommy was a strong, lively child, a nine-pound baby at birth who flexed his legs when you sat him on your lap, already eager to stand. He thrived on three things: food, activity, and love, all of which he received in generous amounts. Dr. Smith used to call him his "little beef cake." Kate would nudge his arm. "Oh, Thomas, don't!" Though she smiled with pride, for wasn't every mother proud to have a healthy, robust child with rolls of fat beneath his chin and dimples on his knees?

When Mickey Jenson was nine years old he dropped a large stone on his foot while helping his father build a fence and lost three of the toes. The boy didn't flinch as Dr. Smith bandaged the wound. At the time, it occurred to Dr. Smith that suffering was a familiar garment to Mickey and he had already accommodated himself to the condition as one adjusts to bad weather.

They arrived at the Zane farm. Mickey got down from the bench and limped up the long driveway that led to Jacob and Tara's log house. Dr. Smith rode on for a half mile before arriving at the maple tree that divided his land and Jacob's property. He and Kate lived in a Victorian-style brick house. The many windows were alight with the warm, welcoming glow of kerosene lamps. Lush, dark green ivy grew up from the ground, winding around the banisters of the front porch and framing the window's wood plank shingles. He drove up the driveway and got down to walk Colonel Scott into the barn. The rain stopped falling and the sun came out. The sky looked bright, washed clean.

Kate peeked her head out the back window. "Hurry inside, Thomas! Sandra is here with the children and they have a song for you!"

He crossed the yard, a slight hunch in his back, and listened to the sounds of happy children at play as he walked up the back steps. Dr. Smith smiled to himself. He hadn't seen his daughter and grandchildren in over a month.

The young family left after supper. It was an hour's journey back to Westville and Sandra didn't want the children to be overtired at school the next day. The large house seemed eerily quiet afterwards. It always did. Thomas wished that he and Kate had more children, but after Sandra and Tommy, Kate couldn't seem to get pregnant again. She once told Thomas that it felt as if her body were mourning for Tommy, thus shutting down the possibility for new life.

Kate went to the piano and began to play. Thomas sat on the sofa beside the window and watched his wife. Her hair was a dark shade of auburn, highlighted with streaks of grey and arranged in a fashionable twist at the nape of her neck. She wore an indigo wrap dress with marrow piping in plain scarlet. As her white, bony hands lovingly brushed the ivory keys, Dr. Smith experienced a quiet stirring that sometimes occurred when he was struck with his wife's natural grace. Then he noticed the bloodstained handkerchief folded in the piano's polished shelf and the quiet stirring disappeared, replaced by a deep sense of emptiness.

He always thought that he would die before Kate. Her health was perfect up until two years ago, and she was thirteen years younger than he. But alas, it was not to be. How would he ever survive without her? They had been together for so long that Thomas was no longer certain as to where the line between he and Kate could be drawn, or if there existed any line at all. He fondly recalled the day that they met. She was a sprite of a girl, with her proper English accent and her sharp, ironic wit. They joked incessantly. He had never met a woman with whom he could truly laugh. In the weeks that followed, the energy changed into something deeply urgent and abiding, an abstract, all-consuming force that transcended both of them.

Kate stopped playing and coughed. Dr. Smith rose from the sofa. "I'll get us some port."

He returned with two glasses and a crystal jug for refills. He noticed, sadly, that Kate only managed a small sip, then resumed playing. Thomas finished his first glass of port, then poured a second one and nursed it. His stomach warmed over with an agreeable, tingling heat and his body, tense from a day of work and the commotion of a house full of children, gradually began to relax. He closed his eyes. The notes swirled about the room—gentle, loving, and yet sated with sadness, a kind of mournful joy.

"That's beautiful. What is it?"

"It's a Nocturne by John Field," Kate replied, continuing to play.

"Have I heard it before?"

"No, Agnes sent it this week. She says it's her favorite. It's father's favorite too."

Kate was till in correspondence with her childhood governess in London, Agnes Frome. Thomas had never met the woman; indeed, he had never met any of Kate's family, for they temporarily disowned her after she came to America to care for a sick aunt, overstayed her visit, and ended up marrying Thomas (a country doctor well below the Rutherford family's monetary status and societal ranking.) Agnes was Kate's only London connection then and now, since Kate's mother died years ago before forgiving Kate, while her father, at the ripe age of eighty-one, was still too proud to write.

He did, however, send Kate her beloved Broadwood on their tenth wedding anniversary. Kate told Thomas that it was her father's way of saying that he cared, that he was sorry. "He shows love through his money," she explained, which, Thomas supposed, was an accurate assumption on Kate's part since her father once showed his intense disapproval of Kate's choice of a partner forty years earlier by cutting Kate out of the family will. With the gift of the piano came a note from Agnes, saying that Charles Rutherford had a "change of mind" and put Kate back into the will that very week.

As if it matters anymore, Thomas presently thought.

Kate was holding the last note when her fingers left the keys prematurely and grabbed for the handkerchief. She coughed until the small veins that ran along her neck grew purple, then bowed her head and gingerly wiped her mouth. "Excuse me."

Thomas swallowed the last mouthful of port and set the glass on the window- sill. "I've been thinking about the young woman that we met yesterday."

"Mary. Yes, so have I."

"Evidently, she's a widow and doesn't have anywhere to live."

Kate gasped. "I was under the impression that her husband was being notified."

"No. I saw Hannah this morning. She said the girl is completely without family—and penniless to boot."

"Poor dear. Whatever will she do?"

"Hannah's prepared to take her on as a permanent guest."

"How kind." Kate stood from the bench and sat beside Thomas on the sofa. "Perhaps I'll ask her for supper."

"Wait awhile," Thomas suggested. "She'll need some time to rest." He stared out the window at the dark field and the shadows of trees that loomed against the clear blueness of the summer sky.

"You're distracted," Kate observed.

"Mmm... I'm thinking about the young woman's eyes."

"Her eyes?"

His forehead creased, as if struggling with a thought. "They were like the eyes of the girls that I used to treat...back in the city."

"You don't think—"

"No, no. But there is pain there."

Kate clasped Thomas' hand in hers, pulling it to her lap. His palm was smooth and strong, a sharp contrast to Kate's brittle bones. "You always see into people, don't you, Thomas?"

He looked at his wife. "I'm not a clairvoyant, if that's what you mean."

Kate smiled. "You saw into me as soon as we met." She let go of his hand and pushed herself up from the sofa with great effort, crossing the room with the crystal jug and glasses in hand. "I'll put these away and we can turn in for the night."

When she came back, Thomas' gaze had returned to the darkness. "I think that I'll stop by Hannah's apartment tomorrow and bring Mary one of Bess' pies," Kate said.

Thomas did not respond. He was thinking of a far-off time in Cincinnati, when he was fetched from his quarters in the middle of the night. He and Kate were newlyweds, and this sojourn to the city was intended to give them some kind of romantic escape from the monotony of rural Ohio life. They stayed only a year, however. It seemed the city contained a volume of poverty and strife that Thomas had never thought possible. It was with great relief that the disillusioned couple returned to the quaint world of Bately, where suffering mirrored the seasons, natural and flowing, sorrowful but always containing hope. Unlike the suffering of the city, which made no sense to Thomas. That suffering was rotten like the garbage and animal feces that filled the streets polluted with violence and hate. On that night, he was taken to an alley where a girl lay dying from her failed abortive attempt. He thought he could handle this, until a few days later. The girl's mother came to Thomas to inquire as to how her daughter died. He told the mother the truth. He asked if there were a father to the aborted baby, perhaps a local mill-worker, who needed to be informed. No, the mother flatly replied. The girl had been repeatedly raped by their landlord since she was ten. He was, no doubt, the father. This is how the family paid the rent.

When he started his work in the slums, Thomas was a storehouse of vitality and idealistic notions, but that particular episode shattered his lofty visions as a small sharp pebble can break a house of glass if thrown correctly and with accurate speed. After he and Kate moved back to Bately, it took Thomas several months before he was finally able to sleep at night.

"You don't think that I should?" Kate asked, misunderstanding his silence.

He forced his eyes form the window and looked at Kate. Her waif-like appearance startled him. It happened often as of late, that shock that ran up his spine when he expected to see her full and healthy, "normal," and was confronted by the severity of her disease. "I think it's a good idea. As long as you're feeling up to it."

"Well, we'll see how I sleep tonight." Kate yawned at the thought of sleep.

They left the parlor and Thomas blew out the kerosene lamp beside the doorway before he closed the door. At the foot of the stairway Kate's body tilted to the side and she fell back on the chair of the hall tree. Her breath was short and her eyelids fluttered queerly. Thomas knelt down, covering her damp forehead with his hand.

"I'm sure it's nothing," Kate said, "only fatigue." She gripped the arms of the hall tree and attempted to stand, then fell back into the seat again, a flash of anger crossing her alabaster face.

"Here." Thomas reached for her.

"No. I can do it."

He forced a casual smile. "Please, Kate."

Her hands formed fists against Thomas' chest as her frail arms lifted and wrapped around his neck. He carried her upstairs and into the bedroom, and placed her on the bed as he once placed Sandra down when she was a child, worn out from a day of play. He walked to the basin, washed his face and hands and dressed down to his undergarments. On the bed, Kate struggled to undo the buttons of her blouse.

"I'll get those," he said.

She shut her eyes, turning her face to the wall. She was proud of herself that morning, when she helped Bess make the pies, then walked over to the barn and spoke with Ben as he fed and brushed the horses. When the grandchildren arrived, she sat on the porch and watched them play in the yard, enjoying a frosted glass of lemonade and sugar cookies with Sandra and experiencing no nausea whatsoever, but feeling like a hapless youth herself. She hadn't even needed an afternoon nap! And tonight, she was ambitious, working on the Nocturne and playing it for Thomas.

Now she paid the price for her earlier delusions. *Such a fool, I am*, she reprimanded herself, *a mindless, weakened fool!* How humiliating that Thomas had to bring her up the stairs, and even more embarrassing, that he had to remove her clothing and see how her body had aged with the disease. He must have wondered how he could have ever made love to this sack of bones.

In the darkness, he reached for her hand. "Tomorrow's a new day," he said.

Kate closed her eyes, weary at the thought.

4

Kate invited Mary and Hannah to dinner on the first Saturday of November. She also invited Jacob and Tara Zane, and the Schenk family (much to Thomas' dismay). It had been months since Kate last entertained in her home. She hoped that she would have the strength to serve the meal by herself, without the aid of Bess Abrams, the family maid.

Bess came to live with Thomas and Kate when Kate's illness first revealed itself. Thomas reassured his wife that Bess's presence was temporary, that she would only occupy Sandra's old room for a few months, until the weather warmed and Kate's cough went away. But by spring, Kate's hacking increased and showed spots of blood. Dr. Smith knew the signs of consumption only too well. He told Kate that she had a nagging case of pneumonia and that it would most certainly disappear when the hot days of summer arrived.

It was difficult for Kate to relinquish her position as the sole keeper of her kitchen, although she immediately approved of Bess. The middle-aged maid was friendly and unobtrusive. The daughter of slaves, Bess had a conditioned tendency to think of her employer's needs before her own. Bess's own life bloomed quickly, then withered. Her husband was killed in the civil war, years ago. Afterward, Bess went from house to house, performing the ancient duties of a cook and confidante.

Bess understood from the start that Kate Smith needed to feel that she was still in command of her domestic affairs, even in her disabled state—*especially* in her disabled state. As Bess helped Kate with the preparations for dinner, she made a point of asking where the Missus wanted things to go, and in what manner she wanted the meal to be served.

Kate supervised Bess's work from her position in the rosewood armchair beside the kitchen stove. Despite the stove's heat and the two afghan blankets that covered Kate's knees, she shivered with cold.

"Need another shawl?" Bess asked.

Kate proudly shook her head. She did not want to look like a sickly old woman, mummified in shawls, when her guests arrived. That's why she chose to wear the most fashionable of her formal frocks. Image was everything.

Bess placed the stoneware crocks of diced vegetables and scalloped potatoes on the window's wide sill, where the draft would keep them cool. She turned the ducks as they roasted on the fire. They agreed earlier that Kate would add the sausage stuffing at the dining table, thus giving the appearance of having cooked the duck herself.

"Will there be anything else, Missus?" Bess asked.

"No, thank you, Bess. Everything looks lovely."

The maid bowed her head and retired to her bedroom to reread one of the dime novels that she recently purchased from a bookstore in town. Dr. Smith lent Bess his magnifying glass when he noticed the maid reading the book with her nose so far down that it nearly touched the page. The device opened up worlds for Bess. She never knew that words could possess such boldness and clarity! She gazed upon each letter as if it were an exquisitely crafted jewel. In Bess's mind, it was.

She entered her room and lit a fire in the small fireplace. The flames were weak at first, but with added kindling, rose in strength and heat. Bess removed her boots and sat upright in her bed, propping two pillows behind her back. She reached for the book on the night table and opened it. Bess pressed the pages to her face, smelling the dry sweetness of ink over paper. She lowered the book and began to read, often speaking sentences aloud. The fire accompanied her soft oration, popping and crackling.

She hoped to complete chapter two this evening. Then she would close her eyes and have a short nap, dreaming of knights in elaborate suits of armor and damsels in distress. Later in the night, when she heard the guests leaving, Bess would discretely re-enter the kitchen and perform the bulk of the clean-up work, perhaps enjoying a plate of duck and potatoes herself. Bess looked up briefly and smiled at the fire.

It was a good, free life.

In the kitchen, Kate pushed her aching body up form the chair and took a slow, satisfying stroll about the premises. The main parlor was polished and well lit with hanging lamps. The dining room also met Kate's approval. The tall, white candles of the silver candelabra were burning and emanated a warm, inviting glow. She left the dinning room and walked down the long hallway with wood-paneled walls covered in oil paintings of solemn children with their pets and still-life's of white cake and summer fruit.

At the foot of the stairway Kate turned to the mirror and scrutinized the image that stared back at her. The cheeks, once pink and round, had sunken into the bones of the face, and the lips were cracked and gray. It was as if all of the blood had drained from her face, transforming the once beautiful woman into a mere skeleton of tired, wrinkled flesh. There was no need for Thomas to tell her that she was dying. She was not a fool

Dr. Smith walked downstairs wearing his gray tweed suit, the one that he set aside for medical conventions in Detroit and the formal dinners that followed the lectures each night. He entered the dining room and lightly kissed Kate's cheek, then stepped back and studied her face. "Feeling well enough for this?"

"Of course I am." Kate forced a jaded smile. In truth, she felt rotten, but she was determined to go through with the evening. It was like passing some sort of final test.

The guests began to arrive at half past six, starting with the Schenks. Kate and Thomas did not care for the minister and his wife, but they felt it their duty as long-time church members to invite them over this evening. The Schenk's daughter, Azalea, joined them. Azalea would not miss a dinner with Jacob Zane present, not for the world. Years back, she hoped that he would ask her for her hand in marriage. She was devastated when he married Tara Nasmith. For many months, Azalea suspected that Tara was with child. But Tara did not get pregnant until well over a year after the vows were exchanged, leaving Azalea and her friends quietly disappointed.

Azalea followed her parents into the main parlor. She was a smaller version of her mother: plump, boisterous in temperament, and bubbling over with carnal desires. She sat on an embroidered footstool beside the fire, her large behind sagging to the floor. When Jacob and Tara Zane entered the room moments later, Azalea pretended to be intent on studying the white-feathered wreath hanging on the wall.

Jacob sat down and ignored Azalea. Azalea thought that he played a flirtatious game. She turned to him and said, in her most distracted, flippant tone, "Why hello, Jacob..." Her eyes fixed upon the young farmer's torso, his shoulder muscles and the nape of his muscular neck. Her mouth watered as a hidden place located between her thighs prickled with excitement.

Tara coolly smiled at her husband. Jacob took his wife's hand and squeezed it in his own. Her smile changed in an instant and she looked at Jacob with affectionate trust.

Drinks were served. Kate made a non-alcoholic fruit punch, a drink which was commonly served with potluck suppers at the church. Azalea followed Kate into the kitchen and asked if her empty glass could be filled with wine, perhaps even a drop of gin.

"Are you sure that your father would approve?" Kate asked.

Azalea glared at her glass in defiance. "Who cares what he thinks, Mrs. Smith? I am twenty-five years old now!"

Kate hid her surprise. Twenty-five years old! Why was it, then, that she always thought of Azalea as being thirteen? Surely it wasn't due to Azalea's innocence. No, Azalea was ten times craftier than her father. Maybe it was the way in which Azalea dressed. This evening she wore a yellow, polka-dotted dress with a bright yellow sash wrapped around her waist. Two rolls of fat bulged in layers over the sash, and one larger, dimpled wave stuck out from beneath. She arranged her hair in two crumpled braids, tied with a satin ribbon, the same color as her sash. She resembled a mismanaged child doll.

Her painted mouth drooped into a pout. "Please, Mrs. Smith. You don't know what it's like to be a spinster at my age. I have to go everywhere with my parents! The least you could do is give me a drop of wine!"

Kate stifled a smile and poured some red wine into Azalea's glass. Azalea quickly drank it down, licked her lips, then requested a second glass. Kate poured again. Azalea drank the wine and held the glass out a third time.

"I'm sorry, Azalea," Kate said "but this is our best wine and I can't pour you anymore."

"Please!" Azalea whined. "Just one more."

The main door opened down the hallway. Kate heard Hannah's voice. "Excuse me," she said, and left the kitchen to greet her guests.

When she returned, Kate noticed that the bottle of wine had gone from being almost full to near empty. She said nothing to Azalea, who sat at the workbench beside the kitchen table, picking at a tray of creamed celery sticks and pickled onions.

"Could you leave some for the other guests?" Kate asked.

Azalea licked her fingers, oblivious to Kate's exasperation. "Who was at the door?"

"Hannah and her young friend, Mary Turner." Kate hoped that the chilliness of her tone would send Azalea away. She enjoyed being alone in her kitchen, and Azalea's presence was the worst kind of intrusion to suffer while getting a formal meal on the table for expectant company.

"The hempen widow!" Azalea shrieked. Her rouged cheeks brightened. "Why did you invite the hempen widow?"

Kate stopped basting the ducks. "Mary is a hempen widow?" Her voice, soft and troubled, could barely be discerned over Azalea's giggles of delight. She reached for the bloody handkerchief on the mantle piece. Her coughs were wet and thick with distress. Keeping the handkerchief pressed to her mouth, she sat at the table to rest.

Azalea continued talking, at a faster pace, each word fueled by meddling intrigue. "Didn't you know? Yes, Mary is Billy Turner's wife. Carrie Seymour heard it from her uncle, who heard it from Billy's brother, Elija. Remember Elija Turner? He was rotten to the core. He told Mr. Seymour his brother, Billy, and Mary were married for over a year, then Mary left Billy when she was with child. Do you remember Billy Turner, Mrs. Smith? Oh, he was an evil boy. Even when we were little, he would stab out the hearts of squirrels and ground hogs and carry them around on a sharp stick. One time, he put a rat's heart in the teacher's drawer and she gave him the licking of his life."

Her enormous mouth, faint purple and pursed at the corners, opened wide as she popped in a creamed stick of celery and started to chew. "What would make a woman marry a man like Billy Turner is beyond me. Not that he was bad looking. Actually, he had a wonderful build and when he took off his shirt—well, why get into what the man looked like. He's dead now, right?"

Kate put the handkerchief, now soaked in blood, on her lap. "I didn't realize that Mary's husband was Billy Turner."

"Didn't you?" A thin stream of whitish drool escaped the corner of Azalea's mouth. "I thought everyone in Bately knew that. And that poor little baby is Billy's child. At least, I'm assuming that she is, although if Mary married a man like Billy, who knows what else she's capable of."

"That will be enough." Kate said.

"I'm just telling the truth, Mrs. Smith."

Kate glared across the table at Azalea. "Some truth is better left unspoken."

Azalea stood from the bench, but not before grabbing a handful of creamed celery sticks to take into the parlor. Several of the polka dots on her dress were stained with small blotches of grease. A long, string-shaped stain of red wine colored the white collar of her dress.

Kate's low spirits were not lifted when she entered the main parlor, carrying the tray of celery sticks and onions. The room was utterly silent, despite the presence of her guests. Dr. Smith stood at the doorway. He shrugged in Kate's direction as if to say, I tried.

In Kate's absence, Mildred Schnek asked Mary about her husband's whereabouts. Mary stuttered a nervous reply, something about her husband's heart giving out while chopping wood last year.

"Was he an older man?" Mildred asked with mock concern.

"Yes." Mary answered. "He was quite old."

Then Azalea entered the room and loudly laughed. "Billy Turner was not old!"

Mary jumped up from her chair and went to Elizabeth, who rolled about in the corner of the room, licking a coin that she had found on the floor in a pile of dust. "No, baby, no!" Mary angrily scolded. Elizabeth wailed. Mary pulled her into her chest and squeezed the girl's round form with all of the consolation that she could muster. She returned to the sofa and placed Elizabeth on the cushion at her side. Elizabeth calmed down immediately, oblivious to the tension in the room.

That's when Kate came in.

Kate placed the tray on the teacart. Azalea went directly to the food. She glanced at the group around her. "I don't see why everyone is acting so surprised. We all knew that Mary was Billy's wife. It's nothing to be ashamed of, Mary." Her tone was sweet, like icing on a cake. "Everyone makes mistakes."

Mary turned helplessly to Hannah. The old woman lay her hand over Mary's knee, saying nothing.

Kate had had enough. She walked to the center of the room and stood before the fire, her petite form silhouetted by the blazing light. Her voice was calm, collected. "If anyone here has a problem with Mary's past, then they would do well to leave our home." Her eyes settled on Azalea. "Will all of you be staying, then?"

"I'm not leaving until I get my duck," Jacob said.

Kate laughed. She removed a white handkerchief form her side pocket and coughed into the yellowed lace. When the coughing would not stop, she rushed out of the room, knowing from the experience that this bout would lead to loud, embarrassing hacks and almost an ounce of fresh blood.

Azalea cast Mary a long, hateful stare. Mary lowered her head. Hannah's hand, previously clenching Mary's knee, relaxed into a gentle, encouraging pat. Azalea scoffed and handed a creamed celery stick to her mother. Together, they obliterated the first row on the tray. Kate came out of the kitchen moments later. She had managed to fix her fair and rinse the blood from around the corners of her mouth.

She passed the tray of food around, allowing time for the group to eat and relax. Then she led everyone into the dinning room, indicating where they would sit. The high mahogany walls were lined with carved mirrors and matching cornices. It seemed everywhere Mary turned she saw her own image. It made her uneasy. Dr. Smith pulled out Mary and Tara's chairs. Mildred waited for her husband to pull the chairs for her and Azalea, but he had already sat down.

The long dining table was covered with a turkey-red tablecloth with a wild rose pattern and Greek key border. Bess had set out the tea leaf iron stone china earlier that day, at Kate's request. The pressed glass goblets were in the popular Liberty Bell pattern and while most of them contained a full portion of dry, white wine, Azalea's glass was only half full. As a shrewd hostess, Kate realized that the last thing she needed was for Azalea's tongue to become any looser than it already was.

The ducks were cooked to perfection: moist, but not greasy, the thin layer of buttered skin crusty, but not dry. Fried green beans and carrots with slivers of almonds were served as a side dish, along with scalloped potatoes in a light creamy white sauce, with a layer of cheese melted on top.

Tara had a small portion of the duck, but requested seconds and then thirds on the beans and potatoes. Her pregnancy was evident, the small indented belly now appearing thick and hard, filling her slender waist. In her fourth month Tara was feeling a wonderful burst of energy and her current appetite was making up for the nausea that she suffered earlier.

In contrast, Mary ate little. She was unaccustomed to rich, heavy foods, and was harassed by memories of the scene in the parlor. She sipped her wine on an empty stomach and took small bites from a buttered roll. *Everyone knows*, she kept thinking. She had successfully deluded herself into believing that only Hannah was aware of her marriage to Billy Turner. Now she felt as if a scarlet letter were emblazoned upon her chest, for all of Bately to see.

Mary wished that she had never met Billy Turner, let alone marry him, but how was she to know what she was getting herself into? At the age of fifteen she simply wanted to settle down and have lots of babies on a farm, a family that she could call her own. When her breasts were no more than hardened bumps that formed a straight, telling fold in her bodice, Mary found herself engaged. Soon after, she purchased her first brassiere with the money that she had saved making quilts.

She wore the brassiere beneath her pink gingham dress on the night that she and Billy visited the justice of the peace. She never dreamt that their union would turn so miserably foul. Billy only slapped her arms and upper back in the beginning, then he used his fists, punching her thighs once or twice. In the final months, the hits became full-fledged beatings that left Mary's face swollen and blue. Now sitting in the company of so many strangers, it all seemed like a nightmare that happened to another girl, a very long time ago.

Dr. Smith brought a high chair up from the basement with a seat that slanted so Elizabeth would not fall. It was a peculiar looking contraption that he constructed for his first grandchild ten years ago. At the time he was so worried that the baby would tip over that he attached several long leather straps to the side of the chair. They wound round and round the infant's form, giving the appearance of a child in a straightjacket.

Kate thought of Elizabeth's needs in advance and warmed a bowl of mashed pumpkin with a sprinkling of nutmeg. Mary fed Elizabeth the pumpkin and the baby groaned with gastronomical delight. At almost four months of age, she no longer possessed the pink, wrinkled face of a flesh-colored raisin; now her cheeks were plump and pleasantly defined and her eyes, once tiny blue slits, had changed into round globes of brilliant emerald light. Her belly full, Elizabeth was content to sit and watch the people around her. She released uninhibited grunts of curiosity and surprise throughout the conversations and loudly clicked her tongue whenever Azalea spoke.

Reverend Schenk spent most of the dinner hour trying to illicit more contributions from Dr. Smith and Jacob Zane. His "vision," as he called it, was to build a Cathedral on "The Hill." He stopped only to add more food to his plate. "But you simply must give more of your inheritance funds to the church, Dr. Smith. And Jacob, even a farmer of modest means is obligated to tithe. You both must have greater faith. Then God will bless you, profusely, with material gain. He will aid Kate's healing, and grant Tara a healthy, newborn son. And most importantly, He will forgive each one of you your lecherous thoughts—the most perverse of thoughts that you store secretly, in the dark corners of your wayward minds. Turn your thoughts to Job. He never questioned the divine plan at work in his life. He never cursed God in his heart. He always believed, and he gave generously all that he possessed. And look at what happened! He was blessed, profusely blessed, I might add, with more property, children, and money than he could have ever dreamt possible." He picked at a string of duck meat wedged between his two front teeth.

Dr. Smith sat back, pondering the Reverend's words. "Isn't that the kind of thinking that got the Romans in trouble?" Rebellion flickered in his eyes. "The selling of indulgences, the building of monstrous cathedrals…faith giving way to the corruption of the world. It's as if your God strikes bargains with his people. If they give him money, he will give them whatever their hearts desire, including eternal absolution."

Reverend Schenk chose his words with care, so as not to lose his temper. "The things to which you refer have nothing to do with what I'm talking about, Doctor."

"Don't they, Reverend? Your way of thinking mixes the spiritual and the material, implying that if a man is truly spiritual, then he will have money, and give money, and prosper yet even more. But is seems to me that the poor and simple of this world are often the ones who express the greatest riches in terms of joy. Turn your thoughts to the Beatitudes."

The Adam's apple in Reverend Schenk's neck grew in size and redness, then quivered. Kate stood from her seat, holding the silver-plated pitcher. "More water, anyone?" She went around the table pouring cold water and when she arrived at her husband's place, let her hand flutter behind his neck briefly. The sharp fingernail settled into his thick skin and she pinched with all of her might. It was all that Thomas Smith could do to hold back a scream, but he definitely got the message that his wife was trying to send.

The group ate in silence, with the exception of Mildred and Azalea, whose vigorous eating sounded like horses chomping at the bushes along a fence. Mary breathed in deeply; she had not spoken a word all evening but now needed to ask a question. "I…I don't know if this makes sense…" she apologized. All eyes turned to her. She regretted opening her mouth.

"What is it, Mary?" Kate asked.

"Well, I've always wondered if Job was sad."

Azalea Schenk released a loud, condescending snort. "Of course he was sad. He was covered in sores!"

Mary longed to flee from the room. "Yes, I know he was sad about that. But in the end of the Book, at the end of Job's life, I mean. Don't you think he must have still been sad?"

"Nonsense." Reverend Schenk shook his head. "He was blessed, dear child, blessed with so much more than he ever had when the book began. And

I might also add that Job's daughters were known for their physical beauty, not unlike yourself." His eyes lingered on Mary's mouth, then trailed down to her hard, milk-filled breasts.

Mary blushed with shame. She felt strangely assaulted, even though she knew that Reverend Schenk was a man of the cloth. Mildred Schenk saw her husband's desire and was secretly enraged, not at her husband, but at Mary, for being such a temptress.

Tara put her fork down. She turned to Mary. "I understand what you're saying, about Job being sad. I've often wondered the same thing. He was rewarded at the end of the story, but look at what he lost before those rewards arrived."

Reverend Schenk looked at his watch, eager to leave. Apparently, no one but him was bothered by the fact that women were freely voicing their opinions about God's word. And they were obviously unfamiliar with the Lord's final response, the scene in which he calls Himself "I Am," because that explained it all.

"So you think that Job was still a man of sorrow?" Mary asked.

"Yes, I do." Tara replied. "Sorrow does not depart the soul, not completely. Not if what one lost was truly, deeply loved. When my children died—"

"What's for dessert?" Azalea interrupted.

"Strawberry rhubarb pie," Kate patiently replied. "And as a special treat, Thomas made the ice cream, so we'll have it *a la mode*."

"Bring it out!" Azalea exclaimed. It was the happiest she'd been all night.

Tara rose from her seat. "I'll help you clear the dishes, Kate." Hannah also helped. Mary wondered if she should join the women, but it seemed they already had too many hands. She remained seated.

Jacob leaned across Tara's empty seat. "Look at Elizabeth," he said to Mary. The baby was fast asleep in her chair, her curly head drooping so low that it touched the top of her chest. Her small hands rested on the tray of the high chair, the pudgy little fingers still clasping the pumpkin-smeared spoon. "I can't believe how she's grown. I can still see the tiny face that looked up at me when I cut the cord."

Mary smiled. "When I think about that day, I'm terrified."

"Me too. I'm just glad that I found you."

"So am I."

He turned away and began talking to Dr. Smith. Mary continued to look at Jacob. The bangs of his sandy brown hair fell forward over his eyes. Mary thought that he looked like Billy, although Jacob's nose was large and crooked, as if it had been broken in childhood. He wore a dark suit, mended at the elbows. The arms rose past his broad wrists and the white-starched collar looked to be strangling his neck. The top button bulged, about to pop off. Jacob tugged at the plaid bow tie. Mary stifled a giggle. He reminded her of a rascal of a boy dressed in his Sunday best, suffering through church service so he could go fishing in the afternoon.

The two men were having an animated discussion. They obviously knew one another well. Each one possessed qualities that Mary never knew existed in the opposite sex. For one thing, they didn't seem to look at her as a woman—at least, not in a sexual sense. Mary felt safe when she was with Jacob and Dr. Smith—like a daughter, or a sister, or a friend.

Her head turned to the open doorway leading into the parlor. She looked into the beautiful room. Each piece of furniture possessed an element that went beyond its functional purpose. The feet of the mahogany ottoman were not square, but scroll-shaped and meticulously carved. The pedestal table was topped with a thick white slab of marble and the cherry whatnot in the room's farthest corner was filled with hand-painted china and delicate vases of crystal and glass. Even the rosewood chairs surrounding the table in which she presently sat had detailed, embroidered seats. Mary felt honored to be a guest in such a luxurious home.

The women returned with two pies sprinkled in sugar, a pail of peach ice cream, and a stack of china plates. Kate rolled out her tea service. The Schenk family divided the first pie amongst themselves, leaving the rest of the guests to share the second of the pies, giving each person one slender slice of dessert.

Elizabeth awoke with a start and began to hysterically scream. She lifted the spoon and flicked it at Mildred Schenk. The utensil missed the woman's large face, but left a spot of orange at the tip of her powdered nose. Mary unloosed the leather straps and brought Elizabeth out of the chair.

"Thank you so much for having us, Kate," Hannah said, taking Mary's cue.

At the door, Dr. Smith helped Mary and Hannah with their cloaks. The women had walked over earlier in the evening and were planning to walk home, but Dr. Smith insisted on bringing them back in his wagon. Mary was grateful. The thought of holding Elizabeth in her arms as they made the long trek back to the church was exhausting in itself.

The other guests finished their pie and joined them at the door, exchanging polite goodbyes. Mary noticed that Mildred Schenk was glaring at her and she could not fathom why. Had the spot of pumpkin bothered her that much?

Dr. Smith took a different road into town. The main road was drenched in mud from the week of steady rain. His wagon got stuck in it two days ago and he had to call upon Jacob for help. The road that they were on was hilly, covered in deep holes and large, jagged rocks. It was a cloudy, drizzly night. Mary wrapped her cloak around her shoulders, thinking for certain that she would wake up the next morning with a stiff neck. This had become quite the recurring discomfort for Mary since Elizabeth's birth, and was no doubt directly related to having to hold the small but heavy load day in and day out.

The cold air made Elizabeth fall back to sleep. Mary was relieved. It was past time for Elizabeth's feeding and she did not want to attempt nursing on the hard, moving bench. She leaned against the warmth of Hannah's shoulder.

"You were quiet tonight, Hannah," she observed.

"I like to sit back and listen," Hannah said.

An uneven line of yellow light hovered in the distance, across an open field. "Is that a house over there?"

"It's an orphanage," Hannah replied. "Run by the Catholic nuns. I'll take you to visit sometime. I used to help with making meals. The nuns are very grateful. Last month they asked me to make some quilts for the children, but my fingers are so crippled."

Mary sat upright on the bench. "I'll make the quilts. Do they have material?"

"Oh yes. Boxes and boxes of old clothing. Why don't you stop by and see them in the morning?"

"I just might do that."

The lights to the orphanage melted into the black night sky. Mary thought of the children asleep in their beds. A quiet ache rose within her chest. When she thought of getting to work on the children's quilts, the ache began to fade.

Kate kicked her husband's leg. "Thomas! Roll over!"

They went through this routine every night of their marriage. Thomas, exhausted, immediately dropped into a deep stupor of a sleep. Kate, tense with restless energy, kicked him to roll over, since Thomas snored when he lay on his back.

His loud snore shifted into a short, startled snort. He rolled over and said, as he had said every night for the last forty-five years, "Night, Kate."

Kate remained on her back, looking up at the ceiling. To her knowledge, she did not snore. The two bricks at her feet were already cold and now her whole body shivered. She pulled at the mountain of quilts and thought about the night. It was not exactly a failure, and yet, with Azalea Schenk's intolerable behavior and Thomas' mischief, she certainly would not call it a success.

But she was pleased with the friendship that Mary and Tara formed. She hoped that Mary felt secure in knowing that she was supported, not condemned. She also enjoyed watching Jacob adore his wife. Kate went soft when she witnessed true, lasting love, especially in a couple so young. It reminded her of the early days that she and Thomas shared.

She quickly reviewed the courses of the evening. Was everything cooked enough? Not over-spiced or bland? Too sweet, too salty? She wished that Thomas was awake so she could drill him with these questions, though doing so would be pointless since she knew what his reply would be: "It was perfect dear, a terrific meal! The best you've ever made."

Kate tossed onto her side. She went for the handkerchief on her night table and expressed a string of muffled coughs. A small amount of hot, salty blood emerged from deep within her chest. The vile liquid traveled up her throat and into her mouth. She nearly gagged before spitting it out. *Next time, I'll use the Belleek ware*, she thought, wiping her mouth. *It's collecting dust in the cabinet and who knows how many more dinners I'll be able to host.*

She was suddenly filled with such sadness. The Belleek ware would not be needed. This was to be the last dinner that she would host, Kate reluctantly understood. Now she was faced with the tortuous task of placing this beloved aspect of her life into a tiny trinket box and slowly closing the lid.

She had collected hundreds of these trinket boxes in the last two years. One contained horseback riding. Another held long, invigorating walks to town that restored her vigor like a splash of cold water to the face. And someday, in the near future, Kate would tuck her daughter and grandchildren into one final, agonizing box where she would also surrender Thomas. Breathing her last, she would try not to cry as she closed the lid.

She heard Bess sweeping the floor in the kitchen below. Kate wished that Bess would come upstairs and sit beside her now. Bess's voice was low and raspy, like water bubbling through a brook. Kate wanted Bess to hold her like a baby, pressing her bony face into her soft, dark bosom. Whispering words of comfort. Words of love.

But these were ridiculous thoughts! "Go to sleep," Kate said out loud. It was her mother's spiteful, uncompromising voice. "Stop acting like a child."

5

Mary left the church with Elizabeth in her arms early the next morning, before Hannah woke up. The upcoming walk was to be a type of pilgrimage, a journey whose steps were comprised of Mary's dark memories of childhood heartache and innocence destroyed. She needed to meet the children of the Little Flower Orphanage and make sure that they were not being hurt in any way. If she saw that their living quarters were filthy, or that they weren't being fed enough, she would return home and speak to Hannah about the matter at once. Together, they could work out a plan. Mary saw herself as a saviour in the situation, and the burden of this self-imposed role weighed heavily upon her as she cut across the commons and left town.

Only weeks before, the foliage that surrounded the main road leading out of Bately was bursting with life—the trees of maple, ash and elm wore festive garments of red, orange and brilliant yellow. Now in November the leaves had all fallen, revealing a grey, barren landscape, harsh in honesty. She walked for several miles, passing the Zane's property, then sat to rest on a tree stump near the Smith's black barn. Her legs were not tired, but her arms ached from holding Elizabeth.

She thought back to her days in the orphanage in Southern Kentucky. It was a terrible place. When the children wet their beds (which they did often, releasing the terror through their bladders as they slept), the sheets were never changed. Urine soaked through the straw mattresses and eventually dried into the beds, leaving a permanent stench of salty mildew in the air. If Mary were to see barn animals living in the conditions in which she and the other orphans lived, her heart would fill with pity, but because the experience was her own, she did not grasp its full horror until years later, when the shredded fragments of her childhood rudely interrupted her daily thoughts.

The children were whipped daily. Large, swollen welts covered their backs and legs, and they were often hungry and parched with thirst.

A boy named Vincent told Mary his trick. "Dream of food at night," he said. "Then you wake up and your belly is full." Mary imagined fresh-baked bread, smothered in butter and blueberry preserves as she drifted into sleep. Vincent was right, it helped.

"And when they beat ya," Vincent advised, "think about your favorite place. But don't close your eyes, that makes 'em mad."

When the sharp leather belt came down on Mary's skin, biting and hot, her thoughts drifted to a mountain valley, bursting with wild flowers and rolling blankets of bright green grass. She lay down and looked up at the soft blue sky. The puffy clouds formed funny animal shapes: fat beavers and graceful deer, mountain lions too. Vincent was right, that also helped.

But Vincent did not tell Mary to see colors, and Mary never deliberately tried to see colors, like she tried to see jam and bread and a mountain valley in the spring. The colors were a gift. The gift frightened Mary. It also gave her hope.

She awoke one cold December morning and saw a trembling hue of gold and lavender that floated over the rows of children in their beds. Mary gasped at its beauty; she had seen nothing like it before. She reached to touch the color. Her hand sliced through it, creating broken wisps of gold and purple that drifted. At breakfast, the children waited for their bread on splinter-filled benches that lined the dining table. Mary noticed that most of the children had ghost-like auras of cobalt and white that wove, like strands of delicate thread, through their hair and limbs. When Mary looked at her own body, lifting her hand or staring down at her legs, she saw the aura's meandering light.

She was part of it.

The big peopled entered the room, carrying baskets of stale bread and pots of weak, clear tea. Their aura's were colored green and red, blackened by spots of brown and singed along the edges. Miss March, a gaunt, hideous woman sporting a cleft lip, lifted a wooden spoon high up into the air and threw it down against the table with a thundering, spine-tingling crack. "Be quiet!" she shrieked. Her aura rose in waves of red, settling over the two workers who stood sneering at her side.

Mary stared, blinked, and stared more. Miss March swung on her heels and slapped Mary across the face. The hard mark would remain on Mary's cheek for days. She shouted that Mary was stupid, dirty. "Stop staring!" Miss March screamed. The white aura engulfed Mary's body, as if protecting her.

She pressed her eyes shut and ate the bread on her plate.

Vincent leaned into her ear. "What's wrong?"

"I see colors," Mary whispered. She wanted to cry. The colors were a curse. They would not go away. In the hours that followed, they would be the cause of more beatings, since the brilliance made Mary look like a lunatic and this made the adults lash out.

The colors remained for three more days. Mary observed them in nature, for example, on the back of a blue jay, or encircling the tiny face of a sparrow or a cat. She gradually stopped hating the colors, and grew attached to them instead. Their beauty left her breathless. She yearned for more—as if yearning for heaven itself. She could barely see straight, the auras were so blinding at times. She stumbled about the orphanage in a state of baffled rapture. The beatings were severe, but after a while, Mary ceased feeling any pain. The colors were so very strong.

By the end of the third day, Mary had fallen in love with the colors. On the final night she turned over in her bed and gazed at the pattern of pinks and yellows that shifted across the soot-covered brick wall. Before the colors came she was dejected, but now she understood that there was more than just this miserable orphanage, the hate of the workers and the fear of the children in her midst. There were colors! Living, dawn-like, sprinkled in silver dew. Mary knew there was a purpose—a pattern behind the pain.

She sunk into a deep depression when the colors disappeared. Her nose started to run and her throat was tight and sore. She was too sick to play and spent most of her days lying in bed, refusing to eat. The adults backed off after that, satisfied that Mary finally knew her place.

Presently, Mary lifted her face into the heatless light of a late autumn sun. She wore her lavender walking skirt with white sprigs of coiled lace lining each side. Her black leather boots were new and sturdy, made feminine by the pointed toes and low heels. A show of white ruffles peeked up from the collar of her cloak, gently framing her chin. If strangers rode past, they would certainly think that she came from money and was either visiting from Cincinnati or the wife of a well-off farmer in the area. No one would guess that she was a hempen widow—unless they were told.

She smelled the coming of winter in the air. Her hands buried themselves into the warmth of her cloak and her face turned away from the wind. The ground before her went dark as a grouping of clouds moved across the sky. The face of a terrified orphan suddenly entered Mary's thoughts. She still felt like that little girl, even though today she was the finely dressed mother of a little girl herself.

She stood and picked up Elizabeth. The baby screamed out in defiance. Her neck locked into her shoulders. She looked at the sky with frantic, outraged eyes. "Now, now." Mary smiled. "It's not all that bad." The sun struggled to break through the darkness overhead as Mary and Elizabeth made their way along the meandering road.

When they arrived at the orphanage, a dim ray of light shone through a crack in the clouds. A little boy leaned against a stone wall, wailing. Mary went to him. "What's the matter?"

"I cut my foot on glass!" he sobbed. Mary looked down at the boy's bare feet. He had indeed stepped on a large wedge of glass and now blood was flowing from an open gash at the base of his heel.

Anger burned in Mary. "Let's get you inside." She entered the brick building without knocking. The little boy followed her into the front hallway. "Hello!" Mary called out.

A nun descended the stairway, the heavy layers of her black dress billowing like fire over the steps. She looked past Mary, at the boy's bloody foot. "Carter!" She rushed to the boy and cradled him in her arms. The boy buried his small face into the nun's broad shoulder, softly crying. The nun turned to Mary. "Excuse me, I'll be with you in a minute."

Mary sat down on a bench at the door's entrance. Looking around, she reluctantly accepted the fact that the orphanage was meticulously kept by the nuns. The hallway smelt of soap and vinegar, and ordered groupings of children's shoes were placed on the mat beside her, each child's first name written neatly in ink across the back of each leather tongue. A carved wooden crucifix hung on the wall—Christ's ribs protruding, the face tormented with pain…and beside this cross, a framed poem written in Old English-style calligraphy:

This way—it is the way where grow the bright-eyed daisies.
He made the daisies, and the Little Way, for children;
They know it when they see the daisies smile and nod.

Elizabeth stretched in Mary's arms, pushing to be set free. Mary placed her on the spotless, hardwood floor. Elizabeth clapped her pink knit booties against the wood panels, looked up at her mother, and smiled. "You are my daisy," Mary softly said. The baby chortled with pleasure.

Mary heard the nun speaking to the boy in the next room. "There now," her voice was calm, comforting. "Don't remove the bandage. And please,

Carter, please put your shoes on before you go out the door."

"But I don't like to wear shoes!" he protested.

"Do you know what, Carter? I don't like wearing shoes either."

Mary heard the little boy gasp. "But you're a nun! You have to wear shoes."

"Exactly, I don't *like* wearing shoes, but I *have* to wear shoes. There are many duties that we must perform as Christians and at times, these duties are tedious and dull. Like putting on shoes. But it pleases the Lord Jesus when we do these duties because they keep us healthy and strong. Now I'll tell you one final secret, and then you must run to Sister Martha and the other children."

"What's the secret?" Carter nearly shouted. The thought of a nun having secrets, being a living, breathing human being, must have been overwhelming to the little boy.

"Do you promise not to tell anyone else?" she teased. "All right then, I don't like to wear this uniform in the summer. It is a Holy uniform, mind you, it's the bridal gown that I was given when I married the Lord, years and years ago—but do you know, there are days when it is so terribly hot. Sometimes, in the scorching month of July, I even remove my petticoats and stockings. One day, I snuck off to the river, stripped down to my undergarments, and jumped in the water for a dip."

Carter giggled. "But you're a nun!"

"I know I am a nun, you silly child. But nuns get hot too."

Silence again. Then Carter's loud sobbing. "I stepped on glass!"

"Don't look at it, Carter. Don't even think about it. The wound will heal, they always do. Will you be strong for me, then? Good! Be strong for the Holy Mother, too. She sees your tears."

Mary heard rustling, then the slamming of the back door and the nun calling out through a window, "Come right back home if you can't catch up with the group!"

She returned to the font hallway, almost tripping over Elizabeth, who crawled for shelter beneath the many-layered curtains of the nun's black skirt. "Oh, dear!" She blushed. Elizabeth's head peaked out from the hemline. The nun leant forward and scooped the baby into her arms. "What have we here!"

Mary rose from the bench. "This is my daughter Elizabeth, and I'm Mary Turner."

The nun nodded. When she looked at Mary, Mary felt as though her whole soul could be seen. Was that the effect that nuns had on people? Up until this morning, she had never met one before. Maybe it was the outfit, which gave the older woman the appearance of an avenging medieval ghost, floating through he dank chambers of a haunted castle.

She shook Mary's hand. "It's a pleasure to meet you, Mrs. Turner. I'm Philothea. How can I help you today?"

"I'm a friend of Hannah Graf, and Hannah told me—"

Philothea's face lit up. "How is Hannah doing?"

"She's fine. Her arthritis has been flaring up, some days she can hardly walk."

She clucked her tongue and shook her head. "Is that so? This has been a difficult time for Hannah, since her husband passed away. Did you know Peter?"

"No. I came to live with Hannah this summer."

"Did you?"

"Yes, I'm a widow. Hannah took me in when I had nowhere else to go, just after Elizabeth was born. She's been very good to us and now I'd like to repay her, in a way. I know it would mean a lot to her if I made some quilts for the children at this orphanage." Mary hesitated. "And being a former orphan myself, I feel a kind of kinship with them, if that makes any sense."

Philothea reached out again and clasped Mary's hand. Somehow Elizabeth's foot got involved in the vigorous exchange. "Yes, yes! It makes a world of sense! We've been petitioning the Blessed Mother for quilts. Only this morning I added a special prayer to St. Teresa too. And now you're here!"

Mary was not prepared for this enthusiastic response. It made her feel needed, appreciated, while simultaneously raising her to the level of Catholic Sainthood, even though she was a Protestant. Or something like a Protestant.

"Come, let me show you the children's beds. That will give you an idea of the sizes that we need." Mary took Elizabeth and followed Sister Philothea up the stairway to the second floor. The children's rooms were as clean as the hallway downstairs. The beds were covered in white linens and thin blankets, perfectly tucked in at the corners and sides. The pleated curtains on the windows were the color of goldenrod and neatly pressed. A red-painted toy trunk stood in the room's corner, containing an assortment of rag dolls and wooden trucks.

"All of these beds need quilts. Not elaborate quilts, just your basic tie. The important thing is for the children to be warm at night. We'll need seven all totaled. Would that be too much?" Philothea turned to Mary, her face still radiant.

"Not at all. I could finish two by Christmas, and the other five by spring."

"That soon! You are a fast worker!"

Mary shifted Elizabeth onto her other hip. "Well, it's not really work to me. It's relaxing. I'd stay up all night and quilt, if I had a choice."

Sister Philothea laughed for joy. "You are an angel! Come, let me show you the nursery."

They walked down a hallway and entered a large, whitewashed room with cribs lining the walls. A small infant, no more than two months old, slept in one of the cribs. A second boy, about Elizabeth's age, was being rocked in the corner by a young, pretty nun. "Sister Margaret," Philothea said quietly, so as not to wake the baby. "This is Mary Turner. She's come to make the children's quilts."

Sister Margaret melted in the chair. "She has been sent by the Holy Mother…" She turned to Mary, her smile of wonder and gratitude widened to the point of cracking. "Your name is Mary. And the mother comes with child…"

"I thought the same thing myself," Philothea said.

Now Mary felt herself being elevated to a level that surpassed sainthood. She was a Catholic miracle, an apparition from on high.

Philothea pointed to three larger cribs. "Each of those will require smaller quilts, Mary, the size of lap quilts, I suppose. We only have three babies with us right now. But if you can manage to make a quilt for each of the eight cribs, we would be deeply grateful." She flashed Mary a beatific smile. Mary knew, without a doubt, that she would be making eight lap quilts.

"Is it too much work for you?" Sister Margaret asked.

"No, they're easy. I can make two in one day, if I set my mind to it."

The sisters exchanged thrilled glances. They stared at her with thankfulness. Mary fidgeted before them. "Hannah said that you have material?"

"Oh, yes! It's in the kitchen." Philothea reached out her arms to take Elizabeth. Mary handed her daughter over without hesitation. How could she not trust these women? Philothea placed Elizabeth in a crib by the window where the baby was happy to squeeze the soft shape of a rag doll, hungrily sucking on the white fabric hand. "Sister Margaret will watch your baby." She led Mary out of the room, down the staircase to a linen closet in the kitchen.

The interior of the closet was so spacious that it could pass for a tiny room. Stacked wooden crates lined the floor, heaped full with children's worn clothing, pillowcases and stained sheets. Mary bent down and examined the top layer of material. "These will be just fine. And I can use the sheets as backing. It'll take me no time at all."

"The wool and heavier linen is in that box to the left. You could use them for the babies' blankets." Mary heard a sudden rush of tumultuous activity approaching the orphanage. "Here come the children now," Philothea said. "I hope you'll join us for tea."

"I'd like that."

An explosion of children entered the front hallway and came bursting through the kitchen's swinging doors. Their cheeks were rosy and their bellies were evidently in need of quick replenishment. They all sat at the table, eyeing the stove and deeply breathing in the sweet aroma of baked cinnamon that leaked from the cracks of the range. The nun in charge, a stocky, frowning old woman, removed her cloak and dark gloves, reached for a dishtowel, and took the bread from the oven.

Mary was surprised at the restraint of the orphans. When the bread was sliced and placed before them, spread with a thin coating of apple butter, they did not eat, but sat looking up at the nun. The noise died down. The nun, still frowning, looked over the group and said with tremendous sobriety, "Now we will make the sign of the cross. We will make it slowly, and think of every word, because God loves that Holy sign." Her pudgy fingers lifted to her forehead. The children followed suit, as together they said, "In the name of the Father, and of the Son, and of the Holy Ghost, Amen." No sooner was the last amen voiced, when most of the children had almost swallowed their slice of bread whole. They were hungry, Mary realized, but not malnourished. The children had good color in their faces, and extra meat on their bones.

Philothea took Mary's hand. "Come join us." Mary sat at the table, surrounded on both sides by inquisitive orphans. Philothea gave Mary a thick slice of bread. "You may prefer preserves to apple butter," she suggested.

Mary swallowed back her astonishment. To be offered preserves in an orphanage touched a sensitive nerve. "I would like some preserves. Do you have blueberry?"

Philothea warmly smiled. "That's our best one."

Mary ate the bread and was afterward served a cup of hot, milky tea. The orphans chattered in her midst. "I like your hair!" one little girl exclaimed. "Where did you get the combs?" She gazed up at Mary with large, adoring eyes. When Mary told the little girl that she was once an orphan herself, the little girl's eyes widened—with hope, it seemed.

"Did a family come and get you?"

"Not quite," Mary said.

"Then you stayed an orphan forever?" the girl inquired.

"Not forever." Mary smiled, reflecting.

The wagonload of nuns made its way into downtown Bately at noon, just as the Women's Missions Meeting was letting out of the church. Sister Martha stopped the wagon and grumbled over her shoulder to the other nuns, "Don't drop any of the boxes or strain your backs!"

Mary stepped down from the bench with Elizabeth in her arms. She stood back to let the nuns disembark. They formed a perfectly straight line and began passing the boxes of material, one to another, leading to the church's front steps. Two hefty nuns waited at the doorway and carried the heavy loads inside, up the stairs to Hannah's apartment. Mary was amazed at the unspoken sense of order that the group possessed.

In the broad daylight, the mystique of the group faded and they looked almost comical in their garb. Mary recalled sketches that she once saw in a picture book on the Arctic North. She thought now that the nuns resembled a flock of penguins, clucking to one another and flapping their wings. They even waddled, due to the cumbersome nature of their vestments.

The Women's Mission Group tried not to stare. They huddled together in a small, tight band beneath a nearby oak tree, as if seeking security in their shared doctrine and experience. Like the nuns, they also dressed in uniform, wearing similar white bonnets, calico dresses and carrying baskets in hand. Their faces were pale, pointed. Mary thought that they resembled pelicans. The two flocks kept a safe distance from one another—it was, no doubt, better that way.

Philothea stood with Mary. "Is Hannah upstairs? Perhaps I should go and say hello."

"She's gone until Tuesday morning."

Philothea's thick gray eyebrows creased with concern. "Is she well?"

"She's just visiting relations in Westville."

"I hope that she'll be home when we pick up the first batch of quilts."

"I'll make sure that she is."

After the nuns left, Mary went up to the apartment and spread a crate of clothing out on the floor. She studied the items as she nursed Elizabeth. Most of the fabric was dingy and earth-toned, but her eyes locked on to a few precious garments of costly velvet, silk, and lace. Mary constructed a quilt in her head, imagining a thick blanket of earthen brown, forest green, and gray patches, with the impulsive triangle of resplendent calico.

She got to work on the first one while Elizabeth napped. She hadn't realized how much she missed quilting in the last year until the needles were in her hands and she experienced the simple, menial pleasure of cutting and folding, arranging and sewing. Mary learned the craft years before, in the hills of Kentucky. She was sent to live with an old woman who produced magnificent products: weaving towels, coverlets and table rugs from wool that was sheared from the backs of family sheep, and flax grown in the garden.

No sooner had Mary unpacked her bags, when the old seamstress called her into the kitchen and told her to get to work. "You might as well learn something useful while you're here." She handed Mary a wrinkled pair of men's underpants (mercifully unstained). "It's the cutting and sewing that'll keep you busy. The caliker is the fun part." Mary watched the woman with the intensity of a hawk. She had the jawbone of a man and fuzzy hair on her chin, but her long fingers possessed the grace and elegance of royalty. Mary imitated their every move.

Her first quilt was a "four-patch." She went on to make a "nine-patch," then a "wild goose chase." The old woman was proud. "You're not as slow as I thought." she reluctantly remarked. Coming from such a critical person, Mary took this as a great compliment. And rightly so. She was gifted at quilting, and many people agreed. "It's like singing nice, or playing the fiddle," they said. "You're real, real good at it, or you ain't."

Within months, Mary's reputation as a seamstress spread throughout the village. Soon women from all over the county came to her door with the patchwork, and cotton and calico lining all ready for Mary to quilt. Most of them could sew themselves, but they heard that Mary did more than sew— she created works of art. Orders even came through the mail. One wealthy man from Boston wanted *ten* Tulip quilts to give that year as Christmas gifts. The pay was generous.

Mary regulated the price by the number of spools of thread used for each blanket, charging one dollar a spool. A single-sized quilt earned her two dollars, baby quilts were sold for fifty cents. With the money that she made, Mary was able to help her guardian with the living expenses, while setting aside a small bundle of savings stored in a sugar tin beneath her bed. Shortly after meeting Billy, Mary took the money that she had saved and purchased a hand-painted cedar chest, two brass candlesticks, a sturdy pot for cooking, and a small brooch with genuine green onyx. She was set to be a mountain bride.

The last project that Mary worked on was an enormous floral quilt. Each of the twenty pink and green blocks contained a different design. The festoons were decorated with cockscombs and sprays of wild flowers, meticulously composed. Mary rarely went outdoors that summer, only to fetch a pail of water or stretch her tired limbs. The rest of her time was spent inside the cabin, working in silence beside her guardian, accompanied by the peaceful hum of the spinning wheel.

When she was finished, Mary folded the quilt on the floor of her cedar chest and gently placed the candlesticks, brooch, and pot on top. Before crawling into bed each night, she would open her cedar chest and look at her dowry, dreaming of the day when she would descend the lush Kentucky hills in a gown of white satin and lace. On her wedding night, she would lay her best quilt over her husband as he slept, as a token of her love.

Billy hated Mary's quilts. He cursed the cedar chest often. They were always moving to escape the law and it was a "pain in the ass" to bring the chest along. What did she need with all of those dam'd blankets, anyway? Billy was so desperate for drink one night that he traded his wagon and horse for a case of whiskey, which meant that the dower chest had to be left behind in their next move. Mary never forgave Billy for that.

She rarely quilted after she was married. She felt anxious and uprooted with Billy, and lacked the security required to create. The few items that she did make were inspired by necessity, like her petticoat. At the time, the shack where they were living didn't have a wood stove or a fireplace. Mary was sick with fatigue from not sleeping at night. She refused to lay beside her husband for warmth; she would have preferred sleeping with the devil himself. So she made herself a petticoat from two of Billy's torn shirts and added a thick interlining of wool. The petticoat kept her legs warm at night, but was soiled beyond repair when she delivered Elizabeth in the field.

Mary's thoughts were sporadic as she worked in Hannah's apartment that afternoon. She remembered the petticoat, and Billy, and the thrill of completing her first quilt. She wished that she had stayed in that mountain cabin with the old lady who taught her to sew. All the time she was dreaming of happiness, she didn't realize that she had true joy right then and there. Thank heavens for Elizabeth. Her daughter's very existence reassured Mary that the choice to be with Billy was not in vain.

Elizabeth awoke before supper and played in her crib. Mary's hands moved across the half-finished quilt, swiftly piecing bits of wool together. She discovered a bright, mustard-colored scarf at the bottom of the crate. It would blend perfectly with the color of the curtains in the orphans' room. As Mary sliced the scarf into small squares, a rush of creative adrenalin ran through her veins. How had she managed to abstain from quilting for over a year? When she had more time, perhaps in the spring, she would make some Daisy Quilts for the babies at the orphanage. She thought of the poem about the bright-eyed daisies and smiled to herself. How good that the children were loved.

Elizabeth's happy noises eventually digressed into frustrated moans and sobs. Mary put her needles down and closed her eyes. Her head was full of colors; some were dull, some vibrant, all of them beautiful and dissolving together as ingredients melt into a thick stew. She rose from the chair and stretched her arms to the ceiling, softly groaning with the simple pleasure that comes from productive work.

The strong stench of Elizabeth's dirty diaper nearly knocked Mary over as she entered Hannah's room. It never ceased to amaze her that her daughter's simple, bland diet, when digested, could produce such a revolting smell. She changed Elizabeth on Hannah's dresser, and brought her into the kitchen where she prepared the baby's meal. The cupboards were almost bare. Mary inwardly reprimanded herself for forgetting to bake bread that afternoon, as Hannah had asked her to do.

Elizabeth ate the last of the applesauce and squash. Mary warmed herself a cup of cider. She had not eaten since mid-morning tea at the orphanage and now her stomach burned with hunger. Hannah stored Mason jars containing an assortment of vegetables and fruit, along with several jars of meat, in the basement of the church. Mary chose to skip supper rather than go downstairs to fetch the food.

Elizabeth was rubbing her eyes at eight o'clock, two hours before she usually went down. Mary put her in the crib and was surprised when the baby fell right to sleep, enabling Mary to return to quilting. She chose two large sections of brown wool and pieced them together, then added an oblong segment of the mustard yellow scarf. The blanket was almost finished. She only had to attach the backing, later in the week.

As she worked, she thought of the preserves in the basement below. Her empty stomach gurgled and groaned. She even started to salivate, thinking about the taste of pickled peaches in her mouth. By ten o'clock, she was so famished that she could have downed an entire jar of beets, which, under ordinary circumstances, she detested. Her mind was made up. She put down the needles and quilting and went to the door. It would be cold in the basement, so she put on her cloak and boots.

The stairway leading to the first floor was lit at its base by a hanging kerosene lamp. Mary took the lamp from its hook and rushed past the minister's office. She noticed a crease of light shining under the door and thought that Reverend Schenk was a hard worker, indeed. She hesitated at the basement door but her stomach roared with hunger—if she didn't eat soon, she wouldn't be able to get to sleep.

The door squeaked loudly as she opened it. Mary stepped, trembling, onto the top step of the stairway. She peered down into the bowels of the church, seeing cobwebs and mice, and a long winding corridor. Mary hated that corridor. She had walked through it once before, with Hannah one afternoon. It felt like the walls would come caving in at any second, burying the women alive.

She ran down the wooden stairway, gasping for breath. The lantern's light barely illuminated the dirt floor before her as she stumbled past two locked doorways and entered a third. The room was filled with old pews, forming a virtual labyrinth for Mary to wind around before arriving at the preserves. She banged her knee on the edge of a pew and almost dropped the lamp. When she got to the shelf, her hand fumbled for a jar of pickled peaches and jar of corned beef.

Clouds of vapor formed on the walls of the jars as Mary took them in her sweaty hands. She pressed them to her bosom and wove back through the cluttered, musty, space. Her heart palpitated and her legs shook visibly as she scurried down the corridor.

A pale face suddenly appeared, as if forming from the darkness itself. Its dark eyes were gleaming. The head was a bulging, luminous egg. Mary screamed.

The mouth moved upwards, creasing into a flat, sinister smile. "Afraid of the dark, little girl?"

Mary screamed again, then saw that it was only Reverend Schenk. She swallowed her fear and laughed in embarrassment. "I'm sorry, sir."

He placed his hand on her hip and squeezed the wool folds of her cloak. A new, darker fear rose up in Mary's chest, primitive but keen. He moved in closer and pressed her body up against the dripping stonewall. His hot breath smelt horribly foul. It climbed, like a furry rodent, up Mary's neck and into her hair. And his body odor! She nearly gagged. It was a putrid combination of spicy sausage and rotting fish.

"Don't be afraid, little girl…" His voice was low and demanding and cracked with excitement.

Mary pushed back and dropped the jar of peaches on the floor. It shattered into pieces, the sweet juice oozing everywhere, turning the cold dirt at her feet into a puddle of syrupy mud.

His hand slipped between two buttons of her cloak, the skinny fingers searching for flesh to grab. Mary looked frantically at her surroundings. Perhaps there was a shovel, or a gun…. As his quivering mouth pressed over hers, Mary lifted the jar of corned beef and smashed it over his balding head. He dropped to his knees, groaning.

She jumped over him and ran through the corridor. Now it truly felt as though the walls were caving in around her, and her lungs burned for oxygen. She ran faster, tripping up the basement steps. In the foyer, she screamed for help and continued screaming as she ascended the second set of stairs. Safe in the apartment, she bolted the door and moved a heavy dresser against it. She placed the lantern on the dresser and blew the flame out.

Her breathing was frantic, choked. She looked into the front room and experienced the strange, discomforting quiet that follows a traumatic event. She went to the daybed and collapsed into its softness, her body wracked with dry, heaving sobs. A preacher—not a preacher! In her turmoil, Mary couldn't help but wonder if there was something in her, some kind of innate evil, or pathetic vulnerability, that attracted this type of thing.

As the minutes passed, her distress transformed into a growing sense of rage. She angrily wiped her tear-stained face with a corner of her sleeve. How dare he! And a man of God, nonetheless! She looked at her surroundings. Up until tonight, Hannah's apartment was a place of security. Now it took on the dark proportions of the run-down tenements and hovels where she and Billy once lived, a prison where she was forced to watch her back at all times.

Mary took Hannah's sewing basket and grabbed a needle and fresh spool of embroidery floss. She wanted to find Reverend Schenk and beat his head even harder with a large, sharp rock. Or better yet, take a sewing needle and plunge it in his beady black eye, twisting it mercilessly in the socket. She decided to make a crazy quilt instead. She found the remainder of the mustard-colored scarf and cut out tiny petal shapes. Her nose was running, and a stray tear slipped down her burning cheeks.

She continued piecing late into the evening, oblivious to the loud, churning pains ricocheting off the walls of her empty stomach. She fell asleep in the rocking chair at two o'clock, the needle clutched tightly in her hand,

and was awakened at dawn by the comforting sounds of Elizabeth playing in her crib. Mary looked down at the square on her lap.

A large daisy with a dangling green stem was set over a man's beige handkerchief. A small knife, made from a mended sock, cut through the base of the stem, and beside the knife, there was a drop of Mary's blood from where she pricked her finger on the needle just prior to falling asleep. Mary spit on the daisy and attempted to scrub the blood away, but it had dried into the fabric as she slept and now gave it the appearance of a flower, crucified.

6

Hannah knew that something was wrong as soon as she came home. Mary's defensiveness only confirmed her suspicions, along with her anxious, childhood habit of picking at the split ends of her hair. She finally broke down and told Hannah the whole story, detail for detail. Hannah was not surprised.

"I should never have left you alone in this church," she said.

"Don't be silly. How could you know that Reverend Schenk would do what he did!"

"I knew."

"You did?"

Hannah suddenly looked very old to Mary. "Jacob has a cottage on his land. I'm sure he won't mind if we lived there."

"You want to move out of the apartment?"

"Do we have a choice?"

"You stay, Hannah. I'll go."

Hannah turned her head towards the window, staring vacantly through the smudged glass pane. Watching her, Mary realized that Hannah was not a bastion of strength. She was a simple old woman, once young like Mary, whose body had aged over the years. When Hannah spoke, she spoke slowly, with a mixture of sadness and resolve. "We'll both go, dear."

The small cottage was made of stone. It was two rooms wide, separated by a short hallway, and one room deep. The outer walls were built of field stones, with cut stones serving as the corners of the house. A porch jutted out from the backside, and beside this, an L-shaped addition where the kitchen and toilet were located. The windows were boarded and the roof was badly in need of repair.

Jacob spent his childhood in the cottage, living alone with his elderly father, the tiny rooms pervaded by an indescribable emptiness. Samuel Zane gradually went senile, at first dropping silverware as he ate and forgetting to put on his shoes, then rocking in the bed with his knees curled up to his chest and mumbling that the room was too cold. In the final months, Jacob left his father in the cottage and farmed the land by himself. He was relieved when the old man died. If he hung on any longer, Jacob would have had to commit him to an institution, and that didn't seem right.

They lived together for sixteen years and, in that time, never had a heart-to-heart father/son conversation. When they spoke, it was about the harvest, the horses and plows, and the building of the barn. It wasn't that his father was an unfeeling man, he was only lost without a wife. Jacob knew that it would be different if his mother were alive, or if his father had remarried. The right woman could have brought tenderness to the household, lightening the heavy burden of getting by from one day to the next. When Jacob met Tara, he thought he had found of piece of paradise.

Tara wanted to live in the cottage, but Jacob absolutely refused. He would build them a log house, with a loft where the children could sleep and a cellar for storage space. Tara insisted that they at least fix up the cottage and use it in the summer time, when they wanted to swim at the lake. Wasn't that what every boy and girl wanted in the hot months of June and July—a home beside a lake where they could cool off whenever they liked?

Jacob agreed, and promised many times to get to work on the cottage and fill it with furniture, but somehow, he never got around to doing it. The memory of his drooling father soaking the bed with urine had a way of keeping him away.

He was glad to give it to Hannah, and threw in a half acre of land to seal the deal. Tara had long since accepted that Jacob was not interested in using the cottage. She now looked forward to having Hannah and Mary living on the edge of their land. She often said that Hannah was for too old to be doing the physical labor of keeping an entire church. Many times, Tara had encouraged Hannah to leave the position and live off the money that her sons sent. But Hannah was too attached to the apartment and its memories of Peter and the boys—until now. Tara asked what made Hannah change her mind, but the old woman would not say.

Mary fell in love with the little cottage as soon as she set eyes on it. Jacob brought Mary, Elizabeth and Hannah up the dirt driveway in his wagon, carrying the last of the three shipments of their belongings. It was a cold and drizzly December morning, on the verge of snow. Walking up the cobblestone path, Mary noticed the outline of a garden behind the stone fence posts. Next spring she would plant tomatoes and green peppers and a row of corn.

They went inside and Mary felt a tinge of disappointment. The tiny rooms were ice cold and smelt of dust and dead air. Cobwebs stretched from wall to wall. Two field mice scurried across the warped floor. Jacob put his hand on Hannah's shoulder and promised to bring them a cat right away.

There was a large fireplace in the center of the sitting room. Jacob made a fire with kindling and logs that he had transported earlier in the week from his barn. They were welcome to his supply. He promised to bring them a fresh load of fuel whenever they ran out. Mary set Elizabeth's wicker bassinet beside the heat of the fire, where the baby could safely watch the group without getting injured in the unfamiliar environment.

Jacob walked outside and unloaded the last of the boxes from the cart. He left soon after that, leaving Mary and Hannah to the miraculous task of making a home rise up from the rubble in their midst. Their first priority was to clean the walls and floors.

Hannah handed a rag and pail of water to Mary. "Have you ever seen such a mess in your life?"

Mary looked about, searching for a ray of hope, a clean floorboard or a hanging lamp. "Do you think we'll be able to sleep here tonight?"

"You'd be amazed what a day of solid work can do."

Jacob and Tara arrived with dinner at six o'clock . By then, the interior of the cottage was scrubbed clean. They sat on the floor and ate slabs of bread and ham. Mary nursed Elizabeth in the kitchen, where an ancient wood stove bubbled and kept them warm. She gave Elizabeth a slice of buttered bread to suck on afterward and placed her back in the crib.

Mary helped Jacob move most of the furniture, scattering the various oak and wicker pieces throughout the house, as Hannah continued to clean. Tara offered to lend a hand, but Hannah insisted that the younger woman sit down and rest. In her sixth month of pregnancy, Tara appeared swollen and inert. Many people asked her is she miscalculated the date, perhaps she was due earlier that she thought? She replied, delicately, that mid-July was the earliest possible time of conception. The baby must be taking after Jacob on its size.

Hannah was right. An amazing amount of work was completed in one day. By the time that Jacob and Tara left, the furniture was in place, the rooms were fairly clean, and two beds were made up with blankets and fresh linens.

Hannah and Mary slept soundly that night, but Elizabeth was restless in her crib.

Mary had dressed the baby in a quilted bonnet and thick wool bunting bag. Elizabeth cried out in frustration, since she was not free to kick her arms and legs. She eventually relaxed by sucking on her fist and making soft, high-pitched sounds. The fire died down in the early hours of the morning. They awoke to the distant sound of roosters crowing. They felt partly frozen, but rested.

The next week found Mary and Hannah busily sorting through the plethora of boxes and wooden crates. Mary hurriedly constructed two pairs of pale blue, quilted curtains from Hannah's old bed sheets. These brightened the dark quarters, while also insulating the windows from the persistent draft. By mid-December, the cottage was in order and Mary was able to return to the orphan's quilts. If she worked with diligence, she could complete the three crib quilts, plus two of the single-sized bed quilts by Christmas, as she had promised Sister Philothea and Sister Margaret.

Jacob stopped by one afternoon to fix the roof. He nailed the loose shingles in place, and put new ones in the spots that were bare. The first snow of winter melted the week before and the current dry weather enabled him to work at a steady pace. On another afternoon, he removed the boards from the windows and placed black shingles at their sides. The run-down cottage suddenly transformed into a home. Mary stepped outside that evening and strolled to the end of the dirt road, then turned to look at the mellow orange glow that shown from the windows.

She walked fearlessly into the woods, eventually emerging on the grassy shores of Spirit Lake. The dark cliffs and shadowy hills seemed to exist in another world, a world formed before the glaciers, before living beings walked the earth. She heard rustling in the woods and turned to see Tara standing only feet away. She glanced at Mary, then gazed upon the hills.

"It's beautiful, isn't it?" Tara asked.

"Yes," Mary agreed.

Tara turned and walked back into the woods. It was a fleeting encounter which left Mary wondering for days.

A few weeks later, Bately held its annual Christmas Dance. Mary was certain that she would not attend, but on the night of the dance, Hannah made one last effort to get Mary to go.

"Jacob and Tara are stopping by the cottage to see if you need a ride," she informed Mary.

Mary looked up from her quilting. "A ride?"

"To the dance."

Mary sighed. "Hannah, you know I don't plan on going."

Hannah walked across the room and placed Elizabeth on the middle of the round rag rug. The baby rose on her hands and knees and started creeping. It was only a matter of time before she would crawl. "Are you sure, Mary? It would do you good to get out and spend some time with people your own age."

Mary returned to her quilting. "I've had enough dances to last me a lifetime."

She had a nice arrangement set up for herself beside the fireplace. The seat was low and comfortable, with a loose, feather-filled cushion tied on its twisted osier, and covered in bright green and scarlet material. On the back of the chair hung a net bag of knitting and needles, and on the low stool at her feet there sat a basket of assorted patchwork. Mary liked that she could go to this chair any time she wanted and merely pick up the basket and continue her work. She looked forward to spending this particular wintry evening in her beloved spot, sipping warm milk and bosco and completing two of the orphan's lap quilts.

She worked for several minutes, purposely ignoring Hannah's eyes upon her. Elizabeth hurtled forward in a clumsy attempt at crawling and fell flat on her face. From the sound of her wails, one would think that she had been seriously injured, but it was only the baby's nature to make drama out of the most trivial accidents. Hannah picked Elizabeth up and cradled her in her arms.

Mary put the needles down. "Why don't you come to the dance with me?" she asked. "We'll bring Elizabeth."

Hannah kissed Elizabeth's wet cheek and tickled her armpit with her finger tip. Elizabeth released a snorting belly laugh, uttering a string of pleasure-filled consonants. "No, no. I'm too old for a dance, and this small one needs sleep. Besides, I want to write to the boys tonight. They sounded lonely in their last letter. They miss their friends in Calgary."

"Why did they leave? I thought they liked it there."

"You don't know my boys. Joshua and Andrew are wanderers, they're not happy unless they're moving on to a new adventure. They seem to think there's money in the logging industry. Joshua wrote in the last letter that the trees on the west coast of Canada are higher and wider that any he's seen in Ohio. They're giant trees, he says. And land is cheap out there. I'm sure they'll make a lot of money."

"But they already have money."

"Andrew says that there's always more money to be made. I wonder if they'll someday ask themselves if their struggles were in vain. Then again, I shouldn't complain. It's the boys who have given me this comfortable life."

Mary experienced a vague gratitude toward Hannah's sons. Were it not for their money and Hannah's generosity, she and Elizabeth would likely be living in a poor house or worse yet, under Bonnie Turner's roof. "When are Jacob and Tara coming?" she asked, removing her thimble and putting it in a dish.

Hannah's face lit up. "They should be here soon."

"I'll get changed." Mary left the sitting room and went into her bedroom.

"Why don't you wear the tweed frock with the blue velvet?" Hannah called out. "And put on the pearl earrings too."

Mary emerged wearing exactly what Hannah had suggested. "You're not trying to get me married off, are you?"

"Not at all, dear. I'd love nothing more than to have you and Elizabeth stay here with me forever."

Mary turned to the mirror above the mantle piece and pinned her hair into a high, apple-shaped bun. Miniature wisps of light blond curls fell behind her ears and the back of her head. Her bodice was curved and cut markedly lower than that of her other frocks, thus highlighting the sharp line of her narrow shoulders and freckled neck. Mary's body had noticeably changed in recent months. It never returned to the thin, girlish shape of earlier days, but transformed into a curved, womanly figure with round hips and a svelte waist.

She turned to Hannah. "Well, what do you think?"

Hannah nodded with approval. "Nice."

"You don't think I should wear the chine? Doesn't this frock make me look pale? Isn't it too low around the bosom?"

"It's perfect, dear."

Mary was on the verge of getting into her nightgown and returning to her favorite chair when Jacob knocked at the door. Her heart sank with disappointment as he stepped inside. "I was hoping you'd change your mind about going."

He removed his black cap and shook off the light layer of fresh-fallen snow. "I wanted to stay home with Tara but she wouldn't hear of it." He turned to Hannah. "How are you?"

Hannah brushed the snow from Jacob's shoulders and shook the collar of his coat. "I'm fine, dear. Isn't Tara feeling well?"

"She's tired. She was half-asleep on the bed when I left her." He looked around. "Where's Lizzy?"

Mary ignored the question. "Maybe I should stay here and you can go home to Tara. Or why don't you go to the dance by yourself?"

Hannah opened the door and handed Mary her scarf and cloak. "Go on now, and have good time." She gently pushed Jacob through the door and whispered in his ear, "Take good care of her."

In the wagon, Jacob placed a bearskin wrap over Mary's lap. Halfway through the journey, he had still not said one word to her. She supposed that most young farmers would have flirted with her if their wife were safely stowed away at home. Evidently Jacob wasn't interested in that sort of game. Mary was relieved—profusely relieved.

She admired the snow-covered fields, the scrawny bunches of grass and spots of brown earth showing beneath the fine layer of white. Her eyes lifted to the sky and she caught her breath. A latticework of large white flakes fluttered, quivering, rising up, then soaring down, their tranquil dance immediately replaced by scores of new, silent, flakes, thick yet weightless, soothing to the sense and seeming, to Mary, heaven-sent.

She remembered a glass ball that she had once seen in a store's elaborate Christmas window display when she was a child. There was a house within the ball, a humble little cottage with shutters and a copper roof, and parked before the house stood a miniature sleigh and a regal white horse. The clerk appeared in the showcase. Upon seeing Mary's curiosity, he shook the ball in his hand. He held it to the window. Mary stepped forward to have a closer look. Tiny white flakes fell from the roof of the ball, landing on the cottage, the front of the sleigh and white back of the horse.

Mary smiled, clapping her hands. "Do it again!" she cried. The clerk did it once more, than placed the ball down and walked away, disappearing into the busy interior of the store.

Mary closed her eyes and imagined that she was actually inside of that glass ball now, sitting beside Jacob in the fragile wooden sleigh, moving, *gliding* forward into the solemn, wintry night. It was a world of ineffable wonder and serenity.

Jacob turned his head and looked at her, his eyes squinting through the snowfall, as though not able to see her clearly enough. She had the urge to lean in closer to his face, in order that he might understand everything that she felt, all that she had known. He reached under his seat and produced a second wrap, this one made out of beaver pelts. "Here, put this around you."

Mary took the wrap and did as he instructed, thinking as she buried her face into the fur's smooth softness and smelling it's dark, musty warmth, that this man Jacob was, like the snow, heaven-sent.

Azalea Schenk nearly wet her petticoat when she saw Jacob Zane approach the Town Hall in his wagon with Mary Turner sitting beside him, *but not his wife*. Azalea had drank an immoderate amount of fruit punch earlier in the night, spiked with strong gin, and giggled to her friends that she no longer felt bashful in the least. Her round cheeks were rosy and her beady eyes glowed with an unruly light.

The front steps were slippery with snow. Jacob took Mary's arm. Some people standing on the grounds noticed this gentlemanly gesture and interpreted it in a considerable darker light. Azalea clutched Jacob's arm when he brushed past and leaned into his startled face. "Where's your wife?" she asked.

Azalea's large size provided her with a legion of glands from which she could sweat, especially when she was drunk. Jacob winced. The putrid odor reminded him of the smell of dead rabbits when they've been left in the traps for too long. He broke free from Azalea's grip and guided Mary into the crowded, smoke-filled room, simultaneously wishing that he had never agreed to come to the dance.

Lines of couples held hands and jostled across the floor like frolicking, spinning tops. The rowdy band was comprised of a fiddler, a pianist, and an elderly blind man sucking on the harmonica. Mary immediately recognized the folk song that they played. She sang it often to Elizabeth before the baby fell to sleep. The present version was loud and raucous and hardly resembled the soothing melody that she loved.

Jacob released Mary's arm and turned to talk with a group of farmers. Mary went cold. For the first time since arriving at the hall, she was on her own. Clumsy dancers pushed past. Twice, she almost tripped. A hulking man carrying a mug of frothing beer came towards her, broadly smiling, and stepped on her toes. She stifled a yelp and went to the farthest corner of the room where a row of wall-flowers were linked, side by side, elbows touching, in a tight, depressing chain. Mary took her place at the end. She lowered her head. It was going to be a long, miserable night.

Jacob appeared to be having a good time. The farmers smoked pipes and fat cigars, one chewed a wad of tobacco and spit the brown bundles of drool into a brass spittoon. Mary found herself wishing that she was a man, and understood why the Psalmist thanked God for such a blessing. Men were like dogs, happily barking and freely tromping about. Women were like nasty, flea-ridden cats, always fighting and scratching, and searching for escape. Mary's back dropped, as if slinking down the wall.

She saw Reverend Schenk standing at the long table of food. He loaded his gaping, crooked mouth with baked beans, simultaneously talking to a small, idolizing cluster of elderly women and men. Older church members loved Reverend Schenk. He often complimented them on their appearance, their houses and jewelry, and their magnificent insights into his sermons.

Dr. Smith entered the room. Mary rushed across the floor to meet him. "Dr. Smith!" she breathlessly exclaimed. He had no idea how relieved she was to see his face—the warm, straightforward eyes, the smile wrinkles that formed shallow dimples at the corners of his mouth.

"Hello, Mary. Do you want to dance?"

She laughed. "Yes."

Dr. Smith was a terrible dancer, but Mary hardly cared. They twirled, bungling about the crowded room. They spoke of Hannah and the baby and Dr. Smith's wife. Evidently, Kate was weaker than ever, but keeping a positive outlook. Dr. Smith stopped talking, swallowed hard, and inquired about the cottage. Had Elizabeth's cold cleared?

Mary stayed at the doctor's side for the remainder of the evening. He was kind enough to introduce her to everyone that she did not know, and include her in the conversations. Azalea Schenk circled Jacob like a meat-deprived, carnivorous bird, at times bumping into him and conveniently snuggling up to his chest. At one point in the evening, she brazenly grabbed his hand and pulled him onto the dance floor. He released himself and walked backwards, hands lifted, professing a sore back from all of the haying that he had done.

It was eleven o'clock and the band was winding down. Several couples left. In an hour, the doors would close. Mary was prepared to go to Jacob and ask if he was ready to leave when someone tapped her shoulder. She turned to face a dark-eyed man smiling at her. He was the same height as Mary, and thin for his size. Though he was not handsome by conventional standards, a certain, untamed crudeness in his demeanor intrigued Mary.

"Mary Turner?" he asked.

"That's right."

"I'm Hannah's son, Drew."

Her eyes widened. "Andrew! What are you doing here? You came all of the way from Canada? Does Hannah know that you're here?"

"I just got back from the church. The new caretaker told me she bought Jacob's cottage." He glanced at his surroundings with calculating eyes. "I was on my way over when I saw that the town had thrown me a welcome home party. My, my, Bately is certainly changing in leaps and bounds. Why, I think Reverend Schenk is soaking money from an old lady that I've never seen before." He winked at Mary. "Can I have this dance?" He reached for her hand and placed his other hand on the ridge of her hip. They walked onto the dance floor and within seconds, formed a graceful pair.

Mary was acutely aware of the people watching her. She heard Drew's steady breathing and smelled the unique scent of his skin. "How did you know who I was?" she asked over the music.

"Azalea Schenk pointed you out to me."

Mary saw Azalea beside the table of food, eating a handful of cookies and openly staring at Mary and Drew. "Why didn't you write and tell Hannah that you were coming?" she asked.

He flashed her a sparkling, reckless smile. "I'm impulsive."

She smiled, almost against her will. "Hannah told me as much."

"Did she?" He pulled her in to his chest and moved his mouth closer to her ear. "Are you impulsive?" he asked. The level of intimacy in his tone made Mary blush. His lips brushed across her flustered cheeks.

Jacob suddenly stepped between them. "Ready to go, Mary?"

"The song isn't finished," Drew said.

"Yes it is." Jacob wrapped his arm around Mary and led her to the door.

Drew followed them outside. "We'll give you a ride back to the cottage," Mary offered. "Where are your bags?"

Drew lifted the large backpack at his feet. "Right here."

For the first time since they met, Mary recalled that Drew was a wealthy man. No one would have guessed it from the looks of him. He wore dungarees, two layers of flannel shirts, and a scuffed, deerskin jacket, a shiny rifle hanging at his side. His boots were worn to the point of ripping, and a bristled shadow on his jaw told observers that he had not shaved in days. Mary recalled Hannah's descriptions of her sons. They were explorers and rebels, definitely not the types to waste energy on playing the game of image and status, no matter what their monetary situation.

The ride home was tense. Drew challenged everything that Jacob said, and Jacob sternly disagreed with the points that Drew was trying to make. Mary sat between them and realized that the antagonism between the two men probably went further back than the events of the evening. Jacob seemed reluctant to drop Mary off at the cottage with Drew.

"Thank you," Mary said.

He snapped the reins without saying goodbye.

Mary opened the cottage door and led Drew inside. The small sitting room was dimly lit with Christmas candles that Hannah placed on the tables and window sills that afternoon. The pressed glass lights radiated soothing hues of amber, amethyst, sea green and cobalt, and produced flickering shadows that danced across the low ceiling and walls.

Mary removed her cloak and scarf and placed them over a chair. Drew closed the door behind him and put his backpack on the floor. "This is nice."

Mary looked at the simple, cozy place with pride. "Do you like it? Hannah and I have been working hard. We're going to paint the walls in the summer, and Jacob is bringing us a cat to get rid of the mice."

"Where do y'all sleep?"

Mary pointed to the direction of the hallway. "There are two bedrooms there, and Elizabeth sleeps in a nursery. Actually, it's nothing more than a closet, but Jacob removed the door from its hinges and her crib fits perfectly. That door leads to the kitchen. I hope you don't mind sleeping here on the floor tonight. The rug is thick, and we have plenty of blankets to keep you warm."

She looked at Drew. There was a glimmer of Hannah in his dark features, but the cynicism in his eyes made him unique. "My mother has written about you in her letters," he said. "I had no idea that you would be this beautiful."

Mary blushed again. "I'll get those blankets." She turned towards the kitchen.

He followed her. "It's true. You were the prettiest girl at the dance tonight."

She hesitated before facing him. "Why are you saying this?"

His gaze lowered to the plush velvet line of her dress, then trailed up her neck to meet Mary's questioning eyes. "Don't know. I just am."

A door creaked at the end of the hallway and Hannah walked out of her room. "Mary, is that you?" She stood in the doorway, blinking her eyes.

Drew went to his mother. "It's Drew, Mama."

"Andrew?" She reached for her son and they embraced. "Andrew? What are you doing here?"

"I got hungry for your Christmas turkey."

Hannah went to the rocking chair and fell back into its seat. She stared up at Drew as if he were a ghost. "Is Joshua with you?"

"No, I came on my own. One of us had to stay behind to watch over the men. Next year I'll stay and Josh'll take the train back. How's that?"

"Oh, Drew." Her voiced cracked with maternal love. "You look well."

"I feel well. We don't have cold winters in Vancouver. I haven't been sick for months. You should see the ocean and the mountains out there! It's like paradise. Sometimes I look around and think of all those crazy stories you told me about Adam and Eve and the Garden of Eden. I think to myself, maybe Mama was right, maybe there is an Eden, and maybe it's Vancouver. In the summer time, the mountains are capped with snow, and Josh and I go swimming in the lake and look up at them. We'll be splashing around in the warm water, looking up at the these majestic mountains covered in white...."

Drew's enthusiasm was contagious. "Have you ever climbed one of them?" Mary asked.

"All the time. We've shot black bears and cougars, and the most amazing birds."

"It sounds beautiful," Hannah replied.

Drew knelt at his mother's feet. "It is, Mama."

The noises caused Elizabeth to wake up. Mary brought her into the sitting room and placed her on the floor. Drew reached down and put the baby on his lap. Elizabeth's small mouth usually formed a rigid square when she was held by a stranger, but it remained relaxed for Drew. He stood her on his knees. "Well, well. You're a night owl, aren't you?" Elizabeth babbled in response, grabbing Drew's nose.

They didn't turn in until after three o'clock. Drew spent that time describing the great Pacific North to his captive audience. His wiry body darted around the room as he spoke, picking up a pillow, placing it back down, tapping his forefinger on the icy window pane, anxiously flicking stray linen from his shirt. His eyes also darted, briefly resting on Mary, then flitting to the side and settling on his mother and Elizabeth.

"None of the houses are more than twenty years old. They're mostly made with wood, not brick. It's a fresh land, unconquered. Josh and I get to feeling like the early explorers sometimes. We'll canoe up rivers and see

Indians living in their tents, or huddled around fires on the beaches. Don't look so worried, Mama, they're friendly."

"And when are you going to find a wife?" Hannah teased.

Drew looked at Mary. "I'm waiting for the right girl."

7

The next morning they ate apple pancakes and cheese at the kitchen table. Mary was touched when Drew offered to feed Elizabeth some strained peas. She sipped at her black coffee, attempting to conceal her growing interest in Hannah's son. Hannah could not cover her own enthusiasm as she refilled Drew's cup with hot coffee and added more food to his plate.

After breakfast Drew asked Mary is she wanted to go for a walk. "I think its too cold out for Elizabeth," she said.

"I'll watch her," Hannah eagerly offered. Before leaving the cottage, Mary discreetly dabbed vanilla extract behind her ears.

It was a cold, sunny day. The land appeared cleansed by the snow. They crossed the field and sighted Jacob and Tara walking at a distance. The couple labored down a steep hill. Jacob held Tara's hand as she waddled in her largeness. Mary thought that she had never seen a pregnant woman look as big as Tara did. One would think she was ten months along, rather than seven.

They got to Mary and Drew and asked if they had seen a cow. Evidently, the animal got out of the barn in the night. Jacob could not imagine how he did it, the door was securely latched. Tara worried that the mindless creature was frozen to death. Jacob said that if they found him alive, he'd have to be shot in the spring, and his carcass sold to the cobbler. Mary and Drew promised to keep a look out; it wouldn't be hard to overlook a frozen cow. The two couples parted: Jacob and Tara heading for the woodland, and Drew and Mary going to Spirit Lake.

The evergreen trees surrounding Spirit Lake were frosted in blankets of white, their branches drooping beneath the weight of snow. Drew took

Mary's hand. "You forgot to wear gloves." He put her left hand in the pocket of his coat, squeezing it in his own. "I'll have to keep this warm for you."

As they walked together, Drew spoke about the trip that he and Josh made to California the summer before. California was as gorgeous as the Pacific North; it was hot in the summers and mild in the winters, and there was an ocean so blue that it almost looked fake. "We want to go back next summer and look for gold," he said. "I don't believe that all of it's dug up—not yet."

They circled the circumference of the lake. Drew helped Mary up onto a large rock and they looked out at the water. "I used to swim here when I was young. Josh and I weren't allowed to come back after Stephen died."

"Who's Stephen?" Mary asked.

"My little brother, the one that died."

"Hannah never said—"

"No, she can't talk about it. She never does."

"How did it happen? When?"

"It was a long time ago. Josh won't talk about it either. It's not his fault, but he thinks it is. We used to tease Stephen for being a sissy. Stephen was an odd boy. We'd be running down the road, hurrying to get into the water for a swim, and he'd be tagging along from behind, just looking at a leaf or a flower in his hand. When we got to the lake, Josh and I headed for the cliffs right away. The jumping was great, we could do triple flips in the air."

Mary shuddered—triple flips! One flip would scare her silly.

"Stephen used to watch us from the shore. If he ever did go in the water, he'd twirl about in the shallow part like a damned ballerina. He wouldn't do laps, and he definitely wouldn't jump from the cliffs. He was nine, and Josh and I had been jumping since we were six, so one day, we thought it was high time for Stephen to start jumping. We dragged him up the hill. He was kicking and screaming. We brought him to the top of the highest cliff, that one over there. Josh called Stephen a Mama's boy...."

"Stephen was crying, shaking. Really sad. He wouldn't step off, so Josh thought he'd give him a little help by picking him up and throwing him over the edge. I guess neither of us thought about the way we did it—we'd have to arch our bodies way out in the air before we curled up to dive or flip. We just didn't think that the reason we never got hurt was on account of doing that special arch that made us land at the deep part of the lake. Stephen's body was twisting when he fell. Shit, he nearly scraped off the side of the cliff. When he hit the water, he must have hit the ground first, 'cause he broke his neck and drowned."

The shale cliffs across the lake took on a horrific shape in Mary's mind. She saw three boys at the tip, then the smallest one falling to his death. "How terrible...." It pained her deeply to think of Hannah grieving for her son.

Drew helped her down from the rock and they resumed walking. A winter bird fluttered in a tree ahead of them on the trail. It's tiny legs sprang off of the branch. It soared into the air, the small gray wings outstretched against the clear winter sky. In one swift, determined movement, Drew lifted his rifle and shot the bird. It appeared to explode into one hundred pieces from the impact of the bullet, bloody feathers flying everywhere, descending to the lake, scattering over the dark ice.

They met up with Jacob and Tara on the way back. Jacob found the cow. She was at the edge of the woodland with her head stuck in a fence. Though the animal did not die in the night from exposure, her eyes were glazed with sickness and her wide face was covered in sheets of frozen phlegm. Tara rubbed her large belly, her eyes filling with tears. "Poor Tillie." She actually wept. Drew briefly glanced at the cow, then at Mary, stifling a laugh.

Jacob visited three weeks later to give Mary and Hannah a kitten. She was a feisty little creature, with black and orange spots and a dry, button nose. Mary came up with the name Patches, and Drew relentlessly teased her lack of originality. She leaned against his shoulder and smiled. Jacob's eyes squinted with disapproval. He looked to Hannah for support, but she seemed pleased with the pair.

Drew needed to return to Vancouver. His lumber company was sending a big shipment of wood to Seattle and Drew wanted to supervise the work. Some of the men got lazy, especially the ones who were doing it as a temporary job and didn't have a family to support. These employees saw the final stage of their work, shipping the wood, as a time of reward for their hard labor in the forest. The days when they were supposed to be guiding the logs down the river, the men chose to spend their time drinking whiskey on the river's banks and racing each other on the logs, tumbling from the unstable vessels into the icy waters.

Drew asked Mary to come back with him. She was speechless. "You can be my wife," he matter-of-factly said.

"I don't know," she stammered. "We hardly know each other."

"That's not true. I've told you everything about myself, Mary, things that Josh doesn't even know."

Mary was flattered. That a wealthy man like Drew should have fallen in love with her, a hempen widow! He never inquired about her past or judged her as most of the men in Bately would certainly have done. And he had the ability to make Mary and Elizabeth's future financially secure, not a small consideration to Mary. After all, her comfortable situation with Hannah could not last forever.

Almost to her own surprise, she heard herself say aloud, "Of course I'll marry you."

He clasped her hands and kissed her on the mouth. "There's a girl. I'll buy another ticket and we'll leave tomorrow."

She pulled back from his embrace. "That's too soon. I need some time to pack, to say goodbye to Hannah and the Zanes."

"All right, come out when you're ready. I'll meet you in Vancouver." His eyes twinkled. "But don't wait too long, I'll start missing you."

They took the stage coach to the train terminal in Cincinnati early the next morning. Drew kissed Mary amidst the hissing of engines and the shrieking of whistles, then wrapped his deerskin coat around her shivering form and hugged her with all of his strength. "Do you promise not to wait too long?" he asked.

She smiled at him with thankful eyes. "I'll be there next month."

8

Agnes Frome was the only child in an extended family of female servants. She worked in the linen room on the Rutherford Estate in Kensington, England, folding towels and sheets, stacking them into large, wooden bins to be sent upstairs each morning. Agnes' mother was a chamber maid and her old, hackneyed aunts cooked in the kitchen.

As a girl, Agnes hoped that she was an orphan, or better yet, a bastard child, with a father that came from good, English blood. When Agnes went for meat or spices at the market, she sometimes turned sharply at a crossing in the roads and peered over her shoulder. Was that her long-lost father, the rich one riding in the gilt carriage? He looked to be interested in her as he stared from his window, and when she caught sight of him, he discreetly lowered his face.

"Father?" she asked under her breath, furthering the fantasy.

The illusion ended when Agnes turned thirteen. Her mother felt she was old enough to hear the startling truth of her paternity. Yes, she was a bastard child, although those were cruel words and she phrased it in a considerably kinder way. No, unfortunately, her father was not of good blood. He was a stupid louse, for after pledging his troth to Agnes' mother, he ran off to the country with a prettier maid. Actually, she wasn't very pretty, but her breasts were larger and bigger than melons and Danny, the horny louse, liked that kind of thing.

If Agnes was disappointed, she didn't show it. The disheartening news only served to strengthen her resolve to rise above her impoverished roots and marry into wealth. Within the space of two frustrating years, Agnes realized that this was an unreachable goal. The snobby Rutherford boys, Arthur, Richard and Rodney, only scoffed at her flirtations. She changed her strategy and acted aloof, but then they just ignored her.

Time was running out. One day, as she studied her white, cunning face in a mirror, Agnes finally admitted that she was homely. It wasn't an easy moment. She liked to believe that her beauty transcended the standard of the day. She likened herself to a portrait of Sir Thomas More's daughter. The girl was prim, unsmiling, with hair strung back tightly from her face. Her dress was bound like a Chinese woman's shoe across her broad, flat chest. Agnes thought that she was breathtaking. Unfortunately, trends in English beauty had drastically changed since the Renaissance. Agnes had no doubt that if she lived in the sixteenth century, she would have snared a rich husband with no trouble at all.

Most women might have given up at that point, but Agnes was a survivor. *Very well*, she thought, *I may not be pretty or have big melons, but I like to read books and I can memorize rows of numbers better than anyone I know.*

So she developed a more practical strategy, whereby she would work hard at her studies (her mother scraped together the coins that she earned as a chamber maid to pay for Agnes' education), and eventually take the position of full-time governess for the Rutherford's grandchildren. She'd be given a large room upstairs, where the decent people lived, and would never have to pick hair from the bathtub drains again.

At the age of eighteen, Agnes effortlessly slipped into the vacant position as head governess for Charles Rutherford's children. Charles and his terrible wife Emily lived in the plushest wing of the Rutherford Estate. Agnes spent her days teaching in the nursery and in the evenings, snuck away to the main building where her mother and aunts prepared her dinner in the kitchen.

It was humiliating for Agnes to spend time with people of the lower class, even if they were members of her own family who loved her more than anything. She felt a bit like a martyr as she hungrily ate the fatty beef, scraped from leftover bones. Her mother and aunts treated Agnes with doting reverence, thus increasing the young woman's already inflated ego.

Agnes despised Charles' and Emily's sons. They were rude and spoilt and, carrying on their father's tradition, relentlessly teased Agnes. The daughter Kate was different, however. She was quiet, sensitive, and excelled at her piano lessons, demonstrating an innate gift for playing even the most difficult tunes by ear. Agnes felt sorry for Kate, to be born into such a hateful family! She sometimes experienced a sense of sisterhood with the little girl. They were both trapped.

Agnes had an affair with Charles Rutherford that lasted, off and on, for over a decade. She fancied notions of Charles leaving his wife, although her overriding sensibility (for in the end, Agnes was an immensely *logical* woman), told her it could never be. Charles continued to laugh at Agnes. He joked that she was uglier than any other women he had ever known, let alone slept with. So what, then, made Agnes open the door for him when he came knocking at night? At the time, all she could think was that her life was fading fast and she had to settle for the meager scraps that were directed her way. And so, in the quiet of her chambers, Agnes hungrily savored every morsel of Charles Rutherford's flesh, just as she savored the fatty meat at dinner hour in the kitchen below.

One night, Agnes opened the door and they both saw little Kate, clutching her dolly, watching them at the end of the dark hallway. Charles stepped forward, about to go to his daughter and make up some lame excuse. Agnes took his hand and hastily closed the door.

They fought inside. "Now she'll tell Emily!" he hissed.

"No, she will not."

"What makes you so sure?"

Agnes wryly smiled. "Do you think that little girl would betray me?"

Charles sat on the bed, unbuttoning his shirt. "You? She doesn't even seem fond of you."

Agnes knowingly shook her head. "Then you don't understand children, my dearest Charles." She sat beside him. "Children are adults, placed in tiny shells. Those hideous sons of yours are greedy, conniving men, and little Kate is a dignified woman. Her sense of loyalty rises above this God-forsaken family, I can assure you of that."

Charles' face reddened with rage. No one spoke that way about his family and got away with it. Were it not for Agnes' kind words about his daughter, he would have strangled her then. "Well, she certainly isn't like her mother, I'll give you that."

Agnes snorted. "Kate will have her pick of London's best men someday, you wait. And I plan on sitting at the front of the cathedral and taking credit for some of it." She stroked his inner thigh. It was a rare moment of intimacy between them. "Kate is the girl I always dreamt of being," Agnes confided. "Not only is she pretty, she's smart in such an inquisitive, original way. She's open, and fresh like dew. She has a quality that one cannot attain through hard work, no matter how hard one tries. A woman is either born with it, or she is not."

"And what quality is that?" He opened her night dress, reaching.

"Kate has genuine lack of concern for money and the possessions that come with it. Do you understand, Charles? One cannot release the potential for being rich, if one has never possessed riches. Look at me, I was born poor and I will die poor, but for the remainder of my life, I shall always lust after money." Her hand rose on his stocky leg. He pressed her back to the bed. "Perhaps that's why I let you use me as you do. Because you have power—and money—and I don't. And we both know it, don't we, Charles?"

Charles simply smiled.

"But Kate is free from the weakness that afflicts most women."

Charles abruptly sat up, the desire draining from his loins in an instant. His eyebrows crumpled with worry. "You don't think she'll run off someday and marry a boy below her? A servant, perhaps?"

"Now that's a tricky question, darling. She may, and she may not. Your despicable wife could drive her to it. Let us hope not. On the other hand, rich or poor, Kate will marry for love. A girl in her circumstances has the luxury of being romantic." Agnes pushed Charles back to her side and rolled her bony body over his. Her spindling arms and legs formed a tight web around his rigid form. She placed her thirsty mouth on a roll of fat beneath his chin. Her small teeth nibbled. "Love is a luxury that I've never been given," she matter-of-factly said. Then she had her way with him, and it felt rather nice that evening for Agnes to be on top.

As fate had it, Kate did marry a poor man for love. His name was Thomas Smith. He was a doctor in Ohio, of all places. As a teenager, Kate went to Cincinnati under the pretense of caring for a dying aunt. The aunt died, but the visit lingered on. Her parents sent one telegram after another, demanding that she return to London at once. Kate finally wrote back, informing them that she had fallen in love that summer and only the week before eloped with a Dr. Thomas Smith. They were presently living in the city but planned to move in the next year to a small town called Bately.

Emily Rutherford was furious. She never particularly liked her daughter, and now she purely detested the girl. She spoke at once to her solicitors and had them cut Kate out of the estate. Charles was silent on the matter. He did not dare stand up to his wife. She set the rules of the household from the day they were married, and to argue would be suicide.

Agnes was secretly let down. She stopped living through Kate's adventures after that. It was fun to watch the girl when she went to balls, escorted by rich, handsome men. Agnes enjoyed helping Kate get dressed and versing her in the etiquette of the day. (She read all of the books on how to behave at such social functions, and knew each rule by heart.) Agnes watched from the sidelines as if Kate's life were an exciting game of polo. When Kate married Thomas Smith, the ball utterly missed the net.

In the next thirty years, the Rutherford dynasty fell apart. Ironically, tragedy befell both of Kate's promising, Oxford-educated brothers. It was inevitable, really, since Charles never thought to mold the character of his sons. How could he, when he had so little character himself?

Arthur married and his wife bore him an heir. The baby choked on a crust of toast at the age of two and Arthur, tormented by grief (he was never told that life could be hard, that trials were to be endured), shot himself in the head.

The second eldest brother, Richard, perhaps the brattier of the two, slipped into a life of debauchery. He gambled away a large portion of his father's wealth, took to drinking hard liquor as soon as he got out of bed each morning, and eventually died of venereal disease at the age of twenty-six.

Rodney, always the underachiever, suffered the least dramatic of the deaths when he died, inexplicably, of heart failure at the age of thirty-two. Inexplicably, because he had never worked one day in his life, and had no knowledge of stress, physical or otherwise.

Emily Rutherford was deeply humiliated by the scandals surrounding her boys, Arthur and Richard, and died of a stroke at the age of fifty-five. Charles hung on to life, but continued to experience it in a bitter frame of mind. Agnes, aging and lonely, tried on one occasion to coax him back into her bed.

They passed each other in the hallway outside of the nursery where Charles' grand-nieces and nephews were citing multiplication tables aloud. Agnes blocked Charles' path and said, as she once said when her wrinkles were not pronounced and the crooked rivers of veins were not etched upon her face, "Why don't you come to my chambers, Charles, for a drink?"

His eyes showed his revulsion. He pushed her to the side and walked off. That's when Agnes knew that she was not a woman anymore, not really.

Charles asked Agnes into his bedroom shortly after Christmas. Her heart leapt with hope. They sat in two wingback chairs by the fireside. Charles sipped warm brandy. Agnes discreetly looked around the room. She didn't see a photo of Emily the Terrible, that was a start.

"It's my daughter." Charles lifted a letter into the air, angrily flapping the yellow page. "She's ill. Her asinine husband wrote to say he thinks she is dying. I'm sure he's wrong. He was most likely educated in medicine by an illiterate mid-wife."

Agnes smiled. She loved when Charles was abrasive—which meant that she loved him often. He was a short man in his youth, and he had shrunk with age. At eighty-one, he appeared shriveled, disproportionate.

His parched mouth curled in revulsion each time that he spoke. "Consumption!" he barked. "That's what the idiot writes. Says Kate is dying." He threw the letter into the fire. The paper rose above the flames, then dashed into the blue center and turned to black ash.

"It can't be, Charles. Kate was always the strong one. The boys were the complainers. I recall one time, I took them horseback riding in the fall. It was a nippy day and the children were under-dressed. The boys whined the entire afternoon, but not little Kate. She jumped up on the wildest of the horses and expended such an amount of energy, she was sweating by the time we arrived back at the stables." Agnes stared into the fire, conjuring up the day in its tired light.

Charles muffled his response. It was a word like "right," or "good." Agnes was relieved to have said the proper thing. The room was silent, then Charles said, "If she is, in fact, dying, and I know that she is not, then she must return to London at once. We'll give her the best care in this household, nurses and the best doctors around the clock."

"Come now, Charles, I'm certain that she'll want to stay in America with her husband. Don't forget, she has a daughter and five grandchildren. That's her home now." One would think that Kate were married yesterday, the way Charles spoke.

Charles swished a mouthful of brandy between his cheeks and swallowed with a sickly gulp. When he spoke, his words were buried in a bubble that formed from the coating at the back his throat. "I would go to Ohio myself, if I could withstand the voyage, but I'm far too old. Perhaps you, Agnes…"

"Me, sir? Go to America?"

"I'll get you the best cabin on the ocean liver of your choice. Have you ever been on one of those ships, Agnes?" He knew that she hadn't. Agnes had lived in the Rutherford mansion every day of her life. "They are wonderful. The ocean air is invigorating, the food is sumptuous, and there are only the best people on board." He hoped that the final remark would get to Agnes, and it did.

"When shall I leave?" she eagerly inquired.

"Soon. I'll make the arrangements in the morning."

Agnes stood from her seat, hesitated momentarily, and upon seeing Charlie's sallow lips curl, turned and left the room.

It used to be that Kate felt better on certain days, depending on the amount of sleep that she got the night before. But now every day was horrible and every night sleepless. It reminded her of the final months of her pregnancy with Sandra, when washing the dishes was an exhausting act, and the mere sight of food twisted her stomach in knots. Back then, Kate only had to think of the end result, a beautiful baby to hold and cherish, and the discomfort seemed a small price to pay.

Dying, in contrast, did not carry with it an air of noble sacrifice. Perhaps it would, Kate thought, if she were a stronger Christian; if she possessed a deeper faith. She wanted to—dear Lord, she wanted to—but her tendency towards doubt was a foundation block of Kate's temperament. No matter how hard she tried to root it out, the skepticism remained—even grew.

Bess sat at Kate's beside, darning socks for one of Sandra's active boys. "Daddy was dancing on the auction block," she said. "They made him dance. I was a girl. I didn't know why I had a big lump in my throat. But now I know, I know. A man stuck his fist in Daddy's throat. He lifted Daddy's lips and was looking at his teeth. 'Good jaw' was all he said, like my Daddy was some kinda barnyard horse."

Kate sadly shook her head, clicking her tongue.

"I never saw my Daddy after that." Bess jabbed the needle into the sock. "I'm sorry, Missus. It ain't right for me to be talkin' to you like this. Not with you ailing and such—"

"Please, Bess, no apologies." Kate pushed up off the pillows with her elbows and threw her legs over the edge of the bed. The sudden movement brought on a fit of coughing. She patted the handkerchief to her mouth. When she put it down, the fabric was wet with clotted blood. "I'd like to eat lunch downstairs today."

"Yes, Missus."

Bess rose and led Kate across the room. They descended the wide, mahogany staircase, arms linked around one another's waists, and entered the parlor. Kate lay back on the sofa, covering herself with an afghan blanket. Bess disappeared into the kitchen and prepared a simple meal that Kate could easily digest—a cup of warm chicken broth, and half of a biscuit with a light spreading of strawberry jam. She made herself a fried egg, boiled potatoes, and a peeled, sliced apple for dessert. They ate together on trays in the parlor, sharing a pot of weakened tea with goat's milk.

Kate lay her head back and dozed after lunch. When she opened her eyes, she looked out the window and saw a horse and buggy coming in the direction of the house. Kate sat up and called for Bess.

Bess appeared like an angel in the doorway. "Missus?"

Kate remained staring at the window. "Now, Bess, who do you suppose that could be coming to visit?"

Bess went to Kate. "I don't know, ma'am. It sure is a fine horse."

The carriage stopped out front. A petite, decrepit old woman stepped down and paid the driver with a bill from her purse. She walked up the dirt driveway and crossed the front lawn. Kate experienced the oddest sense of déj vu. The visitor's gray hair was tied back in a bun so terse that it pulled the wrinkles of her cheeks up to her eyes. Her small frame moved slowly, slouching at a sharp angle over a serpent-headed cane. Watching the stranger, Kate saw a spider.

There came the sound of a wooden serpent's head pounding against the door. Bess rushed to the front hallway, brimming with curiosity, for strangers were rare in Bately, especially at the Smith residence. Moments later, she led the mysterious visitor into the parlor. "A Miss...Frome...is here for you...?" She stepped to the side. The odd little spider walked into the sunlit room.

Kate audibly gasped. There was her childhood governess, standing only inches before her, larger than life.

Agnes forced a paltry smile that seemed to actually battle with the permanent frown that was her face. "Hello, Kate."

"Agnes?" Kate strained to keep her mouth from dropping open.

Agnes scurried across the floor and sat down. "It has been a long time, hasn't it, Kate?"

"Yes...it certainly has."

Agnes rudely inspected the contents of the room with sharp, appraising eyes. "But I thought your husband was poor?"

Kate chuckled, then coughed. Agnes the spider woman had not changed one bit. "I wouldn't call Thomas poor." She wiped her mouth with a yellow handkerchief. "On the other hand, we're not rich like the Rutherfords."

"The Rutherfords, ma'am?" Bess asked.

Agnes shot Bess a hateful look. "Where I come from, servants never intrude on the family's conversation."

"It's quite all right, Agnes." Kate said. "Bess is a friend. And to answer your question, Bess, Rutherford is my maiden name. Agnes was my childhood governess at the home where I was raised near London. In fact, you still work there, don't you Agnes?"

Agnes ignored Kate's question; she wasn't one for small talk. She pointed her cane at a series of paintings on the adjacent wall. "How could you afford all of this on a country doctor's salary?"

"If you must know, Agnes, we inherited the house from a grateful patient of Thomas'. He had no family and wished to give the home to people who would take good care of it."

Agnes coolly smiled. "The rich do get richer, do they not?"

"Bess, please get Miss Frome a cup of tea. She must be parched from her travels." Bess left the room and returned with a fresh pot.

Agnes waited for Bess to pour, requesting a half teaspoon of sugar. She lifted the cup and peeked at its bottom for a sign of its worth. Name was everything, after all. "It was quite a journey," she sighed, taking small, measured sips. "The boat was not extravagant as your father promised. Many of the people were banal and unrefined. The food was overcooked, especially the fish. No doubt, they were worried about poisoning the passengers."

"How is father?" Kate asked.

"As well as any man of his age is, I suppose. At least he is not rotting in the grave, am I right? He asked me to visit you. Your husband wrote and told him…"

Kate loudly coughed. "Thomas wrote?"

Agnes placed her tea cup down. "Didn't you know? He sent a note to your father telling him that you were…ill."

Kate leaned back, deflated. She must be close to death, if Thomas wrote.

"Your father wants both of you to come to London. He'll pay for the entire trip and offer the best nursing care while you're at the estate."

He wants me to close the Rutherford trinket box, Kate thought. It would not be too painful a box to close. The lid had been creeping slowly down to its hinge for the last forty years. "Perhaps in the spring…." Kate offered.

"He insists that you come this month."

"*This* month?" Kate looked to Bess for support. "How could I possibly take a long sea voyage, in my condition, in the month of January? I'll be buried in London, if I do." She wondered if this was her father's devilish way of getting her in the ground beside the other Rutherford corpses. "I could not leave until the month of May, at the earliest."

Agnes placed her cane over her lap. "It's not only you that Charles is thinking about. He is eighty-one years old, Kate, and also unwell. He may not last until spring."

Kate looked down at the afghan, tracing the zigzag patter with her fingertip. "Yes, I understand." She paused and looked at Agnes. She was too hard on the governess, she realized. The severe old woman sitting before her was the closest thing to a mother figure that Kate had during the tender years of her youth. Agnes was admittedly arrogant and proud. She had a mean streak that lashed out and ripped a person's heart with one swift turn of her tongue's icy blade. But she always loved Kate, in her own demented way. Kate's thoughts turned to her father, also cold and arrogant. He was far too hard on her for marrying Thomas, and he didn't stand up to her vicious mother when she cut Kate out of the family will, though he did send the piano in the end.

Kate knew he loved her too.

"Very well then. We'll leave in two weeks. Unfortunately, Thomas must stay behind and care for his patients. Bess, perhaps you'll join me on the voyage?"

"Yes, Missus. I'd like that."

"Good then. It's decided. Bess and I will pack our bags and leave at the end of the month. Will you stay in our home until that time, Agnes? We could make the return trip together."

Agnes rolled her yellow eyes in their sockets. "Gladly! My bags are in the carriage." She snapped her fingers at Bess. "My bags."

Bess held back a quick reply, remembering that this was Kate's family, and dutifully went for the bags.

"I was intending on staying in that despicable hotel in town, what's the name, The Sir Crudor Inn? Sir Crudor, indeed. I'm surprised that Spencer's works are even read in this illiterate country."

"It's actually quite nice."

"Pardon?"

"The Sir Crudor, it's a very nice hotel."

"Yes, well, perhaps. Americans have different standards than those which we fight to maintain in England."

"It will be a pleasure to have you as our guest." Kate weakly smiled.

A crinkled smile formed at the corner of Agnes' arid mouth. Kate was glad that she had chosen to be kind. Agnes really was not that bad. She had certainly encountered worse in her lifetime—her own mother, for example.

9

Bess woke with the sun. Her room was ice cold in the mornings. She dreaded the moment when her feet touched the hardwood floor. She dressed quickly, layering her smock and apron over the wool undergarments that she wore to bed. Warmth was precious in the winter. In the summers she wanted to get rid of it like an unwanted guest. Speaking of unwanted guests....

Agnes was waiting for Bess in the kitchen and immediately complained that the tea was not made, nor were there any fresh pastries to eat. At the least, she required buttered toast. Bess put the kettle on the range and placed two slices of bread onto the rack of the stove. She cringed at the thought of having to travel to England with Agnes Frome. Bess made a mental note to bring a Bible and memorize the scriptures on forbearance and also the ones on keeping a tight reign over the tongue.

She was relieved when Dr. Smith entered the room. "Morning, Bess," he bellowed, full of cheer. His eyes lowered as he sat down at the table. "Good morning, Agnes. How are we doing today?"

"If you insist on asking, *we* are not doing well at all. Your servant was late in the kitchen, and my room was as cold as a mortuary last night."

Appropriate image, Thomas thought. "Sorry to hear that," he mumbled. He perused an outdated edition of *The Bately Herald* and imagined Agnes frozen solid on her bed, her white hands folded neatly over the horizontal crease of the blankets. *Jacob Zane Loses Cow!* The Herald's headline read, and in smaller print, "Finds Half-Frozen Cow Stuck in Fence."

Bess stirred a pot of hot cereal on the range, humming a gospel song. When she saw that it annoyed Agnes, she began to sing the words. She ladled large, gummy dollops into four dishes.

Thomas stood from the table. "I'll bring Kate's upstairs. Fix us a tray with coffee, will you, Bess?"

"Yes, Sa'. How 'bout a basket of muffins, too?"

"Maybe one for me. I don't think Kate will have much of an appetite, do you?"

Bess frowned. "No, Sa'."

Agnes watched Bess prepare Kate's tray. "Does this family not eat proper meals in the dining room?"

"Just on fancy occasions, Miss Frome."

"You Americans! And listen to the way that you speak. One would think that grammar was a lost art in this country!"

"Ma'am?"

"Oh, never mind! I'll have my breakfast in the dining room. I refuse to do as the Romans do…."

Bess shrugged. "That's fine with me, ma'am. That'd be more than fine."

Thomas knocked lightly on the door. Kate sat up in bed. "Come in."

Thomas entered with breakfast. "Honestly!" he mimicked Agnes Frome's flat, disapproving voice. "You Americans! Where is my caviar and champagne?"

Kate smiled. "You are naughty, Thomas Smith."

He put the tray down and nuzzled into her ear, giving her sallow cheek a playful kiss. "Naughty, but nice." He poured his coffee and let Kate pour her own. "I hope I didn't wake you."

She shook her head, swallowing. "I've been up for hours, thinking about the trip. I'm very excited."

"Really? That's good. I was worried that you'd regret your decision."

"Not at all. I understand the voyage will be difficult, but getting out of the house will do me a world of good."

"Are you sure you don't want me to come along?"

"I wish that you could, but I'm afraid this town would fall apart in your absence. Tara Zane's due date is in April, but it certainly looks as though she'll go earlier than that. I'd hate for them to experience another loss without your support."

"You're right. And Bess will take good care of you."

"Of course she will."

"Are you anxious about seeing your father?"

Kate's eyes shifted, deep in thought. "No, I'm not. He's so very old, and

I'm unwell. I'm sure both of us will be at a loss for words. I only hope that my health will not digress." Her voice cracked with fear. "Thomas, what if it does? I couldn't bear to be in England without you when—"

"Sshh," he said, as if consoling a child. "You'll be fine, darling. I wouldn't have written to your father and suggested the trip if I didn't think so as a physician."

"Are you sure, Thomas?"

"I am."

They ate breakfast in silence. Bess came to clear the dishes. Thomas remained with Kate. "I've been thinking about my mother," Kate said. "Perhaps if she were still alive, I'd see her in a different light, as I see father now. As a child, I feared my mother. She was terribly big, over six feet tall, and father was so short."

At this, Thomas laughed. "What brought them together?"

"For all intensive purposes, the marriage was arranged. Mother's family was said to exist at the time of William the Conqueror—"

"Impressive."

Kate chuckled. "Indeed. Father's family is related to royalty too. It was inevitable that the two lines link together at some point. Their coupling seemed to work, despite its emptiness. And do you know, Thomas…" Her eyes twinkled with mischief. "I was thinking only this morning that my father may have *liked* that mother was an Amazon. All of the men in his family were paired with large, intimidating women. I believe that it's due to the lack of maternal affection in their upbringing."

"Interesting…" Thomas enjoyed listening to Kate. Her stories were like Dickens' novels with dark, eccentric characters and complex plots that grabbed him by surprise. He gently patted her hand. "I've got to go. I'll be at the Caplan farm this morning, John's stomach's giving him problems again, them I'm off to the Zane's."

"How is Tara doing?"

"Not bad. She's holding this one differently. I think it might survive."

"Wouldn't that be wonderful!"

Dr. Smith reluctantly gathered his bags and went to the door. Kate looked like a little girl on the bed, she had lost so much weight.

"Have a good day," she said.

In the hallway, Thomas worried that it was the last time that he would see Kate alive. The worry harassed him since he first saw blood in the handkerchief, last May. How on earth would he be able to say goodbye before she boarded the ship to England? But he knew she had to do it. Allowing her to go was the greatest test that his love for her had ever known.

Alone in her room, Kate gazed out the window. Ghostly currents of snow swirled up from the barren landscape, forming powdery tornadoes that faded against the winter sky. Kate thought again of her mother and recalled the day that changed everything. Kate was fourteen years old. She and her mother were sitting side by side in the pristine garden of the Rutherford Estate.

Emily Rutherford drank her tea, her big pinky finger jutting out from the china handle of the cup. A fly buzzed about them. Two young maids, only a year or so older than Kate, stood erect by the fountain, waiting to refill an empty cup, or add more crumpets to the plate. Kate stared at the two girls, for they were quite pretty and interesting to watch. One girl cracked a painful smile, then pressed her lips together.

Kate cocked her head to the side, curious.

The other girl's shoulders suddenly hunched. She appeared to be choking. Kate was ready to stand and be of assistance, but no sooner had she placed her tea cup down, than the maid's shoulders lowered and her face returned to its steady, frowning gaze. It then occurred to Kate, the girls were watching her mother.

She glanced at her mother and saw that the fly had landed on her nose. Kate's mouth dropped open. Her pulse quickened. The fly rose back into the air and landed at the tip of her mother's straightened pinky finger. Emily Rutherford did not flinch. She, of course, knew about the fly's presence, but her overblown pride would not allow her to shoo the fly away.

The girls could no longer contain themselves. One bent over, holding her belly, mutely laughing. The other made a revolting, gassy sound that flew from the tight crack of her lips.

Emily Rutherford jumped from her seat. "That will be enough!" she roared. Kate reddened with humiliation. "You will have your bags packed by this evening, young ladies, and never set foot in this house again!"

The girls sobered at once. They begged for a second chance, they apologized with all of their hearts. No doubt, they both had many family members reliant upon their meager wages. Kate's mother was firm. No one laughed at a Rutherford and got away with it.

In the years that followed, Kate observed how her family controlled the lives of others, demanding unquestioning subservience. In many instances, like the one in the garden, their arrogant behavior bordered on the absurd.

Yes, they were born into money, but did that give them the birthright to behave like pompous buffoons?

Even as a teenager, Kate understood the danger of labeling people as having "good" or "bad" blood, for the tendency created a prejudice whereby one class of human beings set themselves apart as being a more highly-evolved species. It was utter nonsense, and it was exactly why she was only too happy to leave England forever and embrace America. Here, everyone stood a chance, no matter what their lineage—except the Negroes, of course—but maybe, over time, that too would change....

There was something else about that fly.... Kate closed the shutters and prepared for her nap. The fly. Oh yes, now she remembered. She dreamt of flies that night, following the garden incident. In her dream, she stood in a corner of an enormous room. A group of pesky flies hung about her head, dangling from long, golden strings. They buzzed, bumping into one another and landing on her face, and no matter how much Kate swatted and cursed, the flies would not go away. They were tied to strings, after all. Kate whirled in circles and grew dizzy. Then she fell to the floor and became sick.

When she awoke from the dream, she recalled thinking that there was, in fact, plenty of extra space for her to run to and get away from the flies. Why did she remain with them and allow herself to be subject to their pesky ways? Surely, she wasn't afraid of flies on strings, for if she ran, they could not chase her—and even if they did chase her, what harm could an ordinary house fly do to Kate? Kate went back to sleep and decided that if she had the dream again, she would run away from the flies. But the dream did not reoccur. The lesson had already been learned.

Several years later, after running off to America and refusing to return to London, despite her parents' threats, Agnes wrote Kate a long, pleading letter, the gist of which was, "Are you not afraid of the consequences of your actions?"

In response, Kate thought, but never wrote, *What consequences? Houseflies are harmless creatures, after all.*

Bess didn't know why she felt low that afternoon. Maybe Agnes Fromes' belittling jabs got to her more than she realized, or maybe it was the conversation that she had with Kate about watching her father auctioned off on the trading block. Bess loved that old man. He was good, though he claimed to be the greatest of sinners. And he loved Bess and her sisters and brothers dearly, saying that they were the apples of his eyes. So to see him treated like an animal…even today, the memory made Bess's heart ache.

Ben Silas mended a break in the picket fence that lined the Smith's property. He heard Bess's footsteps squeaking over the packed snow as she walked across the backyard and entered the root cellar. She emerged carrying a sack of flour and a jar of preserves.

Ben stopped working and tipped his hat. "Afternoon, Sister Bess."

Bess knew Ben as an acquaintance. He was a deacon at the Black Church of Bately and performed the occasional handy work for Dr. and Mrs. Smith. She'd seen Ben at the front of the church on Sunday mornings, sitting with the row of elders, but she never spoke to him after the service. A swarm of people surrounded the pulpit as soon as the sermon finished. They looked to Ben for prayer and healing, and heatedly discussed rifts among the brethren.

She walked past him now without a glance. "Afternoon, Brother Ben." Her shoulders drooped and she didn't smile.

"Everythin' all right?" Ben asked.

Bess turned and put the sack of flour on the ground. "Well now, Brother Ben, that's an interestin' question."

His eyes twinkled. "Then I'm glad I asked it." Indeed, he did have a way of asking exactly what the brethren needed to hear.

Bess looked up at the sky and inhaled. Exhaling, she asked, "You think we're in for hard winter?"

Ben put the hammer down and joined Bess in gazing heavenward. "It hasn't been easy so far, has it?"

"No, Brother Ben. It's been real hard."

He soberly nodded. In the same instant their heads lowered and their eyes met. "There are ways you can tell," he said.

"What kinda ways?"

"Well, the holly berries, for one, and the stars…"

"What about the holly berries?" Bess was curious.

"If they're real red in the fall, then it's gonna be a long, cold winter."

"Were they red this year?"

Ben slowly nodded. "Mm hmm…"

"What about the stars, Brother Ben?"

His brown eyes sparkled. "The stars? Well now, Sister Bess, the stars are a whole other story…"

10

The creases in Mary's life were finally smoothing out. At seven months of age, Elizabeth had entered an easy stage in which she took two long naps, one in the morning and one following lunch, and slept twelve hours through the night. Mary had forgotten what it was like to feel rested. Her eyeballs no longer resembled cracked porcelain, and her late afternoon headaches disappeared. Elizabeth also nursed with less frequency. She enjoyed a full diet of mashed vegetables, fruit cereal, and small portions of stewed meat. She had even begun drinking goat's milk from a cup, with the aid of her mother's steady hand. All of which meant that Mary was not as bound to her daughter's demanding physical needs.

Mary felt like her days belonged to her again, and she relished in the independence. She busied herself finishing the quilts for the orphanage and used Elizabeth's nap time to work on her crazy quilt. It was in the early stage of creation, with only two squares completed: the crucified daisy, and a ribbon-bound bunch of violets. She thought of the life that awaited her with Drew in Canada. She stitched blue mountains, covered in caps of white, silken snow. She added a round glove of yellow calico, surrounded by bumpy curves of woolen clouds. Her universe expanded—sequined stars, glowing moons, a meandering Milky Way that dipped, teasingly, into another square. Mary felt all of her hopes rushing though her fingers as she worked. She charted her own happiness, taking the needle and thread into new and ever-expanding western frontiers.

At mealtimes, Mary wanted to know everything about the man whom she planned to marry, and what better resource than his mother? She asked Hannah about Drew's childhood. Hannah recounted wild, at times uproarious, stories that depicted a ruffian of a boy with the energy and determination to conquer even the most impossible of tasks, while successfully offending most of the citizens of Bately. On one dreadful occasion, Drew placed hot pepper in the glass of water that Reverend Schenk drank on the pulpit. The minister quietly choked and gagged, but managed to conceal his discomfort. Afterwards, peopled commended him on the conviction which he expressed throughout his sermon. They didn't realize that he was forcing his words out, gasping for breath.

Mary smiled, imagining the scene. "What's his house like?" she asked. "Has he described it in any of his letters?"

Hannah thought. "I don't believe he has. I send all of the correspondence to his lumber company."

"Do you think he owns a mansion?"

Hannah put her fork down, pausing to wipe her mouth. "You'll soon find out, won't you?"

On the first day of February, Mary was awakened from a deep sleep shortly after midnight by a loud knock on the front door. She went to the front room and let Jacob inside. His eyes were frantic and his face was totally white.

"It's Tara. She's having the baby."

"She's not due for another month."

"She's early. You've got to go up to the house and take care of her. I'm going to fetch Dr. Smith."

He left the cottage and rode his horse bareback across the field. Mary ran to her bedroom and threw on her coat and boots. She left a note for Hannah on the kitchen table.

The path to Jacob's house was covered in crusty snow and sheets of black ice. Mary slipped twice as she ran. Her mind raced with foreboding images of Tara giving birth, the lifeless baby appearing blue, wizened. She fervently prayed, demanding that God reveal his mercy to Tara and Jacob, and not His wrath. Mary heard Tara's throaty screams as she approached the log house.

She entered the cabin and found Tara writhing on a bed beside the fire, crying out. Mary rushed across the room and lay her hand over Tara's bare shoulder. She forced a comforting smile. "It's all right, Tara. Dr. Smith will be here in a minute."

"Mary, thank God…" Tara's screams diminished into tired, desperate moans, then faded into silence. She looked at Mary, as if searching for strength. "Tell me the baby will live. Please, Mary, just say it."

Mary reached under Tara's nightgown and gently rubbed her enormous belly. "The baby will be fine."

Tara smiled. Mary was surprised by an overwhelming sense of peace in the room. Tara's belly grew hard, like a rock. Her back arched on the bed and she cried out.

"All right," Mary whispered, her hand circling Tara's womb. "All right..."

Tara's legs folded to her chest. She clenched her teeth and bore down. Mary moved to the end of the mattress and knelt. She saw the baby's head crowning. "That's it. There's the head."

Tara's fists pounded the mattress. Her eyes welled with tears.

"There it is, Tara! Push now."

Tara's screaming peaked. Her head jerked from side to side. Her shoulders slowly dropped and she released a long, frustrated groan. The room was momentarily silent. Again, Mary was aware of the peace. Tara's back arched. Now she was quiet, determined. She pushed until her faced turned red. Mary perched forward and held back Tara's knees. She saw the hard, creamy head pressing against the outer rim of the birth canal.

"Push, Tara, push!"

The head slipped out. Tara fell pack on the bed, panting. "Is it alive?"

Mary looked at the small head cupped in her hands. "I can't tell."

Tara groaned with another contraction and pushed the baby's body out. Mary wrapped the child in a sheet and lifted the small bundle. The mouth opened, the eyes blinked, and the child loudly cried.

"It's alive!" Tara shouted.

Mary placed the baby in Tara's arms.

Tara's eyes suddenly covered over with pain and her back began to arch.

"It's just the afterbirth," Mary said, gently taking the baby and placing it beside her on the bed. Tara screamed more. Mary looked down, expecting to see the hard sac of tissue and blood. She gasped. "Dear God, Tara—it's another baby!"

Tara laughed through her screams. The baby slipped out in one, long push, landing like a ball thrown into Mary's expectant arms. The baby was red-faced and crying and looked exactly like the first.

"Twins!" Mary looked at the first baby's genitals, then the second's. "You have two sons, Tara Rose."

Tara cried. The babies cried. Mary laughed. The room was bursting with joyous praise. Dr. Smith walked in, followed by Jacob.

"Twins!" Mary announced.

Jacob's arms fell to his sides. Mary laughed at the pure bewilderment on his face.

Dr. Smith went to the bed. He cut the cords and examined the babies. He quickly glanced at Tara. Her eyes were closed and her mouth formed soundless words. Jacob knelt at the bedside and brushed the damp hair back from Tara's face. "You did it. Two beautiful sons."

Tara's smile widened as she drifted into a hallucinatory sleep.

Mary helped Dr. Smith examine the babies at the kitchen table. Each one was over six pounds and appeared healthy in every respect. They bathed them, wiping the cheesy mucus from their nostrils and eyes, then bundled them into soft blankets. Jacob stood and went to his sons. He held one, then the other, and tried not to openly weep.

Mary touched his arm. "Congratulations, Dad."

He was speechless, like a small child overwhelmed by his gifts on Christmas day. A child who expected coal in his stocking.

Dr. Smith went to examine Tara. His face darkened. Tara was unconscious. A pool of blood covered the bed. Dr. Smith pressed a blanket to the hemorrhaging region, but to no avail. Soon the mattress was drenched, the entire floor, covered, with Tara's dark blood. A small river wound around the stone hearth and dripped into the fire, causing it to sizzle.

Jacob handed the babies to Mary and went to Tara.

After several, futile minutes, Dr. Smith bent over and touched Tara's neck, then the back of her wrist. He looked at Jacob and slowly shook his head. In the firelight, Mary noticed Jacob's eyes. At first confused, unknowing, they veered into a terrified glare before closing. When he opened them, they appeared empty, hopeless. They weren't Jacob's eyes anymore.

The babies cried in Mary's arms. She carried them down the hallway, into the nursery that Tara prepared early in her pregnancy. Mary sat on the floor and fed them at her breasts. She then placed them in the crib and remained until morning, watching the babies sleep. She heard Dr. Smith leaving, and later, Jacob's muffled sobs.

Though Mary's heart was heavy with grief, the peace that she sensed during Tara's delivery still pervaded the house. When she heard Hannah come inside, it seemed to Mary that the old woman's voice naturally slipped into that holy peace, as if at one with it.

11

They buried Tara the next morning, beside her stillborn children. Jacob showed no grief at the funeral. He stood, rigid, beside the stone that marked Tara's grave. And it was not sadness that Mary saw in his steady, unflinching gaze. It was rage.

Mary and Hannah insisted on bringing the twins down to the cottage and caring for them there. Jacob agreed. He was in no condition to look after the newborns himself and it worked perfectly that Mary could serve as a wet nurse. Tara's mother offered to take the babies herself, and together they agreed that Mary would care for them in the early months, then hand them over to Tara's family before she left for Canada. The arrangement would give Tara's mother time to grieve before taking on the responsibility of caring for twins.

The sleep deprivation that Mary experienced in her early days with Elizabeth hardly compared to the exhaustion that she felt now. During the daylight hours, she squeezed in short, ten- or fifteen-minute cat naps while Ethan and Patrick slept, only to be interrupted by a hungry shriek just as she fell into the luxury of a dream.

At night, she brought the infants into bed with her and fed them, off and on, until the morning. At first, Mary felt selfless and strong, but as the weeks wore on, she only felt depleted, and then resentful. She missed playing with Elizabeth, and was forced to have Hannah compensate for her absence by taking Elizabeth outdoors for long walks and feed her at meal time.

And then there was Drew. Hannah wrote and informed him of Tara's death, and Mary's position as care-giver for the twins. Drew wrote Mary, inquiring if this new development would interfere with their plans to wed. She promised him that she would not go back on her decision, but she did admit that the new situation would stall their plans. She planned on leaving for Vancouver in July. By then the boys would be almost six months old and Mary could have them drinking from bottles when she gave them over to Tara's mother. She thought as she wrote, but did not actually say it, that she would make an unattractive bride right now with her big raccoon eyes. Drew was proud of Mary's looks and she did not want to let him down.

Drew sent a telegram back, saying that he'd wait.

Leaving the two boys in another woman's care would be heart-wrenching, at best. Mary had grown to love Ethan and Patrick as if they were her own. The fact that they were orphans only increased her affection for the helpless little beings.

Jacob came to the cottage each night for dinner. It troubled him to look at the babies. He desperately wanted them to resemble Tara, but they were the image of their father, with their gray eyes and deep dimple in the cleft of each pudgy chin. He held them, awkwardly, and seemed relieved when Mary came to take them to their cribs.

Since Tara's death, Jacob had aged considerably. He lost weight, his hair thinned, and his eyes, previously kind and straightforward, took on an anguished complexity. At one time, Mary felt safe in Jacob's presence. He was the type of person that provided stability and simplicity when others lacked that clear approach. But now his behavior was erratic, moody, and he was often silent for long stretches of time.

"Did you get much work done on the farm today?" May asked over supper.

He sighed, staring at the mashed potatoes on his fork. You'd think those potatoes were crucially important. "Yes," he grunted, making Mary feel as though her question was out of line. Eventually, Mary stopped asking questions. *Let him wallow in self-pity*, she meanly thought.

"It's his way of grieving," Hannah told Mary one night. "We should be patient about these things, he'll improve with time."

Hannah was right; within a matter of weeks, Jacob showed small signs of his former optimistic self. He thanked Hannah for her meals, and Mary for her care of his sons. When he spoke of Tara, it was not with a doomed, darkened attitude, but rather with a sadly affectionate tone that told Mary and Hannah that, though still in tremendous pain, he was learning to accept the loss.

Somewhere in between the endless nursing and the diaper changes, Mary managed to complete the last of the orphans' quilts. Jacob took her to the orphanage the last week of April to deliver the bundle to the nuns. Sister

Philothea was overjoyed. She thanked Mary profusely, vowing to say a Rosary Novena for her every morning for the remainder of the month. The children made a loud racket at the end of the hallway and Mary asked what was going on.

"Come see." Philothea took Jacob's and Mary's coat and guided them into the kitchen. The room was a commotion of flustered nuns and ecstatic children. A group of orphans hovered around a large black kettle in the center of the room, talking to a little boy who Mary recognized to be Carter, the orphan who cut his foot on the first day the Mary came to the orphanage. He was crouched inside the kettle, laughing with pride.

"That's Hansel," Philothea told Mary and Jacob. "Gretel's over there." Gretel was a plump girl with red cheeks and frightened oval-shaped eyes. She stood as rigid as a stone on top of a chair while one nun pinned her costume's sides and another nun hemmed the bottom.

A sliver of a nun, not unlike a black exclamation point, jumped up on the table. Clapping her hands, she scanned the chaos with flat, disapproving eyes. Within seconds, the activity and noise died down.

"She should never stand on the table where we eat!" Sister Martha growled over her shoulder to Sister Philothea.

Mary did not recognize the nun on the table. "Is she new here?" she whispered into Sister Philothea's ear.

"Shh!" Sister Martha hissed. Jacob nudged Mary's ribs with his elbow, chuckling under his breath.

Sister Philothea leaned into Mary and replied, ever so quietly, so as not to be admonished by Sister Martha, "That's Sister Sophia. She came to us this Christmas and our lives haven't been the same. She was an actress in New York, before she was called by the Lord."

"Where is our witch?" Sister Sophia said in a shrill, melodramatic voice. "Witch, witch, where are you?" Her words echoed, as if sounding off the walls of a vacuous cave.

Footsteps descended the back staircase located at the far end of the room. "Here I am!" An orange-haired boy stood in the narrow doorway, his face aglow with excitement. He wore a pointed black hat and a black coat (once a nun's vestment), and thick smudges of charcoal covered his freckled face. The children gasped in horror, much to the boy's satisfaction. He strutted over to the pot, flicking his cloak from side to side, sneering at his fellow orphans and roaring. Mary leaned into Jacob, laughing. Sister Martha shook her head with disapproval.

Sister Sophia jumped down from the table, her skirt rising like a parachute before she hit the ground. She went over to the boy. "Danny, I know you're pleased with yourself, but I must remind you that you're a witch, not a lion." Danny jerked his head forward and roared louder, gesturing to bite off another boy's nose.

"That will be enough!" Sister Martha yelled. Danny withdrew into the safe confines of his cloak. Sister Martha turned to face Sister Philothea. "You see? Didn't I tell you that this play would set off the children? I've spent my whole week taming Danny, and this woman has him acting like a wild animal!"

"But he's not an animal." Sister Sophia sighed. "Why must you use such words, Sister Martha?" She went to Sister Philothea to plead her case. "He's a witch. And I cast him in the part for the precise reason that he is untamed, as a witch would be. Danny has what we call in theater, 'chutzpah.' It's a kind of energy that draws the audience in."

"At any rate," Sister Martha said, "Our order would not approve of a play about witches eating little children. It's heresy, that's what it is."

Sister Philothea wrung her hands, caught in the middle. "Sister Sophia," she said. "Can we change the play a little, perhaps cut out the part of the witch?"

"No!" Danny whined, running to Sister Sophia. "No, don't. I want to be evil, I really do!"

Sister Sophia dropped her hand to his shoulder. "Absolutely not. Danny has been preparing for this part all week."

"Yes!" Danny sobbed.

"Well then, could we tone the part down? You know, make Danny a nice witch, who perhaps sees the wrong of her ways and seeks forgiveness. Yes, she'll be led to our order through the innocence of the children. It could be very nice."

Jacob laughed, then coughed into his hand.

In her anger Sister Sophia pushed her hand off Danny, causing the boy to lose his balance and fall to the ground. "I understand what you're saying…"

Sister Philothea dropped her shoulders in relief, then tensed when Sister Sophia spoke again.

"No, no, and again I say, NO!" Her voice bellowed across the room. The children squirmed with fear. "A witch is a witch, just as white is white and black is black. I'll not have my plays censored. If Danny cannot be an evil witch, then this play is cancelled." She stormed out of the room, her face beat red.

The children whined in unison, looking to Sister Philothea for hope. Sister Martha smirked with triumph. "Well then, it's settled. Let's clean up this mess and set the table for lunch." The children gathered their props in sad acceptance.

"Wait." Philothea raised her hand. The children stopped moving. She smiled. "Danny can be a witch—a terrible, evil witch."

Danny jumped to his feet, roaring at the other children, fierce and victorious. Then it was Sister Martha who stormed out of the kitchen, her normally sallow face also reddening like a beet. Mary sincerely hoped that Sister Sophia and Sister Martha did not bump into each other in the hallway upstairs. She pictured an animated cat fight in her mind, with black fur flying in all directions.

As the children went through their lines, Sister Philothea turned to Mary and Jacob and asked how they were doing. She quickly learned that Jacob's wife died, leaving him with two baby boys, and that Mary was serving as a wet nurse. "She's more than that." Jacob added, "She's loved those twins like a mother would love them."

"Has she really?" Sister Philothea asked. Mary looked at the floor, wishing the compliments away.

Sister Sophia ran down the back staircase and swept into the kitchen, shrieking like a witch, her nose scrunched up and her lips curling. She laughed wickedly. "Where are Hansel and Gretel!" she cried. The children squealed with fearful delight. She grabbed a wooden spoon from the range and glided from one corner of the kitchen to the next, tipping her head and screaming for joy. The children huddled together for protection, while Danny brazenly chased Sister Sophia, pulling madly at her skirt. She stirred the pot with the spoon, licked her lips and pretended to taste. (Carter had long since fled the premises.)

Sister Sophia stopped abruptly, her face relaxing into a mischievous smile. She handed the spoon to Danny. "That, my love, is what a witch does. Now you try."

Danny mimicked Sister Sophia's entire act, right down to the spine-tingling shriek. Mary and Jacob laughed so hard, Mary's stomach began to hurt. Sister Sophia had to restrain Danny in the end, for he was starting to go after the children, poking them with the spoon. She tackled him to the ground, then stooped over his restless body. "Oh, Danny!" Her eyes filled with tears. "You will be a famous actor some day. You will travel Europe and mesmerize the audiences—truly, you will."

Danny hissed like a panther in the clutch of Sister Sophia's grip.

Mary and Jacob sat down with Sister Philothea and watched the remainder of the dress rehearsal. The local priests and several financial supporters were coming that evening, so the pressure to impress was intense. After the rehearsal, Mary went upstairs with the children and Sister Philothea, while Jacob helped Sister Martha bring some loads of wood from the backyard shed into the basement. He told Sister Martha that he had a surplus of lumber from his years of clearing his farm, and that he would bring a shipment over to the orphanage that week.

The corners of Sister Martha's mouth lifted, ever so slightly, taking care not to slip into a full-fledged smile. "We appreciate any help that we can get," she matter-of-factly replied.

Mary placed the assorted quilts over their respective beds and in the cribs. Jacob came upstairs as she was finishing the girls' room and watched as she neatly folded the blankets corners, tucking them into the slot between each mattress and each frame. Sister Philothea stood beside the cluster of jubilant little girls. "Mary, how can we ever repay you?"

Jacob continued to watch Mary, thinking.

"All right girls, you can go to your beds now," Sister Philothea said. The group scattered; each girl jumped up on her bed, feeling the quilt beneath her, touching its patches with her fingertips. For many, it was the first item of value that they had ever owned, for the nuns promised them that they could have the quilts when they left the orphanage someday.

Mary walked over to a sad-faced Indian girl who stood beside the window, looking out. "Why so glum?" she asked.

The girl faced Mary with a pout. "I wanted to be Gretel."

Mary bent down. "Maybe next year you'll be Gretel."

"Next year we're doing Macbeth."

"Macbeth?"

The girl looked at Mary, nodding.

"Well, there are some good parts in that play—I think."

The girl crossed her hands over her chest. She reminded Mary of herself, as an orphan, and the empty feeling of not being seen. Mary reached into her basket and brought forth the last of the quilts. "This is for you."

The little girl's face brightened. "It's yellow."

Mary smiled. "It's a daisy quilt. I only made one of them. I want you to have it."

The girl grabbed the quilt. "A daisy quilt!"

"I can even sew your initials on the corner before I go, then everyone will know that it belongs to you."

The girl flung her thin body into Mary's arms. Jacob walked over. "What's going on here?"

The little girl hopped up and down, making clumsy ballerina moves with the quilt wrapped around her shoulders like an enormous shawl. "This is my daisy quilt!" she told him.

"Aren't you lucky," Jacob said. He looked down at Mary, who seemed to be taking enormous pleasure in watching the little girl dance. Again, Jacob was thinking....

12

Hannah waited for Jacob on the front steps of the cottage. Elizabeth squatted on the front lawn. The little girl wore a pink cotton jersey with a yellow bonnet on her head. She angrily tugged at the bonnet's strings, shouting, "No, no, no!"

Hannah laughed as Jacob approached. "She hates that bonnet!"

He bent over and picked up Elizabeth. "No!" she firmly told him. Her small hands reached out and clutched his chin. "No, Dada, no!"

He looked at Hannah. "Did she call me Dada?"

"Dada!" Elizabeth exclaimed. The bonnet slipped off and she squealed with joy.

Jacob laughed. "Lizzy, you did it—you took off your bonnet!"

Elizabeth clapped her hands, staring at the bonnet on the ground with triumphant glee. Her face transformed in an instant to a look of terrible loss. "Bonny!" she cried, reaching down for the hat. "Baby bonny!"

Hannah picked up the garment, shook off the dirt, and handed it back to Elizabeth.

Jacob followed her into the cottage. "Where's Mary?"

"Sleeping," Hannah whispered. "She was up through the night with the twins. They seem to be growing right now, and they're hungrier than ever."

Jacob put Elizabeth down. The toddler held the edge of a wicker chair and pushed herself into a standing position. "You should have seen how good she was with the children at the orphanage last week," Jacob remarked. "They loved her." Elizabeth plopped her body down at Jacob's feet, resting her back against his shins as if he were a chair. He looked down at her face, so similar to Mary's, then turned to Hannah with a look of consternation in his eyes.

"I've heard some vicious gossip about Mary lately. I'll tell you, Hannah, it makes my blood boil, hearing people call her a hempen widow, talking like she's some kinda whore. It couldn't be further from the truth."

Hannah frowned. "I've heard the talk myself, Jacob. How do you think it makes me feel, with her about to marry Drew? But it's no use trying to change people's minds, they'll think what they want to think, no matter what you have to say."

"She still plans to marry Drew?" Jacob nonchalantly asked.

"Yes, dear, as soon as the twins are weaned."

Jacob could not understand Mary's attraction to a vagrant like Drew, although he could hardly voice his protest to the vagrant's mother. On the rare occasions when Mary did speak of Drew in Jacob's presence, it was with what Jacob thought to be undeserved admiration and respect.

Hannah went to the kitchen and prepared a fresh pot of coffee, grinding extra beans. Mary would need a strong cup after her long night with the twins. Down the hallway, the twins began to cry. Mary emerged from the bedroom ten minutes later with the content creatures cooing in her arms. A faded green nightgown hung from her body, the sheer cotton material fully revealing her naked form. Her hair was gathered into a loose, tangled braid, and she looked to be half-asleep. She walked past Jacob, unaware.

Elizabeth laughed for joy. "Mama!" She skillfully traced the rim of the table with her hand, walking in Mary's direction.

Mary placed the twins on the rug and picked up her daughter. "Good morning, sweetheart. Give Mommy a kiss."

Jacob fidgeted with desire. He saw the forbidden contours of Mary's body, the tempting outline of her hips and legs. He wanted to pull her into the nearby bedroom and take her right then and there.

Elizabeth whipped her body to the side and pointed to Jacob. "Dada, Dada."

Mary pretended not to hear. She went to the kitchen and buckled Elizabeth into her high chair. "I smell coffee."

"Sit down, dear, I'll get you a cup." Hannah placed the steaming mug on the table top, then took the black shawl off her back and handed it to Mary. "Put this over you," she quietly advised.

Mary suddenly realized that she was wearing a transparent gown. She was under the impression that she had on the flannel gown that she wore to bed, but in the late hours of the night she changed into a sheer one, due to the stifling heat. Now she also understood that Jacob had seen her naked body. Her face reddened with stark embarrassment.

"Don't worry about it," Hannah said, reading Mary's thoughts. "He didn't notice," she lied.

Mary put her head on the table and yawned. She peered at Jacob from around the corner of the doorway. He was looking in her direction. She cocked her head and looked at him straight on. "Aren't you joining us?" she asked.

He came to the table and attempted to make light conversation with Hannah as she cooked, but he couldn't stop thinking about having Mary completely to himself in bed. Mary buried her chin into the prickly warmth of the shawl. "Are we still going to town this morning?" she asked.

He couldn't meet her eyes. "Yes. I told Sam Roberts that I'd have the plow to him before ten." He looked down at the twins on the floor. They were fast asleep, their arms wide open, closely resembling two cherubs in mid-flight. He got up from the table abruptly. "I'll wait for you both in the wagon." He lowered his eyes and left.

Elizabeth shouted from the high chair, "Dada!" Her hand saluted the doorway, the fingers clamping up and down in a clumsy attempt at waving.

Mary drank her coffee. "Daddy is in Vancouver, honey," she simply said.

Ted's General Store was empty that morning, with the exception of its owner, who stood behind the counter, sorting chocolates and jelly beans into their designated bins. The bells above the doorway jingled as Jacob stepped inside, followed by the laughter of Mary and Hannah, and the tired wailing of the twins.

Elizabeth gawked at her surroundings from her safe position in Jacob's arms. Though she had been inside the store on many occasions, this one was the first in which she realized that many of the shelves were lined with colorful toys and tasty treats. Her small, pink mouth salivated. A small stream of drool ran down her chin, and she smiled.

"Morning, Ted," Jacob said. "You seen Stan around this morning? I've got his hay in the wagon."

"He's probably at the church meeting," Ted replied. He inspected a half-breed jelly bean: red mixed with yellow.

"What's he doing there?" Jacob asked.

"He's curious, like the rest of us," Stan replied, still engrossed in the unnatural jelly bean.

Mary turned from the fabric. "What's going on at the church?"

"You know, today's the big meeting about Reverend Schenk."

"Reverend Schenk?" Jacob asked. "What about him?"

"Where have you people been? Reverend Schenk wants to resign. Seems a lot of people are criticizing him, saying he's too money hungry and that he likes to flirt with the pretty girls. I even heard rumors that one of the choir girls is carrying his child. God help us all. Wouldn't that be somethin'—another Azalea to bless this fine town. The board of deacons called a meeting for today. Seems they're trying to get him to stay on."

"Is that so?" Jacob asked, genuinely surprised. He assumed most people would want the minister to leave—sooner rather than later. Then again, he did have a way of gathering fat contributions like apples in the fall.

Mary quickly turned back to the fabric. Ethan was rooting towards her breasts, which gave her an excuse to slip away to the bench at the back of the store. She watched Jacob stroll leisurely down the aisles with Elizabeth. He stopped briefly at the perfume display, picked up a blue-tinted bottle, unscrewed the metal cap, and smelled. He screwed the cap back on, placed the glass bottle on the rack, and moved to a line of hammers hanging in lines on the wall.

Mary finished feeding Ethan. Hannah walked over with a small sac of chocolates for Mary. She took Ethan and handed Patrick over to be fed. Mary relaxed on the bench, sucking on a chocolate drop and closing her eyes. Afterward, she burped Patrick against her shoulder and walked over to Jacob and Elizabeth at the cash register with Ted.

"Ah, ah, ah!" Jacob covered a mystery item on the counter with Elizabeth's blue blanket.

She reached for the blanket's corner. He lay his hand over hers, removing it. "Oh no you don't."

"Is it something for me?"

He looked at Elizabeth. "Your mother asks too many questions, Lizzy, did you know that?"

Elizabeth smiled.

Jacob turned Mary around, gently nudged her toward the door. "Go on outside. I'll give you your present before we go."

Hannah waited in the back of the wagon, rocking Ethan to sleep. Mary climbed onto the bench and looked over at the church. "What's going on there?"

"I'm not sure," Hannah said, equally curious.

Reverend Schenk stood speaking on the front steps to a small crowd of people circled in shrimp formation at his feet. It looked as though the entire town had attended the church meeting with the exception of Mickey Jenson, who sat on a stump in the center of the commons, minding his own business and whittling a stick.

Jacob came out of the store and began loading the cart with sacks of flour, sugar, and grain. "Why don't we walk over and see what's going on?" he asked.

Mary shook her head. "I want no part of it."

The crowd gradually dispersed. Reverend Schenk went inside the church. Azalea cut across the commons, heading for Jacob's cart. He jumped up on the bench. "Let's get out of here."

"What about my gift?" Mary asked.

"That's right." He reached behind him for a parcel. Mary was disappointed. It was too big to be a bottle of perfume, as she had hoped. Maybe it was a dress, or a parasol, or material for her crazy quilt. She ripped open the brown wrapping and saw a sturdy pot. "For your stews," Jacob said. "The one you use is too small, the juice is always dripping over the sides."

"It's nice."

"Do you like it? I got the best one."

Mary looked vaguely at the pot, recalling the many nights of exhaustion with the twins, and the nights that were to come. This was her reward—a pot. "Thank you," she calmly said.

Azalea Schenk appeared at her side, pulling Mary's dress. "Mary Turner! Where have you been?"

Mary plopped a chocolate into her mouth, savoring its sweetness. "Taking care of Jacob's twins."

"Have you set your cap for him?

Mary giggled. "No, Azalea, he's all yours."

Azalea let go a loud guffaw, not unlike the sound of wind passing. "I can do better than Jacob Zane!"

"Oh really?" Jacob inquired.

"Yes," she curtly replied. She turned to Mary. "Word has it you're going to Canada to marry Drew Graf."

Mary handed a chocolate to Elizabeth, who promptly put it in her mouth. She turned back to Azalea. "That's right."

"I want to go with you."

"You do?" Hannah asked. Elizabeth jumped wildly about the back of the wagon. A pool of brown, chocolate saliva filled her mouth, dribbling down her chin.

"Yes," Azalea said with tremendous determination. "This town is getting smaller by the day. Daddy is so discouraged about the way that the church is persecuting him. He and mother are moving to Dayton to take another post. Where does that leave me? If I don't get on with my life, I'm going to die an old maid."

"Maybe you'll find a husband in Dayton," Hannah politely suggested.

"Maybe, but I heard the men out west are hungry for brides. There ain't no women out there, I'm told. Those men'll take any skirt they can get."

Mary looked down at Azalea's pinched, pock-marked face. "I'm leaving on the fifteenth of July. You're welcome to join me," she suggested. Jacob was shocked.

The face hidden beneath the layers of make-up brightened. Mary had the urge to pick at the corner, just above Azalea's right temple, and peel the mask right off. "We'll have such fun together, Mary! By the way, is Drew's brother married yet?"

"He's not interested," Hannah flatly said.

That night Mary dreamt of hanging beside Billy on the gallows. His head jerked forward and his hands unloosened the noose from his neck. Jumping down from the platform, he sprinted along a row of train tracks that cut across a vast, barren field. Mary unloosed her own noose and chased after him. The train to Canada whistled in the distance. It suddenly appeared like a metal monster, inches from Mary's form, about to run her down....

Mary shouted in her sleep and awoke, clutching the twins in her arms. She put the babies in their bassinets and went to Hannah's room. The old woman lay sleeping in a fetal position in her bed, her gray face illuminated by a white shaft of moonlight. Mary sat down in Hannah's favorite comfort rocker. It was a simply styled chair, though complex in its cosmetic design, with small wicker rosebuds protruding from the surface of the arms, and intricate figure-eight reed work woven into its back panel.

Patches entered the room and pounced on Mary's bare foot. He circled her right ankle, purring. Mary rocked in the chair and looked at her surroundings. In a short period of time she had grown to love the simple little cottage with its white-washed interior and the little nooks and crannies. It was more than home, it was a living organism that breathed with the cries of the children and the cheerful sound of Hannah's voice. Jacob's nightly visits were familiar and predictable, adding to the rhythm of the place. Mary suddenly understood (and it came as a surprise) that this must be what it's like to be part of a family.

To awaken each day in safety, to know that you are loved, to slip into a routine that brings with it comfort and peace.

She stood up, almost stepping on Patches' paw, and went to the window. In the distance the first floor windows shone from Jacob's log house. A stream of smoke drifted from the stone chimney, lifting to the stars. Mary wondered what he was doing up at this late hour. Her eyes lowered to the ground beside the fence, where she hoped to plant calla lilies and peonies when the warm weather arrived. She smiled at the thought. Flowers would give the cottage a sweet, inviting aroma, thus bringing even more beauty and uniqueness to the domestic organism.

Then her smile faded and her eyes filled with tears. How would she ever rip herself away from this home, this newfound family? She pressed her lips together, sniffing, and angrily wiped at the tear making its way down her cheek. She couldn't stay in Bately forever. She heard the way that people talked about her, all because she was Billy Turner's widow. What kind of childhood could Elizabeth have in a town like this, where she would be mocked as Mary had been mocked, and fatherless too?

It would only get worse if Hannah passed away. Yes, Jacob would allow Mary to stay in the cottage. He was a kind, compassionate man—but the gossip would inevitably escalate. She could hear it now, "the hempen widow" and her daughter living on Jacob Zane's land, caring for his sons as if they were her own. It was scandalous for everyone involved.

"No," Mary spoke aloud, adamantly shaking her head. She had to go to Vancouver and marry Dew, thus making herself respectable. She had no other choice.

13

Kate had forgotten how the brashness of America assaulted her English sensibilities when she first stepped off the boat that transported her from London to Philadelphia, almost forty years ago. In recent months, she experienced the same situation in reverse.

London possessed an air in dignity and old-world establishment which was non-existent in America. As a young woman, Kate reveled in the freedom and rebellion inherent in American beliefs and politics, even in the architectural structures. Now, as a dying woman of fifty-eight, she was coming to appreciate the quiet, austere regalness of England and its ways.

This very idea preoccupied her thoughts on a cloudy day in June as she made her way through Kensington Square. A quizzical smile crept over Kate's face. *How odd*, she mused, rounding a street corner and arriving at Kensington Church Walk. *The things which I despised in my youth are the very things that I have grown to love with age!*

She passed the church whose spire reached nearly three hundred feet, then she meandered through the burial ground. Her feet trekked over the corpses of famous literary figures, theologians, even descendants of the throne. Soon she would also be buried in the earth, the flesh eroding from her body, her brittle bones turning to dust. The image twisted Kate's stomach into tight, tormenting knots. Death. How could it possibly be approached?

She breathed a sigh of relief as she emerged from the cemetery and passed a small parade of shops intermixed with modest houses and flats. Nannies pushed babies in wicker prams with large, wooden wheels. A line of older boys came home from public academy where Kate's brothers studied many years ago.

Kate observed her surroundings with heavy moroseness. Why was she never warned about the speed with which life passes? Perhaps if she knew, she would have savored each moment: holding Thomas' hand in the carriage, weeding in her garden, reading Aesop's Fables to Sandra when she was a small girl.... Kate resolved to love her grandchildren better when she returned to Bately.

The greenish copper roof of the Rutherford Estate hovered like an ominous oasis in the distance. A guard greeted Kate at the gate's entrance with open disapproval flashing across his face. Since arriving at the Rutherford Estate in January, Kate was continually reminded of the fact that her wardrobe did not befit a woman of her stature, even though in America she was often complimented on the way that she dressed. Surprisingly, it was the Rutherford's servants that made her most aware of this fact, through hidden glances and derisive marks. The English were very good at such subtleties in communication.

Now Kate understood that her mother's fanatical adherence to the divisions of class fulfilled the working class' expectations of the well-to-do. The staff at the Rutherford Estate needed to believe the grand illusion that the Rutherfords were grand in stature, brilliant and beautiful at all times. The unspoken belief that the wealthy were somehow smarter, of a higher moral fiber, kept all of English society safely defined—and prohibited revolution at all costs.

Kate wondered if the English had been right after all. In America the masses were encouraged to stand up for their individuality, to forever fight for the truth (or rather, their *opinion* of the truth), and value freedom of thought and speech more than life itself. And look at the young country's history so far: battle after battle, countless religious factions, a country so wounded by its fighting that Kate feared it would never fully recover from the bloody civil war. Then Bess came to mind, and Kate almost could hear her husky voice saying, "Oh no, Missus, it's been worth it all."

Kate rang the mansion's bell. The head servant, Miss Sullivan, let her inside.

Like most members of the staff at the Rutherford Estate, Miss Sullivan was bland and nondescript. Kate had no doubt that in the warm, cloistered atmosphere of the kitchen, Miss Sullivan was probably a vivacious and filthy-mouthed woman, bursting with gossip about the family upstairs. This well-rehearsed, secretive split in servants' personalities always mystified Kate.

As a girl, she would place a glass over the kitchen door and listen to the staff's dark, catty humor, drenched in East End dialect, or thick, Irish brogues. Kate backed off and hid in the corner as the door swung open and saw, to her astonishment, the miraculous shift in countenance as each servant ascended the stairs. The mouths lowered, the eyes lost their light and blackened with reserve.

Miss Sullivan helped Kate with her shawl. "Miss Frome is having breakfast in the north wing, will you join her?"

Kate peered across the hallway into the open doorway of the library where her father spent most of his days. "Is father up and about?"

"Not yet, Mrs. Smith."

"Then I'll join Miss Frome for tea."

"Very well." Miss Sullivan accepted her orders and turned to go, holding Kate's well-worn shawl as though it were a strand of seaweed in her hands.

Kate walked across the front hallway, which was bigger than the entire first floor of her house in Bately. There was a large amount of space between the wall's three doors. One led to a private library lined with two stories of periodicals and books. The other two doorways both led to the same location: a grand, sprawling ballroom where Kate's family once entertained.

The ballroom opened into a dining room with a table that brought to mind a river that had no end. A set of glass doors opened into the garden, at the back of which was an orangery and ice house.

Kate crossed the main hallway and ascended the spiral staircase to the second floor. She steered left, walked down a short set of stairs, and turned sharply to another hallway which took her to the north wing. She came to Agnes Frome's door and knocked twice.

"Enter," Agnes' arid voice cracked.

Kate stepped into the pink parlor. The room was full of frills, dainty fabrics and delicate lace that formed intricate, web-like formations across the windows and paisley walls. Agnes sat, dressed in black, on the cushioned window seat. A tray of empty breakfast dishes sat on the round table beside her. She presently sipped from a white china cup.

'There's an omelet here for you." Her eyes turned to the only covered plate on the tray. "You'll find that the tomatoes are far too runny and the toast is burnt." Her dark mouth curled over the cup's silver rim. She sipped, disgusted, then put the cup down. "The tea is cold and weak. I strongly discourage you from having a cup."

Kate pulled a chair up to the table and removed the cover from the plate. The omelet steamed with heat; it looked very good to Kate. She placed the tray and its dirty dishes on the floor beside her, balanced the clean plate on her lap, and began to eat.

Agnes shook her head. "Where is my chamber maid? These dishes should have been taken away by now!"

Kate wondered how Agnes, who expended so large an amount of energy on the petty matters of life, could handle the real crises that came her way. "It's not worth fretting over," she said. The image of the graveyard from earlier that morning drifted into her mind. "There is really so little worth fretting over in this life," she reflected, "except the millions of moments that we waste—the moments when we fail to love...."

Agnes rolled her eyes. She despised the way dying people spoke—like pious reverends, or lunatics. Watching Kate eat, her face suddenly softened. When Kate looked up, she was reminded of the young, doting governess who taught her in the nursery decades ago.

"You're eating," Agnes remarked. "That's good."

Kate finished the omelet and went to work on the toast, generously covering it with butter and marmalade. "It's the strangest thing, Agnes. I've been coughing less frequently. Yesterday afternoon, I forgot to bring my handkerchief with me on my walk. I feared what would happen if I had a coughing fit without it, but do you know, in the hour that I was away, I did not cough once!"

Agnes frowned. "Don't be too hopeful."

Kate put her knife down. "I'm not a dreamer, Agnes, you know that. I'm only saying that I've been having a good week."

Agnes gazed from the window at the orangery below. "It's wise, not to dream. Has it ever occurred to you that the dreamers in this world are snuffed out? Take Keats, for example, or Mozart. Both men died so young, they were boys, really, and sickly...."

Kate finished her toast and poured a cup of tea. It was piping hot. She cooled it with a spot of cream. "Perhaps they died young because of the energy that they spent on dreaming, which led to their spectacular creations."

"Precisely," Agnes readily agreed. "In order for one to cope with the daily monotony and hardships of life, one must approach it in a detached, glib manner. I understand life to be analogous to a torrid ocean storm. When faced with nature's attack, the wise man, or woman, battens down the hatches and runs to the cabin for cover. The dreamer stand on the deck, her gullible arms wide open, mouth agape, mesmerized by the beauty that surrounds her. Thus, she experiences that rapturous moment and, I might add, she knows it in a way that the practical crew will never grasp—and yet she dies within seconds. Now I ask you, is it worth the epiphany?"

Kate sat back in her chair, stifling a knowing smile. "Your words have me wondering, Agnes, if you aren't a dreamer yourself? Certainly a practical woman could not have conjured up such a poignant image."

Agnes looked at Kate. "Could I have lived to this miserable old age if I were a dreamer? And furthermore, could I have remained the governess of over-spoiled, unappreciative children, never complaining—not even once?" She wanted to add "and never marrying, never having children of my own, *never being loved....*"

A young maid brushed past them and took the tray of dishes. She disappeared quickly, before Agnes had time to criticize the meal.

"Where is your slave friend Bess this morning?" Agnes asked.

"She had breakfast downstairs with the kitchen staff, I believe. She's probably in the library as we speak, making her way through a heaping stack of books."

Agnes' nose pinched into fork formation. "I've never seen anything like it—a servant interested in learning."

Kate held back from reminding Agnes that she was also once a servant with an industrious intellect. "She is a remarkable woman."

"So you say. I must admit, she has helped ease your father's burden in ways that I have obviously failed to accomplish."

"Come now, Agnes. Father adores you, he always has."

Agnes' nose resumed its spoon shape. Her mouth stiffened into a parched smile. "Do you actually believe that?"

"You of all people know that father has trouble expressing warmth. Goodness, listen to the tone he uses with me! Nevertheless, he needs you, Agnes. I dare say, you're the only true friend that he has left."

"I do hope that you're right, Kate. I have always wondered if he loved me more than that dreadful mother of yours."

"Yes. Well, Mother is another story for another day...." Kate looked out the window. The clouds were thick and dark with rain. Despite the dismal weather, she longed to get outside and enjoy this burst of newfound energy. There was no telling how much longer it would last. She rose from her chair. "Let's you and I take a walk before lunch, Agnes. Or better yet, let's go to a restaurant for lunch, then we'll take the trolley about town and see the sights."

"In this ghastly weather! You must be out of your mind."

Kate stooped over and squeezed Agnes' icy hands. Kate's lungs felt light, clear. Her cheeks were rosy and her eyes sparkled. "Oh, Agnes. Don't be a sourpuss!"

"Why I never!" Agnes gasped. "What did you call me? A sour what?"

Kate helped Agnes to her feet. She handed her the snake-faced walking cane and walked her to the door. "A sourpuss, and I challenge you to prove me wrong! Come along, put on your coat. Let's go have some fun."

Kate stopped off at the library before leaving the mansion. Agnes discreetly waited in the doorway. Bess sat at the massive mahogany desk in the center of the room, surrounded by towering stacks of books and magazines. She read aloud to Kate's father, who sat in a leather-upholstered chair by the fire, his eyes scrunched closed, a hot toddy at his side.

"Amphiprostyle," Bess said. "Having columns at each end only." Bess wore a pair of prescription spectacles. She no longer fumbled over words, clutching them as if through a great fog, but now read aloud with eloquence and speed.

"Amphiprostyle," Charles repeated magnanimously.

Bess looked up from the dictionary. "Morning, Missus."

Charles Rutherford straightened in his chair. "Kate," he barked.

"Good morning Bess. Father."

Agnes hovered in the shadows. Kate thought that, by now, the elderly woman would have recovered from her schoolgirl crush on her father, but the passing of years only enhanced Agnes' shy awkwardness around Charles Rutherford. There were those odd moments, however, when Agnes looked Charles straight in the eyes, brazen and unabashed, and in those moments, Kate surmised that there existed an unspoken intimacy between Agnes and her father, not unlike the bond of an unhappily married couple. Over the course of a lifetime the two reluctantly persevered and now, whether they liked it or not, they were finally one.

"Where are you two off to?" Charles asked.

"I thought I'd take Agnes out for lunch, Father," Kate replied. "You're welcome to come along, Bess."

"I gonna read here, if you don't mind."

"Of course not. I know father would like that too."

Charles Rutherford snarled.

"Are you still working on the A's?" Kate inquired.

"Yes, Missus. We'll get to the B's Thursday."

Charles nodded soberly. "If we're industrious. The new spectacles should help."

Kate smiled. She felt a cough coming on. No sooner did she lift her hand to her mouth, when the tickle in her throat disappeared.

Charles reached into his pocket and pulled out a billfold with the family insignia. "Here, take this." He placed it on the table, beside the glass.

"That's all right, Father. I have my own money."

"Nonsense!" he barked. "You're the wife of a country bumpkin. Take the money!"

She went to the table and put the billfold in her purse. "You know, Father, Thomas may not be a man of means, but he is quite intelligent."

"So you say." He dismissed her with the wave of his hand and turned to Bess. "Next word!" he ordered.

Kate closed the door. "Father was in a rather good mood today, wouldn't you say?"

Agnes failed to note Kate's sarcasm. "Yes," she said pensively, stroking her cane. "I believe he was."

They ate lunch outdoors, at a roadside café in Kensington Square. A dim ray of sun peeked through the clouds as a gentle breeze floated past, so gentle, in fact, that it failed to tip over any of the paper items on the table, while filling Kate's lungs with fresh, invigorating air.

Agnes passed up on the offer of dessert, even though they were serving her favorite, cherry cake with a dollop of cream. She acted anxious, distracted, and looked down at her watch from time to time.

"Are you late for something?" Kate asked.

Agnes gazed down at her foot that rested against the table's curved wooden leg. At that precise moment, a pigeon flew overhead and a white dropping appeared on the toe of Agnes' shoe.

"Oh! Will you look at that! The bird!"

Her body stiffened in the chair. Kate restrained from giggling. She expected Agnes to arise and complain about the matter to the workers at the café as if they had a part in the incident.

Instead, Agnes' face whitened and she started to cry.

Her tears were dry, soundless. Her thin body heaved, wracked by emptiness. "The blasted bird!" she screamed. "I'll kill him with my own bare hands, by God I will."

Kate detected vapors of an East End dialect in her speech. It must have taken Agnes years to cover her linguistic roots. She knelt down and examined Agnes' shoe. "Not to worry. Hand me your napkin." Agnes handed Kate her napkin. "There," Kate said. "Good as new."

Agnes sniffed. "Are you sure?"

"Yes, quite sure." Kate looked up at Agnes. "Why the tears?"

Agnes scowled. "Must you demand on knowing my personal business?"

"It might do you well to talk."

"Well, you'll find out eventually. As of this week, I will no longer be employed as governess for the Rutherford family."

"That can't be!"

Agnes lifted a clean napkin and loudly blew her nose. "There are no longer any children at the estate, Kate, or have you not noticed? The last two are enrolled in university for the fall semester."

"But surely father will allow you to keep your room at the house. It's the least he could do."

"Yes, he's offered as much. And I do plan on staying, though heaven knows how I'll spend my days. But that isn't the problem."

"Then what is the problem?"

Agnes stuck her shoe past Kate's head. "Are you sure that you removed all of the dropping? I think I see a speck of white beside the sole."

Kate pushed Agnes' foot back down. Agnes yelped. "My arthritis!"

"Forget the shoe, Agnes. Why are you crying?"

Agnes looked away, sighing. "My salary as head governess has certainly not made me rich over the years, but it has enabled me to purchase my own clothing, books, small gifts from time to time...."

"Is that it?" Kate asked. "You're worried about money? What if we arranged to provide you with a shopping allowance each month? A type of pension. I'm sure that Father would agree."

Agnes shook her head. "Not enough."

"It really should be enough. I see how you live. You don't require that much." Kate leaned forward, her face touching Agnes' sharp knee. "Is there something else I don't know?"

Agnes turned to Kate. "I'm afraid so. I have cousins in White Chapel. Polly and her husband, Dave. They live in despicable conditions, not fit for human beings, really. I'm their sole provider. I have been for many years. Without my money, they shall starve, or die from the winter cold. Already, the doctor's bills are mounting. The cost of medicine these days! Without my income, I don't know how they'll survive. Even with my money, they're becoming too much of a burden."

Kate moved her hand over the governess' bent fingers. She stroked their cold surface.

"Whatever shall I do, Kate?"

"Were you going to visit them today?"

"Yes. I said I'd be there at two o'clock."

"Well then. We'd better hurry, or we'll be late."

"Please, return home. I'm ashamed of their living quarters."

"Nonsense." Kate stood and paid the bill, then helped Agnes to her feet and handed her cane. "Don't forget your hat and gloves. Oh, perfect, here comes the trolley now."

Kate noticed before leaving that Agnes tipped the basket of rolls into her purse.

14

They arrived at White Chapel at half past two. Agnes complained that the section of the city had declined in recent years. Kate saw that Agnes' complaint was, for once, well founded. When Kate was a girl, the East End was one of the favorite local resorts for Londoner's with it's open fields, magnificent trees, and an abundance of healthy air. Today, it brimmed with overcrowded slums, factories and too much smoke.

They walked briskly through the gray, cobblestone streets of White Chapel, pressed in by horse-drawn carts and scattered groupings of depressed, weary East-Enders. They passed a tavern near the docks where a pair of foreign sailors brawled. Kate felt a tugging at her purse. She looked down to see a dirty-faced ruffian politely smiling up at her. "Good day, mum," he said, running off. Kate lifted her purse and held it to her flat chest.

"It's not far from here," Agnes said.

They wove through some of the very alleys and narrow roadways where Jack the Ripper murdered and mutilated his female victims ten years earlier, then entered a small square of buildings at the corner of Flower and Dean Street.

Jewish refugee families were everywhere: sitting on the fire escape stairways, popping their heads from open windows. Clusters of happy-faced children played in the street as skinny Jewish boys returned from the White Chapel Library, toting books and pads of paper at their sides. Their warm laughter and Russian speech lifted Kate's spirits. Unlike the English inhabitants of White Chapel, the Jewish refugees in her midst had hope.

Kate coughed, covering her mouth. When she looked at her handkerchief, she was pleased to see no blood. Agnes led Kate across the square to a narrow building. The roof sloped at a dangerous angle and the walls looked to be crumbling in. The brick surface was coated with grimy layers of soot and Kate could actually see through the open holes that must have let in snow and rain.

They crossed the doorless threshold, walked down a short stairway, and came to a small, wooden door. A trio of rats squeaked in the corner. They ran to Kate and crawled over her boots. She let out a scream. Agnes took her cane and madly slashed at the brazen vermin. "Out! Go, you miserable beasts!"

Agnes removed a set of keys from her purse, brushing off crusts of bread. The rats darted for the food on the floor. Agnes opened the door. Kate followed her inside. The dark room smelled of urine and blood. Kate heard a pain-filled wail, then a series of low-pitched moans. Agnes went to a table and lit a kerosene lamp.

The cloudy light crept across the tiny room, revealing a pair of cast-iron beds, on top of which lay two mounds. *God have mercy*, Kate thought.

When Agnes spoke, it was in a voice that Kate had never heard the governess use before. There was not a trace of criticism or complaint. The tone was falsely chipper, brimming with artificial strength. "Hello, Polly— Hello, Dave! It rained earlier in the morning, but it seems the sun is coming out this afternoon. I saw tulips planted around the fountain beside the bridge, I know how you love tulips, Polly, love."

Agnes bent over and helped Polly to a sitting position in her bed. The old woman blinked at the light, looking briefly at Kate, then at Agnes. "God love you, Agnes. Did you bring any food?"

"Not yet, Polly. I thought my friend Kate could run to the market for us. I'll stay with you and Dave and have a chat." She removed the rolls from her purse and placed them on the bed. "This will keep you until Kate gets back."

Polly grabbed a roll and hungrily ate. Dave turned over in the next bed. Polly reached for another roll. "Take it," she said, stuffing the bread into his open mouth.

Agnes tried to give Kate money as she went out the door, but Kate refused. "The market is two blocks east," Agnes instructed. "Purchase food that's not too hard to chew. Dave hasn't any teeth."

"Don't forget the drink!" Polly said.

"And two large bottles of gin," Agnes added. "The pain, it's so severe."

Kate nodded. "Is there anything else that I can get...that they need?"

Agnes frowned. "Not at the market."

Kate returned an hour later. The ice box contained no ice, only a slimy puddle of black water at its base. Kate put the items in the cupboards, then poured Dave and Polly each a large cup of gin diluted with warm water. She arranged a bunch of tulips in an empty tea tin and placed them on the table.

"How lovely!" Agnes exclaimed, handing the cups to her cousins. "You have your very own bedside garden, Polly. Wasn't that kind of Kate?"

Polly coughed blood into her cup of gin.

Kate and Agnes stayed at the flat for another hour. They changed the bed linens, soaked them in the sink, then hung them on a line to dry. The room was damp to begin with and now the wet linens turned it into a musty cave. Kate wished they had another alternative, but the linens would be promptly stolen if they were hung outdoors.

Dave shivered beneath his thin blanket, watching Kate and Agnes with slanted, empty eyes. Polly reassured Agnes that she'd be able to put the sheets back on the beds herself. Hadn't she done it many times before? Still, Agnes worried. Polly broke her hip earlier that year and couldn't stand up without collapsing back on the bed.

Before leaving, Agnes placed the satiny petals of a yellow tulip in Polly's hair. Polly smiled beneath the fragile floral wreath, a stream of blood dribbling from her chin.

"Isn't that pretty," Agnes cooed. "I wish that I had a mirror to show you how lovely you look!"

Polly weakly laughed.

Kate was glad that there weren't any mirrors in the flat. It wouldn't be right for Polly to see herself looking like that.

Kate skipped supper that evening. She still felt strong, but the events of the day left her without an appetite. Walking through the spacious corridors of the Rutherford Estate, she grieved for the injustices suffered by people like Polly and Dave. Why was she so consistently blessed in her lifetime, while others toiled and fretted their every meal? Surely, they deserved more.

The door to the auditorium was left ajar. Kate walked slowly inside. The posh interior had not changed since she was a girl, although it now appeared faded and antique; the black velvet curtains were covered in blankets of dust; the rows of seats folded upwards and creaked loudly as she pulled one down to sit.

Kate stared at the stage before her. She recalled the marionette show that Agnes arranged for Kate's elaborate seventh birthday party. Even then, Agnes considered Kate's happiness. Kate marveled at the many contradictions in the old governess' character.

A clouded outline of Polly and Dave appeared on the stage: Polly, sitting in her bed, tulip petals adorning her head; Dave, a bumpy, black mound on the sheetless bed. Polly nibbled at her roll. Rats scurried in the shadows. Dave tilted the cup of gin to his mouth and drank.

Kate had not experienced such a desire to nurture and protect since her days as a young mother, with Sandra suckling at her breast. She longer to wrap Polly and Dave in warm flannel blankets and place them in a clean, warm home with a generous supply of bread and warm milk. The thought made Kate smile.

Her lungs tightened, then released. There was no need to cough.

Kate left the auditorium and went to her father's room. Charles Rutherford slept restlessly on the massive canopied bed. Kate sat at his side, nudging him. "Father. Wake up." He didn't stir. A gummy stream of drool ran down his chin, soaking the pillow case. Kate nudged him again. "Father, it's Kate."

His eyes opened. Kate was struck with how much he looked like Polly's husband, Dave. "What is it?" he weakly asked.

"I need some money."

He reached for the billfold on his night table and threw it in Kate's lap.

"I'll need more than this."

He sat up, growling. "Then why did you marry a poor man!"

"It's not for me. It's for Agnes."

"Agnes! What the hell is her problem?"

Kate reached for her father's hand. He recoiled at first, then gave it to her to touch. "Agnes is caring for her cousins in White Chapel. Both of them look to be dying. Agnes pays all of their bills. If you cut off her income, then the cousins are sure to starve."

Charles Rutherford puckered his shriveled lips, thinking. "Agnes shall continue to receive full pay."

"Thank you. And could you possibly give me one hundred pounds?"

His eyes bulged. "Whatever for?"

"I'd like to purchase a small house for Agnes' cousins in Kensington Square where they'll be close to Agnes. I'd also like to employ a live-in nurse and maid."

"Better yet, why don't the sickly imbeciles come live under our roof, eat our meals alongside the family, sleep in my bed for Christ's sake...."

"Please, Father."

"Oh all right! I'll make arrangements in the morning. The money will be deposited in Agnes' account by the week's end."

Kate rose. "Agnes will be so glad."

"Agnes," Charles mumbled, lying down. "That ugly woman will be the death of me yet."

Kate and Agnes went to White Chapel the next Saturday and informed Polly and Dave that they would be vacating the premises that day. The carriage was waiting outside, set to bring them to their new house in Kensington Square.

"But what about Mr. Spurgeon?" Polly asked, truly afraid of her greedy landlord. "He'll send the paddies after us! We didn't give him this month's rent."

Kate sadly smiled. Polly was so accustomed to being trapped, she could not comprehend what it was to be given a way out.

"We've settled the matter," Agnes said in her normal, negative tone of voice. Now that Polly and Dave's situation had improved, she was no longer obligated to act the part of Saint Agnes, much to her relief.

"And a house you say?" Polly asked. "But who will do the cleaning? How will we ever afford the rent?"

"It's all settled," Agnes said, irritated.

The carriage driver entered the apartment, his nose rising with the terrible stench, and helped Dave out of his bed. The old man walked to the carriage by himself. The driver apologized to Polly, then lifted her from the bed. He carried her to the vehicle and gently placed her down on the seat beside Dave. The couple was childlike in their trust; staring with wide eyes from the carriage's window, waiting for Agnes to come outside and take control.

A small crowd of Jewish refugees gathered. Kate and Agnes emerged from the building. "It's moving day," Kate cheerfully informed a young Jewish mother.

The pretty woman slowly nodded, stringing Russian exclamations together under her breath.

As the carriage pulled into Kensington Square, parking outside of the modest brick house attached to a set of fashionable shops, Polly audibly gasped. "The ice box! We forgot the ice box!"

Agnes snorted. "You won't be needing that piece of shit anymore."

Kate and Agnes continued to visit Polly and Dave in their new house on Saturday afternoons. Kate marveled at the transformation in the pair. Dave often greeted his guests at the doorway, cheerfully urging them to come inside and stay for a cup of tea.

Since moving to Kensington, Dave had gained weight. His eyes appeared clear, focused. Polly sat on the pastel print sofa in the main parlor. She spent her days looking out of the bay window, observing the ordered street life below.

In the sparkling new environment, Polly and Dave were full of gratitude. They treated Kate as a benevolent goddess whose generosity knew no end. But as the summer wore on, Polly's attitude changed. She started to make demands; subtle and kind-spirited, but demands just the same. She was getting used to being on the Rutherford dole.

She wanted a better nurse, the current woman was too meddlesome and a "know-it-all." Polly worried that she looked through her belongings when she was asleep at night. Agnes reassured her that the nurse would never think to go into Polly's personal things—disgusting as they were.

"I thought that you'd say as much," Polly sweetly replied. "You've changed lately, Agnes. You're not nice, like you used to be."

Dave looked apologetically in Kate's direction. "The nurse is fine. We're lucky to have any help at all."

"Perhaps she is all right," Polly conceded. "But what about the street noise, Dave? I can hardly sleep at night." She looked at Kate. "It was quiet in our last home."

"Your last home!" Agnes cried, banging her wooden snake on the floor. "Are you referring to that hell-hole where you once lived?" She turned angrily to Kate. "You see? Didn't I tell you that she wouldn't appreciate your graciousness?" She threw her cane at her cousin. "We should have left you both in White Chapel to rot!"

Polly gasped. "Agnes! How you've changed."

Kate intervened. "You'd do well to remember what your last home was like, when these complaints of yours come to mind."

"Perhaps..." Polly said in a small voice. "But it is very hard, being old. Only today I discovered that I'm losing my sight. I have a marvelous view from this window, soon I'll not see it anymore." She coughed, weeping. "If only I could see an eye doctor and get a proper pair of spectacles...."

"There, there..." Dave placed his hand over his wife's knee.

Kate shook her head. She assumed that giving Polly and Dave a safe home would make their troubles disappear. How poor Polly reminded Kate of her own rich father, surrounded by security and support, yet grumbling, as if the world owed her more. At least Dave was grateful, that was something.

She rose from the chair. "I'm going to take a walk, Agnes. Could you tell Father and Bess that I shan't be home for lunch?"

"You'll run yourself down, Kate. Don't be deceived by this sudden burst of energy. Store it up, you'll need it when the disease returns."

"That's true," Polly said.

"Well I don't agree," Kate snapped. "What shall I save the energy for, my deathbed? I'm going to be selfish with it while I can."

"Yes. You do that," Dave said.

The maid came with Kate's shawl. "Where will you be?" Agnes asked.

"I thought I'd take the trolley to that quaint little shopping district that we visited last week."

Agnes retrieved her cane at Polly's feet. "I'll join you."

"No, please. I'd prefer to be alone."

Agnes looked wounded. "Go on then. Leave me with these wretched parasites. Just take care to bring a handkerchief."

Kate's afternoon slipped dizzily past. There were multitudes of sights to see, people to watch, and with the restoration of her health, Kate wanted to enjoy them all. She walked, or rather, skipped, smiling like an elated bride on her wedding day. Kate had ceased bringing her handkerchief outside with her, as a kind of good luck charm to ward off the coughing and the blood. Miraculously, it seemed to work.

She entered a doll shop located in a quiet section of London that overlooked the Thames. She walked through the rows of hand-painted porcelain dolls and eventually asked to see two of the German dolls in the glass case. "These are from the Kestner Company," the clerk told her. "They're very popular with the children this year."

Kate laid the dolls on the lid of the case, examining their faces in the sunlight. They had "sleepy eyes," a subtle trace of babies' pouts, and square-cut porcelain teeth. Their bodies were jointed and they wore velvet green frocks with white knit booties on their feet. They were very expensive, but Kate bought them anyway. One was for her granddaughter and the other for Mary Turner's little girl, Elizabeth.

Kate did not tell Agnes that her reason for wanting to be alone was so that she could enjoy her last journey through London's streets. She planned on leaving for America the next day. She was waiting until the last minute to break the news to her father and Agnes. Though they made a good show of being heartless, Kate knew that they would be upset. Kate wished that she could stay longer, but she desperately missed Thomas and her house, and Bess was dropping hints that she missed her friends in Bately. She even mentioned Ben.

Kate bought a sausage sandwich from a street vender parked outside of the doll shop and walked to a sheltered square that provided a magnificent view of the Thames.

A family ate on the bench beside her. The children were excited to be at a high elevation. One of the mischievous brothers walked along the edge of the stone wall as if it were a balance beam. He was giving his mother the shakes, and he knew it.

"Get down, Jack!" she hollered, the map dropping from her hands and blowing into the fountain. "Do you hear me? This instant. I said get down!"

It seemed Jack was deaf when it came to hearing his mother's terrified orders. The louder she screamed, the riskier Jack's moves became.

Kate finished her sandwich and thought that she might go and buy another one. She had been eating like a horse lately and her clothing was too tight. She smiled to herself. Extra weight was a good sign. Perhaps she would return to America a healed woman.

A beggar pushed a cart full of clothing and miscellaneous kitchen items up the hill. The rusted wheels ground to halt beside the fountain, ruining Kate's view. The mother stood and gathered her children. She discreetly guided them away, speaking in hushed tones. Kate also considered leaving, but how harmless could the old man be? They were both in full view of the main street. If anything were to happen, Kate need only scream.

She lowered her eyes and looked down at her engagement ring, her finger picking at a flake of dirt covering the surface of the stone. She looked up. The old man was watching her. His face was a bag of deeply etched wrinkles; the triangular blue eyes barely perceptible beneath thick folds of brown, weathered skin. He pulled a bag of tobacco from his pocket, rolled a cigarette, and smoked.

He gazed out at the Thames, gingerly placing the cigarette to his mouth, inhaling, then exhaling small gray clouds of smoke. A string of boats split the waters between the Southwark and London Bridge. The middle boat veered off momentarily, then returned on its linear course. The beggar sucked his cigarette until the burning embers touched his fingertips, then threw the butt on the ground and mashed it with the tattered sole of his boot.

He went into the fountain, knelt down, and washed his face. His frail arm lifted, pouring hand-shaped cups of water down his shirt, over his head. He stood erect and stepped out of the waters, wiping his neck and arms with a towel from his cart.

"Good day," he said to Kate, tipping his cap.

"Good day," Kate said.

When he was gone, Kate went to the lookout point, marked by a large, inscribed rock—more like a tombstone than a city marker. Her gaze spread over the expanse of the Thames. It was truly a Father River, timeless, without end.

She started to cough. At first they were small and controlled, but the coughs lengthened—then thickened with blood. The warm liquid filled Kate's mouth. She choked it back, tried to swallow, then opened her mouth and let it come forth, covering her dress in its crimson glow.

Her hand lifted to her heart and pressed its fist over the stain. How could she return home on the trolley covered in blood? She turned to the fountain. The water rose up, sprang forth. Kate hesitated, then climbed over the stone barrier, stepping into the shallow depth. She knelt, allowing the spray of water to pour over her form.

A wave of quiet penitence swept over Kate. Her eyes lifted to the sun, endlessly radiant, pouring forth its healing light. Kate lowered her hands and splashed the water over her face, her hands, the curve of her neck. She stepped out of the fountain. The water dripped form her garment, forming light brown puddles at her feet. She looked down the hill. A group of horrified women stared up at her. A stout, darkly dressed woman left the group and found a paddy. She spoke to him in an animated fashion, pointing at Kate from time to time, lifting her arms in shock. The paddy shook his head and, to Kate's relief, walked on.

Kate sat down on the bench and waited patiently for the sun to dry her dress. It's pale-olive material was now colored dark green, with traces of reddish brown where splotches of blood remained.

She returned to the mansion later in the afternoon. "What happened to your dress?" Agnes shrieked. "Did you jump in the Thames after a coughing fit?"

"Not quite. I washed myself in a fountain."

"Like the beggars do?"

Kate sat down and poured herself some tea.

"I told you to bring a handkerchief with you. Didn't I tell you what happens to dreamers? Didn't I?"

Bess entered the room with Charles Rutherford leaning on her arm. "The bags are packed, Missus."

"Bags?" Agnes looked helplessly at Kate. "You said you weren't leaving until August. You promised—"

"I'm so sorry, Agnes. I've missed Thomas and the grandchildren more than I expected."

"I suppose our company hasn't been enough?"

"Agnes. It's natural that I would miss my husband."

Charles grunted, sitting down. "Let her go, Agnes. She has a mind of her own."

"Thank you for finally saying so, Father." Kate smiled.

Charles hacked into his handkerchief. "You must promise to come again."

Kate went to her father and lightly, fearfully, placed her hand over his bony shoulder blade.

Agnes' face softened, if only for a second. "Yes, Kate. Do come again."

15

Cucumber sandwiches were Hannah's summer specialty. The cucumber slices were crisp and juicy in July, and Hannah's bread was always soft and doughy, never stale. But it was the unusual spread of butter and herbs that made Hannah's cucumber sandwiches the very best. People often asked about the unknown ingredient that made the spread tangy. Hannah refused to say.

She packed ten of them into a basket for Mary, along with a small watermelon, two dozen apple muffins, assorted utensils, and a capped jug of water from the well. Hannah thought about Elizabeth and, at the last minute, added several jars of applesauce and squash, along with ten wedges of "teething toast" that she baked in the oven the night before.

She dragged the basket across the living room floor. "In case you get hungry along the way," she told Mary. She opened the front door and heaved the basket onto the porch.

Mary folded the rest of Elizabeth's cloth diapers into a small suitcase, then tied the two duffel bags at her feet. "I appreciate your thoughtfulness, but Azalea says that most trains offer dining cars nowadays."

"Do the meals come with the price of the ticket?" Hannah asked.

Mary stopped packing. "I didn't consider that."

Hannah went for her purse. "Here, take some spending money."

"No. You've given me enough."

Hannah folded a lump of bills into Mary's hand. "It's Drew's money, remember?"

Mary accepted the money, putting it into the pocket of her skirt.

Jacob came to the door and let himself inside. Mary was glad to see him. Their friendship solidified over the summer months, as did their parenting skills. They were a couple to be reckoned with at the Strawberry Festival the week before, when they won the three-legged race *and* the pie-eating contest. Today he treated Mary with an extra dose of kindness. He understood that she was distressed over parting with the twins. Tara's parents came to the cottage to pick them up the week before. Mary knew that the event would be difficult, but she did not anticipate the gut-wrenching sensations that would overtake her as she handed over the children.

In the days that followed, Mary busied herself with organizing her trip, cleaning and ironing clothing, and generally checking off items on a to-do list that grew longer everyday. She kept a positive facade, but inside she mourned. When she thought of Ethan and Patrick's sweet faces, their happy chortles and needy cries, she recalled the abandonment that she felt after her own mother died.

"Are these bags ready to go?" Jacob asked. Mary nodded. He carried the luggage out to the wagon.

Mary turned to Hannah. "Well, I suppose this is goodbye."

"You have my address, and Jacob's too. If you need anything, please write and let us know."

Mary bent over and took Elizabeth in her arms. "Oh Hannah…thank you again—" She couldn't speak anymore. She only wanted to sit down in the living room and create a new patch on her quilt, then enjoy a leisurely lunch with Hannah and Jacob, afterwards listening to Jacob read aloud. Hannah kissed Elizabeth's rosy cheek. The baby glanced unknowingly about the room.

Jacob poked his head through the open window. "All set?"

Mary hugged Hannah. The old woman's body was pillowy and warm. Mary didn't want to leave its familiar security. Hannah's hand lifted and brushed a long, hot tear from Mary's cheek. "You feel hot, dear. Are you well?"

"I'm tired. I didn't sleep a wink last night."

"There, now. It will all work out."

They walked out to the wagon. Jacob placed the basket of food into the front seat. "Those sandwiches smell good. Can you make me some for supper, Hannah?"

"They're already in the ice box. I've also made a pot of pea soup."

Mary was secretly offended by their casual referral to a point of time when she would be gone. Life at the cottage would continue after that night, and she would no longer be a part of it.

They rode to the train terminal in silence. Mary edged in closer to Jacob. She needed him more than ever. She felt uncertain, overwhelmed. They passed the ditch where Jacob had helped Mary and Elizabeth a little over a year ago. Mary marveled at the changes that had occurred since that day. Jacob steered the wagon into the terminal's busy lot. It bristled with horses and buggies and a short row of coveted automobiles. He turned to Mary.

"What are you smiling about?" he asked.

She placed Elizabeth in the back of the wagon where the curious toddler wandered around the luggage. "I'm remembering the church picnic, when you threw Azalea into the lake."

"It wasn't easy."

"No, I bet is wasn't." Her smile faded.

He put the reins down and leaned forward. "Are you sure you want to go?"

"I have to," she said, her voice oddly devoid of emotion. She glanced back at Elizabeth. The little girl bounced her rear-end against the duffel bag, chanting like an Indian.

Jacob pulled out his wallet and handed Mary a thick wad of bills. "This is for you."

"No."

"It's for your work with the boys. Don't think I'm giving you charity. You deserve a whole lot more than a pot."

She laughed. "I'm bringing that pot with me, you know."

"Good. There's another gift I want you to have."

She sat back, pleased. "What is it?"

He reached under the bench and produced a box wrapped in thin pink paper, a golden bow crisscrossing its front. She removed the paper and lifted the lid. Inside, there was a selection of bell-shaped chocolates, lined in five, delectable rows.

Her hands shook. "Thank you."

"Are you all right?"

She swallowed hard, recalling the first family that took her into their home so many years ago. Elizabeth teetered over the edge of the wagon, threatening to tumble to the ground at any second. Mary jumped off and retrieved the daring little girl as Jacob got down and removed the luggage. He balanced the heavy weight of the duffel bags across his shoulders, carrying the suitcase in his left hand.

Azalea Schenk was waiting beside the ticket booth. She wore an imitation white satin gown with sleeves that puffed like overblown balloons from her arms. Her hair was pinned beneath an umbrella-shaped hat, an assortment of seashells and dry flowers glued to the wide rim. Her parents stood behind her: Mildred, anxiously scrutinizing a train schedule, and the Reverend Schenk, hungrily watching Mary's hips sway as she approached with Elizabeth.

"Mary!" Azalea shrieked, waving frantically. The people in her midst stopped what they were doing and stared.

Jacob dropped Mary's bags at Reverend Schenk's bow-legged feet. "Watch it, farmer...." the Reverend hissed.

"Where's your ticket?" Jacob asked Mary.

She reached into her purse and handed him the yellow card that Drew had sent her in the mail. Jacob took the ticket and went to the booth. Three people stood before him in line. He whistled, looking down at Mary's ticket. He stopped whistling.

"What's this?"

Mary left Azalea and went to Jacob. "Is something wrong?"

"Your ticket. It's an Emigrant Pass."

"Yes, I noticed that."

Jacob's eyes widened. "Do you know what that means?"

"No."

Azalea came over. "An Emigrant Pass! Is that what Drew Graf sent you?"

Elizabeth climbed up her mother's shoulders, pulling a long strand of blond hair from Mary's braid. Jacob took Elizabeth and gave the pass back to Mary. "I'm buying you a better ticket."

"No. Drew sent me this one and I intend to use it."

"Don't be stupid," Azalea jumped in. "Let Jacob buy you a first-class ticket, or at least a second class one. Anything but an Emigrant Pass! By the way, if Drew Graf is a millionaire, then why did he get you such a cheap ticket?"

"That's a good question," Jacob said over his shoulder, expressing rare concurrence with Azalea.

Their curiosity made Mary defensive. "I'm sure it was a mistake. Does this mean you'll be traveling on a different train, Azalea?" she hopefully asked.

Azalea thought about it for several seconds. Above all else, she was a social being who hated being alone. "Well, I suppose I could purchase an Emigrant Pass and travel with you."

Reverend Schenk piped up, playing the role of paternal protector. "Don't be ridiculous, Azalea. Those emigrant trains are ghastly. You'll have a miserable trip."

"Be quiet, Daddy."

Reverend Schenk closed his mouth.

"Azalea," Mrs. Schenk whimpered, "won't you please come to Dayton with us?"

"No, Mother. I've made up my mind."

Jacob arrived at the booth and presented Mary's ticket. The ticket master directed him to the station, where Jacob threw Mary's two duffel bags into a boxcar with one arm, while holding Elizabeth in the other. It seemed he was having trouble letting go of her.

The emigrant train crawled out of the terminal and came to a screeching halt beside the ticket booth. While the other trains in the area possessed an air of romanticism and luxury, with their hunter green cars and golden stripes, and the small windows with lace curtains pulled to their sides, the emigrant train was a sad excuse for a modern-day vehicle. The dirty brown worm was comprised of a score of baggage wagons, followed by the engine, then the Chinese car, the single men and family cars, and finally, at the end of the line, a conductor in his caboose.

"All aboard!" The conductor hollered above the crowd.

Jacob reluctantly handed Elizabeth over to Mary. He leaned into the little girl, his voice cracking with emotion. "Bye," he whispered.

Elizabeth's chubby arm formed the characteristic salute. "Ba, ba."

Jacob turned away. He had felt this pain before—on the night that Tara died.

Mary opened her mouth to speak. Azalea grabbed her arm. "Hurry! It's leaving!" They jumped onto the steps and rushed onto the family car, which was really no better than a long, narrow, wooden box. Mary's thoughts were blurred and anxious, only later did she think that she should have found a window and waved goodbye to Jacob. She followed Azalea's large form down the passageway. Wooden benches faced each other in pairs on either side. Azalea found an empty seat at the back. She plopped her large rump onto its hardness, then released a loud and ecstatic grunt that voiced the immense relief that she felt in being free of her overbearing parents for the first time in more than two decades. Mary placed Elizabeth between them. The little girl leaned against her mother's warmth and immediately fell asleep.

The train started with a jolt, then rolled into motion. Mary removed the money from her pocket and placed it safely in her purse. The man sitting across from Mary watched her handle the bills. His eyes gleamed yellow and he licked his lips. Mary sensed his evil. She shifted on the bench. The thin slab of wood offered absolutely no leg or elbow room, and certainly no space to lie down. She leaned her head back and closed her eyes. Azalea stared out the window, full of chatter. She speculated on the types and sizes of men that she would find out west.

"Are any of Drew's friends rich?" she wondered aloud.

Mary longed to fill her ears with balls of candle wax. Her throat tightened and her face burned. By sunset, she squirmed on the seat with sickness. Elizabeth awoke, groggy and irritable, and cried in Mary's arms.

The man with the evil eyes got off at a station outside of Detroit. Mary was initially relieved, until she saw the new passengers. An emigrant mother sat down with a colicky baby and an older boy who had whooping cough. The train grew cold and dark. Mary stood and brought Elizabeth to the facilities.

Azalea was eating a cucumber sandwich when Mary returned. "These are great! Want one?"

Mary shook her head. Her throat was so sore, she'd be surprised if she could drink a cup of water. Elizabeth stretched towards the muddy floor. Mary put her down and let her crawl about, until a company servant yelled at her. Mary put Elizabeth back on her lap. If she was forced to hold her daughter for the duration of the trip, it was going to be a very long journey, indeed.

Elizabeth screamed within the restraint of Mary's arms. She thrust sideways and scratched Mary's face. Mary put her back down, then saw the company servant glaring at her. She picked Elizabeth up again, causing the baby to throw a massive temper tantrum at the denied privilege. Small beads of sweat formed on Mary's brow and upper lip. The baby across from them screamed louder. Soon Elizabeth and the baby were in a frenzied crying competition. If Mary weren't ill, she would have laughed.

Another company servant entered the car, tugging a small wagon that carried boards and cushions. People gave him money in exchange for the items, then lay the boards across the benches and placed the pillows on top. He came to Mary.

"What are they for?" she asked.

"To sleep on," he mumbled. "Do you want one?"

"How much do they cost?" Azalea asked.

"Two and a half dollars."

"Isn't there a sleeping car?" Mary asked.

He scoffed. "Do you want one or not?"

Azalea handed him the money. "I suppose we'll have to share the bed," she said to Mary.

They placed the narrow board over the benches. The thin cushions were stuffed with straw and covered in cotton and would hardly make for a comfortable bed. Mary wondered how she and Azalea would manage to fit their bodies side by side. She worried that Elizabeth might crawl out from between them in the night.

Mary fed Elizabeth half a jar of squash for supper. Satiated, the little girl sucked on a teething toast and watched the sleeping baby across from her. People were settling down for the night. An elderly man with a goatee played fragments of tunes on a cornet. The boy with the whooping cough hummed, hacked like a barking dog, then resumed humming. Mary wished that she had her health, for if she felt better, she may have enjoyed the moment of respite. As it was, her body ached and it felt like there were sharp shreds of glass penetrating her throat.

She lay upon the board beside Azalea. It was a good thing that she was thin, since Azalea consumed two thirds of the space. They lay their coats over their bodies, shivering. A company servant walked to the center of the car and lit the wood stove. It bubbled and hissed, the red sparks flying from the cracks in the door. Mary wrapped her arms round her daughter and closed her eyes. Elizabeth wriggled, screaming. Mary stroked the little girl's head as Elizabeth kicked Mary's sore stomach. Mary wanted to shake her daughter— her hand stroked harder. "There now, sweetheart," she whispered through gritted teeth.

Elizabeth's energy dwindled and, mercifully, she drifted into sleep. Mary cried to herself. She had not been this sick since after the colors left her in the orphanage, when she was a young girl. The pain in her throat and the intensity of her fever were brutal. She wished for a mother beside her, holding her and stroking her, as she held and stroked Elizabeth now. She slipped into a fiery, feverish sleep. Her dreams were sporadic, but frighteningly lifelike. In one, she walked through a green forest, beside Billy. He screamed at her, enraged. When she argued back, she saw that it was not Billy at all, but Drew. He tackled her and ripped at her dress. At first she was sexually excited, but soon she became terrified, and screamed for him to stop.

She unloosed herself and ran to a peaceful ravine where Jacob was fishing. She sat next to him and they talked. There were shadows in the bushes, eyes that watched the pair. Mary was frightened. Jacob told her not to worry. It was only Mary's father, he explained.

"Is he alive?" she asked.

Jacob didn't answer. The shadows left and the ravine filled with sunlight, joy. Jacob pulled a fish from the water and handed it to Mary. Mary wondered if her father lived within the fish, like Jonah in the whale. The more she stared at that strange fish that Jacob caught, the more she thought of her father. And then, she suddenly *was* the fish. Moving inside of its slippery skin, she felt all holy and pure.

She was awakened at dawn by Elizabeth's frantic cries. Mary's throat was raw and burning, aggravated by the stove's dry heat. She placed Elizabeth down on the floor. When the company servant came over to reprimand Mary, she glared at him with such vehemence that he shrugged and went away.

Azalea grunted, rolling over. She reached into the basket and removed the watermelon. She sat up on the board and sliced into its thick rind with a small knife. "Want some?" she asked. Mary shook her head. It was too painful to speak.

Azalea ate the entire watermelon, making a mess of her white satin dress. They got off of the board and lay it against the side of the bench, placing the pillows beneath them. Mary took the window seat. Azalea polished off the contents of the food basket by mid-morning, with the exception of the baby food, although she did ask if she could have a piece of Elizabeth's teething toast. Mary adamantly refused. Elizabeth wandered freely about the car, bumping into other passengers who spoke to her in warm, foreign tones.

Mary looked out the window. The fields rolled past like an endless blanket containing rippled brown folds, occasionally interrupted by a cluster of bushes or a tree. Wild sunflowers grew along the track in full bloom, and patches of grazing cattle led into dots that transformed into sod houses and small log cabins. Mary thought of her crazy quilt. She wanted to pack it, but Jacob promised that he would pay to have it sent to her. He was sure that it would get ruined in the freight car.

Mary's hand covered her throat and she gently rubbed. The crazy quit was half-finished. It hung on a rack in her bedroom, the best patches facing the window. She speculated on the future colors that she would put into it and realized, gloomily, that earth tones seemed most appropriate.

16

Mary had trouble standing up for herself when she was with Drew. When he arrived two hours late at the Vancouver Train Terminal, she didn't complain, although Azalea certainly made her feelings known while Elizabeth whined with symptoms of an earache.

The toddler came down with Mary's flu as the train crossed the Canadian prairies. The train stopped only at desolate points where there were rarely any outhouses or restaurants. When they entered British Columbia, Mary noticed a greenish-brown secretion dripping from her daughter's left ear, forming sticky knots in the baby's fine hair. An emigrant mother observed that Elizabeth had an ear infection, stating that her own son was cursed with them practically from the day of birth.

"What do I do about it?" Mary helplessly inquired.

"Wait for it to go away." The woman shrugged, glad to not be in Mary's situation. "And hope that the eardrum doesn't burst."

The week crept forward and Elizabeth's infection didn't go away. Her hand pounded her left ear and she incessantly shrieked with the pain. There had to be some kind of costly syrup that would make the ache go away, Mary thought. When Mary met up with Drew she would have him take them to a doctor immediately. But Drew had other things on his mind when he came to get the exhausted travelers. He handed Mary a pitiful bunch of wilted roses and told her that the Justice of the Peace was all set to marry them at City Hall.

"Do you have anything nicer to wear?" he asked.

Mary looked down at her brown plaid dress. It floated on her body like a tent, the hemline brushing against the muddy ground as she walked. After a week in the Emigrant train, she resembled a woman of the streets. "I didn't plan on getting married today. Can't it wait?"

He half-shrugged, "I guess so."

"The baby needs to see a doctor, Drew!" Azalea demanded. "She's been crying like a maniac since we left Calgary. And I've had to put up with it."

Drew gathered Mary's bags and tossed them into the wagon. The vehicle's back-end was warped and the wheels were missing sprockets. Mary wondered why Drew didn't ride a carriage, or better yet, a car. He helped Mary and Azalea onto the bench.

"Elizabeth does need to see a doctor," Mary said, apologetically.

"We'll take care of it in the morning," Drew angrily replied. His eyes scanned the station's manicured grounds, his short fingers tapping his knee. He snapped the reins and reached for a bottle beneath the bench, taking a swig of applejack.

"Can I have a taste?" Azalea asked.

Drew offered some to Mary first. When she refused, he passed the bottle to Azalea. She never gave it back. They rode through Vancouver's busy streets; Mary had never seen a Chinese person in her life until boarding the Emigrant train. She openly gawked as they passed groupings of men and women with what seemed like slits for eyes and hair as dark as the midnight sky. The Chinese sold fruit, fish, and rice cakes. Their round faces smiled through the steamy air, and they spoke in aggressive, chopped tones. Drew didn't exaggerate about the size of the trees in British Columbia. Even in the city, enormous, breathtaking Douglas Firs and Evergreens loomed over the two story buildings. Mary gazed up at their awesome height and felt that they would swallow her whole.

"There's City Hall." Drew pointed to a brick building by the water. "We'll go tomorrow afternoon, after you've had a bath and some sleep."

Mary was ashamed. She hadn't properly washed since leaving Ohio, by the time the train entered Manitoba, she could smell her own body odor and her hair hung in spirals of grease from her scalp.

She expected that Drew would drive them to a large, immaculate house—perhaps a mansion. He took them to his logging camp, located in the neighboring town of Burnaby, in a secluded ocean inlet shaded with trees. The cabins were empty, all except one, and the winding dirt streets were bare. Drew stopped the wagon outside of the largest of the cabins. He put the luggage down in the kitchen and introduced Mary to the two men playing cards at the table. Josh stared openly at Mary, then looked at Drew. "Not bad," he said, as if assessing a newborn calf. He turned to Azalea. His eyes grew. "That's not—it can't be."

Azalea stepped forward, her hands holding her hips. "Hello, Josh."

He blinked. "Azalea Schenk?"

Drew laughed. "I had trouble believing it myself, but here she is, in the flesh."

Azalea pursed her lips, giggling through her nose. The second man, Scat James, rose from his seat and extended his hairy hand. "Good to have you here, Ezra. I'm Scat."

"It's Azalea," she flirtatiously purred. "Like the flower."

"Oh."

Elizabeth knocked her face against Mary's shoulder. "I need to change her diaper," Mary told Drew.

He took her to the bedroom where Mary cleaned Elizabeth on the floor. The baby's genitals were raw and bled from wearing wet diapers throughout the train trip. Mary washed the diapers at stop-off points whenever she had the chance, then hung them on the rack beside the train's stove. The system was not very considerate of others, or efficient, but she had no other choice. Sometimes Elizabeth would have to wear the same diaper for an entire day. Now that they had finally arrived at their destination, the child was truly miserable.

Mary felt guilty for subjecting her daughter to the stress of traveling across the continent. She longed to offer Elizabeth a secure home with a familiar routine. The childhood she never had.

Drew waited by the doorway. He had not acknowledged Elizabeth since their arrival. Mary deeply resented this. She stood and smoothed the crinkles of her dress with her hands, looking about the room. "Is this where you live?" she asked, attempting to guise her surprise.

"Were you expecting something better?"

She did not say. "Do Josh and Scat share this cabin with you?"

"They used to, when the camp was busier."

"I noticed that things were...quiet."

Drew walked around the room, glancing furtively from the windows, drumming his hands over his thighs. Hannah would say that he had a "bee in his bonnet."

"I sold the business. It changes hands this week."

"Sold it? But why?"

He faced Mary. His hands weightlessly touched her shoulders and arms, like stones skimming the surface of a lake. She thought that he would kiss her. He didn't. His head jerked to the side, and he looked at Elizabeth. "She's tired," he observed.

Elizabeth leaned against the wall, her eyelids drooping. Mary picked her up. "Can she sleep on the bed?"

"Sure. I'll wait for you in the kitchen."

Mary heard Azalea roar with laughter when Drew opened the bedroom door. "You've got to talk to this girl," Scat told Drew.

When Drew left the room, slamming the door behind him, the peace was instantly restored. Mary rubbed her daughter's back. She could not deny her tremendous disappointment. Drew wasn't as enthusiastic or charming as he was in Ohio last summer. In fact, he seemed like a different man altogether. Mary sensed that he was now viewing her with critical eyes. And he appeared to be in serious financial straits. The camp had all of the signs of a potentially prosperous logging business, with its giant trees, newly built mill, and cabins where the workers could live. Why then did Drew go and sell it? She quelled her worries by reasoning that he was probably just restless, and chose to move on to new adventures.

Elizabeth rolled on her side. Her small hand reached out and touched Mary's left ear. Mary thought of Ethan and Patrick. She hoped that the grief would diminish, but today she missed the twins more than ever. Her hand warily lifted and stroked Elizabeth's hot forehead with her fingertips. It wasn't only Ethan and Patrick that she missed....

They ate beans and rice for supper that night. By then, everyone was drunk except for Mary. Azalea appeared to be having a terrific time with her new friend, Scat, and her old pal, Josh. (Azalea and Josh despised each other during their school days back in Bately, but with the aid of some strong whiskey, the rift had apparently healed in no time at all.) Drew spent the entire night cleaning his Winchester rifle, which he affectionately called "my lady." Mary was uneasy about having a loaded gun so close to Elizabeth. She kept her concerns to herself, however, understanding quickly that Drew's Winchester was a cherished possession.

When Scat and Azalea started to kiss, Mary left the cabin to get some fresh air. Drew followed her outside and they walked along the beach. "You're not having any doubts, are you?" he asked.

"No," Mary lied, looking out at the water. The Pacific Ocean. It hadn't occurred to her until now. She visualized a map in her mind, with her and Drew teetering on the edge of Canada, and all of her other contacts drifting in the middle of the United States. The image made her dizzy. "Why'd you sell the camp, Drew?" she carefully inquired.

He took a cigarette from his shirt pocket, lit it, and smoked. "I didn't sell it. I lost it in a game of cards."

She turned to him. In the moonlight, he looked devilish and cold. She thought of Billy. Of course—cards and drink.

"It changes hands next week," he said. "I still owe a pile of cash."

"What are you going to do?"

He threw a rock across the water. It disappeared in a blanket of fog. "I'll leave. With you, of course. We've all got to leave. I thought we'd head for California. There's still some gold for mining, and new businesses are sproutin' up every day."

Mary stared at him for a long while, absolutely speechless. He hadn't changed in looks since last Christmas, with his dark hair and magnetic eyes— but tonight he reminded Mary of a frightening black bird prancing about the beach with a shattered beak and broken wings. "You'll find gold," she said, managing her most convincing voice. "You found oil in Calgary, and that wasn't easy…"

"I didn't find oil in Calgary! Who on earth told you that?"

"That's what your mother said. You sent her a big pile of money when you got rich from finding oil."

He laughed. "Sure—sure I did."

"Then where did you get the money?"

He smoked. "I'll never tell."

Mary went cold. In the space of a few minutes, the man she thought she was marrying had drastically, tragically transformed. If he wasn't good for stability, then what was he good for? She turned around on the beach and walked in the direction of the cabin. His footsteps sounded from behind. He caught up with her and circled her neck with his arms. She turned to confront him. He suddenly kissed her mouth, silencing her words. He stepped back and tossed his cigarette into the sea. "Since we're on the verge of being man and wife, how 'bout tonight—"

"No," she cut him off.

They walked in silence. Mary looked to the mountains. If only she could grow wings, flap them hard, and lift herself into the air. She'd sweep into the cabin and retrieve Elizabeth, then sweep back out and fly over the mountains, perforating the fog. Where would they go? Back to Ohio, to see the twins. They'd perch on the mantlepiece and watch the boys as they slept, then Mary would tuck Elizabeth in beside the babies, and soar to Jacob's house, wrapping him gently in her feathered warmth. The fantasy startled her.

"What if we went to Ohio, instead of California?" she suggested. "You could find work in Bately."

"Bately! That's the last place I want to be."

"Why not? Hannah misses you, she wants you there."

"Listen, Mary, my mother is a saint, but she's also very controlling. I can't live with that."

"Hannah is not controlling."

"No? You haven't known her long enough."

Mary shivered. The drizzle was thick and she didn't wear a cloak. British Columbia was considerably cooler than Ohio at this time of year. Drew placed his hand on Mary's hipbone. "What happened to your good looks, Mary? You've gotten skinny as a scarecrow," he coolly remarked. "I don't want a skinny wife hanging on my arm."

"It's all of the nursing. Jacob's twins wore me out."

"Jacob..." he scoffed. "That's another reason not to go to Bately. I can't stand that simple farmer."

The sun came out the next morning and the ooze stopped flowing from Elizabeth's ear. It hardened into thin brown crusts. The little girl woke up smiling, much to Mary's immense relief. When she thought about packing up her small daughter and taking her on another trip, this time to California, her heart grew heavy with dread.

Scat and Josh took Azalea for breakfast at a diner downtown. Drew decided to go with them at the last minute. Mary was glad to have the cabin to herself. She opened the small windows, heated a tub of water, and enjoyed a leisurely bath. The pleasing scent of wet cedar entered the room. Mary removed Elizabeth's diaper and slipped the gown over her head. They played and splashed about until the water turned cold and their flesh was wrinkled like prunes.

Mary wrapped a makeshift toga around Elizabeth, keeping the toddler's bottom purposely bare in an attempt to air out the rash. Elizabeth ran happily about the cabin, frequently sprinkling the wooden floor with tiny spurts of urine. Mary looked down at her own naked body. Her thighs were covered with blue and green bruises where Elizabeth had kicked her during the trip, and her sagging breasts had large stretch marks from nursing the twins. Mary feared that Drew would not be pleased with what he saw on their wedding night. Maybe she could convince him to make love in the dark. She would close her eyes tightly and it would all be muddled, like a dream.

She remembered her first night with Billy. She had only put on the white cotton stockings and the pink gingham dress an hour earlier—it seemed wasteful to take them off so soon, dropping them to the floor in crumpled abandon. Still, Billy was in a rush and Mary was also quite eager to find out what awaited her in the marriage bed. He got rough and talked dirty. Later in the night, she hid beneath the tulip quilt's protective tent, wishing his hands away. She remembered a family from Alabama that she used to live with, in one of her many homes as a child. She remembered how the old grandfather used to fondle her at night, and how she'd play dead in response, fiercely pretending to be asleep and praying that he would go away. He never stayed for more than a few minutes. But he always returned. Night after night, he would come back; and the horrible groping and fondling and fingering would resume.

In the ten months that Mary was with Billy, she never once enjoyed the sex. It seemed that the man got all of the pleasure. This was obvious based on the sounds that Billy made in bed, and the way he wanted her all of the time. Just like the dirty old man from Alabama. One time, in her final days with Billy, she was morning sick and so refused to have sex with him. Billy pushed her to the floor. She fought back, fearing that he would hurt the unborn child. She managed to break free from his grip and went for his rifle.

"Get back!" she screamed. He laughed and walked forward, so she shot him in the leg.

He fell to the floor, writhing and groaning. Mary fumbled for her stockings and made a tourniquet around his shattered shin. She saw the bone protruding. It was white as snow, and surrounded by minced muscle and flesh. He cursed her—oh, how he cursed! She went to the neighbor's cabin and bought a jug of moonshine. Billy drank it all in five minutes and passed out on the bed. Mary watched him sleep, then went to the mirror to fix her hair. Fix her hair! Whatever possessed her to do such a thing, having just shot her husband in the leg? It wasn't her face that stared back at her—the self-satisfied smirk, the crazed glimmer in her eyes. It was more like Billy's face.

"And the two shall be one." She'd giggled to herself.

He'd kill her when he woke up. She knew she had to leave. She gathered the few items that she owned, stole the money from Billy's pants, and left on the train that night. The months that followed were a blur. She worked in Louisville, in a boarding house where she helped to make the meals and clean the latrines, for which she received room and board, then moved on to Lexington, for fear that Billy would discover her whereabouts if she stayed in one place for too long.

As her belly grew, so did her anxieties about what she would do when the baby arrived. How could she keep up her busy work schedule without proper childcare? One afternoon, she bought a peppermint stick at a newsstand downtown and saw Billy's photo on the front page of the local newspaper. He was hanging at the gallows, his handsome head cocked to the side like a flower on the verge of breaking from its stem. Mary's hands trembled as she read the article. Her eyes filled with tears, not of sorrow, but of pure relief and joy. Then she made the difficult decision to take the train up to Bately and visit Billy's mother. Bonnie Turner, while possessing a myriad of vices, would surely help Mary for a time until Mary delivered the baby, got herself a decent job, and saved up enough money to rent a place of her own. Mary had no other choice.

Presently, she put on her bloomers and one of Drew's cotton shirts. Borrowing Azalea's iron, she pressed her yellow chine dress on the kitchen table. It was the nicest garment that she owned, and would have to serve as a bridal suit. When she leaned over to press the sleeves, she felt a warm liquid seeping onto her bloomers. She put the iron down. It couldn't be. After so many months of nursing, she had grown accustomed to the freedom of not having to worry. But now, feeling that sticky substance between her legs, she realized that she once again had the curse.

Drew, Josh, Scat, and Azalea didn't come back until after three that afternoon. They were, once more, all drunk. Scat and Azalea retired to the bedroom.

"Ready to get married?" Drew asked Mary.

She blushed. "Drew, it's not that I don't want to…it's just, I have a certain—problem, you know, a woman's problem. And, well…" her blush deepened. "I just don't think we'd be having much of a wedding night."

He looked down at his shoes in uncharacteristic embarrassment. "I see. Well, we'll wait then. How long would you say these things take to… resolve?"

"About a week," she promised.

Josh and Drew played cards at the table for the remainder of the day. Mary took Elizabeth outside for a walk. A man rode down the hill in a wagon, apparently headed for the camp. Mary met him at the gate and, to her significant surprise, saw that it was not a man after all, but a large woman with a beard. "You must be Mary," she said. Mary put Elizabeth down and walked to the wagon. The unusual woman bent over and held out her hand. "I'm Victoria."

Mary suppressed her laughter—that a manly looking woman would own such a feminine name! Even her voice was that of a man. Mary wondered if the good Lord hadn't made some kind of comical mistake when forming this strange creature in the womb. She politely shook Victoria's enormous hand. "How do you like Vancouver?" Victoria asked.

"It's a very different type of place," Mary said, careful not to let her true feelings show. Had she been honest, she would have sobbed aloud, "I hate it! I miss Bately! I want to go back to the cottage and work on my quilts!"

"That it is," Victoria heartily agreed. Elizabeth crouched on the sand and sucked on a shell. "Is this your child?" Victoria asked. "Drew didn't mention that you had a child!"

Mary mutely nodded, uncertain of Victoria's intentions.

"How old is he?"

"He's a she. Let's see." Mary counted on her fingers. "Almost fourteen months."

Victoria lit a cob pipe and smoked. "She looks like you."

"Do you think so? It's so hard for me to tell."

Victoria opened the sac beside her on the bench and handed two letters to Mary. "These are for Drew."

"You're the postman?" Mary asked.

"Post mistress," Victoria corrected her. "When are you and Drew getting married?"

"I'm not sure," Mary honestly replied.

Elizabeth grunted on the beach, evidently in the midst of having a bowel movement. "That's it," Victoria gruffly encouraged the little girl. "You get it all out! Wish I could do the same, but you know how it is." She turned to Mary. "The bowels get stopped up sometimes. Must be the extra weight."

Mary didn't know what to say to that.

Victoria pulled the reins. "I come by on Tuesdays and Thursdays. I'll see you then."

"I hope so," Mary said. "And thank you for the mail."

She turned to the mountains and smiled, thinking of the odd post-mistress.

17

As Mary bled that week, she observed—and she didn't like what she saw. The camp's new owner arrived on Monday and evicted Drew and his friends from the cabins. Though the loggers were not going to arrive until the first of August, the owner was sending a crew of workers that week to clean up the facilities. Drew calmly inquired if his group could set up tents at the far end of the camp until they left for California in a few weeks' time. The new owner grumbled at the idea, but with a little coaxing from Drew, he eventually caved in and agreed. One could only pity a gambler like Drew whose dangerous habit cost him everything.

On Wednesday morning, Mary walked into her tent and discovered Azalea and Scat, tangled naked in each others arms and legs on the ground. On Thursday, she walked in on Azalea and Josh, in a similarly embarrassing position. A letter came from Hannah that afternoon, along with a threatening note from one of Drew's debtors, saying that he was coming after him. On Friday, Mary walked into Drew's tent and discovered Azalea on the ground with Scat *and* Josh. Fortunately, they were all asleep. Exhausted, no doubt....

She reported the incidents to Drew. "I can't have my daughter around these kinds of people," she complained.

"The hempen widow gets pious." He laughed, penetrating the magazine of his Winchester with a long, steel bristled brush. "I've seen it all now."

"You don't know what it's like when you have a child to raise, Drew. You start seeing things in a different way."

She saw mockery in his eyes. "Is that so?"

Mary wanted to scream out a nasty reply, but something kept her from fighting with Drew. Only later did she realize that it was the irrational fear of being hit, or shot at with the gun. She stormed out of the cabin with Elizabeth in her arms. As she walked, she wondered how she could get out of having to marry Drew. His new life in California would likely be as foolhardy as his time in Canada. Even if he did make some money, it would soon be wasted on gambling and drink.

Mary still had some cash, but it was dwindling fast, and she could no longer afford the price of a train ticket back to Ohio. She could write Hannah. No, she couldn't. It was too humiliating—the whole town would find out. Well then, the answer was clear, she'd break off the engagement with Drew and get a job in the city. The real obstacle was finding work where she would be allowed to bring her daughter along. Perhaps if she took a night shift at a sweat shop, and they allowed her to bring Elizabeth to sleep at her side? It wouldn't be easy, but it could be done.

She passed the mill and saw a group of Indian women and their children eating fish over a fire at the farthest corner of the beach. When Mary first arrived at the camp, she was surprised by the friendly relations that Drew, Josh, and Scat had with the Indians. They often mixed a keg of spirits together and drank on the beach at night. Mary was even more surprised when she saw Scat and Josh flirting with the Indian women when the men were not around, to Azalea's painful chagrin.

Mary turned at the gate and left the camp. She saw a white-shingled house at the top of the hill, hedged in by a small forest of birch and cedar trees. Several wagons were parked in the dirt driveway. Mary approached the house and saw Victoria's large form in the window. Her mood lifted. She decided to pay the post mistress a visit. Inside, the kitchen was full of commotion. Two women sorted mail behind the counter as a Chinese man argued with Victoria.

"He sent it last month!"

Victoria scratched her beard. "I know I didn't give it to anyone else. Maybe it's lying around here somewhere. What did it look like?"

"Never mind that," he barked. "You would have smelled it!"

"Smelled it?"

"Yes. A bear's liver has a very unique smell."

"A bear's liver? Is that what you want? You can't get one of those through the mail."

"My cousin sent it, I know he did."

"He sent it all right! And it stunk up my entire house for a week. I finally had to look inside. It was horrible! I thought someone was murdered. I thought it was a human heart. I threw it away."

"No, no. Don't do that. It has healing powers. Don't throw it away."

"I'm afraid the deed is done." Victoria puffed at her pipe. The man left the house in tears, cursing Victoria under his breath.

Mary walked up to the counter and smiled at Victoria. Elizabeth grabbed an ink blotter and threw it across the room. Victoria's plump face brightened. "Mary! Are you hitched yet?"

Mary's smile instantly vanished. "No, not yet." She looked around. "Do you have a few minutes to talk?"

Victoria walked around the counter, hitting the edge with her enormous hip. "Ouch! Sure. Come into the living room. Here." She took Elizabeth from Mary's arms and handed her to one of the women. "Elsie will take care of your girl." Elsie eagerly took Elizabeth into her arms.

Victoria's living room looked like the interior of a brothel. The walls were painted pink and the furniture was covered with red satin upholstery. There was a round coffee table in front of the sofa, topped with a bowl of hard candies, and a mushroom-shaped lamp with red tassels handing from the bottom if its shade. "We'll have some privacy in here." Victoria put her pipe on the table and sat down. Mary joined her on the sofa.

"Drew told me all about how the two of you met," Victoria said. "At the dance in Ohio. It sounded very romantic. Drew said it was love at first sight. I had a similar thing happen when I was in the circus."

"The circus?"

"You know. My beard."

"Ah…"

"I dated the fat man, the lion tamer, the ventriloquist—I couldn't get a word in edgewise with him." She laughed. "But it was the Master of Ceremonies that changed my world. Do you know what I mean? He *changed my world.* Everything *fit* with the Master of Ceremonies. We talked for hours, about everything. One night we hugged for the first time and I swear to you, Mary, there were forces that held us together. We couldn't let go."

"But you didn't marry him?"

"No. He died in a fire." Victoria took a handful of hard candies from the bowl, then passed it to Mary. "Drew is nice."

Mary said nothing as she took a red sucker from the bowl.

"Scat told me that they lost all their money to cards, but you know, I think that Drew will get it back. He's smart."

Mary looked up at an oil painting of two sad-faced rag dolls on the wall. It looked to be an imitation of an imitation of an uninspired original; the brush strokes were messily bold and seeped onto the canvas as if melting under heat. She sucked her candy. "I don't want to marry him," she flatly said.

"You don't?"

"The only reason that I came out here was because I thought he had enough money to give me and Elizabeth a good life. I'm not ashamed to admit it—I was thinking only of myself and my little girl. But now I see, Victoria. I was better off without him…."

Victoria sobered instantly. "Maybe you should go back home."

"I don't have enough money for the ticket."

"How much do you need?"

Mary shook her head. "I'm not asking for a handout. I thought that I'd get a job in the city and rent a room. If I can save up enough, I might go back to Ohio. Or maybe I'll stay here, if I like it."

Victoria smiled. "You're a proud girl, aren't you?"

Mary sighed. "I'm just tired of needing other people. I want to make my own way this time."

"When are you going to tell Drew?"

Mary slouched down in the chair. "I'm dreading it. I don't know."

"Do it soon. Don't let it drag on."

Mary heard Elizabeth crying in the next room. She stood, turning to Victoria. "I'll do it when I get back to camp."

Drew was looking at maps on the beach with a few of the Indian women when Mary returned. She put Elizabeth down to play with the Indian children. The crew of curious toddlers picked up handfuls of sand and walked down to the water, dumping the sand into the low tide and watching as the tiny white and brown nuggets disappeared in the water's shallow brown depth. They formed a straight, orderly line, each one totally absorbed in the project at hand.

Mary took Drew aside, intently watching Elizabeth's every move as she spoke. "We need to talk," she said.

"What's wrong?"

"Why did you ask me to come out here?"

His jaw tightened. "You know why."

"No, I don't. You don't love me, you don't even know who I am. You found out I was a hempen widow and thought I'd be stupid enough to go along with your crazy plans."

Drew spit at Mary's boot. "Goddamn bitch," he mumbled under his breath. He looked at the Indian woman, Ogema-ga-bow. She tossed her hair over her shoulder and gave Dew a long, thoughtful gaze. Her body was graceful, like a deer. Her brown, toned legs wound around her son. She nestled his dark face into her flat chest. Drew turned back to Mary. "Are you giving me the mitten?" he asked.

"I suppose I am."

His black eyes glazed over with rage.

Elizabeth waddled over to Mary's legs and pulled at her skirt. Mary's hand went down and encircled the safe, familiar curve of her daughter's head. "I'm taking Elizabeth into the city and I'm going to find me a job."

"No you're not."

She laughed nervously. "Yes, I am."

He raised his hand. Mary turned with a start, bending her upper body protectively over Elizabeth and dropping to the ground.

"Are you making a fool outta me, woman?" he yelled.

Mary caught a glimpse of Ogema-ga-bow from the corner of her eye. Was she actually smiling? All of the Indian women were smirking. Mary lifted her head. "Do you think this is funny?" she demanded. They started to laugh.

Drew came forward and kicked Mary like a dog. "At least they know their place."

18

"Leave him, Mary."

"I can't. I'm afraid."

"Afraid he'll beat you?"

"Maybe kill me."

Victoria shook her head. "He wouldn't."

"I know the signs. I'll pack up Elizabeth and sneak off in the night, then he'll find me at the station and beat me black and blue when we get back. That's the kinda game Billy played."

"I'm sorry."

Elsie came to the doorway with a sack of mail in one arm and Elizabeth in the other. "It's getting late, Victoria."

"I'll leave in a minute." She looked at Mary. "Are you coming?"

Mary shook her head. She usually enjoyed going on mail runs with Victoria. It was a chance to get away from the camp, if only for a short time— but today she was overcome by sadness and fatigue. Drew's recent behavior had a way of draining the life out of her.

"Are you sick?" Victoria asked. "You look peaked, and you've lost more weight."

Mary shuddered at the possibility. She knew that she looked haggard when she arrived in Vancouver. The stress of the last few weeks must have drained her of what little health she had left. Even her clothing reflected her unfortunate circumstances. Her three dresses, previously bright and in good condition, were now dirty and ragged from overuse and improper washings. Through some ironic twist of fate, she had come full circle, returning to her days with Billy as an impoverished, frightened woman fighting like a wild animal to survive.

"I need some rest," was all that she said.

"Can you and Jane watch Elizabeth for a few hours?" Victoria asked Elsie.

"Sure."

Victoria patted Mary's hand. "You go back to the camp and have a nap. We'll feed Elizabeth her supper tonight."

"Are you sure?" Mary asked, looking for reassurance.

"Go on now. Elizabeth needs a healthy mother."

Mary reluctantly left the refuge of the post office and descended the hill to the camp. She crossed the grounds and heard noises coming in the direction of the tents. Mary cringed, thinking of Azalea's escapades. She passed the men's tent and heard a husky laugh, then the seductive murmurs of a woman making love.

"Drew?" She opened the leather folds of the door.

A weight came crashing against her, pushing her aside for immediate escape. Mary turned on her heels and saw the Indian woman, Ogemah-ga-bow, skirting around the cabin. She ran down the beach, her long brown legs thrusting over the sand, the hide-skin garment clinging to her muscular back.

Mary entered the tent where Drew scrambled about, getting dressed. He threw his shirt over his shoulders. "What are you doing back this soon?" he demanded.

"I don't understand you, Drew! Why are you holding on to me? Take Ogemah to California—her husband's dead, she'll do it."

Drew followed her out of the tent and grabbed her shoulders. "You're not getting off that easy."

"Let go—" Mary tried without success to pry his fingers away from her throat as he shook her.

Drew might have strangled her then, were it not for Azalea and Josh. They came out of Azalea's tent and took hold of Drew, guiding him away with promises of malt liquor.

Azalea walked back to Mary. "What happened?"

"He was with Ogemah."

"What did you expect?" Azalea asked. "Why don't you just satisfy him? Why do you have to be such a tease?"

Azalea went back to Josh and Drew. Josh was comforting his brother and also encouraging him to allow Mary to leave. "Take Ogemah to California," he said.

Drew's body trembled on the beach. He spit into the water, glaring in Mary's direction. "Mary's coming with us."

They left the camp soon after, leaving Mary to figure out a way of escape. She walked to the beach and looked out at the snow-capped mountains. They were breathtaking in their beauty, but to Mary they had come to symbolize all of the broken promises and dreams of Canada. It was the land of milk and honey, that's what Drew told her in one of his letters. Come join me in the land of milk and honey! Now Mary scoffed at his words.

What was she to do? Her past with Billy was repeating itself. She felt like a fool for making the same mistake twice. Didn't she see the signs in Drew last Christmas? He wasn't temperamental or controlling. If anything, he was charming; bursting with energy and long, colorful tales. *That's the first sign*, Mary chastised herself. The extraordinary charm and charisma, and the splendid stories of a better life, just over the horizon. The dream was always somewhere else. Never in the here and now…

She had haunting thoughts of taking her life. She envisioned the calm surrender of slitting her wrists. Nothing stopped her, except for Elizabeth. She turned on the beach and headed back to Victoria's house. One of the painters stopped her along the way. He was washing out his pails at the latrine and soaking the brushes in a puddle of water. He stepped forward, lightly touching Mary's arm.

"You all right, miss?"

She tried to smile. "Yes, I'm fine." The sound of her own voice startled her. A tear escaped the corner of her right eye, furthering her shame.

The painter surprised her by lifting his hand and gently wiping the tear. "Things will get better."

She pressed her eyes shut. His words were like a balm on her open wound, at first painful, then enormously soothing. She opened her eyes. He was still looking at her face. It seemed he was searching for clues that he could leave her- that she would be safe.

"I'm just going to visit the post office and pick up my little girl," she said.

He nodded. "Then I'll get back to work."

As if in obedience to her command, he returned to scrubbing the pails, softly whistling. Mary looked at the back of his head. His hair was reddish-brown and trailed down to the collar of his shirt. His shoulders were broad and his shoes were covered in streaks of brown and white paint. Yes—he was, in fact, made of flesh and bones, though he served as an angel for a very brief moment in time.

She walked on to Victoria's house, pausing to look at a red flower that grew in the crevice of a moss-covered rock, it's fragile roots enveloped in sand and brittle twigs. Her hand lowered, hovering over the delicate plant, and picked it. The pedals quivered with the rupture, but stayed intact. She placed the flower on the windowsill when she entered the house. Elsie sat at the kitchen table, eating cornbread and chicken with Elizabeth on her lap. She looked up from her meal as Mary walked inside.

"I thought you were having a nap?" she asked, licking the chicken grease from her fingers.

Elizabeth smiled at Mary, and the young mother knew she had made the right choice to return to this world.

"I couldn't sleep." She picked up her daughter and pressed her to her chest. The little girl had never felt so good, or smelled so incredibly sweet. Mary's mouth lowered to the mop of curls, brushing them with her lips, kissing the back of her ear lobes, murmuring, "Elizabeth, I love you, sweet baby…"

Elsie's eyes narrowed with curiosity, though she returned to eating. Victoria came up the driveway in her wagon and entered the house. "Mary? You're supposed to be sleeping."

Mary put Elizabeth down on the floor. Standing, she almost lost her balance. She was fatigued beyond her limits, so weary that she could not speak.

"What happened? Drew didn't—"

Mary's stomach turned over. She worried that she would vomit right there. "Can I sleep here?" she asked.

Victoria stopped asking questions and led Mary and Elizabeth upstairs to the master bedroom. Mary lay down with Elizabeth on the maple and pine rope bed and lifted the layers of blankets over them. The toddler lay still in her mother's arms, listening as Mary sang. She pressed her head into Mary's bosom, searching for her mother's nipple. It had been weeks since Mary nursed, but now she unbuttoned her dress and gladly gave the little girl her breast.

Mary woke up four hours later, alone in the bed. She heard Elizabeth's happy noises in the room below, accompanied by Victoria's hoarse, bawdy laughter. Mary lifted herself onto her elbows and peered out of the octagonal-shaped window beside her bed. Dark and raining, the day mirrored her mood. She lay her head down on the pillow and listened to the rain pattering on the steel roof. The bliss of safety. She was blessed with it in Hannah's cottage, and yet chose to move on. Why did she repeatedly choose to leave places of simplicity and love? She vowed at that moment to never chase illusions again.

She left the bed's warmth, washed her face with cold water in the basin, and walked downstairs. The kitchen was full of Chinese women who had prepared Victoria and her friends an elaborate dinner: steamed fish and assorted vegetables on large platters of brown rice. They invited Mary to come and join them. She took her place beside Elizabeth who was eating tiny bits of rice, one at a time, while dropping the fish and vegetables to the floor.

Drew came for Mary at nine o'clock. He made a point of complimenting Victoria and the other women on their appearance and kissed Mary on the cheek in front of the group, leaving Mary to wonder if they thought she was a lunatic for not wanting such a devoted man. He even took Elizabeth into his arms and spun her about, but it only made the small child dizzy and confused. As they walked back to the camp, Drew apologized for being with Ogemah-ga-bow and promised never to be unfaithful to Mary again.

The rain poured down. "Don't make me go to California," she was pleading now.

"You're the one who wanted to come out here and be with me."

Mary wondered if she was crying, or was it merely the cold rain on her face? "I changed my mind. I want to live alone, with Elizabeth."

He took her hand and pulled it into his coat pocket, at first stroking her wrist, then pinching it. "You're staying with me."

The fir and cedar trees hovered around Mary, fencing her in. In the distance the mountains were covered in a thick grey mist. They seemed to be in retreat, moving away from Mary each time that she stepped forward, teasing and relentless.

The workmen had left the camp that afternoon and locked all of the cabins. There was a broken down shanty beside the gates. It was unlocked and empty so Drew and Josh took down the tents and moved what little food and belongings the group had into the shack. He opened the door for Mary and led her into the dismal space. Azalea sat on the bed with Josh and Scat, drinking Old Orchard from a large, ceramic jug.

"Well look what the cat dragged in!" She laughed.

Drew sat beside Mary on the floor. He laid his hand over her thigh, a gesture that did not go unnoticed by Azalea. "Is she warming up for you, Drew?" Scat reached his hand under Azalea's skirt. She lay back on Josh's lap, smiling. "I hope you boys have some lambskin tonight," she said.

Mary turned Elizabeth's head away from the scene. She mournfully rocked her daughter, thinking of ways to escape. Drew took his maps out from under the bed and perused them. He circled several locations with his fingers, then folded the maps again and placed them back under the bed. He took his "lady" off the wall and shined her with cottonseed oil, then loaded her magazine with eight shells.

Azalea finished the whiskey and Scat opened a second jug. Mary leaned against the wall as Elizabeth dropped onto her lap and sucked her thumb. Mary closed her eyes, blocking out the repulsive sounds of Azalea and Scat. Minutes passed, maybe hours. She sat up with a start.

"Elizabeth?" She blinked back the haze of sleep.

Josh and Scat tossed the terrified little girl back and forth on the bed. Mary saw red. Her hands fumbled for Drew's rifle. She jumped to her feet, pointing the gun at the bed.

Drew jumped up. "Mary!"

She pounced away like a cat. "Get back!" Her eyes darted around the room, settling on Josh. "Put her down," she slowly said.

He dropped Elizabeth to the floor. The little girl ran for cover, hiding beneath Mary's skirt. "Give me back my gun," Drew said.

She faced him and pressed the long barrel to his chest. His hand lifted to remove it, but lowered as she cocked the lever. "I've got your lady." She laughed. Her knees shook with fear. She felt Elizabeth's fingernails digging into her thighs—strangely, the little girl did not cry.

"Give me the gun, Mary."

"I want all of you out of this shanty right now, and don't ever come back."

"We're not going anywhere," Drew said. His voice sounded higher than normal, giving Mary a sudden thrill. Drew was afraid. Now who had the power?

"Then I'll have to shoot you." She coldly smiled.

"You wouldn't."

The adrenalin rushed through her body, almost sexual in its heat. She put her finger on the trigger. "It wouldn't be the first time I shot a man. This time, I aim to kill."

She saw the beads of sweat form over his upper lip and felt the same jolt of excitement as after she shot Billy in the leg. It must have shown on her face. Drew swallowed hard. "Let's get out of here."

Azalea, Scat and Josh got up without questions, quickly packed their bags, and left the shanty. Mary watched them from the doorway. Azalea's feet were bare, her boots held at her side, and her bodice was partly open, with Azalea's large, banana-shaped breasts swinging in the breeze. "Drew!" Mary called out. An observer would think that she was a concerned wife. "You forgot your maps!" Drew came back to the shanty and took his maps, then stormed out cursing.

Mary slammed the door behind him and bolted it. She went to the window and saw that it didn't have a lock. She took a broom and wedged it between the ceiling and the window's middle rim, still holding Drew's "lady" in her left hand. Elizabeth's moist, warm breath rose up her thighs. Poor baby, she had forgotten all about her. In her fear, the little girl had even moved with Mary as she walked across the room, following, step by step, under Mary's skirt.

She lifted her skirt and scooped the frightened little girl up into her arms. "What were you doing under there?" She laughed. Her laughter quickened, growing louder, and her body bent over with convulsions on the floor. She dropped the rifle and squeezed her daughter so hard that the little girl wriggled for release.

Mary got hold of herself, then went back to the window to make certain that they were actually gone. The camp appeared empty. The trees stood like shadowy monsters against the misty night. Why had Josh and Scat not tried to jump her and take the rifle? It wouldn't have been that hard to do. Perhaps they were cowards, or perhaps they were just plain stupid. Whatever the reason, Mary was thankful to be free.

A deep peace filled her. She turned from the window and looked down at her daughter. Elizabeth had climbed upon the bed and was currently rocking her body against the wall. "I'm sorry, darling." She went to Elizabeth and held the pudgy white hand in her own. "Everything will be all right now. I promise."

19

The wind blew all night. The shanty rocked on its flimsy foundation, then the rain changed to sleet and large sheets of ice coated the walls of the shack. The old wood stove struggled to release a bit of warmth. Mary finally fell asleep shortly after midnight. The sound of a large weight impaling itself against the shanty's front door woke her up only minutes later. She gripped the gun and pointed it at the doorway. Her heart pounded, waiting for the second thud. None came. She crawled across the floor, alarmed by another thud, this one pounding against the adjacent wall. She peered out of a crack in the boards. Her stomach tightened into a hard ball of fear. It wasn't Drew, as she had feared, but a large cougar that circled the shack, throwing his entire body against the walls, then pouncing back and circling again.

He was a beautiful creature. His golden-brown pelage shone smooth and was lightly shadowed in the yellow moonlight, the muzzle and strong tail painted in strips of black. He moved silently, secretly, about the sandy grounds. Mary understood that he was hungry, for he had come down to the mainland from the mountains, a rare occurrence. Did he smell human flesh? She didn't want to find out.

She slipped the tip of the gun into the crack—it fit perfectly. The cougar sat on a grassy hill in front of the shanty, the long hind legs giving him the appearance of moving forward, although he was still. Mary pulled the trigger. The loud blast woke Elizabeth and she screamed out for her mother from the bed. Mary cocked the bolt a second time. Racing spurts of fear and the instinct to protect flooded her body. The cat fled into the forest. She waited several minutes, to be sure, then went over to Elizabeth and stroked the hysterical toddler's head, carefully placing the rifle beneath the mattress of the bed.

Beads of sweat sprinkled Mary's brow, dripping like melting ice down the sides of her face. She lay back on the bed and held Elizabeth.

Rock-a-bye baby, on the treetop,
When the wind blows, the cradle will rock,
When the bow breaks the cradle will fall,
And down will come baby, cradle and all.

It seemed the baby in that macabre song was just as terrified as Elizabeth was right now. Needless to say, hours passed, and Mary still could not get to sleep.

The first noises that morning came from the window, followed by the sounds of a hammer trying to pry open the door. Mary jumped up from the bed and hurriedly searched for the rifle, her hand fumbling across the floor. Where was it? A foot came through the doorway and pushed down onto the floor of the shack.

Mary found the rifle beneath the mattress. Her fingers went for the bolt as she mentally counted the number of shots there were left. Two strong arms wrapped around her back. She attempted to turn, but couldn't. "I'll shoot!" she screamed. Elizabeth cried out in her sleep. The breath was hot upon her neck. A bearded face leaned into her ear. The stranger grabbed the gun from Mary. It fired as it flew across the room.

Mary turned and saw the salt and pepper whiskers through her tears. "Victoria?" she laughed with relief. "Victoria! What are you doing here?"

"I heard a gun shot in the night. It wasn't Drew, was it?"

"No, they left. I was shooting at a cougar."

"A cougar? Is it gone?"

"He ran away."

Dawn's light entered the shanty on a cold, wet wind that blew through the large hole that was once a door. "Get your bags," Victoria said. "You're coming back to the house."

Leaving the shanty, Mary wished that she had a match and some kerosene to burn the wretched structure down. She crossed the beach and threw Drew's rifle into the water, as far out as it would go.

"Good girl," Victoria said.

Victoria was the first to see the man leaning against the front gates. "Who do you think that is?" she asked.

He stood beside an automobile and smoked a cigarette. His clothing looked expensive. The trousers were neatly pressed and a bright yellow handkerchief peeked out of the pocket of his coat. He tipped his bowler hat at Mary and Victoria. "Good morning…" He paused. "…ladies?" Mary presumed that he was the new owner of the camp. He approached them. A long wisp of smoke rose from his red, swollen nose. "Do either of you know a man named Andrew Graf?" He spit the cigarette from his mouth. It landed at Mary's feet.

She pressed her boot over the cinder. "Are you looking for him?"

He licked his bottom lip. "No. I like to throw people's names into the air, just for fun." His icy gaze slithered over her body, traveling from her head to her boots, then back up to her head. The cold eyes deliberately overlooked Elizabeth, perched on Mary's hip. "You're a scrawny little thing, aren't you?"

"And you've got an ugly face," Mary sneered. She had had enough of mean-talking men.

Victoria's hand reached for Mary. "Keep walking," she quietly warned.

He laughed. "Then you do know Andrew Graf."

Mary stopped and turned. "What makes you think that?"

"Because you talk like a tart, and that boy likes tarts."

His words stung. "Drew left for California. You won't find him here."

"What part of California?"

"I don't know. Does he owe you money?"

"You might say that." He went back to his car and got inside. Passing Mary and Victoria, he slowed. "I hope you're not living alone here," he said, pointing his words at Mary. "There are more men coming to collect, and let's just say that they might not be gentlemanly like me. Do you hear what I'm saying, skinny lady?" Mary did not flinch. He pressed the gas pedal and sped away, honking the horn as he ascended the wooded hill.

Over breakfast, Mary and Victoria discussed options for Mary's future income. They looked through the help-wanted ads in the *Vancouver Sun*, but the pickings were slim, leaving Mary discouraged. Victoria assured her that there were many jobs available in the city, even for a young mother wanting flexible hours. She just needed to go into town and speak directly with the shop owners.

Victoria looked around the room. "Where did Elizabeth go?"

Mary jumped up from the seat. "I forgot all about her." She found Elizabeth upstairs with her face pressed to the windowpane in Victoria's room. She was looking at Elsie's horse in the driveway, saying "Doggy, doggy!" Her pink tongue licked the glass.

Mary looked out the window. A young woman moved up the driveway and crossed the front lawn. She was the most extraordinary young woman that Mary had ever seen. She wore a simply-tailored Albert overcoat, calf-length and obviously designed for a man, with breast and hip pockets and a half circle cape resting on her narrow shoulders. A pyramid of packages leaned against her upper body, threatening to topple over at any instant. She stopped to blow a long, frizzy, red sausage curl out of her eye, then resumed walking, taking graceful and yet orderly steps. Very orderly steps. Mary took Elizabeth from the bed and went downstairs.

The orange flame for a girl spoke with Victoria at the counter. "I have the address." She put a slip of paper into Victoria's plump hand. "It's in Boston, they'll ship it to you free of charge. The formula itself is expensive, but believe me, it will change your life. I tried it myself. I had an embarrassing light orange mustache over my lip. I rubbed this formula on it one night, and the next morning, it was gone."

"I can still see it, Colleen," Victoria said. "There's a little bit of peach fuss under your nose."

"But it used to be much worse! And now it's colored white, see? Not red."

Victoria adamantly shook her head. "I've come to accept my beard. It's part of who I am."

"Victoria! You have a pretty face. You do. Why don't you try—"

"No." Victoria handed the slip back to the girl. "Now tell me where these packages need to be sent."

"All right. This one's to Colorado, these two are to Seattle, and this letter goes to my parents in Utah. I shouldn't be sending any of the packages, to be quite honest. I'm running low on money. My hours at the mill were cut in half this week."

"Is that so?"

The red flame nodded, her neat coat wrinkling into a disheartening slouch. "I'm the best secretary they have, too, but the new supervisor overspent last spring's budget and now he has to cut everyone's hours. They only want me to come in on Wednesdays and Fridays. I don't know how I'll pay the rent."

Mary stepped forward. "Do you need a roommate?" she asked.

Colleen turned to Mary and gradually smiled, revealing a set of white, perfectly straight teeth. "I didn't think of that! I have a double bed. There's plenty of room."

"It's a good idea," Victoria agreed.

Colleen looked at Elizabeth. "Do you have a job?" she asked Mary.

"I'll need to find one."

"Well, what can you do?"

"I can quilt and sew. I can cook, clean, those kinds of things."

"That's good. You shouldn't have too much trouble. Perhaps a restaurant, or one of the hotels?"

"I just don't know what I'll do about my daughter," Mary thought aloud.

Colleen knelt down and smiled at Elizabeth. "Hi there." Elizabeth smacked her lips together, making the sound of a kiss. Colleen looked up at Mary. "I can watch her, if you get work on the days when I'm home. We'll just have to make sure that our hours don't cross. When can you move in?" she eagerly asked.

"How about today?"

"Let's go," Colleen said.

They left Victoria's that afternoon with Elizabeth and took the tram back to the boarding house. Mary had never been on such a speedy vehicle in her life. It whizzed through the thick forests and grassy fields. Colleen pointed out the mill where she worked, which was only a mile or so away from the post office and logging camp. The tram left Burnaby and plunged into the heart of Vancouver, stopping at several depots along the way. Colleen pulled the bell as they approached a residential section comprised of small shops and newly built, grey-shingled Queen Anne style homes that lined the sloping hills. She took Mary's duffel bag and Mary held Elizabeth as they walked up one of the steeper hills and turned into the walkway of the boarding house where Colleen lived.

Her flat was in the basement of the enormous, three-story home. The door was hidden beneath a vast floral garden of blooming tulips, lush ferns, and verdant shrubs. She opened the cast iron gate and led Mary up the winding cobblestone walkway. Mary's head bowed so as not to smash into one of the many drooping branches that hung like spider webs overhead. Mary was pleased with the flat's interior. It was far from extravagant, but it was clean.

The one-room space contained a double bed, a dresser, and an old, scratched deacon's bench that lined the longest of the walls. Its left leg was missing and two bricks held it up for support. There wasn't any dining table or chairs, but a nice gas stove stood in the corner of the room, alongside an icebox that looked to be new. A frail, rickety washing stand, ewer, and basin stood in the other corner of the room. The carpet was threadbare, but would serve to keep one's bare feet warm on chilly nights. Mary noticed only one source of light in the premises, which was a portable peg lamp, set on the windowsill.

"Well?" Colleen asked, removing her overcoat. "What do you think?"

Mary nodded with approval. "It's very clean."

"That's my virtue and my vice," Colleen said, brushing lint from her mannish-styled shirtwaist. "I hope you're not a messy person, are you?"

Mary put Elizabeth down on the floor. "Well, I wouldn't say I'm messy, but I'm not that neat either."

"That's all right. As long as you pick up after yourself and help clean the dishes. I don't want any bugs."

Mary shook her head. "Definitely not. No bugs."

Colleen walked across the room to a hanging mirror and attempted to roll her hair into a chignon, ornamenting it with lace. She worked at it for several minutes, then dropped the brush to the dresser. "This blam'd hair! I hate it."

Mary looked up from the bed where she was unpacking her clothing. "Really? I love your hair. It's so thick and red."

"Exactly. That's what I hate. I want it straight, controlled. You know?" She walked to the bed and sat down. "You'll like this bed. It's stuffed with feathers. When I moved in last summer, it stank so terribly! I emptied all the feathers and washed them in a tub of suds. They're as good as new now."

Mary sat down beside Colleen. "I don't think I've told you my name yet. I'm Mary."

"Mary, it's a pleasure to meet you. Call me Colleen." The two young women shook hands. "Where are you and Elizabeth from, Mary?"

"Everywhere. I grew up in Tennessee and Kentucky. Before I moved out here, I was living in Ohio."

"What brought you to Vancouver?"

"It's a long story," Mary said, growing tired at the sheer thought of recent weeks. "What about you?"

"My brother came up here to cut wood. He used to write our family in Utah and tell us all about Vancouver. I suppose it was my adventuresome spirit that made me come here."

"Do you like it?" Mary asked.

"I'm not sure yet. I miss my parents, and my little brother. They're in Salt Lake City. But I'm going to visit this Christmas, so that'll be fun." She looked at Mary. "How old are you?"

"Nineteen."

"Really? Me too. Gee, nineteen and you have a baby. I wish I had a baby. Where's your husband?"

"He died."

"You're a widow?"

Mary nodded.

"We've got another widow in this boarding house. Delila. You'll like her."

"Are you going to mind having Elizabeth sleep in bed with us at night?" Mary asked.

Colleen shook her sausage curls. "As long as you keep her on your edge. I'll be worried that I'll roll on top of her and smother her to death."

A long, uncomfortable silence ensued. Two strangers, brought together by financial need, about to share the same living quarters—the same bed. "I'd like to look for work this afternoon," Mary said. "Do you have any suggestions?"

"There are lots of shops on Chestnut Street, where the tram let us off. Try the dry goods store, and the diner, too. They might need a waitress. Why don't you leave your baby here while you look?"

"Will you mind?" Mary asked.

"No. It might help you get a job, if they see you without the child."

Mary went to the basin and opened her carpetbag to retrieve her toothbrush and baking soda. Her hand fingered a strange-feeling, small packet at the bottom of the bag. She pulled it out, curious, and was shocked to find that Azalea had somehow stored some lambskin condoms in her bag. She hurriedly deposited them back in the bag, thankful that Colleen had not appeared to notice. She then dutifully brushed her teeth, making certain to get at all angles. "I'm so glad that you're a clean person," Colleen observed, watching her new roommate from the bed. "Most girls our age already have rotten teeth."

Mary washed her face and changed into her yellow chiffon dress, keeping her arms pressed to her sides to conceal the sweat stains. She bent down and hugged Elizabeth. "Mommy will be back later," she promised. She was relieved to see Elizabeth go over to Colleen and crawl into her arms.

She went from shop to shop to café, even taking the tram deeper into the commercial district of the city. She was offered several jobs, but none of them had the flexible part-time hours that she needed to accommodate Colleen's schedule. It was getting late and she worried that Colleen might not have fed Elizabeth yet. Mary took the tram to the Central Park crossing, then waited on the bench for another tram that would take her back to Chestnut Street. An old oriental man sat beside her with a bag of ice pressed to his chin. His pain was evident. His body quivered, and he groaned.

"Sir?" Mary asked. "Are you all right?"

He couldn't speak English. His small, dark eyes rolled back in their sockets, and he pointed aggressively to his mouth.

"Do you have a toothache?" Mary asked. She opened her mouth and pointed to her back teeth. "Tooth hurt?" she said slowly, as if talking to Elizabeth.

"Oooohhh…" he groaned, nodding.

"Are you going to see a dentist?"

He stared at her with vacant eyes. Mary looked up and down at the street. It was unlikely that she'd find a dentist in this kind of neighborhood, but it was worth a try. She helped the man from the bench, doing her best to gesture with her hands that she was going to take him to find a dentist. She smiled, patting his arm, hoping that he'd trust her enough to be led. They walked two blocks and miraculously, Mary discovered a shop with a large, tooth-shaped shingle hanging from its door. She brought the old man inside.

The waiting area was packed with people, all in pain, holding towels and ice, and even raw, red meat to their faces. One lady had a set of artificial pewter teeth set on her lap, the rusted wires sticking out of their sides. She gave Mary a gaping, toothless grin. Mary sat down with the oriental man. His eyes lit up, focusing on Mary, and understanding that she had taken him to a place where he was going to be fixed. The dentist emerged from the back room. He appeared flustered and jittery and tremendously stressed. "Samuels?" he called out.

The old lady with the wired dentures rose anxiously from her chair. Her teeth fell to the floor. "I'm next!" she scowled. "I've been waiting here all morning!"

"You're not in pain. You can wait."

"I cannot wait!" She barged past him and plopped herself into the chair in the next room. He shrugged at the other patients and apologized.

A little boy went to him, pulling at the tails of his black coat. "Please, sir! My tooth hurts!" Following suit, the oriental man stood from his seat, rubbing his jaw line, looking to the dentist with needy eyes.

"A new patient." The dentist sighed. He went to the desk and asked the oriental man his name. Of course, the man could not reply.

The little boy started to cry and the old lady with the dentures called out from her chair, "Yoo hoo! Doctor!"

Mary got up from her seat and guided the boy back to his mother. She then went to the desk. "I'll have him write his name down, sir. Is this your appointment book?"

He managed a feeble laugh. "You could call it that."

Indeed, the book had names written between the lines, scratched out, new names written in the margins, and ink blots everywhere. The desk was a mess of stray papers and sketches of artificial teeth. Mason jars lined the interior of each open drawer, containing gold and silver fillings, and human teeth pulled out of corpses. The dentist returned to the back room and Mary went about the challenging task of calming down the occupants of the cramped waiting room. She wrote all of their names down on a new page, ripping the old one away, then set the new one to the side so the ink could dry. She arranged the mason jars in categorical lines: gold teeth, porcelain, silver and falsies with wires, then stacked the papers in organized piles and dusted off the desktop with the corner of her sleeve.

The dentist emerged with the lady at his side, proudly displaying her new, white porcelain mouth to Mary before she left. Mary waited until the dentist was ready to work on the old oriental man, for she worried that he might not know his way back home. Her presence was requested from the back room. The oriental man sat down and the dentist handed him a tin cup full of strong-smelling brandy. He gestured for the man to drink. The man lifted his hand in protest. The dentist pressed the cup to his aching mouth and forced the potent concoction down. The old man gagged, but drank some.

"Hold his head back for me," the dentist told Mary.

She did as he instructed. He looked at the old man's rotting tooth, lanced the gum, and produced a rusty pair of iron forceps. The old man's eyes widened with terror. Before he could say anything, the dentist pulled his hand with a violent jerk and extracted the large, black tooth. The old man howled like a wild animal and, in between vigorous swallows of blood, was given another cup of brandy. This time, the sweet, liquid painkiller was not refused.

Mary helped him from the seat, gently dabbing his mouth with a towel from the shelf. She led him to the basin where he rinsed his mouth. He then shocked her by taking her in his arms and swinging her about the room, so glad was he to be rid of the pain. He went to the dentist and bowed with his hands in prayer position; two, three, four times, over and over, repeating what must have been "thank you" in Chinese. He produced a big wad of bills from his wallet. The dentist picked two out, refusing to take more, though the Chinese man begged him to do it.

The dentist stopped Mary when she went to the door. "Young lady, I could use your help in this office."

"Are you offering me a job?"

"You could do exactly what you did today. Take the appointments, keep the patients calm, and hold their heads when I need to extract."

Mary nodded, thinking. "I could to that."

"I'm willing to pay ten dollars a week."

"Ten dollars?" Mary gasped. She paused. "I can't work on Wednesdays and Fridays."

"That's fine. Come in on the other days. The office is closed on Sunday mornings, but I'll need you here on Saturdays, and Sunday afternoons. That's my busiest time. Some evenings, too. I'll pay you eight dollars a week."

The oriental man looked up at Mary and the dentist as they spoke, having no idea of the transaction at hand. "I'll do it," Mary said.

"Good. My name is Dr. Griffith, and you are…"

"Mary Turner."

He shook her hand. "Mary, we'll see you tomorrow morning at eight o'clock sharp." He went to a green cupboard behind the desk. "One more thing, I'll need you to wear this nurse's uniform."

Mary took the white cap and the long, pinstriped dress. "I'm not a nurse."

"You just have to look the part, the patients won't know."

On the walk back to the tram, the oriental man hopped about, smiling at passersby. They both boarded the tram to Chestnut Street. They walked up the aisle and sat down together on the rattan seat. Arriving at Chestnut Street, the old man pulled Mary in the direction of a produce store at the foot of Mary's street.

She reluctantly allowed him to take her into the shop and soon understood that it was his family business. His stout Chinese wife greeted him with smiles and chuckles of amazement upon seeing her husband's giddy, painless expression. He spoke to her in Chinese, pointing to Mary. The wife went to Mary and said in broken English, "Thank you. Thank you, lady." She bowed, lightly touching Mary's hands, then bowed again. Her husband went to her side and they both bowed in unison like strange little birds, pecking.

"You're welcome," Mary said. She bowed back. "Goodbye."

"Food?" the wife asked. "We give food. Money too—" She turned to her husband, tapping his square behind where his wallet bulged from his pocket.

"No," Mary lifted her hands in protest. "I have a baby at home," she pointed out the window. "I need to go home to my baby."

The wife nodded in acknowledgment. "Baby," she agreed. She turned to her husband and told him something in Chinese. Mary spotted an open closet where a row of brilliantly colored silk kimonos hung. She couldn't resist the urge to walk over and examine the exquisite material. The old woman went to her side. "Canada food, make fat!" she said, patting her large belly.

"Are these yours?" Mary asked.

The woman nodded, then rubbed her belly and hips. "But fat."

"They don't fit you anymore?"

"Fat!" The old woman laughed. She took the kimonos from their wooden hangers. "For you. Take. Please."

"No. I couldn't."

The old man rushed over, eagerly nodding his head. "Please, take," the woman urged.

Mary hesitated, but eventually accepted the colorful garments. Their material was smooth, like ice, each dress hand-woven. It must have taken the creator hundreds of hours to make. The old man took a crate from the back of the closet and folded the kimonos inside. He handed the crate to Mary, bowing.

"Thank you so much," Mary said, amazed at her good fortune.

Mary left the little shop with the crate of kimonos and walked up Chestnut Street. Material, a job, and a flat with a nice roommate—the night from hell had led into a heavenly day. A band of bright-eyed adolescent girls wearing blue plaid uniforms and tasseled caps emerged from a large brick building at the foot of the hill. Mary glanced at the inscription on the stone gate: Miss Croft's Academy For Young Women

A private school for girls. Mary had never heard of such a thing. An animated trio of Miss Croft students cut in front of her, leading the way. She eavesdropped on their conversation.

"I don't see why we have to read him," one girl whined. "His ideas are outdated. Who cares about the dietary laws of eating fish!"

"I do. I'm starved."

The middle girl shook her head. "Erasmus is wonderful. He was the one true prophet of the enlightenment."

"Balderdash! You heard what Mr. Skylark said. He was a Judas in his day. He spoke like a religious philosopher, but he lived a very sinful life."

"He did? What were his sins?"

"I don't know. I'm going to ask my tutor tonight."

"Whether we agree with his ideas or not is irrelevant. Daddy says that we read Erasmus in order to learn logic. He's smarter than Socrates or Plato, that's what my father says. He should know, he's a professor of philosophy."

"Then I suppose I'll have to read him, if I'm going to be a teacher."

They turned onto a cross street and headed in the direction that led to the finer, larger homes in the neighborhood. Mary walked for another block, thinking of those girls. They were like members of another species, possessing the outspoken confidence that most females lose before the age of twelve. What would it be like, to be born into such privilege? She would certainly never know.

She arrived at the boarding house and heard Elizabeth's laughter pour out of the open window as she entered the floral garden. When she opened the front door the scene that presented itself was both shocking and humorous. Elizabeth ran about the room, her sopping wet diaper dragging across the floor, leaving a thin, wet streak. Colleen lay outstretched on the deacon's bench, her wild hair even wilder than before, if that was possible, and gasping for breath. The previously ordered apartment had transformed into a cluttered mess of dirty dishes and clothing scattered everywhere.

"I had no idea!" Colleen exclaimed. "Are all children like this?"

Mary put the crate down and Elizabeth ran into her arms. "Mommy— hug!"

Mary looked up at Colleen. "I hope this won't change your mind."

Colleen smiled, sitting up. "Actually, we had a terrific time. But you're going to have to buy a pram so I can walk her to the park and get some fresh air. I'll go insane if I have to stay in this small flat with her all day."

"That's a good idea. I'll get a big one, and she can sleep in it at night."

Colleen went to the icebox and poured Mary a glass of cider. "How did the job hunt go?"

Mary sat down and drank the cider. "Good. I found work at a dentist's office, as a secretary and a kind of…nurse."

"You did? That's wonderful. How's the pay?"

"Eight dollars a week, plus Sundays off."

"And you don't have to work on Wednesdays and Fridays?"

Mary shook her head. "Only some evenings, and weekends."

Colleen lifted a kimono from the crate. "What are these?"

"Kimonos. I met an oriental couple, and the wife gave me all of them. They don't fit her anymore."

"For free?"

"Well, I helped her husband get to the dentist. The poor man was in terrible pain waiting for the tram. They were so thankful that they gave me those."

Colleen's pretty face scrunched up. "Are you going to wear them? You'll look a little silly...."

"Sure," Mary teased. "Isn't that the Gibson Girl look?"

Colleen's red mouth dropped in horror. "No! That's not the Gibson Girl look at all!" She smoothed her skirt and shirtwaist. "'This is the Gibson Girl look."

Mary laughed. "I know. I'm going to cut them up and use the material for quilts. I'll need to buy some cheaper material too, to blend with the silk. I'll sell them when I'm finished. Maybe I can rent out a window in one of the local shops."

"Do you have a sewing machine?"

"Not yet. I'll make the first batch by hand."

"You know, these would make beautiful quilts. I bet the oriental people would buy them by the dozens. Some of them have a lot of money, you know."

Mary nodded. "That's what I'm hoping for. I can make different designs that will suit their tastes, you know, like dragons and frogs and things."

"Can I buy one, when I get some more money?"

"I'll make you one for free."

Colleen went to the mirror and tried once again to roll her hair into a neat chiffon. She smiled at Mary's reflection. "I'm so glad you're here, Mary. We're going to be great friends."

Elizabeth, having expended huge amounts of energy that afternoon, climbed onto the double bed and instantly fell asleep. Mary lay down beside her, on her back, and closed her eyes. She was happy— more than happy; her heart was bursting with joy. She found herself praying. The sentiments of gratitude sprang up from within. They melted her fears and granted her hope.

20

Jacob inherited forty-two acres of land when his father died. At the time, twenty acres had yet to be cleared. Jacob threw himself into the backbreaking labor with the energy that only a man of his age could give to the task. He chopped down trees, broke apart their stumps, and pulled rocks and tree roots from the bowels of the earth. Over the course of three years, the Zane homestead transformed into a prosperous farm, yielding bountiful harvests of corn, hay, and tobacco.

At night, Jacob often left his house and strolled along the path that bordered his land. He gazed with pride at the moonlit fields, looking forward to the day when he could purchase more land and have the twins help him with the work. When Mary left for British Columbia, however, the farm didn't seem that important anymore. His evening walks, once the favorite part of his day, became lonely, frustrating times when Jacob was seized with feelings of futility.

He remembered his father; a man who worked hard every day of his life, stopping only when the senility set in. And yet, what was the purpose? True, he provided for his son, giving Jacob shelter and a full belly of food each night, but there was nothing other than his work when the day was done: no friends, no laughter, no spontaneity or joy.

Now Jacob realized that his father's life was a series of missed opportunities. When Jacob suggested that they clear the other twenty acres and plant more corn and hay, his father stubbornly refused. "Be content, Jacob," he advised in earnest. "Pay your small debts, don't chase large ones." While the work ethic was a backbone of Jacob's German upbringing, too much ambition was a sin.

The same could be said about women, affection, and love—the stuff of great poetry. Jacob's father discouraged him from ever marrying, but if he did decide to go that route, then he should do it later in life, when he had a clear head and could handle the responsibilities. Jacob grew up thinking that the magical age of thirty-five changed a boy into a man and until that day, it was useless trying to act like an adult. After his father's death, he understood that the teaching he received was not worth living by, for it was inspired by fear, not practicality as he had once supposed.

The realization got him to marry Tara when he was nineteen years old. She was also nineteen. They were happy, and grew happier, although the stillborns had a way of dismantling their strength. In the end, he had no regrets about marrying his first love, clearing the land, or building his log house. The decisions weren't hazardous, they were wise.

Why then did he not have the initiative to propose to Mary before she left? She appeared to love his sons, and Jacob even began to wonder if *he* didn't love *her*. It didn't seem possible that he would desire another woman so strongly only months after his wife's death, especially one who was so different from his dark-haired, vivacious Tara. And yet, Jacob could not deny that his feelings for Mary went beyond physical attraction. While she lived in the cottage he wondered what exactly it was about her that stirred in him in such strange, dark ways. In her absence, he came to understand that it was Mary's tender, honest response to life that drew him to her as a moth is drawn to light.

He had heard rumors about her background, and many of them were confirmed by Hannah herself: that Mary grew up an orphan, and that her marriage to Billy Turner was a violent one in which she barely escaped alive. She was broken—shattered, really—and yet it was that overriding aspect of her character that not only made Jacob want to love her, but also want to learn from her brokenness by acknowledging his own. As for the fact that she was fair-haired and freckled and shy around those whom she did not trust (most people, it seemed), it was better that way, for Jacob wanted no painful reminders of Tara in the living. The prospect of a romance with Mary possessed qualities of freshness and novelty.

Jacob had to admit that Tara's death instilled fear in his heart—a feeling that was absent until that time. Even after the stillborns, he encouraged Tara to try to conceive again, telling her that they had to have faith. When he saw those healthy newborns on that winter night, his faith was strengthened. He knew that is was right to hope. But when Tara began to bleed, when her body lost its life, becoming so strangely cold and limp on the bed, Jacob experienced the same fear that trapped his father's soul, that made the old man isolate himself from the community, blaming others for his own unhappiness rather than examining himself.

Loving Mary meant the risk of getting hurt. She could die in childbirth, like Tara did, or she could stop loving him. Better to be alone and safe, he reasoned. After she left, he paid the price for that faulty reasoning. He wasn't prepared for the biting sting of loneliness. Yes, he was lonely after Tara died, so lonely that he banged his fists on the wall at night because there was no one to talk to, no one to touch, but at least he had Mary and Hannah in those days of grief, and as least the townspeople were sensitive to his needs, frequently stopping at his house to give him a meal or simply asking after his well-being when he went into a store, gravely nodding their heads, the tears of compassion rising in their eyes.

When Mary left, that all changed, almost overnight. Hannah got busy with activities in the church. There was a lot to do now that Reverend Schenk was gone. A new minister needed to be found, visitations had to be made to the shut-ins on the town. The cottage was often empty when Jacob went over for dinner; the walls echoed the faded sounds of babies crying and Mary's voice. Jacob ate in silence, looking about the room. He could sense his father's shadow looming in his mind as a nightmare is retained the morning after it's dreamt. Eventually he stopped going to the cottage for his evening meals and ate at home instead.

Hannah was usually evasive when Jacob asked if she had heard any news from Mary or Drew. Mary said that she would send a telegram when they were married and the telegram had yet to arrive. "I'm sure she's busy," Hannah said, careful to cover her concern. "They're probably on their honeymoon as we speak."

Mary as Mrs. Drew Graf. The thought made Jacob seethe.

Sister Philothea wasn't aware that Mary had left. She came to the cottage one summer evening as Jacob was trimming hedges, taking advantage of the cooler temperatures. The nun came up the driveway on her wagon, her black vestment billowing in the wind as she stepped down from the bench. "Hello, Jacob."

He put the clippers on the grass and crossed the yard. "Sister, how are you?"

"Very well. Thank you so much for bringing the quilts last spring, the children are extremely pleased. And the wood, too. The wood! We have enough to get us through the entire year, thanks be to you."

"I'm glad to be of help," Jacob said.

Philothea glanced about the front yard, then fixed her eyes on the windows of the cottage. "Is Mary home? I'm hoping that she could make a few more quilts. We have two new boys and—"

"She went to Vancouver."

"Vancouver! That's above Washington, isn't it? What is she doing there?"

"Getting married."

"Is she?" Her voice dropped. "You don't seem very pleased."

Jacob went back to the hedge and returned to clipping. Philothea walked over.

"The children will miss Mary. One of our Indian girls took such a liking to her. Every night, she wants me to comb and braid her hair and make it pretty, 'like Mrs. Turner's,' she says. It was short when she arrived at the orphanage last summer, but now it hangs down her back. She spends her days trying to pin it into a bun, 'just like Mrs. Turner's bun,' she says." She suddenly stopped talking, and searched Jacob's face. "Mary isn't in any…trouble, I hope."

Jacob clipped a crooked black branch that strayed from its bush. "That depends on how you define trouble."

Philothea crossed herself. "Goodness, no—what's wrong?"

"She's too good for the man she's marrying, is all. Her fist husband was a bad egg, I think the second one's a bad egg too."

Sister Philothea looked skyward, pressing her hands together. "What can I do to help?"

"Nothing. Once Mary's mind is made up to do something, she won't turn back."

"Yes, I know the type. We have children in the orphanage who defy our authority every step of the way. They just won't listen to good sense. I'm prone to the vice myself."

Jacob stopped clipping and looked closely at the nun. If anyone would help him, it was she. "Why don't I give you her address in Vancouver?" he suggested. "Ask her if she's married yet, and if she didn't marry, ask her why not."

"I'll do that. I'll have the children write letters too."

"Good idea." *Anything to make Mary homesick,* he strategically thought.

At the end of August, Jacob was deep in his field, plowing, when he looked up from his work and saw a bright orange light in the front windows of his house. He wondered if it was the sunset, which had a way of shining through the windows at this time of day. But the light trembled, glowing. Then he noticed billows of smoke lifting from the roof. Jacob ran through the field and, as he approached the log house, saw the extent of the fire.

He ran to the Smith farm and told Bess to go into town and alert the fire department. He then found Ben, and they grabbed two large pails from the barn and carried them to Spirit Lake. It was a useless effort. By the time they returned to the house with the water, most of the first floor was destroyed. The red and yellow flames pulled up through the roof with awesome strength. Jacob ignored Ben's protest and ran inside. He took some belongings from his bedroom: the title to the farm, and the family Bible with photos of Tara pressed between the pages.

Jacob and Ben watched the house burn to the ground. Jacob was reminded of how a house of sticks would look if it caught fire—fragile and insignificant, seized by forces that far surpass the structure's meager strength. It was a humbling experience. As the flames ripped through the kerosene-soaked logs that formed the sidewalls of the house, the fire department arrived. Jacob told them not to bother bringing their hoses to the lake. It would be a wasted effort. Dr. Smith arrived in his wagon and stood beside Jacob in a stance of silent support. He stayed until late in the evening. By that time, the log house was nothing more than a smoking pile of ashes and cindered stone.

Dr. Smith rested his hand on Jacob's shoulder. "Are you all right, son?" Jacob went to the spot where his front door once stood and kicked a black brick.

"I was planning on building a new one anyway."

"At least the barn made it," Ben said, returning from the barn. "The animals aren't harmed, that's a blessin'. Nothing worse than cleaning up carcass."

Hannah came up the hill from the cottage. She embraced Jacob, then stood back and wiped her eyes. "You'll stay with me, until you can build another house."

"Thanks, but I think I'm going to need some distance from the farm."

"Come back to my place," Dr. Smith said.

"Can Kate handle having company?"

"Sure. She'll be glad."

Ben spoke, a tinge of affection in his tone. "Bess'll stuff you with corn biscuits and hotcakes every day, and she makes a mighty good mince pie."

"Ben's right," Dr. Smith agreed. "Bess takes care of us. She's worth her weight in gold." Ben nodded his head with pride.

"All right." Jacob smiled. "You've sold me. I wish I had some bags to pack, but it looks like the fire burned all of my clothes."

"You can wear some of mine," Dr. Smith offered.

Kate removed her silver necklace and placed it on the top drawer of her wooden trinket box. She was about to close the lid, then stopped herself. The lid would stay open today.

When Kate left for England last winter, she anticipated the trip to be a time of closure, when she would bid farewell to her London connections and return to Ohio to die. In England, she was surprised by the ever-unfolding story that presented itself: Agnes, her father, Polly and Dave, and cherished moments like washing herself in the fountain by the Thames, or smelling the delicious aroma of oranges on the trees in the garden of the Rutherford Estate. Strolling about the grounds, Kate was struck by the continual overturning of nature and its offspring: blooms, followed by decay, and again such beautiful blooms...

It was a pilgrimage, Kate's trip to England—but the final destination was not that of physical healing, as she had hoped mid-way through the journey. No, it was a spiritual healing of sorts, whereby Kate understood that all of life is dying, then rising, and she could partake in this awesome mystery if only she surrendered herself.

She tried to communicate this newfound wisdom to Thomas upon her return to Bately, but the pearls were placed before swine, so to speak. Not that her husband was a spiritual swine—of course not, he was good and true, worthy of every morsel of Kate's admiration and respect. It was only that he had not been given the gift that Kate had received; he had not been lowered, through wretched circumstances or terminal disease, in order that he might be lifted up. No doubt, his day would come, as it comes to the living of every generation.

She barely survived the ocean voyage back to the continent, and the train trip from Philadelphia to Bately wasn't any easier. Kate pressed her face into Bess' shoulder as a sick child seeks comfort from her mother. "There, there...it won't be much longer," Bess hummed in Kate's ear. When Kate saw the dull white light that emanated from the Bately train station, she clapped her hands with relief. In a matter of minutes she would be safe in Thomas' embrace.

Kate's condition worsened in the weeks that followed. Her aching muscles kept her from sleeping at night. When she moved on the bed, shocking bolts of pain traveled up her limbs. Kate swore that she could feel the disease devouring her insides like a horrid parasite, overtaking her flesh so that Kate's spirit had no choice but to turn heavenward. This too was a gift, for Kate no longer feared death, but now looked forward to the day when her pain would disappear and she could finally fly free, disencumbered. She contemplated the mystic's words: "My soul is restless, until it finds its peace in Thee." *Yes,* Kate reflected. *St. Augustine understood.*

Not a day went by in the last thirty years that Kate did not think of her little boy Tommy who died when he was four. The ache never went away, although the process of mourning did change shape. It grew muted with time, then surprised her with a cruel stab of pain when she least expected it: walking past his bedroom, or even seeing a little boy nuzzle into his mother, then push off, bursting with independence, heading back to the recess ground where the other boys played. In the final days of Kate's life, she thought of Tommy more than ever. She eagerly anticipated the day when she would see him on the other side. She wondered if he would have aged in heaven, although she suspected that heaven would be a timeless realm, in which Tommy remained youthful, though now inhabiting a different, resurrected form.

By August, Kate could not get out of bed. She resigned herself to spending her waking hours sitting propped up on pillows, staring out the window. The fields glistened green, backed by a vast blue sky. Kate fondly recalled the summer day that Thomas proposed behind his father's barn. It was a good thing that their engagement was short, since it was all that either of them could do to keep their hands off each other, and back then they were so desperate to follow the rules of the church.

The honeymoon was beautiful. Thomas did not work for three days. They spent long, lazy hours in the single bed of their apartment, exploring one another with childlike awe. The quarters were cramped, dark, and dismal. Roaches cut across the floor, fleeing from the window's light, at times crawling across the lovers' faces as they slept. Kate hardly cared, since Thomas's devotion had a way of holding her every thought. On the final afternoon, the landlady visited and gave them a bottle of champagne.

Kate drank several glasses, feeling both sinful and adult. Now she chuckled at the memory. Yes, the champagne certainly helped, for that last, passionate session of loving making was still clearly etched upon her memory.

And afterward, as she bathed and dressed, splashing generous amounts of perfume over her satisfied flesh, Kate relished in a lingering sense of womanhood. Her body felt like a present that she freely gave to her husband time and time again. It was a present that never lost its surprise, nor did she lose the inherent pleasure to be found in giving it away. She tingled from head to toe, having tapped into a secret that she was never told, but figured out on her own. Sex was not a burden to be born, as her mother had sternly instructed. In fact, a woman could also experience the momentary rapture whenever she wished, given the right movements and pressure applied.

Kate clung to Thomas in those early months. The fact that her parents rejected him, and nearly disowned her for marrying him, made their passion that much more intense. Thomas was not just her husband—he was her mother and father, a devoted sibling and trusted friend. She said to him often, "You are all that I have." In response, he loved her better, since Thomas found his greatest satisfaction in providing care to those in need, and Kate's unsurpassable English beauty made the service quite enjoyable, to say the least.

Did she think back then that her flesh would change as it did, that the beauty and firmness of her face and body would not last forever, but would sag, wrinkle, and eventually be consumed by sickness and eventually decay? No, she clearly did not. She saw elderly woman all of the time, and attended many funerals over the years, but Kate, in her own, quiet attitude of self-importance, assumed that the natural course of life would overtake everyone except herself. And perhaps, she now reasoned, this is the most profound pleasure of youth: the very denial that age will ever set in. The false assumption that age will devastate all of one's elders, but never inflict itself upon the generations of which one is a part. Yes, she and Thomas were like little Greek gods in those days, or so they believed.

In July, Kate was pleasantly shocked to see Bess and Ben locked in an embrace beside the garden. Bess was only a decade or so younger than Kate, and Kate had never considered the possibility that the maid could have eyes for the hired help. Kate wished that she had binoculars, to see the pair better. She had grown so intolerably bored with bed rest and was desperate to enjoy a real-life romance. Ben came to pick Bess up for church that Sunday, and the next Sunday. On the following Monday, he chased Bess through the field and kissed her so hard on the mouth that Kate found herself catching her breath as she watched in bed.

They were married the following Sunday, July 17, 1896, after the church service at the Black Church of Bately. Kate apologized profusely to Bess that morning. She so wanted to see them exchange their vows, but the trip into town would wreak havoc on her body, which was already sapped of its strength. She gave Bess her best pair of sapphire earrings, insisting that she keep them as a gift.

Thomas came into the room and handed Bess two round-trip train tickets to Niagara Falls, in the Negro train, of course. "I hear there's a magnificent suspension bridge over the water. Ben will love it."

Bess was beside herself with gratitude, at first refusing the gifts. "Don't be ridiculous," Dr. Smith said. "This house would have fallen apart without you and Ben to keep things in order."

He turned to Kate, but she already knew his thoughts. "You're quite right, Thomas. I've been too weak to prepare the meals. Bess has been a wonderful help."

Thomas helped Bess fix her hair in front of the mirror. Kate watched on, advising that Bess powder her cheeks with blush. "It's in the top drawer," she weakly said between coughs.

Thomas showed Bess where to put the rouge. Bess had never powdered her face before, and Thomas had watched his wife perform the task hundreds of times. "I had some trouble getting those train tickets," he remarked, stroking Bess' bronzed cheeks with a piece of gauze. "I asked for two round trip tickets. The ticket master said, 'Where to?' and I said, 'Why, here of course. They're round trip, aren't they?'"

"Oh Thomas," Kate groaned. "Your jokes get worse with age." She looked at Bess's reflection. "Are you nervous?" she asked.

"No, Missus."

"That's good," Thomas said. He put the container of blush back into the drawer and turned Bess to face him. He fixed the bow around her waist, then straightened the shoulders of her dress. "Ben will be a fine husband. You couldn't pick anyone better than Ben."

Bess beamed at Dr. Smith. Kate remembered the exhilaration of being in love, when the mere reference to the beloved fills one with joy. Then after the consummation, it's as though one has entered another sphere. *When does that end?* she wondered. The birth of a child certainly has a way of mellowing the fire, and the passage of time, with all of the little conflicts that arise from everyday life. The meshing of two personalities, two minds. It was a miracle, really, that anyone stayed happily married at all. But there existed an unknown component, almost chemical, that seemed to propel two separate beings together, bonding them into one.

In the weeks that followed, Thomas and Kate spoke often about Bess and Ben, wondering if they had reached the falls, and how they enjoyed the sights. Kate recalled their own, simple honeymoon. Thomas touched Kate's face and rubbed the backsides of her frail arms. They both surprised each other by making love one night. It had been almost two years, but even more surprising was the fact that Kate enjoyed the gentle exchange, despite the pain that rushed through her body, threatening to extinguish the pleasure every step of the way. Afterward, lying in her husband's arms and desperately trying not to ruin the mood by coughing, Kate turned her face to his and said that this night was also a gift. Softly kissing Kate's forehead, Thomas agreed.

Presently, Bess came into Kate's room to fix the bed sheets and give Kate her syrup. She told Kate that Jacob Zane's house burned to the ground and that he was downstairs in the parlor with Ben and Dr. Smith, his face covered in soot, but otherwise in good condition.

"My." Kate coughed. "First his wife, then his house...."

"He doesn't seem bothered in the least," Bess remarked, stirring the cough syrup. "Says he planned on building a new house anyway."

"Yes, but the memories of Tara—they'll all be gone now. I'm sure he feels sadness, he must be covering it."

Bess sat Kate up and put the spoonful of black liquid to her mouth. "Did you ever think Jacob and that girl Mary Turner would get together?" she asked. "Me and Ben thought they sure made a handsome couple."

Kate pressed her chin to her chest and swallowed. "Mary and Jacob? But she was engaged to Hannah's son after Tara passed away, wasn't she?"

Bess wrapped the spoon in a napkin and screwed the cap back onto the bottle. "Don't know, Missus. I just thought they, well, never mind. Ain't none of my business—"

"You thought Mary was interested in Jacob?" Kate inquired. The months of bed rest were making her shamefully nosey, she realized. Still, she had to know. "Did Mary say anything to you, Bess?"

"No, but sometimes, the way Jacob looked at that fine girl Mary—just made me wonder. Made Ben wonder, too."

"Jacob looked at Mary? He was interested in her?"

"It's nothing, ma'am. Probably all in my head."

"No, I don't think so. You have a sixth sense about these things. I must admit, I am surprised that Jacob would be interested in another woman so shortly after Tara's death, but stranger things have happened. Is Mary Turner married yet?"

"I don't know that, Missus. No one's heard nothing since she left. Not even Hannah."

"I wonder…"

Thomas quietly entered the room. The curtains were drawn. He was never sure of when his wife might be asleep. She was like an owl these days— awake throughout the night and napping through the day. He went to Kate's bedside and placed his hand over her leg. "Did Bess tell you about the fire?"

"How sad for Jacob. Did he lose the animals too?"

"No, the barn survived."

"Poor boy. What next?"

"Would you mind if he stayed here for a few months, until he can build another house?"

"Of course not. He can stay in the guest room, or on the third floor."

"He has a lot of work ahead of him." Thomas sighed. "I hope the weather holds up. Maybe he can finish building by Christmas."

The almanac says it's gonna be a mild fall," Bess said, walking to the door. "Gonna' be dry, too."

Thomas nodded. "That's good to hear." Bess bowed her head and left the room, gently closing the door. Thomas looked at Kate. "Are you up to seeing Jacob now? He'd like to say hello."

Kate coughed into her handkerchief. Thomas handed another one to her, for the first was soaked within seconds. "Perhaps after supper, when I have my second wind."

Thomas rose from the bed, briefly looking at the ingredients on the label of one of Kate's bottles. "About the morphine—"

"Yes. I've decided. Bring me some tomorrow."

"You've been very strong…."

"But I'm human, after all."

"We all are, Kate."

21

Jacob decided to order a home from the Sears catalog for the sole reason that the idea was a new one. Most farmers lived in cabins or hewed-log houses, while rich residents of Bately had architects come in from the city and design a mansion to suit their needs. The Cape Cod style houses in the Sears catalog were modern structures and no one in Bately owned one to date. Jacob wanted to be the first.

The weather did hold up in the weeks that followed. Jacob started on the foundation before the blueprints came in the mail, then put up the sides of the house in a matter of days. Several men from the community helped out; many of them owed Jacob favors and were happy to pay him back. Jacob was strengthened by their response, and while he had often begrudged petty details of small-town life—the gossip, especially—he now realized that these vices were insignificant in light of the support that he presently received.

The new house was a sharp contrast to the log house that Jacob built for himself and Tara eight years earlier. The log house was seven rooms long, in a direct line, with small spaces for sleeping in the lofts. The Cape Cod house was painted pale blue on the outside, with black shingles framing the windows. It had an entry hall and parlor, with a pantry and a long kitchen behind them, and a stairway leading from the corner of the kitchen to the upstairs bedrooms. The first bedroom was small and could serve as a nursery, while the master bedroom was considerably larger with two bay windows that let in warm blankets of sunlight in the afternoon. Jacob considered adding an ell, or a one-story extension, then realized that the decision depended on the outcome of the next few months, since a bachelor would have no need for more living space, while a family man would.

He went back to the Smith farm late in the evenings, sometimes having worked on his house beneath the light of the moon, and enjoyed one of Bess's sumptuous meals. She put a teaspoon of maple syrup in his baked sweet potatoes, and melted butter over top. With this mouth-watering side dish before him, the meat on Jacob's plate appeared irrelevant and tasted bland. Ben was right about Bess's gift for making mince pies, but he failed to mention her talent for squash pie, apple pie, and even coconut pudding.

After dinner, Jacob frequently drank coffee in the parlor and talked to the newlyweds, Bess and Ben, while Dr. Smith spent his free evenings upstairs with Kate. Bess and Ben possessed a security in one another's presence that Jacob had only witnessed in people who had been together for many years. They were not doting on one another, devoured by lust, but instead looked at Jacob straight on and pulled him out of himself, serving his needs rather than feeding their own.

Ben was a spiritual man, Jacob quickly learned, often quoting long passages of scripture and saying prayers before dinner was served. One night, as the group sat in silence by the fire, Jacob looked at Ben and imagined a jeweled-crown sitting atop the little man's brown, balding head. The oddest thought then occurred to Jacob, that this person before him, the son of slaves, now a handyman, would someday rule over him and the Smith's in another sphere. This is what Tara's death had done to Jacob. It was as though he were part-crazy at times, with one foot on this earth, and the other foot in a surreal plane of existence where he imagined that Tara was, and where a big part of him secretly longed to be.

Jacob chose to sleep on the third floor, since he did not want to impose on the Smith's by interrupting their daily routine in any way, especially with Kate so ill. The third floor was private and spacious, offering three bedrooms to choose from. Jacob picked the largest room, with the biggest fireplace and the longest bed, so his feet wouldn't hang over the mattress when he slept. It also had a sitting room where he could read. He was often so tired at night that he fell asleep in the wingback chair with the fire's warm flames lulling him to sleep. Other times, he merely closed his eyes and imagined what his new house would look like when it was finished. He strolled from room to room, seeing the beige and brown rag-rug carpets on the floors downstairs, and the woodwork on the walls, then walked up the stairway and entered a small room, the nursery, with his children asleep in their beds, then into the master bedroom where Mary waited in the sunlight, her arms outstretched, welcoming him.

On one night the stroll through the house spiraled into a dream, in which

Mary's face emerged from the darkness of the kitchen, clearer than life. It was not a perfect face, for it was as if an artist had painted it and let the brush stroke an extra dab of pink above the left point of her upper lip simply to bring a noticeable flaw to the otherwise flawless mouth. The same held true for the nose, which, while being small and smooth, was too slender. The cheekbones were perfect; high and strong, they foretold a beauty that would endure, becoming more marked with age.

But the eyes! Were they green, or hazel, or blue? They contained scattered fragments of each hue, intermixed with slivers of nervous light. Jacob woke with a start, the image of Mary's eyes etched clearly in his thoughts. A sense of well-being overwhelmed him, confirming his earlier suspicions. He did love Mary, and he wanted her as his wife. And Tara understood. He wasn't sure how he knew this, but he did.

One day, Kate called Jacob into her room. His heart filled with compassion when he saw Kate's fragile form lying listlessly in the bed. She pointed to the walnut bookshelf, to a wrapped package on the bottom. Jacob brought it over to Kate.

"Open it," she said, her voice hoarse from coughing. Inside was a porcelain doll. "It's for Mary Turner's daughter, Elizabeth."

Jacob stared at the doll. "It looks like her."

Kate weakly smiled, rolling up onto her elbow. "That's why I bought it. Every little girl..." She madly coughed into the sheet. "...needs a doll."

Jacob stroked the smooth white face. "Do you want me to send it in the mail?"

"You could. Are you in contact with Mary?"

"No. Hannah is."

"Tell me, is she married to Drew Graf?"

"Hannah says she hasn't heard."

"But wouldn't they have told her, if they were married?"

"You'd think so."

"They probably..." She coughed. "...aren't, don't you think?"

Jacob put the doll down. "I hope she didn't marry Drew," he confided.

"Why not?"

"Mary's too good for him. I know everyone talks about her being a hempen widow, like that's some kind of crime, but she's a fine woman, really. She loved the twins, she nursed them and rocked them. She treated them like they were her own. She's a good mother to Elizabeth, too. She's patient, affectionate…. I don't know what she sees in Drew Graf. All he sees in her is her looks. Granted, she's a pretty woman, but she's much more than that. Drew won't appreciate her the way—" He stopped abruptly, his face coloring.

"Go on, you can say it."

He looked away.

"This doll might break in the mail," Kate said. "You should deliver it by hand.".

"What if she's already married? I'll look like a fool, going out west."

"Would it bother you, Jacob—to look like a fool?"

"No."

Kate squeezed his hand, her own fingers brittle with disease. "She might need you."

"I asked her at the train station if she was sure that she wanted to go. She said yes."

Kate's smile lowered. "I see."

Jacob put the doll back into its box, neatly layering the folds of tissue over the stuffed, lacey form. Bess walked into the room, looking unusually discouraged. The small lines around her eyes and mouth were clearly visible.

"What is it?" Kate asked.

Bess placed a white card beside the multitude of medicine bottles on Kate's table. "A telegram from Miss Frome," she answered in a small, yet angry voice. "She plans on coming here to visit—*again.*"

Kate sat up in bed, grimacing with pain. "Agnes is coming?"

"Yes, Missus."

"Who's Agnes?" Jacob asked.

Kate smiled at Jacob as Bess rolled her eyes. "You'll find out soon enough."

Agnes did not give her hostess very much warning concerning her visit. She arrived in Bately two weeks later. The passenger that shared the seat with Agnes nearly ran out of the car, audibly complaining to family and friends about the "cranky old bat" who made his journey to Ohio unbearable.

Agnes was glad to be with Kate, although she complained constantly that Bess and Ben were far too affectionate in public. According to Agnes, the newlyweds even kept her up at night by knocking the bed frame against her wall. She heard terrible, despicable noises coming from the next room, including old Ben taking the Lord's name in vain. Also, the young farmer named Jacob stayed up too late on the third floor, walking noisily about the creaky boards in the hours when decent people were asleep. Additionally, Agnes sorely missed her English diet of fresh crumpets for breakfast and kidney pie for lunch, and could not fathom as to why Americans ate so much farm produce! The added bulk always gave poor Agnes the most terrible cramps and runs.

If Agnes was like a mother to Kate, she was the prototypical mother-in-law to Thomas. Whereas once he was patient and tolerant of the old woman's ways, by the second week of her visit he found himself grumbling and even shouting back at her when she made the smallest opinion about Bess and Ben, or the way that the household was run. Agnes thrived on this new dynamic between herself and Thomas, for she missed the biting conversations that she and Charles had so enjoyed over the years, the energy of which fed Agnes' aggressive personality.

Kate was physically at the end of her rope, at times moaning loudly in her bed. In the rare moments when she could open her eyes and look about with a perception that was not distorted by bodily discomfort, she marveled at the colors with which her final days were painted. The grandchildren visited on Sunday afternoons, taking care to be quiet when they played in the parlor and kitchen, so that Nanna might sleep upstairs. One at a time, they visited Kate's dark room, at first timid and frightened, then warming up rapidly and relaying their vibrant tales of girlhood heartache and competitive sport. Kate inwardly smiled, knowing that each one viewed his or herself as existing in a universe that, being full of adventure and possibility, spun only about themselves. Sandra and Donald always came in last and told Kate about life on the farm and the latest episode with one of the children; a first step was taken, there was yet another problem with discipline. Kate closed her eyes and listened. She was too sick to respond.

Hannah visited one evening with sugar cookies, an inappropriate gift, since Kate could only eat plain chicken broth and juice these days, but Hannah had not seen Kate for months and therefore had no idea of the rapid rate at which her friend's health had digressed. Kate wanted to ask about Hannah's son Drew, and whether or not he was married to Mary Turner yet, but her throat was dry from coughing and when she spoke, her words formed cracked whispers that faded as soon as they emerged. She was glad when Jacob came into the room and initiated the questioning himself.

"Have you heard from Mary?" he asked Hannah.

"No. Drew wrote, though."

"Are they married?" he directly asked. Hannah shook her head. Kate's heart leapt when she saw the hope that suddenly livened Jacob's face. "They're not married?" he asked.

"No, it seems not." Hannah's disappointment was evident and almost as great as Jacob's relief. "Drew says they're not getting along. Mary's having second thoughts. Drew sold his business and they're living in tents with Josh and a friend."

"Tents?"

"Drew wants to go to California, to find gold."

"Hold on a minute." Jacob sat beside Hannah at the foot of the bed. "Did you say that they're living in tents?"

"Two tents, one for the women and one for the men."

"This doesn't add up. First he sends Mary an emigrant pass, now he has her living in a tent? What about Elizabeth?" Now anger entered his tone. "Is the baby in a tent all day long?"

Kate propped her head to the side on the pillow. This was getting very interesting, indeed.

"Where's Azalea?" Jacob asked. "Is she still with Mary?"

"Yes, Azalea's there. Drew says she's been a wonderful friend to Josh and their friend Scat."

"Scat?"

"It's an odd name, isn't it?"

Jacob rolled his eyes. "And you haven't heard from Mary?"

Hannah frowned. "It's not like her, is it?"

"No, Hannah—it's not."

Kate was sure that Jacob would leave for Vancouver that week, but he continued to build his house and come home late at night, talking in the parlor with Bess and Ben. On Sunday morning the entire group, except for Kate, went into town. Bess and Ben went to the black church, while Thomas and Jacob took Agnes to the white church. They came home together and ate a tender roast of pork for lunch, with gravy and potatoes. Thomas went upstairs after dessert and told Kate that the service was the best he had ever been to at the church. Reverend Schenk left Bately shortly after seeing Azalea off to Vancouver, bringing with him half of the congregation. His adherents were wealthy and loyal, sharing the unspoken belief that Reverend Schenk was their personally funded door to the Kingdom.

Today, Mickey Jenson gave the sermon. Mickey was once the runt of the schoolyard, who took the other children's punches and merciless teasing all because he walked with a limp. Lame Mickey, who, as an adolescent, had a pale face covered in large, puss-filled craters that resembled strawberry preserves on bread. Today, that same Mickey shone before the congregation as the true leader that he was. He went to the front of the church, not having been asked to preach, opened the Bible, and read three psalms aloud. He went on to speak about David's heart-wrenching lament with the sincere and sober authority that comes through a lifetime of personal suffering.

"Kate, I wish you could have been there," Thomas said. "Mickey's voice was stirring, and his simple thoughts, provoking. He stuck with the scriptures too, and didn't blow off hot air talking about what the latest theologians and scholars have to say. You know how Schenk used to love doing that. No, Mickey was honest, right to the point. He had all of us captivated. We insisted on having him back next week."

Kate coughed, straining to speak. "What did Jacob and Agnes think?"

"Jacob liked it well enough, and Agnes, well, you know 'The Queen.'" He winked. "Hannah took Jacob aside after the service. He was quiet on the ride back home."

Kate closed her eyes, pulling the blanket to her chin. *Please go to her, Jacob* she thought, directing her wish to the third floor.

22

The month of August was a blur. Mary created five quilts that sold in a matter of hours from the front window of the dry goods store on Chestnut Street. On the days when she was not quilting and watching Elizabeth, she went to work at Dr. Griffith's office. She soon acquired the lingo of the trade, advising the patients on which rinses and tooth powders actually worked (most didn't—they were nothing but costly placebos, and some actually cracked away the plaster of the teeth), and what types of dentures carried the most biting strength. (On this subject, she kept quiet about the fact that even the best artificial teeth lasted for no more than five years. Although, with the invention of rubber, the industry was steadily improving. Dr. Griffith even predicted that by the turn of the century, dentures might stay intact for up to ten years, maybe more. Mary could hardly imagine such a marvel.)

She took the tram back to the boarding house after her long days of work, with the hysteria of the patients in pain ringing in her thoughts. Colleen was doing a great job with Elizabeth. At times, Mary even felt a twinge of jealousy when she saw the little girl run to Colleen's arms, preferring the fiery redhead to her own mother. On Thursday nights, Mary treated Colleen and Elizabeth to ice cream at the local confectionery. Financially, Mary was doing better than Colleen, and did not mind carrying the brunt of the responsibility with the rent and food. It was the least that she could do, in light of Colleen's dedicated childcare.

Colleen constantly edged her way onto the topic of sex when they sat together in the back booth, licking their ice cream cones.

"Tell me, what's it like?" she repeatedly asked.

"Great!" Mary replied this time, mistakenly thinking they were discussing Mary's chocolate ice cream. "Next week I'm really going to take a risk and try something different."

Colleen gasped. "Like what, Mary?"

"Strawberry," she said, as though sharing a scandalous secret.

Colleen's shoulder's dropped. "I'm not talking about the ice cream, Mary. I'm talking about, well, you know."

Mary bit into her cone. She easily forgot that, although she and Colleen were exactly the same age, their life experiences were considerably different.

Colleen's almond brown eyes sparkled. "Is it fun?"

Mary sighed and wiped Elizabeth's sticky mouth with a cloth napkin. "I thought I told you already, it's a woman's lot. Close your eyes and bear it."

Colleen was genuinely disappointed. "But you can't mean it, Mary. Delilah upstairs says it's like dying."

Mary smirked and chomped into her sugar cone. "I'd rather be alive."

On their way out of the confectionary, Mary bought a newspaper and tucked it into the back pocket of the pram. It was a magnificent September evening. The previous three days of pouring rain, while irritating at times, now produced a wealth of greenery that gave the moist air an even sweeter, fresher aroma than its usual cedar-flavored scent. Mary breathed in deeply, and slowly exhaled. "Colleen, I've never been this happy before." Her steps were brisk, her arms swung like pendulums at her sides. She was aware of the change in her appearance since moving into the flat. Her figure had returned. Her complexion was rosy and clear—all the result of a proper diet, consistent, eight-hour sleeps, and a life devoid of poverty or fear.

And she was also aware of the men who looked at her as she walked along the sidewalk while Colleen pushed the pram. It came as a surprise, that she and Colleen were viewed in similar ways—both attractive women in the prime of their youth. It was an optical illusion, Mary thought. In her heart, she felt old beyond her years, perceiving herself as an elderly woman whose next obstacle was death, rather than life. But she was content with that perception. It was safe and did not involve any more uncertainties, or anymore suffering. No more marriages or childbirth—no potential for pain or grief. Only a simple life with Elizabeth, followed by eventual death—and death was safe.

Back at the flat, Mary worked on an oriental-style crazy quilt after Elizabeth went to sleep. Quilt sales were far surpassing her modest expectations. Ten new orders had come into the dry goods store earlier that week, leaving Mary to wonder if she shouldn't order a few rods of the expensive silk material and have it sent from China, since she only had four more kimonos left. And then there was the dilemma of balancing her quilting with the hours that she spent at Dr. Griffith's office. Eventually, she would have to choose between the two and of course, she knew that the quilting would take top priority. Dr. Griffith would not be pleased if she handed in her resignation. He had come to depend on her organizational skills in recent weeks—more than that, he greatly appreciated the way in which Mary stifled peoples' complaints when they had been waiting for too long, or were in severe pain.

She adjusted herself on the Boston rocker, a present to herself that she purchased at a moving sale the previous weekend. The spindle-backed chair was a classic, with its cyma-curved arms and seat, and gilt-stenciled designs. Mary had never felt so proud as when she purchased the rocker with her own, hard-earned money. She experienced the same flush of confidence as she bought Elizabeth's wicker pram and rolled it back to the flat. She was truly self-reliant for the first time in her life.

"Mary!" Colleen screamed out from the deacon's bench. Elizabeth rolled over on the mattress of the pram, but did not waken. Mary put her needles down and went to Colleen's side. "Look at this," Colleen smacked her index finger into the middle of the newspaper's front page, almost tearing it with her enthusiasm. "We should enter Elizabeth."

Mary peered down at the advertisement for Vancouver's cutest baby contest that had Colleen so worked up. The prize for the cutest child under the age of two was a five-dollar note and two free meals at a fine, French-cuisine restaurant. "Elizabeth would definitely win." Colleen spoke as a proud aunt. "She's the prettiest little girl I've ever seen. She has that adorable little dimple on her chin, and such big, blond curls. Everyone stops me when I walk her through the park. Everyone says she's as cute as a button."

"You don't have to convince me," Mary readily agreed.

"It says all entries must be submitted by September twenty-third, at the town hall. I can do that tomorrow, on my way to work."

"When's the contest?"

"The second Saturday of October." Colleen flipped a wild red curl from her powdered brow. "Elizabeth is going to win that contest, Mary. I just know it. But we'll have to feed her lots of food in the next few weeks, to get her chubby and even more dimpled. Not too much, though. We don't want a little dough ball on our hands."

Mary smiled at the serious look on Colleen's face, greatly pleased that her friend adored her daughter so much.

Colleen rolled up the newspaper and swatted it against the windowsill. "These ugly spiders!"

Mary stepped back. "Where is it?" Her fear of spiders had grown tenfold since living at the flat, where the insects came in from the garden, often late at night. In Ohio and Kentucky, she was usually exposed to daddy longleg spiders, and even those harmless creatures gave her the creeps. But in Vancouver, at this damp time of year, the spiders were thick, sometimes furry and black, with long legs and bulbous heads. Truly dreadful creatures. They skimmed over the hardwood floor, always evading the quick, violent deaths that Mary and Colleen strove to administer.

The spider presented itself. It was at the edge of the brick that held up the deacon's bench. It seemed to stare up at Mary. Though she couldn't see its eyes (if, indeed, it had eyes), she could almost sense its defiant, "come and get me" stance. She pounded her boot at the corner of the brick. The spider furtively fled, scurried up the white-washed wall, then stopped abruptly at the windowsill.

"Get it!" Colleen shrieked.

Mary grabbed the newspaper and pressed it down, smudging it against the board with all of her strength. She lifted the paper, victorious, only to find that the spider had, once more, evaded death.

Agnes read Keats from the window seat, the black, leather-bound book opened before her at arm's length. Her eyes pinched up as she read in the sliver of dim light that peeked its way through a break in the drapes. They squinted to the point of closing. Her slender back was severely crooked. Her head hung from her shoulders like wet laundry on a line, and her face thrust forward with the effort of reading. Her dry, purposeful mouth made short and choppy opening and closing movements. Kate watched Agnes and listened, absorbed by the words:

That spreading in this dull and clodded earth
Gives it a touch ethereal—a new birth;

The purple mouth closed. The skeletal faced turned in the direction of Kate on the bed. "Understand this," Agnes instructed, her aged voice cracking with self-imposed authority. "Pan brings together the mortal and the immortal, but not in a way that transcends the mortal and joins with the immortal. No, not at all. Pan is the virtual concurrence of the two." Her face jerked back to the position of reading. Kate closed her eyes.

Be still a symbol of immensity;
A firmament reflected in the sea:

Again, Agnes stopped reading, this time to put the book down and rub her eyes. "I must not overdo it." She rose from the seat. Her back turned and she pulled the drapes apart, peering through the opening at the fields below. "More rain," she complained. "It never ends! I almost broke my neck walking down the steps this morning. That slave Ben should take care to keep the steps salted. That is what you give him room and board to do, after all, and he certainly reaps the rewards of his meager labors at night, with his Negro lover, Bess."

A jolt of laughter rose in Kate's chest, at once smothered by a larger, harsher bolt of pain. It had only been raining for two days, and yet Agnes made it sound as though they were in the midst of torrential floods. Furthermore, didn't Agnes know that Ben and Bess were husband and wife? Of course she did, she was merely looking for a way to criticize the pair, and the implication that their nighttime activities were somehow illicit helped the negativity of her cause.

Dearest Agnes, Kate thought, *as if you are one to judge!* She recalled the night, decades ago, when she saw her much-revered father slipping into Agnes' chamber. Even then, there was a derisive intimacy between the two of them—one could not call it love.

Agnes placed the book of poetry on the top shelf of the cherry bookcase. She went to Kate and gave her a substantial dosage of morphine, her own hand quivering with pain as she lifted the spoon to Kate's half-opened mouth. "We memorized all of Keats work when you were a child of twelve. Do you remember, Kate?" Agnes asked. She placed the spoon back on the dish, her eyes avoiding Kate's pale face.

I remember, Kate thought. *I had broken my leg falling from my horse that autumn. You had me study in bed. Then, after some time, I moved to a chair and rested my foot on the ottoman. "Your legs may be idle, but your mind shall stay alert." Those were your exact words, Agnes. Your hair was pitch black in those days, and your skin was just as sallow, but smooth, like murky ice. When father entered the room, your eyes twinkled and your words rolled with a lilt when you spoke, as if singing a song to father. You see? I remember it all.*

Thomas knocked twice and entered. Agnes scuttled across the floor and slipped past him in the doorway. "Going to reprimand Bess?" he inquired.

She stopped in her tracks, as if stung by a hornet. She turned and faced Thomas. "Listen up, young man." Thomas smiled, taking the compliment. "I will not be mocked. And I will have you know that your two slaves stole off at dawn and have not been seen since!" A dry snort of triumph moved up her nose, and her nostrils flared.

"Thank you for the update," Thomas kindly replied. "They went to Cincinnati for their church picnic."

Agnes angled her beady eyes to the corner of their sockets. "Slaves enjoying a day in the city! I should only be so lucky!" She scurried down the hallway, maintaining a good pace for a woman of her age.

23

The night before the cutest-baby contest, Mary and Colleen drugged Elizabeth with Dr. Winslow's Cough Syrup for Infants, which contained a trace amount of morphine. It was Colleen's idea. Mary reserved the expensive medicine for nights when Elizabeth had ear infections and could not fall back to sleep. Tonight was the exception. Colleen wanted to make tiny braids in Elizabeth's wet hair in an attempt to enhance the toddler's curls as she slept that night. The plan was this: when Colleen removed Elizabeth's braids in the morning, her hair would topple to her shoulders in downy golden spirals, just like a china doll's. Elizabeth screamed out in protest, her face turning to shades of red, and then one shade of light purple as her pudgy legs wildly kicked at Colleen's freckled arms.

"Forget the braids," Mary said. "Her hairs is fine as it is."

"How about some of that syrup?" Colleen suggested. "That'll surely knock her out, then I can finish the job."

"Are you sure…?" Mary asked.

"Are you sure you want to eat a genuine French meal?"

Mary fetched the syrup from the cupboard and gave a teaspoon to Elizabeth. She swallowed it like candy, and cried for more. Within minutes, she lay prostrate on the bed, her little head bobbing from side to side as Colleen tilted it at various angles and braided the blond wisps together. Finished, she turned to Mary. "What about her skin?"

"Her skin?"

"Maybe I should rub some of my night cream on it, you know, to soften it."

"She's fifteen months old, Colleen. Don't you think her skin's soft enough?"

Ignoring Mary, Colleen went to the dresser and brought back her tin of cream, reading aloud the printed description on the back: "'This wonder lotion removes wrinkles and blemishes like waters from the fountain of youth, while giving cheeks a fresh, rosy glow...' The judges will love it, Mary. Her cheeks will be like rose petals, velvety and soft."

Mary sighed. "Do what you want, Colleen. I don't see that it matters much, anyway."

Colleen covered Elizabeth's face with generous amounts of the wonder lotion, rubbing the leftovers in her palms onto her own rosy cheeks.

Nestled in her wicker pram, Elizabeth was as still as a stone that night. In the morning, she stared up at her mother with dazed, euphoric eyes. Small rivers of drool trickled down her mouth and chapped the skin on her chin, turning it into a bright red blotch. Mary's eyes widened. *Her skin.* The child's cheeks had broken out into a horrible rash that trailed all of the way behind her ears and down her neck. It was red and bumpy, like a severe case of adolescent acne. Mary shrieked for Colleen's immediate assistance.

Colleen ran to the pram—then also cried out. She went to the sink and wet a washcloth. She tried desperately to wipe the rash away, but the scrubbing only made it worse. "It will disappear," she reassured Mary. Colleen tried to unravel Elizabeth's braids. The wet strands had dried into knots in the night. Elizabeth hollered as Colleen tugged at the twine. Mary paced the room, wringing her hands, feeling the unease of knowing that her child was in pain, coupled with the guilt of knowing that she gave Colleen the authority to undertake this crazy scheme.

Fifteen minutes of torture passed. Colleen dropped her hands in defeat. Mary stopped pacing. "We can't bring her to the park looking like that!"

Elizabeth pouted angrily in the pram. Her hair stuck out in all directions, as if she had just viewed a demon from hell. Her eyes were puffy from the morphine, and her rash spelled out the letter O on her round face by starting at her forehead, circling over her plump cheeks, and then meeting back at her forehead again.

"We'll have to cut it off," Colleen said with determination. She got the sheers from Mary's sewing basket.

"No! Not the curls!"

"I'm sorry, but the knots will get worse if we leave them in. Don't worry, she'll look sweet with short hair."

Elizabeth resembled a shorn poodle (with a terrible rash) when the procedure was complete. Mary quietly wept, feeling as though someone had stolen her beautiful baby and replaced it with... she hated to admit it, but replaced it with an ugly one. Colleen giggled into her hands. "Poor, dear Elizabeth!"

"I suppose I wouldn't like French food anyhow," Mary quietly remarked, defeated.

It seemed that all of Vancouver's residents with small children went to Stanley Park for the cutest-baby contest that day, each one believing that theirs was the cutest baby in the city. The infants were lined up in their respective strollers and prams. Some were dark-haired, other's fair; many were oriental, most were Caucasian—and beautiful. The judges strolled up and down the grounds, carefully inspecting each child's face. They arrived at Elizabeth.

"Was she born with those bumps?" a judge asked.

"No, sir," Mary said. "It's a rash."

"Oh dear!" A woman judge approached from behind. "What a dreadful-looking child! Why does she stare at us so?"

"Dr. Winslow's syrup, I'll bet…" another judge remarked, clucking his tongue. He looked sternly at Mary. "Did you give that syrup to your child?"

"Yes, sir. Last night I did," Mary confessed.

"Horrible stuff!" the woman judge bellowed. "Makes the children into zombies!"

The judges moved on, failing to make one single mark on their pads for Elizabeth. Colleen was infuriated as they walked through the park later that afternoon. "They didn't even look at her eyes, Mary. Everyone notices Elizabeth's eyes. They're like emeralds." She stopped abruptly at the playing field where a fierce game of rugby was underway. "Just a minute," she said to Mary.

Mary obediently stopped the pram, pulling at the brake. "Do you know any of them?" she asked. A varied assortment of rugby players ran and collided before them, their tanned bodies wrestling one another to the wet earth.

"I don't think so," Colleen thoughtfully replied. Her brown eyes followed a handsome player as he tackled two members of the opposite team, grunting for show as his body fell to the ground with a loud thump.

"Let's go," Mary unlocked the brake and pushed the tram forward.

Colleen remained still. "Look at how sweaty and dirty they are," she observed, her voice feigning disgust.

"Aren't you coming?" Mary asked, growing impatient.

Colleen slowly nodded, her eyes still pinned to the field, as if drugged by the mass of flesh in movement. "They are quite sweaty, aren't they?" she said, mesmerized.

Mary forcibly gripped Colleen's hand and guided her away. "Yes, Colleen. Now come with Mother before you get yourself mixed up in their game!"

It was a glorious day. They ate a picnic of ham sandwiches and melon, and then walked to the beach. They both napped in the sun, gratefully absorbing its warm autumn rays. When they awoke, they built intricate sand castles and energetically conversed until the sun went down. Needless to say, Elizabeth slept soundly for the entire day.

Back at the flat that night, Mary went to the basin to brush her teeth and wash her face. Her fingers unloosened the blue ribbon that held her braid intact. The blond hair fell about her shoulders in a rippled mass of golden and cream-colored waves. She combed out the tangles and leaned forward to examine her scalp in the mirror's hazed reflection. Her hair was getting quite dirty. She had not bathed for over two weeks. In the morning, she would iron her grey tweed dress and soak herself in sudsy hot water before going to work later that afternoon. Colleen's reflection hovered in the corner of the mirror's glass. The fiery red head was preparing for bed. She tucked the frizzy flames of red hair into a white bonnet and tied the modest cap at her chin. She dramatically yawned. "Ready for bed?"

"One minute." Mary stripped down to her slip and went to Elizabeth's pram. "Fast asleep," she whispered.

Colleen smiled up from her pillow. "She's a sweetheart. Even if she isn't the city's cutest baby."

Mary peered down at her daughter. A melancholy smile lifted the corners of her mouth. Sometimes she had trouble believing that this fantastic little creature actually formed within her womb. She bent down and kissed the warm cheek. "Goodnight, Elizabeth." She crawled into bed beside Colleen and gathered the quilt about her chin. "It's getting cold. Do you feel the chill?"

Colleen rolled on her side, her back facing Mary. "Winter's almost here. I hope you won't be too lonely when I'm gone for Christmas."

Mary stared tiredly at the ceiling, watching the slow drifting blue and yellow shadows that formed from the street lamp beside the window. "Sometimes I miss Ohio." She yawned. Colleen had already fallen to sleep and was softly snoring.

Mary closed her eyes and remembered the twins. In solitary moments, she ached for those children as though they were her own. She remembered Hannah and the cottage; Dr. and Mrs. Smith; and the quaint simplicity of Bately. It seemed like a lifetime ago, like another woman who inhabited that world of maternal sacrifice. Did she actually care for another woman's infants, nursing them at her breasts and attending their every need, day in and day out? She closed her eyes and tried to conjure up an image of the boys. She saw two bald little heads and round, grey eyes that closely scrutinized the rosy curve of Mary's nipple as they steadfastly drank her milk. Mary smiled in the darkness. *Poor dears*, she thought, *having to stare at my awful breasts all day long. But they didn't seem to mind.* She laughed to herself in the dark.

The image soon transformed into that of their father, Jacob. She saw his strong cheekbones and weathered face and the grey, aching eyes. The eyes shifted, smiling, as Colleen's eyes would sometimes smile. They were the eyes of a friend—one to be trusted, never feared. The mere thought of Jacob was always pleasant in Mary's mind. It had a way of lifting her mood, removing the loneliness, and filling the void. In the darkness she fantasized about the feeling of his hands touching her flesh and exploring her with delicate precision...then his body moving over hers. These were Mary's secret thoughts, ones that were reserved for the darkness of the night, when reality merged with dreams and her daytime fears were tempered with the bliss of sleep.

24

Kate looked up and saw Thomas' face leaning over her in the candle's flickering light. Was he that old already? It seemed only yesterday that his skin was tight and young, his eyes clear and illumined with energy. Thomas was always going somewhere, putting on his coat, taking if off in the kitchen and hurriedly grabbing a bite to eat, then rising while still chewing the last part of his meal and putting on his coat again. "Back soon," he promised. Sometimes his appointments would lag for hours.

But today he moved slowly—too slowly, it seemed to Kate. *Is something wrong?* she wondered. She wished that she could ask the question aloud, but the morphine consumed her senses and anchored her tongue at the base of her mouth.

He lifted her head and put the spoon to her lips, then tilted her face up in order to allow the syrup to dribble down the back of her throat. He wiped the corners of her mouth. She thought she saw a tear trip over the crease of his bloodshot eye. *Why the tears, Thomas?* she asked with her thoughts. He caught his breath and looked away.

Bess appeared at Thomas' side. "The minister is here," she quietly said.

No, Bess, I don't want him here! Kate thought vehemently. *Send him away, you know better!*

Thomas nodded. "Send him in."

Kate looked up at her husband with frustrated eyes. A young man appeared at the foot of the bed. She strained to see his face. It was not Reverend Schenk, as she had expected in her drugged stupor. It was Mickey Jenson who presently stood before her. Little, sickly Mickey—and yet, he looked strong today. She vaguely remembered that Mickey was the new minister at the local church, and that Reverend Schenk had resigned, surrounded by scandal. Her heart filled with relief.

Thomas spoke quietly with Mickey. He kissed Kate's hand and left the room. Mickey came forward with a Bible tucked under his arm. An unusual layer of light spread across his face—like a sheet of sunlight, but whiter, and softer, and not entirely of this world. He stared at Kate for a long moment. She felt the young man was reading the depths of her soul. He opened the book. "The Lord is my Shepherd," he began.

Kate closed her eyes. The psalm from her girlhood. She had memorized it under Agnes' instruction, years ago, as an intellectual exercise. Today the words carried life. Kate repeated them after Mickey in her thoughts. He prayed for her after that and discreetly left the room.

Kate lay in the darkness, understanding that the end was very near, and understanding, also, that it was not really the end, but the beginning of something other than what she had ever known. She was sad, and afraid, and yet strangely excited—as if about to take an incredible voyage. She saw her little boy's face. It was the way that it looked when he was waiting for dessert, with wide, brown eyes that shone with anticipation. His hands were neatly folded before him. Tommy was waiting for his mother to come to him.

Bess entered the room and cleared the empty glasses and sticky spoons from Kate's bedside table. She leaned over and straightened Kate's blankets and sheets, paused, and reached out to touch Kate's feverish cheek. "You all right, then?" she softly asked.

Kate tried to smile at Bess with her eyes. Did Bess see? She must have, because she sat down on the bed and started to talk. Kate was grateful for her presence. With the deterioration of her body, it seemed most of her visitors assumed that her mind had also deteriorated to the same disastrous degree. True, it had been numbed and slowed by the morphine, but she could still listen, and reason, and feel. Even Sandra and Donald spoke to her like she was a child.

"I'd do anything for him," Bess was saying, her hands wringing in earnest. "We were happy on our honeymoon—those tickets to the falls were a blessin'." She laughed, fondly gazing into the darkness as if seeing the steaming fall before her as she spoke. "But now that sista' of his is makin' us miserable! I tell you, things were fine until she moved back inta town. She tells him what to do—acts like she's the missus, and I'm a nobody—a nothin'! I ain't a nobody, am I?"

Kate tried to communicate a "no" with her eyes, but it seemed Bess was more interested in unloading her inner turmoil than having it resolved. Which was fine with Kate. "I should put my foot down, shouldn't I? Just walk up to her and say, 'That'll be enough, Masie, you ain't the woman of the house. You git on now, Masie, and leave me and Ben to enjoy the happiness the good Lord's been givin' us.'"

Kate yearned to speak aloud. When Bess rose from the bed, it seemed a weight had been removed. She walked to the door with a visible lightness in her step. Later that evening, Kate heard Bess and Ben laughing in the adjacent room.

At nine o'clock that evening, Thomas came to give Kate her medicine and change her bedpan before going to sleep himself. (He slept on the sofa by the window ever since Kate had returned from England and was frequently up with her in the night, feeding her more morphine, or adding more kindling to the fire.) His lips brushed across her forehead. "Night, Kate," he said in a low voice of resignation.

Her eyes followed him as he walked to the window. Yes, he was definitely moving slower these days. The hunch in his back was more pronounced. Is it sore, Thomas? she wanted to ask—but it seemed she could no longer care for him as he steadfastly cared for her.

She watched him lie on the sofa and close his eyes. He instantly fell to sleep. Kate closed her own eyes. Sleep was still far away. Lately, she wasn't certain of when she slept, or for how long, since the morphine led her into dizzy spells of darkness and when she finally managed to open her eyes, the pain racing through her flesh, she wondered if she had been asleep at all—or merely over-medicated.

A stream of loneliness entered the room, then another, and another, until the powerful surge of currents surged into a sea. Kate felt that she was drowning, and she could not cry out for help. *It's only the morphine,* she thought, desperately rising to the surface.

She began to pray: *The Lord is my shepherd, I shall not want.* Splinters of pain filled her stomach, and then moved back, crackling up her spine.

He maketh me to lie down in green pastures. She imagined lush valleys and white sheep, wandering about.

He leadeth me beside the still waters. Kate saw the Little Miami River flowing past. She sat on a hill beneath an apple tree, tossing stones and watching them form ripples in the water. *Yes,* she thought, *This is nice…*

Kate filed her hair with silky white apple blossoms and gazed up at the warmth of the sun. *He restoreth my soul.* The heat splashed down upon her, warming her bones with heavenly light, caressing her like a lover, and lifting her wary spirit into… into what?

An element filling the space between;
An unknown—but no more.

Elsie and Jane worked behind the counter of the post-office. Victoria was in the kitchen, baking cinnamon bread. Her large body stooped over the iron range, the salt and pepper beard hanging from her chin, ending in a point, and covered in bits of dough and flour. Mary approached from behind and wrapped her arms around Victoria's upper body.

"Hello, beautiful," she chimed.

Victoria turned. "Mary! Where have you been? Shame on you for not visiting!"

"You wouldn't believe how busy I have been," Mary said, sitting at the table.

"I'll make us some tea and we'll chat. Just let me get this bread in the oven." Victoria finished her work and wiped up the messy range, then served Mary a cup of piping hot tea. "How is the living arrangement working out with Colleen?"

Mary blew on her tea. "Just wonderful. She's been like a second mother to Elizabeth."

"And the flat?"

"Oh, Victoria—I love the flat. It's very simple, but cozy. I'm just glad to have a safe home for me and Elizabeth."

"You deserve it, Mary. You really do." She lightly touched Mary's sleeve. "Look at you! You've put on some weight, you look wonderful!"

The compliment warmed Mary, like the tea. "Honestly, I've never felt better in my life. I've been quilting again, and the Dry Goods Shop downtown sells the quilts for me. I've made good money, Victoria. I'm even putting some savings aside to buy a sewing machine."

"How's Elizabeth?"

"She's thriving, too. She's getting so big, and saying a few words. Thank heavens she sleeps most nights now—straight through till morning. So I feel very rested."

"Did you find a job—other than the quilting?"

"Sure did. I'm a secretary for a dentist in town. His name is Dr. Griffith."

"Tell me, what does your dentist charge to pull a tooth? I've got a rotten one in the back of my mouth. Hurts like hell."

"Extractions range from fifty cents to a dollar."

"That's reasonable. Give me his address before you leave."

Elsie entered the kitchen carrying a large brown envelope. She handed it to Mary. "This came from Ohio last week," she said.

It was a package from the Little Flower Orphanage. Mary excitedly tore open the seal. A plethora of paper snowflakes fell out on the table before her. They were made of thin, white paper—very crudely cut—the edges frayed and torn, with small, dirty fingerprints covering the sides. Mary imagined the children working on the project in the kitchen of the orphanage, fighting for the scissors and proudly showing their artwork to Sister Philothea and Sister Martha, who approvingly watched on. No doubt, Sister Martha thought the idea was ridiculous—a waste of time.

"We've also had some letters from Hannah Graf," Victoria said, "but they've all been addressed to Drew. Does she know that the two of you have split up?"

Mary shrugged, sipping her tea. "I have no idea if Drew is in touch with her. She must not know that he left Canada, or she wouldn't be sending the mail here in the first place." She lifted the brown envelope to her nose in an attempt to catch the orphanage's gingerbread aroma. She then unfolded the letter from Sister Philothea and slowly read:

November 15, 1896

Dearest Mary,

Forgive me, I have wanted to write this letter for some time now, but with the children and all of the chores, I have not had the free time. I went to Hannah's cottage in July and spoke with your nice young friend, Jacob Zane. The poor man, he must be lonely without his wife. I do wish I knew a nice, Christian woman to introduce to him—do you know of any young, available young woman who might be interested in Jacob Zane?

Are you married? Jacob did not know if you were married yet. He expressed some concerns on the matter. Are such concerns valid, or am I simply being overly anxious about your welfare? I am sending this package to the logging camp where Hannah sends all of her correspondence to her son, in hopes that you will receive it in due time.

I do wish that you came to the orphanage one last time to say good-bye. Little Lydia misses you so. Every night, she asks that I pull her hair up into a very high bun, like Mrs. Turners, she says, and she loves that daisy quilt that you made her. She carries it about the house all day long!

The snowflakes are from the children. Winter has arrived in Bately, and soon we will take our little ones coasting on the hill by the river. Did you know that I've even been known to ride down that hill myself? Last year's production of Hansel and Gretel "went off without a hitch," as Sister Sophia would say. Danny was marvelous in the part of the witch and do you know, I ended up playing the wicked step-mother when Sister Sophia came down with the flu? Now we are busily working on a Greek production, Oedipus Rex, which seems rather adult for small children, but Sister Sophia feels strongly about the matter, so who am I to interfere? As you know, my dearest Mary, I am never one to interfere with the will of God.

With Love and Salutations,
Sister Philothea.

PS If you are having doubts about marrying Hannah's son, please let me know and I will take up a collection in Bately and have you and Elizabeth returned at once. Also, let me know if you have any interest in Jacob Zane.

Sister Philothea's PS was not the most subtle in the world, but Mary knew that the cheerful Mother Superior had the best of intentions. So, news must have spread quickly about her troubles with Drew. Just as well. She'd prefer the speculative gossip over having people think that she was actually married to the scoundrel. She wondered what Hannah thought about the matter, or if she even knew at all. No doubt, she would be disappointed. In retrospect, Mary wondered if Hannah had a hidden agenda, unknown to even herself, in which Mary's calming presence in Drew's life would somehow settle him down and possibly bring him back to Bately.

She visited with Victoria for another hour, then left the post office and boarded the nearest tram. The vehicle sped through the unpopulated forests and fields of Burnaby. Mary gazed out the window at a pair of mountains topped in white snow and standing side by side, reminding her of a pair of pointed breasts. Colleen thought so too, as did most of the city's residents. The tram slowed as it entered downtown Vancouver. Mary pulled the cord and sounded the bell as it approached Chestnut Street. She glanced through the window at the familiar stores, houses, and trees. She marveled at the way in which she slipped with ease into this city neighborhood in recent months. One year ago, she would have never guessed that she would be living on the west coast as an independent woman with an income of her own. Until this summer, she had always assumed that a woman required a man's financial and emotional protection. Now she knew better.

Carla, the owner of the dry goods store, greeted Mary on the sidewalk with a cheerful smile. "We sold every one of your lap quilts over the weekend, Mary." She went into the store. Mary followed her to the cash register where Carla removed a crisp, twenty-dollar note, along with a slip of paper citing rows of new orders for lap quilts and crazy quilts. "Can you make rag dolls?" she asked.

Mary took the slip. "Is there an order for one?"

"There's an order for three! And the customer wants them before Christmas."

Mary nodded while scanning the list. "I can do that."

"Now about the material from China—"

"Hold off on that order, Carla. The prices will probably drop after the Holidays."

"Smart girl. You know, maybe you should run a shop of your own?"

Mary smiled. "Someday, but it will take some planning. And I have to save up some money."

"Well, when you're ready to get started, you could lease some space with us," Carla suggested.

Mary absently took a pencil from the counter and wrote some notes on the slip: rods of material to be ordered, along with spools of white and black thread. Soon she could afford a sewing machine to help alleviate her late-night labors. "I don't know, Carla, I don't want to go under in my first year because I'm lacking in customers. But someday, I would like to get a place on this street. I even have the name picked out. I'll call it 'Mary's Closet.' I'll sell my crazy quilts, and my linens and towels. There are so many new people moving to this area, and most of them probably need new bedclothes. The only linen shop I know of is over an hour away."

"Mary's Closet. I like it. Why don't you start the operation in my back room after Christmas?"

Mary looked up from the list, intrigued. "What would you charge for rent?"

"Oh, next to nothing, I suppose. Your being here at the store will probably help our business. Come with me, let me show you the space." Carla led Mary through the shop to a side door that opened into a dark, dusty storage room, sufficient in size to suit Mary's business needs. A set of boarded-up windows faced the corner of Chestnut Street. Mary walked over to the windows and unloosened a shingle. She peered out at the busy intersection, then turned and explored the tiny room. A tall set of shelves lined one wall, where Mary could stack an assortment of linens and towels. The two bay windows on the adjacent wall were exceptionally large for such a small space. They had wide ledges at each base, perfect for displaying Mary's show quilts to passers-by on Chestnut St. "Name your price, Carla," she said.

"I've decided—no price. You can have it for free."

"Free? What's the catch?"

"Darling, your quilts have brought us plenty of new, paying customers."

"And what about a cash register. Could I share yours?"

"We have a spare one you can use. The drawer gets stuck from time to time, but it should work well enough if you keep it oiled."

Mary was speechless. She glanced at her surroundings, envisioning a fresh coat of pale peach paint on the walls, and white curtains gathered at each window's edge. But what provided the sudden lurch of adrenalin was the image of the stenciled sign that she would hang out front, facing the street: MARY'S CLOSET

It was the beginning of a dream. First she would have one shop, then a second, and a third. She would dedicate her entire life to the pursuit.

"I can have it cleaned out for you by the first of the year," Carla said.

"That might be too soon. I'll need to quit my job with Dr. Griffith, and I really should give him two months notice, don't you think?"

"The first of March then?"

Mary embraced her new patron. "How can I ever thank you?"

"Keep bringing me business. That will be more than enough."

That afternoon, Mary skipped like a child all of the way down Chestnut Street, then broke into a sprint as she rounded the corner and caught sight of the boarding house. The air had cooled dramatically the night before, and its invigorating chill filled her lungs. Colleen spoke with the upstairs tenant, Delilah, on the cobblestone walkway. Elizabeth sat upright in the wicker pram, tightly wrapped in Mary's yellow shawl.

"Colleen!" Mary called out, gasping for air. She waved the twenty-dollar note in one hand, and the order slip in the other. Colleen parted with Delilah and pushed the pram forward to meet Mary on the hill. Mary lifted Elizabeth out of the pram and spun her over her head in the middle of the street. She felt like a giant that possessed inhuman strength. "Would you like to go to Miss Croft's Academy someday?" she asked her daughter. "Mommy will make bunches of money, and send you to that fine school!"

In her excitement, Elizabeth drooled all over Mary's face. Mary put the child back in the pram, and wiped herself with the yellow shawl.

"What in heaven's name happened to you?" Colleen asked.

"Carla is giving me her back storage room to use as a shop. My own shop, Colleen! I'll be my own boss. The room is wonderful. The windows face Chestnut Street, right at that busy intersection next to Vine."

"Your own shop?"

"That's right. And I'll make so much money, if these orders keep coming in."

Colleen heartily laughed. "I can hardly believe it, Mary. When we first met, you had nothing but the clothes in your duffel bag. Now look at you!"

Mary slowly shook her head, sharing in the wonder of it all. "Why don't we try that fancy French restaurant for lunch?" she suggested.

"I just ate."

"We'll go to a tea room, then—for pastries."

25

At a local tearoom, over apple dumplings and chocolate cake, Mary openly shared her dreams for the future with Colleen. The business was important, to be sure, but Mary's greatest hopes involved Elizabeth. The little girl could attend Mrs. Croft's Private Academy, and then go to an upper-level school of her choice.

"Don't spoil her," Colleen warned.

"I won't. But I want to give her opportunities. Elizabeth will never know the feeling of being trapped. That's what money, and schooling, does, Colleen. It gives people freedom."

"I am happy for you, Mary."

Mary licked her fork. "None of it would have been possible without your watching Elizabeth. I owe you a great debt."

"You owe me nothing, Mary. It has been fun."

"Well, I know she's not the easiest child in the world." Mary ordered a glass of milk and a second apple dumpling for Colleen.

"Oh, Mary. Take it. I couldn't possibly eat more."

"All right then. I'm famished. I skipped lunch today."

"Can I see the package from the nun?" Colleen asked. Mary pushed the envelope across the table. "I can't believe you were friends with a nun, Mary."

"Why not, I'm friends with a Mormon, aren't I?"

"Yes, but being a Mormon is a far cry from being Roman Catholic. Besides, I'm not exactly a practicing Mormon. I drink tea and coffee from time to time. If anything, I consider myself a Protestant, like you." Colleen took out the snowflakes and Sister Philothea's letter. She began to read, and suddenly looked up at Mary. "You were going to get married? You didn't tell me that."

"I don't like to talk about it. It didn't work out."

Colleen resumed reading. "She says this man Jacob was concerned about you. Do you think he was jealous?"

"Colleen, please. I don't want to talk about it."

Colleen finished reading and put the letter and the paper snowflakes back in the envelope. Mary took the last bite of her dumpling and washed it down with milk. She paid the bill at the cash register. Colleen followed her out of the shop, pushing Elizabeth in the pram. She quickened her pace as they walked along Chestnut Street. Elizabeth clapped her hands. Colleen broke into a gallop. Mary followed at her side. Mary hoped, as they ran, that the pram would not hit a rock or loose cobblestone and tip over, spilling Elizabeth to the ground. The cold wind blew the little girl's bonnet to her neck; the trimmed blond curls lifted into the air, and her cheeks turned red with the thrill of the race. They turned in the direction of the boarding house. "Weee!" Colleen screamed.

Mary gasped for breath. "Careful, Colleen—the pram might tip over!"

"No it won't. Look at Elizabeth! She loves it." Colleen recklessly wove the pram around the various trees and street lamps that lined the hill on which they lived. Mary ran forward and opened the front gate. "Hurry up, Lazy Bones!" she yelled down at Colleen. She laughed, gasping for air, and turned to enter the garden. She bumped into a man who waited beside the front door. She saw the buttons of his wool coat first, and looked up at his face.

The familiar grey eyes smiled down at her. "Hello, Mary."

Her mouth dropped open. "Jacob?"

Colleen zoomed the pram into the garden. She stopped abruptly and stared at Jacob. Mary also stared, incredulous. In her absolute shock, she failed to introduce him to Colleen. "Dada!!!" Elizabeth merrily cried.

Colleen's eyes widened. She turned to Mary. "Do you know this man?"

Jacob stepped forward, removing Elizabeth from the pram. "Lizzy, how's my girl?" The child leaned her forehead into Jacob's shoulder, suddenly turning bashful.

Again, Colleen asked Mary. "Do you know this man?"

Jacob carried Elizabeth to the door, where a china doll sat on the steps. He picked up the doll and showed it to her. She touched its painted mouth. Jacob looked over at Mary. "It's a gift from Kate Smith. She brought it back from London for Elizabeth."

Mary walked forward. "It's beautiful. Thank her for me, please."

"Excuse me," Colleen demanded. "But who is this man?"

"This is Jacob, from Ohio."

"The father of the twins?"

Jacob smiled. "Mary told you about me?"

"Oh, yes! She talks about you often."

Jacob appeared pleased by this information. He looked at Mary. Her eyes darted to the ground. Her throat was dry, and she swallowed several times. "Why don't we go inside," she suggested. She unlocked the door and opened it for Jacob and Colleen. In the doorway she paused, partly wishing that she could turn and run away from what awaited her in the flat.

Jacob entered the modest but clean space. He looked around. "So this is your home?" he asked.

"This is our humble abode," Colleen cheerily answered for Mary. "Let me take your coat, Jacob. By the way, my name is Colleen. I'm Mary's roommate… and Elizabeth's faithful caregiver when Mary is at work."

He handed her his coat and she placed it on the bed. Mary still couldn't lift her eyes from the floor. She walked to the deacon's bench and sat down.

"Can I get you a drink, Jacob?" Colleen inquired. "Perhaps some cider?"

"Just water," he replied. "If you have it."

Colleen filled a glass at the basin and handed it to him. "Did you travel here on the train?" she asked.

He nodded, looking over at Mary. "I got here this morning."

"Where are you staying?"

"A hotel on Fourth Street."

"The Landsdown Inn?" Colleen asked.

"Yes, that's the one." He drank his water, studying Mary. "How are you, Miss Turner?" he playfully asked.

She finally looked up, still unable to meet his eyes. "Fine," she replied.

He handed the empty glass back to Colleen. "I gather you didn't marry Drew Graf?"

She shook her head, tremendously embarrassed.

"That's good news." He smiled. Mary said nothing.

"How are your baby boys, Jacob?" Colleen asked.

"The boys are doing well. Though they miss Mary something awful."

Elizabeth eyed Jacob from the corner of the room. She walked to him and placed her head tenderly against his knee. His calloused hand lowered to her head. "I missed you, Lizzy." Elizabeth drooled on his leg, leaving a dark spot.

"What are you doing here?" Mary finally got the nerve to ask. Colleen sat forward and looked at the pair with great interest.

"I was worried about you," he said.

"Isn't that sweet," Colleen observed.

"Well you shouldn't be worried. I'm fine."

He warmly smiled. "I can see that."

"Mary has a job at a dentist's shop," Colleen proudly explained. "And she's been working every night on her quilts. You should see them, they're very pretty."

"Are you selling them?" he asked Mary.

"Yes. I've sold twenty-five since August."

"Can I take you out for supper?" he directly asked.

"Well, I just ate two desserts at the pastry shop—"

Colleen laughed. "Mary, don't be silly! The man took a train all of the way across the continent to see you, the least you could do is have supper with him!"

"Yes, of course," she apologized. "I'll have supper with you. Maybe we could take a walk through the park first." She turned to Colleen. "Could you suggest a restaurant?"

"There's a nice one at his hotel," she excitedly replied, as if about to join them on the date.

"Perhaps you could watch Elizabeth?"

"Of course. You two go out and have a wonderful time."

Mary went to the basin, removed her hairpins, and combed her hair so it flowed down her back in a soft, alluring fashion. She turned to Jacob, who was staring at her. "Ready to go?" she asked. He jumped to the doorway, more than ready.

At dinner, she barely touched the food on her plate, the coupled result of having a stomach full of pastries, and nervous butterflies. After dinner, they drank fresh, strong coffee. Mary still couldn't believe that Jacob had come all of the way to Vancouver to see her. She was touched by his concern for her well-being, and also a trifle irritated by his assumption that she needed his assistance. She assured him several times over the course of the meal that she was really, truly fine. If he had come out to visit her in July, he would have encountered a much different situation. This fact she carefully omitted from their conversation.

"Is Hannah disappointed that Drew and I aren't together?"

"I don't think so. She wanted me to come out here and see how you were doing. I guess she got a letter from Drew a few weeks ago—from California. I think it worried her, what he had to say."

"What did the letter say?"

"I don't know, but she came up to me after church and suggested that I come out here and check on you and Lizzy." He leaned forward. "What did happen between you and Drew?"

Mary shrugged, partly ashamed at having been involved with a low-life like Drew Graf. "I thought he was a different man. I believed all of Hannah's stories, about Drew and Josh being wealthy, and having a fine home out here."

"I gather they weren't as wealthy as you were told?"

Mary sipped her coffee. "Seems they did make some money, probably through gambling, then spent it all before I arrived. It wasn't just the lack of money that broke it up, I can assure you. Drew treated me like a dog. When I tried to break off the engagement, he acted like he owned me. He wouldn't let me go."

"Why not?"

"I think it humiliated him, Jacob. A man like Drew doesn't like to be made a fool—especially by a woman." She sighed and gazed out the window at the harbor below. The blue water was framed in a glorious spectacle of mountains and rolling hills, all covered with fresh toppings of snow. She turned to Jacob. "Isn't it beautiful out here?"

He looked at her intently, his eyes brimming with kindness. "It surely is."

On impulse, she reached across the table and touched his hand. "Thank you for coming out to see me. You've been like family. Like the brother I never had."

"You know I care deeply about you," he quietly replied.

She let go of his hand. "Tell me, how are the twins?"

"Well, you wouldn't believe how they've grown."

"What do they look like now?"

"Patrick is the bruiser of the two. He can barely crawl, Mary—he's so blasted fat! You wouldn't believe your eyes."

"They're already crawling?"

He nodded. "Tara's mother told me they both started the same day. They did the same thing with eating solid food, too. Ethan looked at Patrick, then Patrick looked back at Ethan, like they were deciding together."

"And how has Tara's mother been with them? Is she tired?"

"She is. She spoils them, too. Every time I go over there, she's fixing their clothes and changing their diapers even though they don't need changing. One day, I walked in and she was combing their hair. The boys are almost bald, mind you, but she was combing anyway."

"What color is their hair—I mean, the little that they have?"

"Mostly blond, though Ethan is turning a little red, believe it or not."

Mary giggled. "They sound adorable." She finished her coffee and looked around the spacious dining room. It was festively decorated for the holidays with holly and ivy, and hanging sprigs of mistletoe. Apple-green taffeta curtains softened the small-paned windows and blended in with the oriental carpets in their red and pastel tones. A small group of musicians played Bach in the corner of the room, beside the bar, giving a deceptively soothing atmosphere to the busy surroundings. Each table was packed with finely-dressed patrons. A low-pitched chatter hovered in the air, intermixed with the clinking of glass and chinaware, sometimes interrupted by the occasional roll of loud laughter from one of the larger groups.

Mary looked down at her grey tweed frock. "I feel underdressed."

"You look terrific, Mary. I've never seen you look so good."

"I want to buy a whole new wardrobe. But there are a few things that I need to purchase first."

"Such as?"

She tossed her hair back, quite pleased with her recent accomplishments. "Well, a sewing machine, for starters. I'll have enough money for that next month. And I want to get Elizabeth a proper bed—with a bar, to keep her from falling out at night. Let's see..." she paused to think. The waiter came over and poured more coffee into their china cups, moving to the next table with perfectly ordered steps. Mary leaned forward. Her mouth lifted into a secretive smile. "Can I tell you something that makes me happier than anything else in the world?" she asked.

He adored her. "Sure."

"I've been given a shop on Chestnut Street. For free."

His eyes lost their light. "A shop?"

Her enthusiasm increased, overshadowing his abrupt change of mood. "I'm going to call it Mary's Closet. I'll sell my quilts, and also other types of linens—sheets, blankets, towels. A lot of people come to the boarding houses around here with only one trunk or suitcase, and certainly no linens to speak of. There's a high demand for quality linens in this city, Jacob. I'm sure of it. If the business does well, I might even open a second store in the East End. What do you think?"

"I don't know," he flatly replied.

She lifted the cup to her mouth. Her lips settled on the rim. "I know it's a risk," she went on, blowing at the hot coffee. She took a small sip and smiled.

"I think I can do it, though. My quilts have been disappearing like hot cakes off the grill. I've got backup orders that will keep me busy till spring. It seems more orders come in by the day, too. And do you know what else?"

He dismally shook his head.

"There's a private school at the bottom of our hill." Mary mimicked a stuffy English accent: "Miss Croft's Academy for Young Women. I see the girls getting off the tram every day. They have starched uniforms and cute little matching hats. I want to save up and send Elizabeth there when she's older. She'll have a proper education. It will open up doors for her, Jacob. You see, I don't want my daughter to be a rich man's doll—or worse yet, a poor man's wife. I want her to go to university and get a proper education and be self-reliant. Just think, Elizabeth could be a teacher, or a nurse. She could have her own, independent life."

"She is as smart as a whip," he admitted. He gazed sadly at Mary. Seeing the forlorn look in his eyes, she suddenly understood. In coming to the west coast, this man had more than brotherly motives. "I had no idea that I would come out here and see you so free," he honestly commented. "I'm proud of you, Mary."

"Thank you." She gladly took the compliment, but also felt selfish for being so insensitive to his needs. She gathered up the courage and asked straight out, "Did you travel out here to bring me back to Bately…so I could be with you?"

"Yes. That's exactly why I came out here."

"When did this all happen?" she wondered aloud. "This change of feeling?"

"After Tara died. Remember that day at the orphanage?"

She nodded.

"You were great with those children. It seemed you understood them. And I watched you with the twins, too. You're a good woman, Mary."

It all made sense to her. "So you want a mother for your boys, is that it?"

"It's more than that, Mary. I want you. I couldn't stop thinking about you after you left. I even dreamt of you. Would you consider coming back to Bately?"

"I don't know—"

"My log house burnt down. I've built a new one. I was hoping that you could help make it a home. We could have the twins back from Tara's mother, and have Elizabeth. We'd be a family. I know it doesn't sound as exciting as what you have right now…."

"Are you asking me to marry you?"

"Yes—I suppose I am."

"Well, this certainly comes as a surprise. It's just not what I want."

He lowered his head, saying nothing.

"I wouldn't be happy in Bately, Jacob," she explained. "The people judge each other so. I have a fresh slate out here, you see. And now, with this plan to start my own business, and all the money I hope to make. Well, it just wouldn't make sense to give that all up and return to Bately."

He was overwhelmed, and devastated, by the abundance of new information, most of which depicted a very different woman with a very different future than what he had imagined back in Ohio. "How do you feel about me?" he reluctantly asked, not wanting to be wounded any more than he already was, but knowing he had to find out.

"I think about you from time to time, Jacob. You've been a wonderful friend. All the thoughts I have about you, well, they're always good." Seeing his face suddenly brighten with hope, she pitied him, not wanting to let him down. "But I wouldn't make a good wife, Jacob. Not after everything that I've been through."

"Hannah told me that Billy beat you."

She nodded. "Things weren't good with Drew, either. Don't you see? I can't be with another man again. You deserve a woman who'll be obedient, someone who will want to be your wife. I'm afraid, with all I've been through, I'd be very unhappy—even bitter in the role."

"You wouldn't be bitter, Mary. If anything, I'd say the pain has softened you."

"You don't know me, then."

She finished her coffee. The silence stretched between them, reaching awkward proportions. She studied his face, the broad shoulders and arms, and couldn't help but view him in a sexual light. "I do get lonely," she admitted.

He sadly smiled. "So do I."

Again, she reached for his hand. "Would you..." she paused, seeking the courage to find the right words. After all, she had never proposed this type of thing to a man. "We could go upstairs," she suggested. She waited nervously for his response. She became aware of the noise from the tables in their midst, and even worried that people nearby had overheard her daring proposition.

"Upstairs?"

She glanced at him and lowered her eyes.

"You mean—"

"Yes," she interrupted, not wanting him to speak the reckless idea aloud.

"But you won't come back to Bately with me? You would still expect me to return on the train alone?"

"It would just be for one night, Jacob. Since we're both so lonely—we both need comfort."

He sat back in his chair, still digesting the startling proposal. "And you don't want to marry me...? You just want to go upstairs, for one night?"

"What's stopping us?" she boldly asked.

"Making a child, for one thing."

"I have something for that," she shyly said. She could run back to the flat in no time and take Azalea's condoms from the carpetbag.

He rose from the table. She noticed his hands formed fists. "Well what are we waiting for?" he asked. "Let's go upstairs."

About fifteen minutes later, she returned from the flat with the condoms.

He was waiting for her in the hotel room. The drapes were pulled across the windows, with the bed awaiting them in the darkness. Mary had no fear, for she knew that Jacob was not like Billy or Drew. He was not a violent man. More than anything, she wanted to lie naked in his arms and experience the wonder of being held by a good and gentle man. She had never known that comfort before. He closed the door behind her. She turned and sunk into his arms. His face was warm, and his mouth wet and inviting. As they kissed, she dropped her cloak on a nearby chair. Her hands moved up and delicately moved through his thick hair. Her heart was racing with desire; for the first time in her life, she desperately wanted this to happen. She stepped back in the darkness and unbuttoned her bodice, then stopped. She caught him looking at her in the room's dim light—the look of adoration had completely disappeared, and now his eyes were sorrowful with yearning, and yet somehow distant and emotionally removed.

"Maybe we shouldn't do this." She slowly buttoned her bodice back up. "I'm sorry to lead you on. Really, I am." She walked to the door.

He followed her across the room, touching her shoulder as her hand dropped to the brass knob. "Wait, Mary—"

She faced him. The love in his eyes caressed her, and she was truly frightened by the seductive power that those eyes possessed. They could ruin her life, if she let them. "I know you want to be with me." His voice grew raspy with desire. "I know you love me too. Please, be my wife, Mary. I'd do anything to have you stay here with me tonight."

She pushed him away. "No. That's not it. You don't understand. This has nothing to do with love, Jacob. I only thought, since we're both adults, and we both have needs, it might make sense to share a bed for one night." In actuality, her thoughts went beyond such logical reasoning. In fact, her desire was fueled more by anger and a sense of entitlement. For once in her pitiful life, she wanted to do something bold and freeing. She wanted to take control of her own destiny, thus controlling her own pleasure, rather than having a man assume his rightful dominance.

His arms lifted, wrapping around her and forming a blanket of protective warmth. Every instinct instructed her to give in to this all-consuming energy, to accept his proposal and not only lie with him for the night, but even return with him to Bately and stay with him for life. It took all of her inner resolve to break free from his loving grip and open the door. She ran down the hallway. He called after her. She descended the stairway with no intention of ever turning back. Outside, it rained ice pellets. She walked for miles. The streets were slippery, and the night air was freezing cold. She made a large circle of the downtown district and reluctantly returned to the horse stables beside the inn. She looked up at the window of Jacob's room. He had pulled open the drapes. The lamp light shown from the mantlepiece, although she couldn't see him inside. She re-entered the hotel and trudged up the stairway. Arriving at the second floor, she knocked twice on Jacob's door. He quickly opened it and pulled her back inside. "Have you changed your mind?" he asked.

She shook her head. "I just came to fetch my cloak. I left it here."

He released her and went to the chair. He carried back the cloak and wrapped it around her shoulders, buttoning the collar. "I remember the last time I helped you with your buttons," he said, stifling a mischievous grin. "Do you remember?"

"I don't recall your ever helping me with my buttons, Jacob Zane."

"'Course you do. In the field. When Elizabeth was born."

She tried not to laugh, but instead forced a serious tone. "Let me be frank with you. I can't go back to Ohio and live on your farm. And I'll tell you why not. It's a life of drudgery. Look what poor Tara went through—the miscarriages, and all that hard work, with your long hours in the field. I want to be free of that, Jacob. Please. If you genuinely do love me, then please give me that freedom."

His hand lifted to trace the curve of her chin. "You'd better go, Mary. It's getting late."

"Do you plan on leaving tomorrow?" she asked.

"Is there any reason for me to stay?"

"No."

"I wish I never met you, Mary."

"And why is that?"

"When I go back to Bately, I'll still love you—and want you. And I'm going to keep on wanting you."

"It will go away," she said. She personally knew how quickly romantic love could fade.

He shook his head. "This kind of love only grows."

26

He was waiting at the foot of the cobblestone walkway early the next morning as she left the flat to go to work. A wave of relief swept over her when she saw him, for she had suffered a sleepless night believing that she would never see him again. "What are you still doing here?" she happily asked.

"I just came to make sure that your mind was made up."

"It is," she quietly said. "By the way, I'd like to apologize for asking you up to your room last night. I didn't mean to be a tease like that."

He smiled. "You certainly have a mind of your own these days."

"Still, there's no excuse—"

"Well, I should have declined the offer to begin with."

She looked at him. What was it about a man in a coat? The image of warmth, shelter. The old instincts resurfaced, and again, she dutifully fought them back. "Why didn't you play the part of a gentleman, Jacob? Why didn't you say no?"

He stepped forward, standing only inches from her desirous flesh. "So now you think I'm a monk, is that it?" he inquired, holding back a grin.

She took two steps back, in fear of pressing her body to his and kissing him fully on the mouth. "Jacob, I am staying in Vancouver. My decision is final."

Flurries of snow drifted in various directions through the damp, grey air. Jacob rubbed his hands together, breathing over them. "OK," he said. "But can I visit with you, for just a few more days?"

"I'm not changing my mind." It was bad enough that she led him on the night before, she was determined not to be so cruel again.

"I didn't say you would. I miss you, Mary. I can't tell you how lonely I am in Bately. I just want to talk to you—as a friend. We have a lot of catching up to do."

In the distance, the tram approached. "I'm going to be late for work. I'll meet you back here for lunch. Maybe we can take Elizabeth to the park this afternoon." She turned and walked down the hill.

"Is there another beautiful baby contest?" he asked.

She laughed, picking up the pace. "Did Colleen already tell you about that?"

"See you tonight," he called out.

Mary ran down the hill and rounded the corner, her hair blowing in the breeze, with tiny snowflakes speckling the long blond locks. She waved at Jacob as she climbed up the steps of the tram. He watched her from the top of the hill, his frame set like a rock against the clod, slate-colored sky.

Jacob was waiting for her at the flat when she returned from work that day. Colleen had prepared them a pot of chicken soup and conveniently left the apartment to visit with her brother for the evening. Mary heated the soup on the range and fed Elizabeth first. The little girl was tired from a day of play with Aunt Colleen. After devouring a bowl of soup, she fell asleep in Jacob's arms as he gave her a cup of warm goat's milk. He gently placed her on the bed and then joined Mary on the bench where they ate some soup themselves. They drank tea afterwards. "I'd like to show you Mary's Closet," she said, somewhat uneasy about bringing up the subject of her new business. "Would you like to take a walk to the dry goods store tonight?"

"I suppose," he reluctantly replied.

Mary introduced Jacob to Carla when they arrived at the shop, then took him to the back room. "It needs some work," she said, loosening a shingle from the window.

He went to her side. "Do you want me to remove all these for you?"

"That'll be great. I'll ask Carla for a hammer."

When she brought the hammer back to Jacob, she felt an odd mixture of excitement and guilt for having him help her with the project that would ultimately drive them apart. When the shingles were removed, a blanket of late evening sun came into the room, bringing the small space life, and enhancing Mary's mental picture of her future shop. In her mind's eye, she saw pastel-colored sheets and towels stacked upon the shelves, jars full of bath salts and bars of soap, and ornate quilts hanging from the wooden racks beside the windows. Despite this vision, she felt inexpressibly sad, knowing that Jacob would not be a part of the dream.

She returned the hammer to Carla and went back to the small room. Jacob sat on the windowsill, gently stroking Elizabeth's chin with his fingertip, just as he had touched Mary's face the night before. He looked up at her and their eyes connected, communicating in the sun's dim light. "I'm sorry," she said.

"What will it take to convince you to come back with me, Mary?"

She warily shook her head. "I am so, so sorry...." In her mind, there was no hope for him. Nothing he could say, or do, would win her hand in marriage.

"You're sure you don't mind my staying for a few more days—maybe a week or so—just to visit?"

Her face instantly brightened. "Of course you can, Jacob."

Indeed, Jacob stayed for the entire week. And Mary's physical desire for him intensified with each passing day. She was tempted, on more than one occasion, to give into his sweet kisses and tender words. At the docks one afternoon, Jacob placed his hand on her shoulder as she pushed the pram along the boarded peer. She didn't move his hand away, but secretly hoped that it would remain on that very spot for the entire afternoon. Elizabeth fell asleep with the motion of the pram's wheels rolling over the weathered boards. Several minutes later, they arrived at Stanley Park. Jacob guided Mary into the woods, to a clearing that was buried at the foot of a steep hill, hundred of yards away from the main pedestrian path. Now they had entered the danger zone, to be sure.

Mary placed the pram beside a cluster of ferns, in the shade of a giant willow tree. She lifted its hood and wrapped Elizabeth in a thick coating of blankets and lap quilts, then she eagerly returned to Jacob on the frost-covered grass. This was all under the pretense that they were just "good friends"—merely out for a casual stroll on a frigid Sunday afternoon. Although in her heart, Mary knew otherwise.

His hand moved from her shoulder to the edge of her hourglass-shaped waist. She willingly placed her body back on the cold moss, drugged by the aroma of verdant earth, intermixed with the smell of his flesh. He lay down beside her and kissed her mouth with urgency. His face moved over hers, and their mouths briefly separated. She gazed up at his eyes, as if in a trance. "I do love you, Jacob," she softly confessed.

"Mary... I love you too. More than life..." His mouth covered hers and lingered across her neck, flooding it with tender, hot kisses that made the bumps rise to the surface of her skin. It seemed her heart was on the verge of crumbling with years of suppressed yearning—a lifetime of longing and unfulfilled needs. She never knew that a man could get her so worked up inside—and best of all, it seemed that she had a great deal of control, for she only had to look up to get an inkling of Jacob's subservience to her. His expression was immensely loving, and yet, pained with months of tortured aloneness.

He unloosened her bodice, murmuring her name, passionately kissing her bare breasts and lifting the hem of her skirt. She eagerly helped him to loosen the layers of material and unfastened the buttons of his pants. Seconds later, he was deep inside of her. She groaned, wanting him to penetrate harder, until their bodies were completely joined as one. Her hands moved across his buttocks and thrust him farther inside. He cried out sharply in the cold winter breeze, inciting a force so powerfully strange that it stirred like a tempestuous storm within Mary's groin; this rolling surge of energy rose to an intense climax of pure, painful pleasure, and for the first time ever, she cried out in a lost void of agonizing ecstasy.

Afterward, the lovers lay silently together in that clearing in the wood, barricaded by ancient cedars and firs. It was a secret, magical place.

Eventually, Elizabeth broke the euphoria by awaking in her pram. Mary and Jacob hurriedly dressed and went to the child. Jacob lifted Lizzy to his chest. He turned to Mary. The small, pointed shadows of willow branches sliced across his form, intermixed with glowing white slashes of sunlight. "Does this mean you'll come back to Bately?" he asked.

She brushed the wet leaves from her lavender skirt, not knowing how to reply. "I just don't know, Jacob. All I have to do is think about what the future holds. Life as a farmer's wife in Bately—"

"It will be a good life," he promised.

Her face dropped. "And more children…"

He put Elizabeth down to run on the ground. "But you love children—"

"Of course I do."

"Then why don't you want more?"

"God forgive me, Jacob. They'll be like chains, holding me down."

"Children grow up, Mary."

"But the needs never end. Elizabeth has drained me. What will it be like having more, in addition to the twins?"

"You've had to do it all on your own with her," he argued. "But once we're married, I'll be around every day to help you."

"I just don't know, Jacob." She sat on a nearby log. "The more we discuss it, the more of a trap it becomes…."

He knelt at her side. "A trap? Do you really believe that?"

She mutely nodded, grieved at having to destroy his expectations after the wonder of what they just experienced.

He took her hands. "Mary, darling. Have you forgotten what it was like when you cared for the twins?"

"Hardly. I was exhausted night and day. I never had time to take a bath or eat a meal. I couldn't even go outside for a walk on my own, Jacob, without one of them screaming for me. It was like being in a prison."

He sat beside her on the log. "There were days when you were beaming, Mary. I remember. You loved my boys, they were like your own children."

She saw their faces in her mind and smiled in spite of herself. "Is that what it will be like?" she asked. "One ounce of joy for a ton of sacrifice? I fear I'll lose myself again."

"That is fear speaking, Mary. It's not the truth."

"It is the truth, Jacob. It's my truth. I'll lose Mary's Closet. I'll lose my dreams."

Elizabeth crawled to them in the clearing and confidently climbed up on Jacob's lap.

"Let's go." He lifted Elizabeth in his arms and helped Mary to her feet. "Maybe the walk home will clear our heads."

Mary pushed the empty pram alongside Jacob and Elizabeth as they crossed the park and headed back to Chestnut Street. They stopped at a street crossing. Jacob's mouth lowered to the side of Mary's nose. "What are you doing?" she asked.

"Kissing your freckle," he said. His lips moved to her chin. "There's another one." His mouth tilted to the side of her ear. "And another—and another."

She leaned against him and Elizabeth, laughing. "You are a silly boy."

He lifted her arm and kissed the elbow. "How many of these things do you have on your body, Mary Turner?"

"Wouldn't you like to know." She winked. He placed Elizabeth in the pram, turned, and scooped the child's mother into his arms, twirling her in the winter air. Mary saw the green, green leaves and the clear blue sky, and felt that she would burst with love for him.

They ate again at the hotel, later that night. "I've been living with the Smiths since my house burnt down," he told her.

"How is Kate?" Mary asked.

"Not well. She'll die any day now."

"And how is Dr. Smith?"

Jacob poured Mary a second glass of wine. "He puts up a good front."

"He is a kind man, isn't he? They were both very good to me when I first arrived."

"That's their way," Jacob agreed.

"And what about Hannah?"

"I haven't seen her much lately. I stopped going to the cottage after you left. She keeps busy with her church work."

Mary sipped at the sweet white wine. "It's hard to believe that Drew and Josh are her sons."

"Isn't it? But the son that died, Stephen, he was a nice boy. I used to be friends with him. It was hard, when he drowned like that. I couldn't understand why it had to happen."

"How old were you?"

"Thirteen."

Mary was struck with how little she really knew about this man that she loved. "What was your life like, Jacob?" she asked. "Before you were married to Tara—before I knew you?"

"I guess I was a typical farmer's son. I worked in the fields with my father when I wasn't in school. He taught me everything about farming that I know today."

"What was your father like?"

"Quiet, simple. He couldn't read or write. He was from the old country."

"Which one?"

"Germany."

"And your mother?"

"She died when I was born."

"Were you lonely, without a mother?"

"I suppose I was. What about you? I can picture you as a child—you must have been a cute little thing with all those freckles."

She laughed. "The freckles have always been there. But I was lonely, too—without a mother or a father. I think I was a shy girl. Not at all like Elizabeth. The more I got moved around from family to family, the shyer I got. I used to worry that if I talked too much, people wouldn't like me. Seemed like I was always afraid." Her mind turned to the old man from Alabama. Would she ever share with Jacob what that man did to her at night? She suspected that she would tell Jacob someday, because she knew he would understand.

"I hope you don't feel that way now," he said.

"I'm getting over it. Seeing the way Colleen stands up for herself has certainly helped."

"She's a firecracker, that one."

"Isn't she? I love her. I've never had a friend like Colleen."

After dinner, he walked her to the flat and they spoke in the garden outside. "My train leaves tomorrow," he said.

"So soon?"

"It's been over a week, Mary. I need to get back to the farm. You'll need to decide tonight. Will you come back with me, or not?"

"I'm sorry, Jacob." She wept.

He was not moved by her tears. "You're staying?"

She slowly nodded. "It's what I need to do—for me."

He jerked his face to the side, as though she had slapped him with her words.

"Goodbye, Mary."

"Then this is it?" she asked, but he had already turned away and left the garden.

Mary walked into the flat. Without him, the large room seemed eerily silent and empty, mirroring the way that she felt inside. Colleen had left a note for her on the deacon's bench. She had taken Elizabeth to visit with her brother and would be back before ten o'clock. Mary sat at the deacon's bench, remembering every detail of their time together in the clearing. Mary's Closet paled in comparison. She rose from the bench and put on her cloak, then took it off. Five minutes later, she put her cloak on again. She stared out the window, desperate for Colleen to return. Colleen did not return until almost 11 o'clock. "Where have you been?" Mary asked like an angry mother whose daughter had been out too late.

"Didn't you get my note? I took Elizabeth to see my brother."

"Yes, but it's late."

"I'm sorry. The tram took forever to arrive." She removed her Albert overcoat and boots. Elizabeth remained sleeping in the pram, and would do so for the entire night. "When did Jacob leave?"

"Hours ago…"

"That early? How come?"

"He's going back to Ohio in the morning."

Colleen put on her night shirt. "He's very in love with you, Mary. He even told me so."

"I love him too, but I don't want to go back and get married, Colleen."

"It's your decision," Colleen said.

Mary's eyes widened. "I thought you wanted me to marry him?"

"Not tonight, Mary. I've got other things on my mind." She crawled into the bed. "My brother's moving back to Utah next month. He wants me to go with him."

Mary rushed over to the bed. "You can't go, Colleen. I need you here!"

"You don't understand, Mary. Things haven't been going well at the mill. They want to cut my hours again. I can't let you keep paying all the bills."

"I don't mind. Once my shop gets busy, I can hire you as a full-time nanny."

Colleen pulled the covers to her chin. "I miss my parents, too, and my little brother, Hal. You don't have a family—that's probably why it's hard for you to understand."

"But what about Elizabeth? You've been like an aunt to her."

"It will be hard to leave my baby," she reflected. "But you'll find another mother's helper. There are a lot of immigrant women in the city—"

"Not like you!" Mary nearly whined like a child. "They won't love her like you do, Colleen."

Colleen pressed her eyes shut, as if willing the conversation away. "I'm going back to Utah, Mary. I have to."

Mary fell back on the bed. She'd have to find new childcare for Elizabeth, placing her most beloved possession with a stranger. Until she got a solid financial grounding with the shop, she'd also need to find a new roommate in a city full of strangers. The puzzle wasn't fitting together as smoothly as she had previously thought. She undressed and put on her nightgown. "Did I make a mistake, refusing Jacob's offer?" she asked.

Colleen suddenly came to life. She sat upright, the bonnet slipping from her head, and the mass of red curls falling carelessly to her shoulders. "I think you should go to him, Mary."

"I do miss Ethan and Patrick," Mary reasoned aloud.

"Mary—don't delay this. You must go to him before it's too late."

"What about Mary's Closet—all my dreams?"

"Oh, those ridiculous dreams! Please go to him, Mary."

"Living on a farm is hard work, Colleen. I'll need to bear more children, to help Jacob manage the land. He has over one hundred acres. I'll be pregnant off and on for another fifteen years, with babies sucking at my teats all the livelong day."

"But when your children have grown—"

"Then I'll have grandchildren, Colleen, and I'll be too old and tired to do anything else. Who's to say that Jacob will live a long life? What if he dies early, and leaves me with a farm and children? Then I'll have to remarry, I'll have to find some old gizzard and share his bed each night!"

Colleen giggled. "Oh Mary, you're such a practical girl. Love isn't practical, you know that."

"All too well, I'm afraid."

"You can't plan out every day of your life, Mary. You have to take risks."

"Don't you see, Colleen? I don't want risks! For the first time ever, I feel like I'm in control of things—like I have choices. If I marry Jacob, then I'll cut off my freedom overnight. I'll be trapped again."

"But you're not trapped if you're happy. Jacob would make you happy—I just know he would."

"Do you really think so?" Mary asked, wanting encouragement.

"Yes! Listen, Mary. Elizabeth will grow to be a woman someday. You may have friends out here, but you'll never have a family to call your own, except for Elizabeth. And she won't want a lonely mother. You will be lonely when you're old, Mary. I guarantee that. Do you really want to grow old alone?"

Mary didn't reply. She was thinking about the feeling of Jacob inside her, earlier that afternoon; her heart tensed within her chest, beating like a drum. The image of them coupled in the forest caused her pain—a marvelous, joyful pain, that made her willing to jump off the highest cliff and take the inevitable plunge, if only to re-enact the wonder of making love to him once again.

"Go to him," Colleen firmly said.

"Now?"

"Of course, now. Go to his hotel before it gets too late."

She pressed her eyes shut and gripped her fists beneath the covers. "I can't, Colleen."

"Then it's your loss." Colleen angrily sighed. She lay back on the pillow. "If a man like Jacob loved me, I'd run to him this instant. There would be no question in my mind."

Mary stared up at the ceiling, pondering Colleen's innocence. "Do you know what my problem is? I know too much—about men, about what can happen when things go wrong."

She rolled onto her side. It didn't take long to fall asleep, after the day of fresh air and "exercise" in the woods. Although, her dreams were muddled and fragmented, reflecting her troubled state of mind.

She awoke with a start. Morning's first light brightened the room. Mary got dressed, brushed her teeth and hair, and scrubbed her face. She wrote a note for Colleen, and silently left the flat.

Outside, the street was empty, lifeless, and silent. The trams were just starting their morning runs. She waited on the park bench for the first one to arrive. She boarded it with two early-morning passengers and they traveled along Vancouver's hilly wet streets that wound down to the waterfront. She descended the tram and ran to The Landsdown Inn. At the stables, she looked up at the window of Jacob's room. The lantern was not lit, and she feared that he had already left for the train station. He suddenly appeared at the window, as if sensing her presence outside. She ran into the hotel and met him in the lobby. They tightly embraced, then walked together to the second floor. Once inside the room, Jacob pulled the drapes and undressed Mary, one garment at a time.

The train did not leave until two o'clock that afternoon. Time was on their side.

Jacob guided Mary to the bed.

27

It had the shape of an hour-glass—a peach-colored, chiffon hour-glass, with ivory lace trimming that traced the sleeves and the v-shaped opening of the waist-length jacket. The blouse was off-white and ruffled, its buttoned collar securely fastened with a silver brooch. Mary studied the reflection staring back at her in the mirror as though it were not her own, but rather the form of a stranger looking at her with surprise. From her position in Colleen's arms, Elizabeth also stared gapingly at the stranger with wide, mesmerized eyes. "Mama?" she asked.

The owner of the boutique came up from behind and propped a small hat on top of Mary's head. It perfectly matched the color of the dress, with a peach-tinted satin ribbon woven through its straw rim. "You have to put your hair up for this hat, in order for it to look right," she advised. She reached into her apron pocket and removed several long, black hairpins. She loosely tucked Mary's hair beneath the rim of the hat, pinned it, then brushed out a thick wave that trailed Mary's high forehead, enhancing her strong cheekbones and the length of her freckled neck. Mary shook her head in utter amazement. She looked like a sketch from a Parisian fashion magazine.

"You look so beautiful," Colleen said.

The shop owner stepped back and nodded with approval. Her eyes lowered to Mary's boots. "Those won't do at all," she said. She unlaced the boots and pulled them off, causing Mary to brightly color when her torn wool stockings were revealed. "Give me a pair of beige court shoes with a Louis heel." She snapped her fingers at the shop girl. "Size eight, I'd say, and some cashmere stockings. The off-white ones."

Mary removed her old stockings and the shop owner promptly discarded them in the wastebasket without asking Mary's permission. The new stockings and court shoes were a perfect fit. The clerk handed her a white cotton petticoat. "This will give a bell-shaped curve to your skirt. Go on now, put it on, you haven't much time before your train leaves for Ohio."

Fully dressed, Mary stood to her feet and examined the final product. "Now you see that clothes make the woman," the woman said, giving Mary's reflection a satisfactory nod of approval.

Colleen went to the shelf and brought back some accessories: small white gloves and silver clip earrings to go with the brooch. "Try these on, Mary. Then we must pay for the suit and leave. Jacob is waiting with the bags at the station."

They were about to leave, having paid the bill, when the owner took Mary by the hand. "Dear child," she quipped. "You won't go out of my shop until you learn how to walk in that dress." She led Mary to the center of the room and firmly pressed her fist against Mary's back. "Posture is everything, you see. Never forget good posture. Now stand upright with your head held high, young lady. That's right. Thrust this forward, keeping your shoulders down. Good, good! And you must lift the corner of the skirt with your fingers right here, at the side. That's it. Your hand must rest naturally on the back of your hip, to display the lower edge of the petticoat." It seemed entirely too difficult for Mary to remember everything, but she did as the shop owner instructed, and left the boutique that morning resembling a wealthy debutante.

They made the burdensome journey to the train terminal amidst the sounds of bells ringing and Christmas carols, and arrived at half past one that afternoon. At the station, Jacob was waiting wearing a black Mohair suit and a new pair of lace-up patent leather shoes. It seemed he had done some shopping that day as well. His hair was even oiled and slicked back from his face.

He balanced his own luggage in one arm, and took Elizabeth from Colleen with the other arm. Colleen helped Mary with the parcels, including a dark-green satin dress that she had purchased for Mary as a wedding gift, with a low neckline trimmed in black velvet. There were also new undergarments for Mary, including a satin nightdress and a bulging sack full of new cloth diapers and smocks for Elizabeth. "I wish that I could watch you say your vows." Colleen sniffed. A single tear slipped down her smooth, powdered check.

Mary took her friend's delicate, manicured hands in her own. "I'll write," she promised.

"No you won't! You'll find another friend in Bately, and you won't care about me anymore." Her pink mouth formed a gorgeous pout, one that could send men to war.

"Come here." Mary hugged Colleen, smelling the soapy aroma of her freshly-washed mop of red curls. She stepped back and looked at Colleen's pretty face in an attempt to memorize each detail—knowing that it was the last time that she would ever see her first, real friend. "Don't forget to tell Victoria and Elsie I said goodbye. And tell Dr. Griffith and Carla both that I am so sorry it had to work out this way. I didn't intend to leave them in the lurch."

Ignoring Mary, Colleen stooped forward and flooded Elizabeth's head with tear-stained kisses. She ran from the scene, unable to say a final farewell.

The train was scheduled to leave at two o'clock, but it did not arrive until three. It was an unusually mild December day. A haze of warm, white light encircled the afternoon sun. They would be traveling first class, on a hunter green, gold-striped train with white lace curtains in the windows—just like the train that Mary had yearned to board when she left Ohio, so many months ago. The ticket master helped Jacob and Mary with their belongings and led them to their own private compartment. "This definitely isn't the emigrant train," Mary approvingly observed.

Elizabeth went directly to the bed and started to bounce. Her thick legs stretched before her, flying up into the air. The ticket master hooked a long, crib-shaped basket above the double bed. "The baby sleeps here." He had a thick, Scottish brogue.

"I see." Mary touched the basket. "What a good idea."

The ticket master placed a small box of chocolates on the bed, alongside a single white carnation. He then stamped their tickets. "Enjoy the trip." He tipped his hat and left the compartment.

Jacob put his suitcase on the rack beside the bed. "I think Elizabeth needs a nap," Mary said.

"You two stay here and I'll take a look around. They tell me there's a chapel in the last train. Thought we might get married tonight."

Mary lifted her hand to her mouth. "So soon?"

"Are you having second thoughts again?" He smiled.

She went into his arms and tenderly kissed his cheek. "There will be no more second thoughts on this train, I promise."

Jacob left the compartment and Mary pulled the shades over the two windows. The train jerked into full motion and glided over the tracks. The small space was extremely quiet and dark. Elizabeth went to sleep immediately. Mary thought back to her trip across Canada in the emigrant train. How could she not have suspected back then that something was amiss? One would think that her years as an orphan and her marriage to Billy would have made her considerably more shrewd. But in a strange way, the experiences seemed to have made her even more gullible and needy—more desperate to latch on to false promises of security. The lesson was learned. She felt confident that she was not making the same mistake again.

She found Jacob in the gentlemen's car later that afternoon. He was part of a foursome of opinionated men talking politics and smoking fat Cuban cigars. Jacob leaned back in the seat, listening to the debate with sparkling eyes. One big bellied curmudgeon of a man with a slicked-back moustache and diamond cuff links pointed with great gusto to an article on the front page of the Ohio newspaper. "You stupid men are all blind, I tell you," he growled. "The economy is going to crumble, mark my words. This here United States of America is too goddamn regional. We're not setting our sights on expansion. That's the name of the game, gentlemen. Expansion. And this idiot president of ours doesn't know the first thing about it."

Mary approached the group. "Excuse me, miss." The opinionated curmudgeon rose from his seat. "I didn't know a lady was present...."

Jacob stood and introduced Mary to the group. "Gentlemen, this is my soon-to-be-wife, Mary."

"Well, well." The old man puffed at his cigar. His curled mustache lifted with his smile. "You're a lucky man, indeed. When's the big day?"

Elizabeth thrust forward from her position on Mary's hip, reaching for the man's fat cigar. He pulled it away, grinning.

"Tonight," Jacob announced, looking at Mary. "I've arranged for us to get hitched in the train's chapel."

The man pulled out a black leather appointment book. "What time?"

"We need to talk to the minister to set the time," Jacob said, more to Mary than to his new friend. "Why don't we do that right now, Mary?"

"Go on then." The old man pushed the pair down the narrow aisle. "I'll pop my head in the chapel in an hour. Hope to see you there."

They walked through the ladies' car, which was smokeless and clean, then the dry coach, through the parlor and dining car, and entered the chapel at the rear of the train. It was a simple little room, obviously Protestant in décor, with a plain, corpse-less wooden cross that hung on the front wall, and a few tired old people that sat in the three rows of leather, fold-out chairs. "Is the minister around?" Jacob asked no one in particular.

"The service starts in five minutes," one woman whispered in reply. She placed her hand on the chair. "Come, join us."

They sat down, with Elizabeth receiving her very own chair, and were given hymnals. The minister entered shortly thereafter. He tripped like a circus clown down the aisle, fell to his hands and knees, and sprung up. The passengers gasped, but no one made comment. He was quick to reassure the traveling worshipers that he was not injured; it was only the train's jerking movements that would throw him off balance from time to time. The organ came to life with a low-pitched chug, not unlike the sound of the train moving over the tracks, followed by a haphazard cadence in G major, and hymn number 54. "Hark the Herald Angels Sing" made a weary start. It grew in momentum so that by the time that the third verse began, the spirit of Christmas had crept its way into the tiny room.

Mary looked out the window. The car was surrounded by mountains, and a light snow fell outside. The white flakes swirled in tiny tornadoes, with some of the larger ones sticking to the glass and melting. More carols were sung, followed by the Christmas story, read by the minister from the Gospel of Luke. He blew his nose twice, one blow for each nostril, and said the benediction. As the worshippers dispersed for dinner in the adjoining car, Jacob stepped forward to inquire if he and Mary could be married that very night.

"Oh, my!" The baby-faced minister fumbled for his Bible, calling the worshippers to a halt. "Ladies and gentlemen, this gentleman has made an interesting request. He'd like to marry his lovely bride tonight. Will some of you stay with us as witnesses?"

Murmurs of excitement sounded through the room. Several older women worshippers immediately sat back down. One offered to hold Elizabeth as Mary and Jacob stepped up to the stage, assuming a stance of solemnity. Then Jacob's companions from the gentlemen's car entered the chapel, towing glasses of scotch in hand. "Beverages in the next car," the minister called out with disapproval.

They left and returned without their glasses, and with a few more men and women from the saloon, many red-faced and giddy, ready for some entertainment. They lined the walls of the chapel, eyes fixed upon Mary and Jacob. The minister flipped open his Bible, dropping several loose pages and kneeling to pick them up. A few drunken Catholics thought that he was signaling a period of prayer, and fell to their knees on the carpet.

Jacob said his vows first, then Mary. When it came to the part of exchanging rings, Jacob surprised Mary by reaching into the pocket of his jacket and producing two plain gold bands. He put Mary's on first, and she returned the gesture. The minister's eyes watered as he announced the pair man and wife. Jacob tenderly kissed Mary's forehead, then her lips. The older women wept, but the drunken guests that lined the walls were not the least bit satisfied.

"Come on then, blote!" one called out. "You can do better than that!"

"That's right," his lady friend said in crackly Newfoundland dialect. "Come on, lover boy, pucker up!"

All seemed to agree—they wanted more of a show. Mary eyed them from the stage and, in a moment of sheer brazenness, took their challenge to heart. She stepped forward and planted a long, wet, and extremely passionate kiss on Jacob's mouth, leaving him no option but to lift his hands around her and return it with a passionate kiss of his own. The wall of people cheered as if at a ball game. The organist accompanied the frenzy of excitement with an upbeat chorus of "Joy to the World." Then the party people rushed forward and pushed Jacob and Mary down the short aisle into the dining car. "Time to wet yer whistle," the lady from Newfoundland announced.

"Thank you, Reverend," Mary waved back at the minister.

"Come see me in the morning," he called out over the bustling crowd. "I'll have the papers ready for you both to sign. Remember now, sleep in separate quarters tonight until the legal papers are signed—and Merry Christmas!"

The older woman that held Elizabeth followed Mary and Jacob into the dining car. "I'll watch the little girl while you eat," she offered.

The rich old man with the moustache approached with a bottle of champagne. As luck would have it, he was the owner of the entire train line and one of the wealthiest men in America. "To the newlyweds." He popped the cork. "Your meal tonight is on the house."

Their meal consisted of Roquefort cheese and water crackers as an appetizer (washed down with bubbly champagne), peach fritters and duck in wine sauce, and mince pie for dessert. Before leaving the table, Mary reached into her pocket and presented Jacob with a sterling silver watch and chain that she had purchased at the dress boutique earlier that morning with the money that she had been saving for her sewing machine. It was a solid, well-built watch and would last him many years. They retired with Elizabeth to the second room of the posh dining car and joined the animated conversations of the passengers.

"The Ringling Brothers and Barnum Bailey Circus, now they know how to travel," one outspoken Irish man exclaimed. "They use over one hundred railway cars, most for their animals."

"No?" one woman cried out.

"He's right," Mary joined in, warmed by the champagne. "I took my daughter down to the rail yard before they left Vancouver. It was quite a sight. They had elephants, and zebras, and exotic animals. They formed a parade right down Main Street, and they loaded everything into the big boxcar. The rail yard smelled like manure for days."

"Did you see any ladies with beards?" Jacob asked, thinking of how Colleen described Mary's friend, Victoria.

"I don't believe I did." She smiled. "But I saw the fat lady—as big as a house—and the fire eater, and a couple of midgets, too."

"Midgets!" The Irish man exclaimed in a hushed tone of inebriation. "We've got a whole family of midgets back in Montreal. Little French Catholics. Their oldest boy is a midget priest. As sure as the pope is Catholic, that midget gives the Mass every Sunday, be it rain or shine."

Mary looked about her as the discussion progressed, or rather, digressed, into talk of Siamese twins joined at the hip and clowns that dressed like ladies, even stuffing their brassieres and walking with a feminine gait. The seats were cushioned and golden tassels hung from the arms—a far cry from the uncomfortable benches of the emigrant train. The curtains were made of velvet, and oil paintings lined the floral-papered walls. Hanging chandeliers circled overhead, each one containing five branches that dipped at sharp angles from a spherical golden center. Mary had trouble actually believing that she was inside a train, and not someone's extravagant living room. Only the sound of the wheels rattling over the rails, and the occasional shriek of the train's whistle warning animals to scatter away from the track, confirmed the fact.

Elizabeth rested against her mother's bosom and quietly sucked her thumb. Jacob's arm went around Mary on the sofa. She snuggled gratefully into his warmth. Her limbs tingled with excitement, longing for another exchange like the one she had so enjoyed earlier that morning in the darkness of his hotel room. She closed her eyes and listened to the hushed conversations of the porters behind her.

"That haughty bitch said that the linens weren't folded. She's a liar. They were folded, every one of 'em. Do you know how much she tipped me after I ran to her beck and call for over an hour? One cent! Did you see the rings on her fingers? That bitch gave me one cent!"

"Listen there, Sam. I've told you a hundred times that the rich ones are the cheapest. Was she a snot from England?"

"Sounded like she was from the East Coast—she had a Yankee accent."

"There you go—Easterners are the worst tippers. You know who's best?"

"Who might that be?"

"The show people. Don't laugh. Show people have big hearts, especially when they get a little sauce in 'em."

Jacob's hand moved over Mary's knee. "Getting tired?" he asked.

"I am. Do you want to go back to the bedroom?"

The group around them began to listen to their intimate conversation. "I thought you'd never ask," he said.

"Wedding night, is it?" one man asked. He elbowed Jacob's ribs. "Ain't you the lucky dog?"

They said goodbye to the group and returned to the compartment. Elizabeth lay on her stomach in the basket above. She didn't seem at all frightened by the strange contraption, most likely because she was depleted of all reserves from the busy wedding day, and also pleased to finally have a comfortable bed to herself. She closed her eyes, sucking her thumb, and fell into a deep sleep.

Mary and Jacob crawled into the narrow bed. Mary closed her eyes, reveling in the comfort of Jacob's presence beside her. Beneath the covers, his hand moved, ever-so-slightly, becoming even gentler, to the point where she could barely feel his fingers over her skin. She kissed each of his fingertips and moved her body closer into his rising warmth. She sighed, loosening each limb to a state of relaxation that verged on sleep. Her arms lifted and she pulled her satin gown over her head. She kissed his mouth longingly, lingering…. He also sighed, and she knew that he needed her too. She took his hand and placed it on her inner thigh. He pressed against her, growing in urgency.

The compartment closed in around them, its curtained walls, and the softness of the marriage bed. She hungrily breathed his scent and tasted the flesh of his neck.

For one, timeless instant, he was all that she could see.

28

They sent Hannah a telegram on Christmas day. It was her job to tell Tara's mother that they would be coming for the twins before the first of the year, and also to visit Dr. Smith and make certain that they did not mind Jacob and Mary bringing the children back to the house for a week or so until the Cape Cod was completed. If it was a bother to have guests with Kate in her condition, then they could easily stay with Hannah at the cottage. As it turned out, Dr. Smith was more than happy to have the newlyweds and their children living on the third floor. The Smith household was currently oppressed with the gloom of Kate's imminent death. The sounds of small children and the lightness of new love would keep Dr. Smith from slipping into the deep depression that he fought against every day. Even in the company of Bess and Ben, he felt utterly hopeless and alone. As for Kate, she was too ill to be aware of the Zane's presence, anyway. Her days and nights were spent in a stupor of morphine. On two occasions, she had slipped into an unconscious state, emerging only minutes before Thomas contacted the relatives.

Hannah waited for Mary and Jacob's train to arrive at the station in Bately. It was an unusually cold day. The mild temperatures had ceased just after Christmas, effectively reversing the proverbial saying, "in like a lion, out like a lamb." Hannah was wrapped in a long fur cape and fur mitts. She wore three layers of wool socks inside of her boots, and a body-length pair of long johns beneath her dress. Still, she shook with cold. She left the little brick building and walked eagerly to the platform as she saw the train approaching on the railway that stretched from horizon to horizon, across the barren white fields.

Mary was the first to emerge, followed by Jacob, holding Elizabeth. Hannah embraced all three at once. "Congratulations!"

Mary was relieved to see the genuine happiness on her old friend's face.

Months later, Hannah finally asked Mary what happened between her and Drew in Vancouver. What was Mary to say? If she told the truth, it would ruin Hannah's image of her "prosperous" sons. So, playing the role of a courteous coward, Mary simply evaded the question, saying only that she and Drew had differences of opinion about childrearing and finances, which, technically, was not a lie.

"I see," Hannah said, sensing there was so much more to it, but deciding not to probe further.

They went to Tara's mother's home to pick up the twins. Mary stared at them all of the way back to Bately, while Elizabeth showed off to her new little brothers beside her mother in the back seat of the cart. In upcoming months, the little girl would shove the babies and slap their legs when Mary turned her back, enraged that she was no longer the focus of her mother's devotion, although as years progressed, all of the children became close friends. As the eldest, Elizabeth naturally assumed the part of the strong-willed leader; Ethan was her mischievous partner in crime; and Patrick was the "tattler"—running to Mary and Jacob and relaying terrible tales of his brother and sister's sinful deeds. Occasionally, the roles reversed, and Elizabeth and Patrick became the best of friends, excluding Ethan from their fun. As adolescents, the twins bonded, leaving the girl, Elizabeth, out as the shunned older sister in a vicious twist of fate. As adults, the passions mellowed and each one appeared to forget the dramatic sagas that defined their childhood, leaving Mary and Jacob to understand that their fears of family division were all in vain. Of course, more children were to come, thus complicating the dynamic, inevitably layering it with more conflicts, more traumas, and thankfully, more love.

On New Year's Day, Mary helped Bess to prepare a mouth-watering New Year's dinner. The new minister, Mickey Jenson, was to join them. Other than that, the group was limited to Dr. Smith, Agnes, Bess, Ben, and the children. It was an informal meal and they ate quietly in the dining room, so as not to waken Kate upstairs.

"It won't be long now," Dr. Smith said, referring to Kate's death.

For once, Agnes did not fight back. "Where will she be buried, Thomas?" she asked.

"In the backyard. Beside her garden."

Agnes went for her cane. "Put that blasted thing down, Agnes," Dr. Smith said with his voice raised. "I won't have you pounding the floor in protest and waking up Kate. She asked to be buried by her garden, and I'm honoring her wishes. The cemetery is too far from the farm, anyway. I'll have to drive five miles just to visit."

Bess's tone was soothing, and directed at the grieving husband. "I'd like to see the missus buried beside her garden. That way, I can have a chat with her when I work outside."

Ben cracked a black walnut and picked out the meat. "Don't forget, she's gonna be in heaven, worshipin'. And she'll see that little boy of hers again. That little one she's always talkin' about, Tommy."

Mickey agreed. "She'll have work to do, too. Heaven isn't just a long vacation with the angels. There will be a mansion, with rooms for each of the departed, and we'll have jobs to do. I personally think we'll be given tasks based on the gifts we had here on earth."

"You mean, I'm gonna bake?" Bess asked.

"I don't see why not," Mickey replied. "The Lord ate fish in his resurrected form, so we'll all be able to eat in heaven."

"Food in heaven," Ben dreamily remarked. "Ain't that a relief!"

"I guess I'll be a farmer," Jacob reasoned, not very thrilled. Mary thought of her mother for the first time in years. Perhaps she would finally meet the woman that she never had the opportunity to know.

Dr. Smith appeared wary of religious talk. He stopped eating and left the table. Agnes sipped the puree of tomato soup from her spoon. A blood-like rim hedged over her thin upper lip. "I don't believe any of it. I never have." She rearranged the napkin on her lap and seemed to enjoy that everyone was looking at her, shocked. "Don't look at me that way," she instructed, "as though my soul will burn in hell for eternity. By the way, there's an important item that we failed to discuss. This is the possibility that Kate may be buried alive before her actual, medical death. Who is to know the final hour? Poe discussed this matter at great length. Frankly, it terrifies me that the significant determination of time of death shall be placed on the shoulders of a country bumpkin like Thomas. I can see that idiot accidentally burying his poor wife alive. He's just the type to do it."

"Don't be ridiculous," Jacob said.

"No, she's right," Bess readily agreed. "I also hearda' folks getting buried alive. A lady in Mason got herself buried alive only last year."

"It happens all of the time in England," Agnes joined in. "There are special coffins, with bells at the heads, designed to warn the grieving family. If the corpse returns to life, he or she simply tugs at the little bell—"

"Thomas will make sure that his wife has stopped breathing before he buries her," Mickey intervened.

"I wouldn't be so sure, Mr. Southern Preacher," Agnes shortly replied. "I fully intend on having a shovel placed by Kate's coffin so she can dig herself out in the event that she awakens post-mortem."

Bess went to the kitchen and rolled out the teacart that carried the main entrée: boiled salmon with anchovy sauce, and browned potatoes and carrots with apple jelly on the side. Mary helped serve the meal. She cut smaller portions of the fish for the children, carefully picking out the bones. The group ate in solemn silence. As dessert was served, the Smith's daughter Sandra stepped into the room. She had stopped bringing her husband and children to the house weeks earlier. It upset the grandchildren to see Nanna in such a delirious state. Sandra usually visited in the evenings, sometimes relieving her father of his duties so he could get a proper sleep on the sofa in the parlor. She had long talks with Bess in the kitchen before bedtime, often reviewing her mother's life. Together, they pulled fragments to the surface of their discussions as one would go through a treasure chest.

"It doesn't seem like she had enough time here," Sandra once reflected.

"But the missus' life was full," Bess said. "That all that matters."

The house was steeped in tension and sadness, although on the third floor, it was a different world altogether. The children were Mary's greatest joy. They reminded her of bear cubs, the way they crawled about and playfully wrestled, butting heads and murmuring tender noises of affection. They shared a nursery at the top of the stairway, comprised of three wooden cribs, lined up side by side. In the mornings, they awoke with a domino effect: first one, then the other, then the third, and the hallway rang out with the sounds of their chipper squeals.

Mary was still floating from the honeymoon and the novelty of being in love for the very first time in her life. She knew that this romantic fervor would not last forever. If it did, she would surely burst apart. She only had to look at Jacob and a vast tumult of emotions rose to the surface: joy, gratitude, and blind devotion. The nighttime routine remained the same. They would lie in bed talking about the day's events, then this would lead to kissing, and passions were inevitably roused....

Later that evening, after the kitchen was thoroughly cleaned and the left-overs placed in the ice box for lunch the next day, Mary worked through a heaping pile of books and mail-order catalogs depicting various styles of furniture and interior design. She had already ordered the downstairs furnishings, due to arrive at the end of the month. There was no need for wallpaper on the first floor, since it was paneled in light oak wood, to match the fireplace's molding in Country English style. Jacob had built a slender window above the front doorway and the zipper-cut beveled glass arrived the day before. Mary watched him install it. She then took a few steps back on the driveway, squinting her eyes. Yes, it was perfect. It was simple, and yet dignified. Jacob walked to her side. "Do you like it?"

"I love it," she answered. "To think, you built this home with your own two hands."

His arm circled her waist. "I had some help."

"Still, you're a hard worker, Jacob. And you've prospered because of it."

On a whim, she chose a red, shell-shaped basin and sink for their bathroom, and had the floors tiled with marbleized battleship linoleum, imported from Japan. She laughed as she made the order, realizing that the bathroom would be the most extravagant room in the entire house. The master bedroom was her favorite room, however, with walls covered in a pattern of coral and praline on sand, giving the large space an airy, almost ethereal ambience in the daylight hours, especially when the winter sunlight reflected the whiteness of a fresh-fallen snow and filtered in through the lace curtains, casting intricate shadows over the bed and floor.

She heard Jacob walk up the stairway. His footsteps stopped in the hallway, where he peeked into the nursery. He resumed walking and entered the sitting area of the third floor bedroom, carrying a large crate. He placed it beside the fireplace. Shaking the snow from his coat, he simultaneously leaned over and cupped Mary's face with chapped, ice-cold hands. His frigid lips pressed over hers, melting.

"You're back early," she said. He usually worked on the interior of the Cape Cod until after ten o'clock, and it was only eight o'clock.

He removed his coat and sat across from Mary in the wing chair. "It was too cold to keep going." He unlaced his boots and placed them on the fire's stone hearth. The pellets of ice and snow turned to slush and droplets of muddy water that dribbled down the leather and formed puddles beneath the soles. "I can't remember temperatures this low since I was a boy. Jake Sanders says his cat froze to death in the barn last night."

"How terrible," Mary said. "Are our animals safe?"

"The horses and cows should be fine. And I made a bed of hay and blankets for the dogs." He glanced at the book on Mary's lap. "Any more orders?"

"Just material for the downstairs curtains. I'm tempted to purchase a Queen Anne clock for the parlor, but I don't want to exceed our budget."

"Let's see how next year's harvest turns out." He looked over at the crate, rose, and walked to it. "I stopped by Hannah's on my way back, she gave me your crazy quilt." He took the quilt from the crate and handed it to Mary. "She wanted me to tell you to add more bright colors—I think she said some satin and calico."

Mary gazed down at the quilt and stroked the daisy patch, remembering the incident with Reverend Schenk in the basement of the church. A lifetime ago. What would Jacob do if she told him? Probably leave for Dayton that instant, find Reverend Schenk, and beat him to a pulp. She spread the quilt on the floor to get an overall impression of the patches that had been completed and the ones that were to come. Hannah was right; the quilt possessed too many dark colors and plain materials, perhaps reflective of Mary's somber mood at the time of its initial creation. She would make a new square that week, using fabric that was festive and bursting with newfound hope.

"I hung the globe lanterns outside," Jacob was saying. "One at the front door, and the other one on the post at the foot of the drive. Abe Jenkins helped me with the doors this afternoon. The brass hinges look real nice."

Mary lifted the quilt and shook out the dust. She folded it with care at the foot of their bed, then walked to the fireplace and sat on the hearth beside Jacob. He smiled at his wife. "I passed Agnes in the hallway on my way up here. She scared the living daylights out of me. I thought I saw a ghost."

Mary shook her head. "Her stories of dead people coming back to life gave me quite a scare."

Jacob took a catalog from the floor and browsed through it. Mary watched him in the firelight. The shadow that he projected was dark and looming, with hands cutting like bats across the wallpaper as each page was turned. Feeling playful, she stood and sat on Jacob's knee. He placed the catalog on the hearth. Her face lowered to his, its shadow dipping on the wall's canvas. His hands lifted and he deftly unloosened the pins from her hair. It fell about her shoulders in a cascade of blond and golden wisps. His face lowered to her bosom, burying itself in the honey-scented flesh. She pressed him against her, as she often did with the children. "Thank you for coming to fetch me," she said.

"Thank you for coming back."

The fire's orange glow filled the room, decorating the walls. Their shadows blended into one form on the canvas; the arms and hands moving like small birds soaring through the orange light. The shadow lifted, as if in flight, as their forms rose from the fire's hearth and moved across the room, lowering to the bed….

29

In the month of February, Elizabeth was up through the nights with a series of worsening ear infections. Mary had grown accustomed to losing sleep since motherhood found her in the field. She found herself going to bed every night with the anticipation that she would be rudely awakened by her daughter's cries. Fortunately, the twins were heavy sleepers, and did not wake up to the sound of their sister's distress. There wasn't much that Mary could do. She held her daughter, rocked her, and prayed that each infection would disappear. One night, she sat for two hours and waited for Elizabeth to return to sleep. Then she placed the little girl back into her crib. As she went into the hallway, she heard the sounds of Agnes and Mickey Jenson's voices drifting up the stairs.

Mary put on her robe and went to the second floor. Agnes and Mickey were quietly conversing in the hallway outside of Kate's room. Mary went to Mickey. "Is everything all right?"

"Kate's about to leave us," he whispered. "You can see her now, if you want."

"Are you sure?"

He nodded.

Agnes and Mickey followed Mary to the deathbed, where Dr. Smith sat beside his wife. Bess and Ben stood behind him. Ben's thin brown hand lay over Dr. Smith's hunched back, and Bess silently wept. Her tears dropped to the bed, as if christening Kate's atrophied legs. Mary stood with Agnes and Mickey at the foot of the bed, keeping vigil.

Kate's breathing was raspy and slow, almost non-existent. Her face was colored in a dim shade of blue. Dr. Smith held her hand, his own face devoid of color. All thoughts were focused on Kate's breathing and when it would stop. Ben went to the night table and lifted a saucer of oil. Making the sign of the cross over Kate's cold forehead, he mumbled a blessing of release. Bess glanced at Mary. With the meeting of their eyes, Mary couldn't help but slip into tears. She hardly knew Kate and yet she felt, in a blurred and inexpressible way, that a piece of herself was lying before her on the bed. Here was a glimpse of her inevitable destiny.

Kate's motionless body suddenly arched and her chin thrust forward. There was a prolonged, burly breath that seemed to shake the very core of her slender chest. Mary's heart leapt with hope, thinking that Kate was returning. Dr. Smith groaned in a low, angry tone. Ben's hand gripped Dr. Smith's shoulder, and Bess audibly sobbed; all three had seen death many times before, whereas for Mary, this was her first exposure to the final gasp at life. Kate's frail body collapsed back on the bed. Her hands, previously clenched into fists, relaxed, their wrinkled palms opened to the ceiling.

Mary saw luminous colors of white and yellow suddenly lighten the room. She looked at Mickey, to get his response, but apparently everyone else was oblivious to this blinding light. Mary clutched the bedpost, wanting to voice the beauty in her midst. Then the colors disappeared, and she was left with the morose picture of Dr. Smith bending over his wife, loudly sobbing in his loss. Ben and Bess walked to the others at the foot of the bed. "Let's leave him alone."

Mary went to the kitchen with Mickey, Bess, and Ben. Agnes stoically returned to her room. Mary didn't think that she would cry as she did with the others, but she grieved deeply that night, sharing in their immense sorrow for the woman of the house. They sat at the kitchen table, and Bess slipped into song. Her grief took on a poignant, wounded sound. At dawn, Mary walked upstairs. On the third floor, she was stunned to discover Agnes standing in the nursery, beside Elizabeth's crib, with her back turned to the door. She held the weeping toddler in her arms. Her voice had lost its usual hostility, and now quivered with tenderness as she spoke. "There, there, child...." Mary stepped into the room. Agnes turned sharply on her heels. Mary caught the actual moment when Agnes' face changed. Its lines, seconds earlier, soft and loving, tensed into deep crevices of hate. "Your daughter was crying," she scolded Mary. "And that lazy husband of yours didn't even get up."

Mary walked over and took Elizabeth. "Thank you, Agnes."

At the door, Agnes turned back to Mary. Her beady black eyes looked at Elizabeth. "She reminds me of my Kate, when she was small." Her thin lips shook and her nose began to run, although her eyes stubbornly refused to produce any tears. She pointed the cane into the hallway and turned it on its axis, leaving Mary to wonder if she was too quick to judge the caustic woman after all.

Two weeks following Kate's death, Mary and Jacob moved into their new home. Jacob went back to working in the barn, while Mary cared for the children, spending most of her time in the kitchen, busily cleaning and preparing the meals, and also completing her crazy quilt and mending the children's clothing at night.

Agnes intended to leave Bately the following Saturday, and it was all that Dr. Smith could do to keep from kicking her out of the house and paying for her to stay at the Sir Crudor Inn prior to her departure. Agnes possessed little sensitivity to the fact that Dr. Smith's emotions were raw and needed to be treated with care. Bess had learned to stand up to difficult people through her dealings with Maisie, and now she told Agnes that she should just stay away from him, but it seemed that this advice only served to egg Agnes on. She pestered Dr. Smith incessantly, first about the gravesite, insisting that they put a bell in the coffin, and then about Bess and Ben and the fact that Bess received some very expensive jewelry items in Kate's will. It wasn't enough that Agnes was given all other items of jewelry, including Kate's finest cameo and pear necklace—no, the governess wanted more.

There was a particularly bad row one morning before Dr. Smith was to leave for Cincinnati to pick up some medical supplies. Bess and Ben were to join him. Ben wanted some new tools, and they could be purchased at considerable savings in the city. Bess was looking forward to taking the day off and spending some time with Ben. His sister-in-law, Maisie, had not let up on them in recent months, and Bess had drained her supply of emotional strength, what with also having to deal with Kate's death. She wanted the day in Cincinnati to serve as a type of vacation, after which she and Ben would return to the lighthearted union that came so naturally during their courtship.

But Agnes had other plans. She was extremely jealous of the trio and was genuinely hurt that they did not invite her to join them. To Agnes' way of thinking, Dr. Smith and the slaves required chastisement for going into the city that day. She chased Dr. Smith out to the barn, madly swinging her cane into the icy winter air. "The slaves must stay behind and prepare my lunch! One would think that they are royalty, taking days of leisure whenever they please! Do you hear me, Thomas?"

Dr. Smith ignored Agnes as he brushed down the horses and hooked them up to the carriage. Bess and Ben came outside, and Bess lifted herself onto the vehicle. Agnes shrieked, "Look at the slave woman! She thinks she's the Queen of England!"

Dr. Smith quietly laughed, although his eyes held no joy. "You're one to talk, Agnes."

She angrily poked her cane at his foot. "Yes, I certainly am one to talk. And I'll remind you that your elders are to be respected, not mocked."

Ben climbed up to the front of the carriage and lifted the reins, eager to get the devil out of Bately before Agnes murdered them all. He looked at Dr. Smith. "All set, sir?"

"Am I ever," Dr. Smith replied, getting into the carriage and closing the door as Agnes continued to shout out a string of obscenities. His last image of Agnes still living was that of her face, pressed against the carriage window, the long nose rippling with rage, and the small white fists clenched and pounding the glass. When the group returned to the farm later that night, they found Agnes' body huddled into an angry ball on the snow bank beside the barn. It seemed she had suffered some kind of heart attack or stroke shortly after they left. Over the course of the day, her body had completely frozen and was now mummified with rigor mortis on the ground.

"A fitting death," was all Dr. Smith could say.

Bess felt guilty, thinking that if only she and Ben had stayed at the house that day, they could have helped Agnes. Ben consoled her, also feeling guilt. Thomas dug the hole himself and lowered the coffin. For good measure, Ben threw his best shovel into the ditch. Dr. Smith filled the hole with dirt, and placed a wooden cross on top of the mound. "That'll be all I need," he muttered, walking back to the house with Bess and Ben, "Old Agnes digging herself out of the grave, coming back from the dead to make my life a living hell...."

Agnes never did wake up. Her body decomposed beside the garden, where Kate's tulips and peonies bloomed each spring, just after Easter.

30

1898

She was an anachronism, with rolls of flesh that dimpled beneath the uncompromising glare of the noonday sun. The dress, faded yellow and tattered, had a polka dot pattern, once the rage of Ohio school girls, but today a comical remnant of fashion history that bordered on nostalgia. Two stubby pigtails stuck out from behind her ears. These were braided and tied with fringed, pink ribbons at each broom-like base. She moved along the length of the clothesline, stopping momentarily to re-clip a crooked item, or pick up a smaller garment that had blown off in the breeze. Her hands dipped into the basket, producing more wet clothing such as children's shirts and men's underpants. At the end of the line, the anachronism dropped her wary body onto the garden bench and looked upon the product of her morning's work. She felt no pride, but only relief that it was done.

She produced a small, tinted bottle from the pocket of her apron and daintily drank the last of its contents, lifting the chipped rim to her mouth and sipping as if the toxic mountain whiskey were a refreshing cup of tea. Within seconds, the bottle was empty. She looked over her shoulders, searching for more. She often kept bottles hidden in the bushes or the gutters, or behind rocks in the fence where the squirrels and the other rodents lived and pounced from the tinted glass sides as they climbed the fence's low height.

But this was the month of September—the month when it happened two years earlier. "It" was the pivotal turning point of Azalea's young life, when lusty adolescent fantasies twisted into something altogether dark. She had only wanted to have fun. Being out west was a liberating experience, in its conception, when Azalea realized that the religion of her father was nothing but a crock of hypocrisy and lies. She recalled her parents' faces as they would forcibly shift whenever their carriage entered the town. Proudly entering "their" church, they greeted the parishioners with caring, concerned tones—these being the very same people that they viciously attacked within the cloistered confines of the parsonage each night.

Life was different in Vancouver, and especially in California. There weren't many churches out there. People were free to act as they damn well pleased, and they didn't put on any airs. Azalea happily released the misguided notion that a woman had to marry in order to live a satisfied life. Indeed, she came to understand that marriage was a restrictive and confining institution, just like the churches where her father preached. Rules, rules, rules: don't do this, don't say this, and above all else—don't have any spontaneous fun! It came as a pleasant revelation when Azalea realized that she wasn't meant for marriage after all. She loved men—oh, how she loved them! And it was this very aspect of her character that made Azalea want to spread herself out, so to speak. The more, the better—the more often, the merrier.

Over time she made a business of the adventure. Gifts and money came in return for healthy romps in bed. They sometimes lined up at her doorway, when she lived in San Francisco. It seemed once she left Drew, Scat, and Josh, Azalea's reputation spread. Here was a working woman that would do anything a man requested—and with tremendous pleasure, to boot.

Until that horrible night, when it happened.

The man seemed so charming and polite, like a grateful little boy. She took him into her room and, seeing his shyness, wondered if perhaps she was to have to honor of deflowering this lovely creature. He put the money on the table in advance. She was pleased to see that the pay was generous. Azalea guided him to her bed, where she had given pleasure to over one hundred men in the course of that month alone. At first, he was docile—submissive, even, and she thought that he would probably want to be roped to the headboards, as some of the shy ones seemed to enjoy. But somehow, in the course of the evening, the young man seized control. He produced a broken bottle from his coat pocket and mercilessly raped her for several hours.

The pain, the blood, but more than these—the terrible humiliation—the violation. His obscenities were steeped in hate—the desire to destroy. Eventually, Azalea passed out on the bed. Her body was discovered by a customer, later the next day. She lay in a sickening mess of blood and bruised, shredded flesh. She was lucky to have survived.

He cut her lips apart. She wasn't pretty to begin with, but there was something horrific about having to spend the rest of her life purposely avoiding mirrors.

She returned to Dayton where, upon seeing the spectacle of their fallen daughter, the Reverend Schenk and his wife, Mildred, ordered her to leave. Where would she go? Her thoughts turned to Bately.

The town continued to prosper in the years that Azalea was out west. This was the result of the new train line, and also a fertile byproduct of trading along the Miami River. Azalea located work right away, first as a dishwasher at the Sir Crudor Inn, where she had a room above the kitchen and three meals a day. However, when her drinking interfered, she was fired and forced to leave the premises and never return. She took various housekeeping jobs after that, preferring the ones where she was given a room and hot meals, although with time, word circulated that Azalea Schenk (poor, poor Azalea—the minister's fallen daughter? The one whose mouth looks like cut up sausage? Yes, that's the one) was a bad worker and a drunkard. Better to hire a railroad tramp than hire Azalea Schenk.

She took work where she could find it. She swept barns, weeded gardens, and cleaned other people's garments and hanged them out to dry. She had no home to speak of, and often slept in the leaky shed behind Ted's General Store where she kept all of her belongings and a blanket in the corner beside the shovels and rakes. In the winter she was known to go to the church late at night, the same building where her father once preached, and Mickey Jenson would let her sleep in the boiler room, where it was warm.

He took pity on the minister's fallen daughter. He always welcomed her inside, sometimes having a steaming pot of vegetable soup to offer her. In another day, Azalea would have tried to seduce Mickey, or at least have some fun openly flirting with the celibate man; but the shy boy with the broken bottle had also broken Azalea's spirit, leaving her bitter and unforgiving, though grateful for Mickey's kindness. She had come to learn the hard way that compassion was a rare commodity in this world—virtually extinct in regards to a woman's sexual sin, though considered "virility" in the male counterpart.

A little boy ran across the sprawling lawn of the estate, heading directly for the clothesline with his muddy dog. He grabbed at two white shirttails and hung from the garment as though it were a swing. The dirty dog jumped up and bit a pair of damp trousers, tearing the hem. Rage filled Azalea. It rose up her throat and tasted like bitter bile. She jumped from the bench and whipped her empty bottle at the boy. He continued to hang from the shirttails, laughing in defiance. The bottle flew over his head and landed on the driveway, shattering over the cobblestone.

"Git, git out!" Azalea ran to the boy and yanked him from the shirt. She angrily threw his small body on the grass as if he were a bushel of hay. The dog left the trousers and turned on Azalea, attempting to procreate with her right leg. His tremendously long red tongue flapped wildly from his slobbering mouth. Azalea pounded the mutt's matted yellow back with her clenched fist—simultaneously shouting at the boy, who was now in a fetal position, crying on the grass.

The lady of the house emerged from the back porch, evidently having witnessed the entire scene. With hands on her broad hips and a face that flashed indignation, she stormed over to Azalea and slapped her hand across the shredded face. "You miserable creature! How dare you—HOW DARE YOU?"

The dog released his grip from Azalea's leg. The boy took him by the collar and ran back to the house. "I'm sorry, ma'am," Azalea mumbled, lowering her head.

Again, the woman slapped her, this time missing Azalea's face and hitting Azalea's neck with her jeweled hand. "I was warned about you, but the Reverend Jenkins told me to show some charity. I'll never make that mistake again!"

Azalea craved alcohol. She always did when things like this happened. Her mouth was parched and her hands trembled from withdrawal. She glanced furtively about the yard. Was there any booze? Dismal and defeated, she remembered again that this was September. She looked at the woman who fumed before her. Azalea formed a pitiful smile with what was left of her mouth. "Could I have my pay now, ma'am?"

"Surely you're joking. Get off of this estate before I call the servants to lead you away. And don't you ever set foot on the grounds again, Azalea Schenk!" She shook her head in vehement disapproval, "To think, after all that your good parents have given you—the opportunities, the support! And now, you disgrace them by becoming a drunkard and a whore. God help the Schenks, to be shamed by a daughter like you!"

Azalea's body slouched into the shape of a dying willow tree. Years before, she would have fought back and stood her ground. Today, she accepted her lot. She left "The Hill," where the wealthiest residents of Bately lived, and descended to the village below. It was a Sunday. Azalea rarely found work on Sundays. Most of Bately's citizens adhered to the laws of the Sabbath. The fact that she was given a job that morning was unlikely to repeat itself.

She could walk out to the Zane's farm. Mary was good about giving her a meal and a small job to do, knowing full well that the coins would be used by Azalea to purchase some cheap bourbon or moonshine to help her through the chilly autumn night. But now Azalea sadly realized that, this being Sunday, the stores would be closed and bourbon and moonshine would not be available. Also, the Zanes were probably at church, and Azalea did not want to go to church.

The day of sobriety stretched out before her—long and devoid of hope.

Across the commons, the tall, white-washed doors opened and the civilized residents of Bately slowly filtered out. Azalea turned in the opposite direction and made her way to the train depot. It was her favorite pastime, to sit and watch the travelers board the powerful vehicles. Sometimes, if Azalea thought long and hard enough, she could capture the momentary flutter of excitement that she herself felt when she left Bately and went out west, only two years earlier. It helped if she was intoxicated, then she actually imagined that she, too, was a traveler waiting for her escape. She fantasized about going to the East Coast this time around, and meeting up with a wealthy older man who wanted nothing more out of life than to shower Azalea with gifts and liquor and take her on luxurious trips abroad. Some afternoons, Azalea was carted away by the ticket masters, the drool dripping down her chin, as she audibly described her elderly rich lover to the faces of sheer repulsion that hovered over her. Oh, how she resented their judgmental faces! They were like rain clouds threatening to storm on her sunny, drunken day.

This afternoon, the station was close to being empty since most of the lines were closed on the Sabbath. Azalea sat on the bench beneath the stairway of the signal tower. An engineer descended, angrily clapping his hands for Azalea to go away. "Don't worry," she told him, "I'm as dry as a desert." The clarity of her eyes told him that she spoke the truth. Plus, she didn't have that ridiculous smile plastered across her shredded face, the one that she would get whenever she started rambling about her mythical fiancé. The engineer allowed her to stay on the bench, figuring that there was no harm in a sober drunk.

Azalea's stomach grumbled. The stale bread that Ted had thrown her for breakfast had already digested, and now her empty stomach burned with hunger. Ted didn't seem to mind that Azalea slept in his shed. His only rule was that she vacate the premises each day before daybreak, when the townspeople could see her and her presence would have a poor effect on business. One night, Azalea offered Ted payback for his charity. Ted replied with some kind of an excuse. Later, tugging at her shredded lip, Azalea knew the real reason why he refused.

The noonday train approached in the distance. It arrived at the depot with a chilling shriek of its wheels, then a clamping down as the brakes released. The side door opened and the passengers emerged: an ordinary pair of middle-aged farmers, followed by their chatty wives, then an elderly couple. Seconds passed, and another wave of passengers flowed forth from the second car. The groups departed to the parking lot. One woman remained on the platform as the train crept into the terminal, evidently having nowhere to go.

Her eyes were gray and tired; the rims were circled in pink. She was of average height and weight, and her clothing, while appearing new, was garish and obviously tailored with the intention of revealing the little amount of cleavage that the middle-aged woman possessed. Her hat carried enormous, floppy feathers that warily drooped, as if fatigued from the trip and the heat of the day. Seeing this stranger, Azalea was reminded of the sour taste of apples and eating them before they were ripe—in the late summer time.

She had no luggage, only a small imitation velvet purse. She walked over to Azalea, removed a flask from her pocket, and offered her a swig. Azalea grabbed the bottle, then, gathering up the little self-control that she possessed, forced herself to take slow, measured sips. "Don't hold back," the woman reassured her, instinctively knowing that this pathetic creature was a drunkard thirsty for brew. "There's plenty more where that came from."

Azalea's face lit up. She tilted her head back and guzzled the contents of the flask. The woman laughed. "I like a woman who can handle her drink."

"What brings you to Bately?" Azalea asked, handing back the empty flask.

The woman sat beside Azalea on the bench. "Thought I'd start a business in these parts, a kind of high-class saloon."

"The people in this town don't approve of that type of thing," Azalea slurred.

"Oh, don't I know it!" the woman exclaimed. "Tell me, are you a working girl?"

Azalea knew this woman wasn't referring to hanging laundry on the line. "Used to be, out West. Then some mean man went and cut up my mouth."

"Well then, you could work for me, in my saloon. I'll have a room upstairs where the boys can relax."

Azalea adamantly shook her head. "Men don't wanna' kiss a mouth like this."

"Who said anything about kissin'?" the woman elbowed Azalea. "Besides, I've known a man or two who likes that kinda freakish thing."

Azalea straightened herself on the bench. "All right. I'll work in your saloon. But I think you should move it down to Cincinnati. They're too religious in these parts."

"Wish I could—but I gotta stay in Bately. Seems I got me a grandchild here that I ain't never met."

"Is that right?"

"Yes, ma'am. My son died a few years ago. Got himself hung at the gallows for a crime he didn't even commit. His wife had herself a baby, and now I hear she lives in Bately. Mind you, she'd never think to tell me I had myself a baby granddaughter. She's just gone and cut me outta her life, like she's some kinda goddamn princess, and I ain't got a pot to piss in."

"You're Bonnie Turner!" Azalea gasped. "I remember you. We used to steal apples near your cabin in the summer time, when I was a girl. And you would chase us through the meadow with your shot gun, remember?"

"And who might you be?" the woman asked with interest.

"Don't you recognize me? I'm Azalea Schenk, the reverend's daughter."

Bonnie Turner let loose a loud gasp. "No! Glory, how you've changed! Tell me then, do you know that cherry, Mary Turner?"

"Sure I do. She's called Mary Zane now."

"I tell you what, I have a fresh bottle of bourbon right here in my bag. I'll give it to you for free if you take me to see her. Will you do that, Azalea?"

"Now that all depends. Where are you sleeping tonight?"

"The only inn in town, I suppose. Is it still called The Sir Crudor?"

"Yes, ma'am. And I'll make you a deal. I'll show you where Mary lives, for the bottle of that bourbon in your purse, and also, I get to share your bed tonight."

Bonnie's eye brows lifted. "I don't like me the sound a' that!"

"I need a good night's sleep, is all," Azalea honestly explained. "And a hot bath, too."

Bonnie nodded. "The working girl has fallen on hard times. I understand." She stretched out her hand. "You've got yourself a deal, preacher girl."

Azalea winced. "Don't call me that."

"All right then, I'll just call you Azalea, like the flower."

The mutilated mouth lifted into a childish grin. "Like the flower—that's right."

31

Mary didn't like Sundays. Having to keep her four young children still in the pews of the church for over two hours was a truly impossible task. Or maybe it was the slower pace of the Sabbath that she detested, with the afternoons dragging on without anything to do, except minding the children and serving the meals. Not even cooking was allowed. They had to eat cold meat, apples, and hard-boiled eggs. By four o'clock, her body felt like lead and her head always ached—as though pounding from a week's worth of pent-up fatigue.

Elizabeth and the boys played with wooden trucks beside the barn. Mary watched them from the kitchen window, occasionally shouting a command or a rebuke. They shouted back, "Look, Momma, look!"

And, not really having seen what they wanted her to see, Mary would reply, "That's good, Ethan (or Patrick, or Elizabeth)."

The baby slept in her wicker pram beside the kitchen table. Mary wiped her hands dry and went to the peaceful form. She leaned down and kissed little Rose's cheek. The tiny hand reached up and formed a dimpled fist. Eight months old. Rose smiled and laughed during her waking hours, crawling with reckless abandon and looking up with wonder at her siblings' boisterous activities. She was Mary's easiest baby yet.

Mary's open palm circled the curve of her womb. Already, there was another on the way. This child was not planned, and Mary wondered how she would get through the exhaustion of the next three months of pregnancy, followed by the early months of a newborn's sleepless demands. The tasks stretched out before her and coated her days with depression, especially when she was tired.

Jacob napped upstairs. Mary moved quietly about the first floor, picking up the children's toys. She sat down on the sofa beside the window where she could keep an eye on the children and started to stitch her newest quilt. As usual, her creations kept her sane. She worked on her quilts throughout the days and late into the evenings, at times placing the needles down to enjoy the wonder of the unborn baby's kicks and gentle rolling within her womb. Jacob's child. She imagined what it would look like—a fusion of Elizabeth and the twins, and closely resembling Rose. It was as if she intuitively knew that she was carrying yet another girl, for the quilt's final squares were noticeably feminine—mostly pink and red, and full of ripe strawberries, while others depicted lime-green corn stalks with tiny pink hearts dangling from the husks. She embroidered large initials for each family member: J, M, E, P, E… and then an S, for the child soon to be born.

The front door swung open and Elizabeth ran inside. "Mamma! My grandma's here!"

"Is she now?" Mary got up from the sofa, pleased that Tara's mother had come to pay a surprise visit. She reached for the railing to keep from fainting on the spot when she saw Bonnie Turner standing beside the twins in the side yard, with Azalea Schenk swaying to and fro at her side, a bottle in her hand. Mary took a deep breath and walked over. "Bonnie," she said. "What brings you to these parts?"

"I thought I'd meet my granddaughter. She is the only family I got left, Mary, now that Billy and Elisha are dead."

Mary forced a smile for the children's benefit. She stepped forward and leaned into Bonnie's ear. "You watched that godforsaken son of yours beat me black and blue and you did nothing about it," she vehemently hissed. "Get off my property now, before I chase you with my husband's gun!" Mary stepped back, towards the children, and again, cracked an artificial smile. "I'm sorry you can't stay for tea, Bonnie. But it was certainly thoughtful of you to stop by and say hello. Goodbye now."

Bonnie's eyes narrowed, prepared for a fight. "Oh, ain't you the special cherry, now, in your fancy clothes, with your fancy house? Azalea's told me how you went and made yourself into a mighty fine and proper woman. But I'll have you know, Mary Turner, I remember when you were nothing but a little orphaned whore hanging onto my son. Billy beat you for good reason. You were a sorry excuse for a wife!"

Elizabeth looked up. "Mama?"

"Go get Daddy," Mary calmly said. Elizabeth ran into the house. Mary stared Bonnie down. "I mean it, Bonnie. You leave my land, and don't you ever come back here again."

"I'll have you know I plan on stoppin' by every day to see my only granddaughter. And I plan on startin' me a fine saloon here in Bately, with rooms upstairs where people can sleep."

Mary closed her eyes, wishing her former mother-in-law away. Jacob emerged from the house with Rose wailing in his arms, and Elizabeth aggressively leading the way. "She says you're not my real daddy," Elizabeth was telling Jacob.

He walked to Mary's side. "Leave this farm right now," he firmly said.

"She only wants to see her grandchild," Azalea said in Bonnie's defense.

Mary glared at Azalea. "I can't believe you brought her out here today, Azalea! After all I've done for you."

"She would have found your house anyway," Azalea slurred in reply.

Mary looked at Jacob with pained, desperate eyes. "Bonnie says she plans to stay in Bately and start another saloon."

Jacob loudly scoffed. "The people will kick you out again, Bonnie. You have a reputation in this town."

"And your whore for a wife doesn't?" Bonnie snapped back.

Elizabeth started to cry. "Mommy, make her go away!"

Bonnie caught sight of the bulge beneath Mary's white apron. "Glory be, woman! Are you with child again? You're like a rabbit these days."

Jacob's hand went for Bonnie's back. "That'll be enough." He guided her to his wagon. In fact, it was more like a long, forceful shove. He rode Bonnie and Azalea back in to town and dropped them off at the back door of The Sir Crudor Inn.

Mary and Jacob did not talk about Bonnie Turner until well after the children went to sleep that night. Mary sat up in bed, sipping a cup of warm milk. This was her feeble attempt to put out the burning sensation in her throat, the consequence of eating raw onions at dinner that night. She watched Jacob undress and felt the sudden urge to make love. He walked over and sat on the edge of the bed. She finished her milk and wrapped her hands around his waist. Her hands lowered....

He lay beside her and they kissed, but his movements were far too slow and restrained for what she wanted right then. She climbed on top of him and lifted her gown, pressing her pelvis into his. It was lust, plain and simple, and she took great pleasure in the assertive act. Later that night, Mary expressed her deepest fears to Jacob as they lay together in the dark. "It has taken me three years to get rid of my reputation as a hempen widow in this town," she said. "And people know better than to talk about Billy to Elizabeth. Why did Bonnie have to come back and ruin everything?"

Jacob stroked her hair. "Don't worry now, Mary. People stopped seeing you as Billy Turner's widow a long time ago. As for Elizabeth, we'll just have to help her make sense of it as she gets older."

"You'd be surprised how quickly people will remember my past, Jacob. Especially with Bonnie Turner's help. She's not a quiet woman, and I fear she means to destroy me. She'll go telling everyone our business, and she'll start getting Elizabeth involved in her wicked games. Poor Elizabeth. She'll have to go to school some day and have the other children tease her about having a prostitute for a grandmother. She'll hate me for it, Jacob. I just know she will."

"Shhh...Elizabeth won't ever hate you, Mary."

Nevertheless, the next morning, when Elizabeth came to the kitchen table, Mary swore she saw Billy Turner's hateful look in her daughter's eyes. The blatant defiance—the flippant disregard for her mother's authority. She feared she was imposing all of her traumatic memories on the innocent child. It wasn't right. Elizabeth merely had a strong temperament. She was born with it and in many ways, it was a gift, although at times Mary felt like throttling the little girl when she got sassy. This morning was one such time.

Elizabeth's eyes were puffy from a restless night's sleep. Her movements were jerky and aggressive, as if somehow out of sync with the family rhythms that surrounded her. When Mary asked the child to go get herself dressed, she whipped a crust of toast in mother's face, shouting "NO! You do it!" Mary pulled down the little girl's bloomers and gave her a stinging slap on the rear end. A day of Bonnie-induced battles had begun.

By suppertime, Mary avoided her daughter, having reached an unspoken agreement with the three-year old—you don't cross me, and I won't cross you. Jacob came inside from a long day in the field and the family sat down to eat. Halfway through her meal, Elizabeth threw her fork at baby Rose. Jacob ordered her to stand in the corner. She glared defiantly at him. "You can't tell me what to do! You're not even my real daddy. Billy is!"

Mary picked up a saucer and threw it across the room. The dish shattered against the wall, covering the range in glass splinters and chunks. "Stop it, Elizabeth!" she screamed. Her hands were shaking on the table. "You are never to mention his name in this house again, do you understand—

NEVER!" Elizabeth cowered in her seat. Her bottom lip quivered and her freckled face turned bright red.

"Go upstairs to your room," Jacob commanded.

The little girl rose from the chair. Passing Jacob, she clutched his muscular arm and cried loudly into his shirt sleeve, "I'm sorry, Daddy. I won't say it again."

He patted her shoulder. "All right, Lizzy. It's not your fault." He glanced at the terrified twins. "Boys, go upstairs with your sister."

"But we haven't eaten yet!" Ethan wailed at the injustice.

"Bring your plates with you."

The motley crew promptly evacuated the premises. Jacob left the table, placed Rose in her pram in the parlor, and returned to the kitchen to rub Mary's neck. Her head was pressed against the table. "Why did she have to come back and ruin everything?" she murmured in despair.

Jacob knelt on the floor and lifted Mary's face in his hands. "I'll make her leave."

"How?"

"I've been thinking. I got some money saved up. I was going to buy new equipment in the spring. I think I should give it to Bonnie, instead, with the understanding that she's never to set foot in this town again."

"Bribe her?"

"That's right."

"It doesn't seem right, Jacob."

"I don't care what's right and what's wrong about it, Mary. I won't have my daughter asking me every day about Billy Turner. I don't want that man's ghost in our life."

"But, Jacob, we need that money. Besides, you remember the sermon at church this Sunday. We have to find room in our hearts to forgive our enemies."

In response, Jacob scoffed.

In bed that night, Mary's womb tightened into a hard ball. The pain was enough to bring her out of a deep sleep. She rolled over and nudged Jacob. "I got cramps."

He reached over to stroke the unborn baby that was hidden in Mary's flesh. "You're tense. Relax."

She breathed deeply. "Maybe some milk—"

He got out of bed and put on his overalls. "I'll be right back."

The cramps lessened by the time he returned. Mary rubbed her belly and sat up to drink the milk. "It's feeling better."

He got back into the bed. "Good. Keep breathing. This thing with Bonnie has you upset."

She slept for a few hours and dreamt of Billy beating her. She was in the cabin where they lived when she was newly pregnant with Elizabeth. His fists were pounding at her stomach, and she cried out: "Don't kill the baby—don't kill the baby!" She awoke in a cold sweat, with her lower regions squeezed within a vice of excruciating pain. She nudged Jacob. "Wake up!"

His hand sleepily reached for her womb. "Just relax…"

"Help me!" she screamed.

He sat up with a start and looked down at her face. It was an unhealthy hue of pinkish-yellow, and covered in tiny beads of sweat. He pulled away the covers. There was blood between her legs. Tara. It formed a brown pool on the mattress, and dripped over the post to the floor. He grabbed his coat and boots. Seconds later, she heard him riding away from the house on his horse.

Elizabeth came to the doorway. "Mommy?"

Mary reached for her daughter.

"Mommy? There's blood!"

"It's all right." Mary forced a reassuring voice. Her fists clenched with the contractions. Elizabeth's eyes widened with terror. Minutes later, Hannah entered the room.

She touched Elizabeth's head. "Go back to your room, dear."

"But Mommy—the baby…"

"Go on now, do as I say."

Elizabeth left. Hannah went to Mary's side. "Oh Hannah," she wept. "I'm losing the baby." Her strength was dwindling and the long, hard contractions were secondary to the sickening dizziness and the enormous desire to sleep. She visualized her own body on the bed, the blood being sapped like syrup from the tree. She thought of Tara, feeling a strange kinship with the departed soul.

"The baby will be fine," Hannah said, stroking Mary's head. She pressed the sheet between Mary's legs, covering her horror at the sight of so much blood.

Mary fell back into darkness, at first hearing Hannah's words: "Don't leave, Mary… stay with us…" then hearing nothing and seeing only a turbulent flow of tattered black light.

When she opened her eyes next, she thought that years had passed away, although it was only a few hours since Jacob had left on the horse. Sunlight poured into the room, engulfing her in its golden heat. Jacob sat at her side. Dr. Smith spoke to her from the end of the bed. "How are you feeling, Mary?"

"So tired…"

"The bleeding has stopped. You'll be fine now, dear."

She felt somehow different—vacant. "Did I lose the baby?"

Dr. Smith nodded. "I'm afraid so."

Her crying had no sound—just long, hot tears that flowed down her face and continued to flow, off and on, for the remainder of the day. It was bitter grief, liquefied. Dr. Smith gave her two pills and some clear syrup. "Are you hungry?" he asked. She shook her head. "Then get some sleep, Mary. You close your eyes, and go to sleep."

She looked over at Jacob. "Where are the children?"

"Hannah's with them."

She closed her eyes and heard Dr. Smith gather his bag and instruments and softly leave the room. She opened her eyes moments later to see if Jacob was still there. He stood before the fireplace with his back to Mary. He removed the family savings from the cigar box on the mantelpiece. Mary eyed a wooden crate on the floor with a blanket folded inside. "Is that my baby?" she asked.

He looked down. "I'll take it out of here."

"No. Please. Don't."

He looked at her with concern.

"I'm not ready to have it put in the earth. Not yet."

He folded the bills into his pocket. "I'll be back for lunch. Hannah's got everything under control downstairs."

"Where are you going, Jacob?"

"To see Bonnie. She's the one that killed our baby."

"Don't say that."

"I'll say whatever I goddamn please. That bitch killed our girl."

A girl. The morbid announcement was a knife in Mary's heart. "It was a girl?"

He nodded. "She looks just like Rose." The tears seeped into Mary's mouth, salty and warm. "Bonnie got you so worked up that you lost the child."

Jacob angrily left the room. Mary shivered in her bed. She had never seen Jacob so bitter—so full of hate. She forced herself up from the bed and lifted the swaddled corpse out of the crate. She carried it to the bed and held it to her breasts as though she had just given birth. In a way, she had. She lifted the blanket's edge and peered down at the smooth pink form. The skin was slightly blue. Six months of created flesh. The limbs were perfect. The eyes were closed, as if asleep. She could already see the lashes. They were the color of sand, and the fine, blond hair that appeared on the head and tiny eyebrows. The corpse was no larger than Mary's open hand. The fingers were white spikes, and the feet, like miniatures on a doll. Mary named her then.

Outside, Elizabeth ran in circles around the barn. She lifted up the rocks and peered around the trees. Jacob took little notice of her until he got up on the wagon and heard her calling out: "Baby! Baby! Here, baby, baby!" Her high voice chimed in the crisp, autumn air.

"Lizzy, what are you doing?" he asked.

She ran past the wagon, stopping briefly to look beneath each wheel. "Tryin' to find the baby."

"Rose?"

"No, Daddy, the new baby. Hannah said Mommy lost it."

"You won't find the baby out here," Jacob quietly said.

She looked up, confused. "Where then?"

"The baby died last night, Lizzy. That's what Hannah meant to say."

Her face screwed into a grimace. She looked older, and serious. "Oh." She turned from the wagon, and walked to the house with sinking shoulders and a lowered head.

"Lizzy—" he called out. She faced him. "Are you sad, Lizzy?" he asked.

She shrugged, slowly raising her head. "I suppose."

He looked at his daughter. She was the picture of Mary, with long, blond hair, green cat eyes, and a fierce, determined manner with which she held her chin. Desperate not to show her true feelings—keeping everything hidden, where it was safe. "You're a good girl, Lizzy." He snapped the reins. "Take care of your mother today."

Lizzy recognized that she was given a great responsibility. "I will, Daddy," she promised.

It was a typical weekday morning in town. Mickey Jenson greeted Jacob from the church steps as he drove past, but Jacob avoided eye contact. Mickey excused himself from the conversation he was in and walked after Jacob's cart. It stopped outside The Sir Crudor Inn.

"Where you going, Jacob?"

Jacob gave the minister a chilly smile. "None of your business, Mickey."

He followed Jacob into the lobby, reaching for his arm. Jacob pushed his hand away. "You're not planning on hurting Bonnie, are you?"

Jacob sneered. "No, I'm just going to give her some money to get her ass out of this town." He turned to the front desk. "What room is Bonnie Turner in?"

The clerk eyed him with suspicion. "Fourteen."

"Don't waste your hard-earned money, Jacob. You have to forgive her."

Jacob scoffed, looking Mickey in the eye for the first time that day. "Let me tell you something about forgiveness, Mickey. Mary lost the baby last night because she was so set on forgiving Bonnie Turner. She almost died. You see, the problem with your style of religion is that it's not practical. I'll be damned if I see that woman destroy my whole family by degrees."

"Who's to say she'll never come back, once you've given her the money?" Mickey challenged.

"Is that all you have to say?" Jacob asked.

"At least let me go upstairs with you."

Mickey followed Jacob to room fourteen. Jacob pounded the door so forcefully that he nearly broke it down. "Hold your horses!" Bonnie's groggy voice came from the other side. "You men have no patience!" Azalea groaned in the background. Bonnie opened the door wearing a skimpy red negligee. A syrupy smile oozed from her gaunt face. "Oohh my!" she sang out. "A preacher and a farmer. Now this is interestin'."

It didn't take Jacob long to convince Bonnie Turner that she should take the money and return to Kentucky—provided, of course, that she never set foot in Bately again. Jacob was one hundred percent certain that Bonnie could be trusted to honor the deal. How? He threw in an additional term that he had failed to mention to Mickey downstairs: if Bonnie ever came back, he would have her killed. He had connections, even as a farmer. It was as simple as that. Seeing the look in Jacob's eyes, Bonnie knew the farmer meant business.

Hannah ran to meet Jacob at the barn when he returned. "It's Mary," she said. "She left with the dead child. I tried to stop her—"

"Where did she go?"

Hannah pointed north, in the direction of Spirit Lake. Jacob ran through the field that led to a small apple orchard. Most of the trees were already picked bare, the season being almost over. Wreaths of worm-infested apples encircled each of the trunks. Thoughts of regret raced through Jacob's mind as he wove his way through the lines of twisted trees. He failed to comfort her after she lost the child. He was too absorbed in his own rage—and trying to find a solution to the mess that Bonnie Turner had made. The image of Mary crying in the bed lingered. He could have taken her hand—held her in his arms. Why hadn't he thought to do that? It just didn't seem the time, was all. It seemed like action was in order—not complacency.

He stopped at the edge of the forest and heard Mary's sweet voice singing a lullaby. Jacob calmed his breathing and peered through the trees. He saw Mary's willow-like form moving deeper into the dark forest, blanketed by rocks and branches, and wild birds prancing through the leaves. Jacob stepped into the wooded lot and followed the slice of violet that was her dress. She went to a secluded wild garden, placed the crate on the ground, and removed her straw hat. Jacob entered the garden. Mary looked up at him with sad, sedated eyes. Her arm reached forward. "Join us," she said.

He walked over and knelt at her side. She carried a small garden shovel, and now used it to dig a hole. She stopped and looked up at the ceiling of branches overhead. "It's peaceful here, isn't it?" Her hand went to the edge of the crate that served as both bassinet and coffin. Mary's beloved crazy quilt filled the narrow space, creating a worthy shroud. "I named her Sarah. It reminds me of the wind, blowing in the winter time." She delicately touched her favorite square—a single white snowflake tangled in a vine of crimson thorns.

Jacob took the shovel from Mary and finished digging the shallow grave. He placed the swaddled form inside and sprinkled it with soil. "Sleep well, Sarah," he said.

Mary lowered her head and prayed for the soul of the daughter that she would never know. "Do you think she's safe?"

"She's safe." Jacob filled the hole with fresh earth, then stood and helped Mary to her feet. "How are you feeling?" he asked.

"I'll be OK."

Overhead, the wild birds sang out in discordant song. They formed groups that hovered over the trees, dispersing, getting ready for their winter retreat.

Jacob and Mary left the woods and walked with hands linked through the apple orchard. Entering the field, Mary's surroundings took on the life of a portrait: the golden stalks of corn, the house on the bluff that stood as a beacon, watching over them. The sun dipped down in a translucent ocean of yellow and purple clouds. Their children played beside the barn with delicate frames that formed cameos against the sky's gleaming light. Hannah stood at the porch and waved as she saw Jacob and Mary approach.

Mary turned her head and caught a glimpse of Jacob's profile—simple but proud. The profile of a farmer, and she was a farmer's wife. And yet, in this simplicity, their world possessed such riches—such purpose. The dimensions stretched our before her, presenting divergent angles and meanings, melding together at moments like this and fusing into one point of truth which, in its clearness, could not be defined with words.

Sarah was part of the portrait. In the ground, in the breeze, whistling like a winter wind—warming them as the sun's rays beat down upon the harvest in the summer time. Death flowing into life—pain, trembling into waves of joy. Mary resisted the passing of the moment, for it was a timeless moment, and she knew, even as it happened, that it would never reoccur. It passed, as everything passes, as she would someday pass: into the breeze, up to the heavens, over the fields and skies, bits of her soul weaving through the apple trees and feeding the white blossoms as they grow. A life lived to its fullest and ending before the truest joy was to begin.

Printed in the United States
28602LVS00004B/23